LEANING
ON

WATER

JOAN JUNE CHEN

Leaning on Water

First edition published in February, 2018
First printing in February, 2018
Alternate cover edition published in April, 2018

ISBN-13: 978-1985705043

ISBN-10: 1985705044

For my family

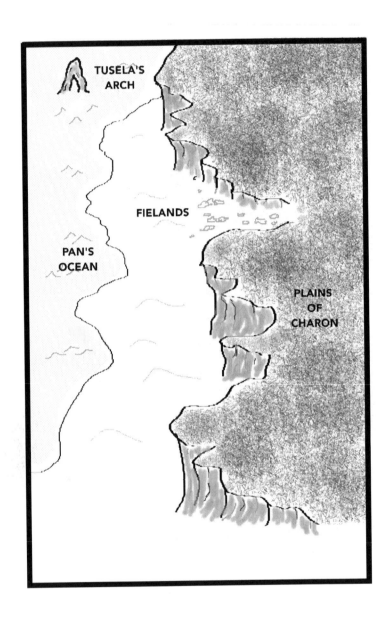

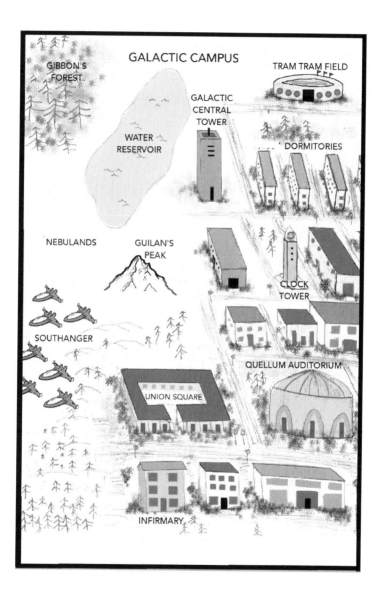

You are officially entering the Erlion System. Words and phrases unfamiliar to you may be found in the digitek's emergency glossary located at the end of this journey.

LEANING ON

W ATER

It all starts with imagination. The courage to dream. The ambition to take the first step of bringing that dream into reality. The endurance to take the next step and the thousand steps that follow. And the stubborn willpower to get up again and again after you falter, until you reach the finish line.

(Excerpt from *The Thoughts and Memoirs of Livinthea Park*, star year 8117)

I

LIVI: GUILAN'S PEAK

THE MORNING AIR FEELS GOOD against my face as my legs beat hard against the dirt path up to Guilan's Peak. My thighs are starting to complain, but just a little farther, and I'm almost at the top. It will be worth it, I tell myself.

It has been two weeks since the last Quadrati breach, and things around the Galactic campus have finally started to settle down. This last attack by those metal droids, we were lucky. Though a whole fleet of our Tullies was decimated, at least no civilians were captured. Galactic Central even rescheduled our annual Luthati training drill for later this morning. The Galactic higher-ups decided to replace our training fleet with fully functional mockups of the enemy spacecraft, the Quadrati Buggards. Maybe I *should* have stayed in bed.

Training drills aside, I'm eager to get back into my usual morning run with the other cadets, anything to help clear my mind. Double doses of Dr. Kang's healing salve have worked wonders for my cuts and bruises from the last breach, but sleep has been far from restful.

When I finally reach the top of Guilan, my thighs burn, but the view really is worth it. Guilan is the highest point overlooking the Galactic campus. From here I'm greeted by a golden sea of clouds, edged by the fire of a coming sunrise. Already the light chases the shadows from the trees far below. Seeing the whole of Galactic and the waking whispers of life, it's hard to fathom that just a millennium ago, before humans arrived on Cerulea, only a few wild plants and animals populated the planet. Now patterns within chaos dot the landscape, the telltale structure of civilization.

"For someone who is just recovering from her sickbed, Livi, you sure are doing a heck of a job of it." Jia, my best friend, cuts into my thoughts as she comes panting up the dirt path behind me, swiping at the beads of sweat running down her forehead as she stutters to a stop. She slumps back against a rough boulder, catching her breath.

Remeni, our fellow Team Horizon cadet, catches up a few moments later, then practically collapses onto the ground. Between heaving breaths, he complains, "Livi, whatever Dr. Kang has been giving you, I think I need some of that too."

Remeni and Jia are like the pesky older brother and sister I never had. Though they're always teasing me, if I were ever in the midst of a Quadrati attack, I know they would have my back.

"Well, it's about time you guys showed up. I was beginning to think I would have to enjoy sunrise all by myself." And it's as if the universe is actually listening. For just as I say it, Altheria and her two sister suns peek over the horizon. I turn to watch. It is breathtaking every time I see it. Even Remeni stills for a moment.

Jia turns to face me. "Did you hear, Livi? The Kyvoxes from the Polaria division have already arrived. After that flu that went around last week took out half of our Kyvoxes, Galactic Central thought it was a good idea to get some extra help around here with drills."

"Kyvoxes from Polaria?" My pumper does a flip. I was hoping to get through the next few weeks without any *distractions*. The Choosing Ceremony is coming up in two weeks after all.

"Rumor has it that there are quite a few that are rather easy on the eyes. But that's top secret." She waggles her eyebrows at me.

"Well, in that case, I can't wait to see them." I roll my eyes, trying to ignore the sudden touch of queasiness that sits in my stomach. *What if I see him?*

I turn to head back, when Jia stops me, her face suddenly serious. "By the way, Livi, I never got a chance to thank you for covering me during the last Quadrati breach. Stars only know what might have happened if you hadn't come back for me."

I'm a little embarrassed that she still remembers. "No big deal. I just happened to be in the right place at the right time. You know you would have done the same for me," I remark truthfully.

Jia looks at me quizzically. "Funny how you do seem to end up in all the right places more than the rest of us mortal beings."

"My dear Jia," Remeni laughs, "I think it's called skills. Livi's just too modest to admit it." Remeni turns to me. "Though don't let your head get too inflated, Livi.

Remember we still have the Luthati drills today. I just heard the winning team gets a free day on the beach, no duties, no drills, and an extra week's allowance. I for one would like to cream Team Lunai, especially that draggart Cadet Wilkie. Yesterday I saw him practically cheating on his quantum test."

Jia adds, "Yeah. You know he only made it into Galactic because his father bought him a spot."

I look at my digital. "Well, none of us will be creaming anybody if we get ourselves kicked out of Galactic. We'll be late for the Luthati drills if we don't get ourselves off this hulk of a mountain now."

"Uggh, don't remind me," Remeni mutters.

"Last one down flies tail position," Jia calls over her shoulder as she sprints back down the way we came. A dirt plume kicks up in her wake.

"And it's not going to be me, if I can help it." I laugh and sprint down after her.

"Hey. But we just got here! Can't you guys just take it easy for once in your lives?" Remeni shouts after us as he scrambles up. "Wait for me!"

II

LIVI: THE NEBULANDS

"**L**IVI, TRY TO LEAVE some of the nuggins for us too, okay? Remember, not everyone is as stratospherically gifted as you."

Remeni stands next to me now as we don our flight suits. He throws me a teasing smile. "The rest of us need to look good at least some of the time you know. The Choosing Ceremony is coming up after all."

"And go easy on such a fine, young, strapping Galactic cadet as yourself? Why on Cerulea would I ever want to do that?" I give him a mischievous smile as I clip my faceplate in place. After all that has happened, it feels good to be back flying with my troop. "And I dare say that Jia thinks you look good all the time anyway. So what if you make Beacon or not."

"Livi does have a point there." Jia bats her lashes and gives Remeni her puppy dog eyes. "Beacon or not, makes no difference to me."

I laugh at Jia's comical face. "Told you. But I promise I'll leave at least *one* nuggin for you, Remeni. And that's only because I'm just recovering from my sickbed." I give Remeni a playful slap on the shoulder.

"Thanks, Livi. You are *so* generous," he remarks sarcastically, but winks at me with a crooked smile.

As we tromp onto the launching field, the vibrations of the Buggards' engines surge all around me, from the ground under my feet to the chilled air. As I step closer to the alien ships, I have to pause a moment to take them all in. The Buggards never cease to amaze me. The grey metal bullets gleam like daggers in the sunlight. They're small but fast. Their sharp edges and sleek lines rest on winglike haunches, and it's not hard to see why they're so agile.

Floating above the ships awaits the Nebulands, an aerial arena that Professor Hensly once described to me as the most treacherous land mine imaginable, only without the land. The air is littered with booby traps—two-hundred-kilometer-per-hour wind cyclones, ferociously hot fire walls, the Flying Blades of Anduria that can slice through metal like bread, and finally Fizwold's collapsing gravitational tunnel, which can ensnare even the largest Tracker ship.

We may complain about the drills, but all cadets know this training could mean the difference between life and death someday. After one of the Quadrati Buggards was downed, our scientists replicated the ships down to the most minute details—from the strange icosahedral patterns embedded in their walls to the last seamless bolt. If any one of us ever gets captured by the Quadrati, we'll at least have a fighting chance.

Giving Remeni and Jia one last salute, I peel off and climb into my Buggard. As I strap myself into the seat, I take a quick glance around. Yes, it actually feels good to be back in the pilot's seat, even if it is an alien ship.

I run my hand over the familiar toggles and switches of the control panel. As I throw on the engines, the wind whips around the ship, and it's as if I can sense every air molecule that courses by. I have never been able to explain it, but algorithms like three-dimensional landscapes of color and amorphous shapes start running through my head. I can predict what each little motion of my hands on the control panel will do. Like every ship I've ever piloted, I know the Buggard and its capabilities like I know myself, maybe even better.

The start signal streaks across the arena in a rainbow of colors. My body launches into reflex mode. *Fire propulsion jets.* My head hits the back of my seat as my Buggard arcs into the arena, a full second ahead of the others. Within moments a flash of crimson catches my eye. No question about it. It's the first nuggin. *Forward thrusters. Now.* The nuggin weaves in and around the wind traps, just past the flaming walls of fire. Its four spherical choppers catch the sunlight in flashes of orange and white. My body crushes into the back of my seat as I accelerate ahead of all the other cadets, twisting and twirling to avoid any of Team Lunai's disabling shots. My fingers fly over the control panels of their own accord, and I weave between the blades of the Andurian metal and past Fizwold's gravitational tunnel before it sucks me in. *Close.* And within seconds I'm in range of the nuggin. *Got you.* I fire an electrical bolt.

The nuggin bursts in a haze of smoke and flame.

"First down. Great job, Livi!" Jia's voice crackles into the comms unit as I blink through the smoke.

But before I can reply, another flash of crimson catches my eye as a nuggin streaks past, only this time one of Team Lunai's members is already after it. It bursts into a ball of flame.

"Dang it," Remeni curses into the comms unit as his Buggard whizzes by. "I should have gotten that one."

Within a matter of seconds, another nuggin zings past me, its metal choppers whirling close to my right wing as it does a crazy dance and then shoots straight up towards Altheria.

"Not so fast, little buddy," I say under my breath, twirling the ship and climbing skyward. As I gain altitude, I squint against the blinding rays of Altheria. Then I spot it. *There.* Just before the nuggin can disappear into a tuft of clouds, I lock my missiles on target, releasing them in the same movement. Boom! Crack! The nuggin splinters in a flash of colored lights even more beautiful than the first.

"Way to go, Livi!" Remeni's voice blasts into my helmet. "And forget what I said about leaving some for me. You get as many as you can. We need that extra allowance!"

Nuggins fly at us from many directions now. Remeni and Jia start to get good hits themselves. We're ahead seven to six.

But mid-competition, Jia's voice spikes across the intercom. "Crimeny! That draggart Wilkie clipped me!" Jia's ship drops off the radar. "Sorry, guys." She's been disabled.

Now it's just Remeni and me left against the three Lunais.

But I'm in the zone, the ship a natural extension of myself. Spin, twirl, launch, strike. Veer left, bank right, dive, climb. Arc. Fire. The Buggard obeys my every notion. The nuggins have no chance. Soon the arena is littered with tufts of smoke, slowly dissipating with the gentle winds. But when I glance at the levitating scoreboard, I realize that Team Lunai has fared well also. Sure, it's two against three, but we're tied seventeen to seventeen. And there's only one nuggin left. *No room for mistakes.*

In the distance, the last nuggin zips past the wind trap ahead of me. *I've got to get it.* I push my thrusters to the right, narrowly avoiding a Flying Blade and swerving by a Lunai member so closely that I can see the whites of his eyes. *Wilkie.*

Just as I'm about to fire on the nuggin, it drops out of sight. Quickly, I scan the perimeters. And when I spot it, I have to squint my eyes to be sure of what I'm seeing. What in the name of Altheria?

"Did you see that?" Jia's voice blares in my ear. She may be out of the game, but she can still see everything going on.

"I know right? I thought Galactic restricted flying in that area," Remeni shouts back over the intercom.

"Well, not anymore apparently," I yell back.

The last nuggin has pitched straight down into Gibbon's Forest, the plot of thick trees and brambles that lies beneath the southern perimeter of the Nebulands. Decades ago, Gibbon's Forest was declared off-limits. Too many training accidents and a number of untimely cadet deaths occurred there. And the forest has only grown more dense and treacherous since.

I drop the nose of my Buggard.

"Wait, Livi! What are you doing?" Remeni's voice crackles. "Maybe that holiday on the beach and extra week's allowance isn't worth it."

"Well, if I don't go in, I'm sure Team Lunai will. And I do not like to lose. It's worth it, Remeni." Gritting my teeth, I nosedive right in after the last blasted nuggin, weaving in and out of the cyprian trees that threaten to slice through me. A disabling fire pings close to my left wing, but luckily I swerve just in time, and it misses me. My eyes whip over to my radar. The three Lunai members are right on my tail.

"Infinite black holes," I mutter under my breath. I may be a good pilot, but even I know three against one, especially within Gibbon's Forest, are not good odds.

"Don't worry. I've got you, Livi," Remeni calls out. He fires at them, disabling two of the Lunai team ships, one right after the other. "Take that!" He whoops.

"Thanks, Remeni!" I call out. There's only one Lunai member left, but he's close on my tail. *It's Wilkie.* I can't let myself get disabled. Letting the nuggin out of my sight momentarily, I pull out one of my oldest tricks. In one tight arc, I slingshot my ship upwards and yaw to the left around a giant cyprian tree, nearly clipping my right wing in the process. Gravity then whips my ship back down and around directly behind the last Lunai team ship. I shoot a disabling beam. *Direct hit.*

"That's for clipping my best friend!" I shout.

Now it's just the last nuggin. I spot it whizzing ahead of me in brief flashes of crimson as it heads deeper and deeper into Gibbon's Forest. The nuggin threads through a dense canopy of trees like no nuggin I've seen before. *Who on sweet Cerulea is controlling this thing?* I promise to head over to Galactic Central and give him a piece of my mind later, that is, if I make it out of here alive.

The trees are so dense now that it takes every ounce of my concentration to fly the Buggard without getting my wings lopped off. Algorithmic shapes and colors whirl in my head, an orchestration of movement and mass, finding patterns within a patternless landscape. The ship, the air, the trees, and the wind pump through me like the blood in my arteries.

Slowly but surely, I gain ground on the nuggin. But where is it heading? Then I know. Fizwold's Tunnel. Lying just above the southernmost edge of Gibbon's Forest is the collapsing gravitation tunnel. And if the nuggin reaches it, we forfeit the allowance.

Remeni's voice cracks over the comms unit. "Livi, forget what I said about it not being worth it. Go get that last nuggin."

"Whatever you say, boss." I bank right to avoid a tree and tilt the Buggard's nose sharply upwards. I slam my thrusters hard, spiraling and twisting to avoid a quartet of cyprian trees, each one trying to derail me with its long branches. I tilt and spin, trying to get a straight shot through the trees. And then finally, I've got it. Just as the nuggin reaches the gaping mouth of the tunnel, I let loose the last missile I have and hold my breath. The missile screams through the narrow slivers of light that bleed between the trees and finds its mark in a blinding array of blues and golds.

"Woohoo!" Remeni hollers ecstatically.

"You did it, Livi!" Jia cheers so loudly, her voice vibrates clear through my head.

I let out the breath I was holding, pulling up and away from the canopy of trees. The Buggard shudders in relief as much as I do. "Thank the stars," I sigh, crumpling back into my seat. I'm just about ready to pass out. "Let's bring these darn Buggards home."

When I land, I open the cockpit door and throw off my helmet, the cool air a welcome relief to my flushed face. The first to greet me are Jia and Remeni, along with the rest of Team Horizon—Rox, Keria, Haven, and Song—not far behind. And as I descend from the Buggard into the cacophony of cheers, I'm surprised to see what seems like the whole of the Galactic campus as well. I recognize even many of the Kyvoxes and my professors cheering amongst the crowd.

Remeni and Jia rush at me with a bear hug, nearly squeezing the daylights out of me. "Those were some seriously deranged moves, Livi!" Remeni calls out.

Before I can answer, a familiar voice booms from behind me. "Yes, very impressive indeed."

The celebrating immediately stops, and I dig my head out of the tangled mess that is Jia's hair to find myself looking into eyes like the endless depths of space and time. Kyvox Keenon Young.

III

LIVI: THE PAST RETURNS

NOW I HAD HEARD that my old childhood friend made Kyvox, but it has been four long years since I last saw him.

Does he even recognize me?

He certainly looks different. He's no longer the skin-and-bones boy I joked around with back in Traxos when we snatched ripe red plums off the fruit vendors' carts. There's no question that time and whatever training he's been receiving in Polaria has been good to him. His fitted black Kyvox uniform emphasizes how his shoulders have broadened, and he's now at least a foot taller than me. A day's worth of light stubble lines the hard angles of his jaw. But his eyes are the same, glittering pools of dark midnight. If he recognizes me at all, his stony expression gives nothing away.

But we *were* good friends. Best buddies in fact. Until one day things changed. And he went off to Polaria and never came back. Though I suppose I can't blame him, not really. What did I expect? A holomessage every star week telling me how he was doing? No, I can't really blame him for what happened to our friendship because in truth, I was mostly to blame.

Professor Hensly steps out from behind the Kyvox. Warmth creeps into my face as I realize that I've been staring.

"Professor Hensly." Dragging my eyes away from the Kyvox, I salute my quantum physics professor while Remeni, Jia, and the rest of the cadets abruptly do the same.

"Team Horizon, I would like to congratulate you for winning the tenth annual Luthati drills." Professor Hensly's eyes flick from Remeni to Jia, and then come to rest on mine. "No one has been able to successfully navigate Gibbon's Forest for quite some time, Cadet Park. That certainly was a well-earned field trip to the beach and an extra week's worth of allowance."

Clapping and cheering erupt around me. I never particularly liked being the center of attention. "Thank you, Professor Hensly," I manage to reply and shrug. "It was a team effort of course." I glance over at Remeni and Jia, who grin back at me.

"Of course," Professor Hensly replies. He turns to the rest of the cadets that have gathered. "That's it for the show. Time to report to your first sessions. Team Horizon, stay with me."

All the other cadets hustle off. Jia, Remeni, and the other members of Team Horizon remain, looking quizzically at each other.

"Team Horizon, seeing as Kyvox Scott has taken ill, Galactic Central has had the good fortune of recruiting the Head Kyvox from our Polaria division to replace him as your unit leader." He turns to the young man I know so well, or at least *used to know*. His next words ring in my ears. "May I present to you Kyvox Young."

Professor Hensly nods at Kyvox Young, and only then do I snatch another glance at him. The Kyvox greets the others with his charismatic smile. The glint in his eyes reminds me of his former self, the one who snuck out with me for scrabbling games of Scrimt. The one who always won. No matter how hard I tried, his drone could always fly through the mine-infested maze to the finish line even before mine had made it halfway through. We were an impetuous and scraggly pair back then. How he and I both made it to Galactic is a wonder.

The Kyvox dips his head back at the professor. Professor Hensly continues. "And you've already had a rapid-fire introduction to his tremendous piloting skills." Dr. Hensly smiles, the light catching on his crooked teeth.

It takes me a moment to connect the constellations. My jaw sags open, and my head jerks to the side to face the Kyvox. My mouth is forever forging ahead of process and cognition, and I blurt out my thoughts before good sense and restraint can stop me. "*You* were controlling the nuggins?"

Just with that, his walls are up. And like the torrential Andurian rains, the Kyvox drenches me with his cool gaze. "Yes, Cadet Park. Professor Hensly has been reintroducing me to some of the interesting training games you play as cadets." He looks intently back at me, nonblinking, even as the tumultuous winds whip waves of his hair across his face.

Although I know I should try to reconcile and mend our long-lost friendship, all I can feel right now are my hands balling up at my sides. The arrogance of his current manner bulldozes over any favorable thoughts I might otherwise have had. I take a step towards the Kyvox. "*Games*? And you mean to tell me that our last run through Gibbon's Forest was *your* handiwork? You nearly got me killed." Here I go again with my temper.

Jia, who is standing right next to me, elbows me hard in the ribs. Her eyes flash widely at me as she whispers frantically, "Livi! What in the hellas are you doing? He's a Kyvox, for stars' sake."

But I've already slingshotted too far, from ecstatically happy, to utterly bewildered, to seething mad. And there is no going back.

The Kyvox takes a step towards me, so close I can feel his breath cascading down onto my face. He stares back at me, his gaze locking hard onto mine, unwavering. "You're just as strong willed as before, Cadet Park. No one *forced* you to go after that last nuggin. You chose to go after it of your own accord."

So he does recognize me. I have to admit—he has a point there. But I'm still so mad, I'm not ready to let him off so easily, my new trainer or not. "That area was restricted," I say through gritted teeth.

"I'm afraid *that* was my fault." The professor actually hobbles forward, planting himself between me and the Kyvox.

Who he thinks he's protecting, I'm not sure.

"I failed to debrief Kyvox Young on the usual parameters, and he didn't know that Gibbon's Forest was off-limits. Before I realized what was happening, you had already dived in after that last nuggin, Cadet Park. Anyway, the drill was an excellent demonstration of *both* of your abilities." Dr. Hensly looks between the Kyvox and me. "Now if you'll excuse me, I have another meeting, and you all have your first sessions to attend. Dismissed."

Except for the Kyvox, the rest of Team Horizon disperses. Jia tugs at my arm. "Come on, Livi, we better hurry. We're barely going to make it to quantum as it is."

But for some reason, my feet don't move. "You go on ahead, Jia. There's . . . there's something I need to speak with our new Kyvox about."

Jia gives me a questioning look, then glances back and forth between the Kyvox and me. Her eyebrows arch high, but she grumbles low, "Okay, but don't do anything I wouldn't do." She gives my hand a squeeze and hurries to catch up with the rest of Team Horizon, leaving me standing alone on the launching field with this stranger who was once my best friend.

IV

LIVI: TRUCE

THE TWO OF US STAND AWKWARDLY for what seems like an eternity on the island that is Tullies Field, the rest of the world pure background noise to the thunderous silence swallowing us.

Though I could reach out and touch him, he might as well be on the other side of Pan's Ocean, for that is how far away he seems to me right now.

In my mind, I'm replaying the regretful last words we said to each other four years ago, just as I'm sure he is doing. Until finally, I can't take it anymore. I'm the first to break. "You never forgave me, did you?"

"I don't know what you're talking about." His voice curdles cold while he eyes me stonily.

"When you wanted us to forget about Galactic and pursue a different life together, and I wouldn't," I prod. He continues to look back at me, eyes sharply bladed. The hard depths of his gaze gauge me, reading me. But I will myself not to break. "You never forgave me for that did you, Keenon?" I take a chance that our history still means something to him and put my hand on his shoulder. "What happened to you at Polaria?"

He flinches at my touch, as if I've burned him, and my hand falters away. His eyes train on a light in the distance for a long moment, the taunting wind whipping through his dark hair. His shoulders are rigid, but then he takes a deep breath in. And when he looks back at me, some heat has crept into his stony expression.

"Nothing *happened* at Polaria. It just wasn't where I wanted to be, away from you. You were the only family I had left, Livi." He hesitates a moment, a lock of hair strays at his left temple, and I resist the urge to reach up and tame it. "I thought I meant something to you too, but when you wanted to go off and join Galactic, well I had never felt so lost."

"But you got into *Polaria,* Keenon. Only the best get chosen. How could I let you give that up?"

"Well, I would have." Again, he turns away from me, the muscles in his jaw feathering.

I had no idea I hurt him so badly, and now I'm at a loss for words.

The memory comes flooding back, a neighbor's boy I had seen wandering outside our house along the banks of the Ion River, eyes red and puffy. Though he seemed older than me—already half a head taller at that time—I took his hand and led him into my Grandpa Wren's house. That's when he told me what had happened. It was the first of several Quadrati attacks. He had seen his parents taken before his eyes.

I can't deny that he was family to me too. Loved him like family in fact. Both of my parents were gone, and though I loved Grandpa Wren, he was always too busy

Joan June Chen

making ends meet and trying to survive the loss of his only daughter. But one day I had the strange sensation that things were growing into something different, and it scared the hellas out of me. I wasn't ready. Perhaps Polaria was only an excuse for what I was not ready to face.

Despite the years apart, when I look at his hurt expression now, I still see hints of the boy I once knew, and my throat aches. I wonder if I made a mistake.

I'm about to apologize, to tell him that perhaps I was wrong and should have chosen differently. But in the next instance, Keenon straightens his back and looks me in the eye, his gaze a little less bladed, a little more like the Keenon I knew long ago.

"But I'm past that now, Livi. My years at Polaria have given me a strength and purpose I didn't have before. So in that respect, I suppose I should thank *you* for that." And now it's his turn to put his hand gently on my shoulder. "Let's just move forward, shall we?" He pauses a moment and actually quirks a small smile. "Especially since I'm to be your Kyvox now, isn't that right, Cadet Park?" And to my surprise, he offers his other hand to me.

A part of me feels confused. And some strange sense of loss seeps in through the worn seams of my heart, as if a ship has sailed away with someone dear and is now out of reach. But I know it's for the best. I clear my throat and look him straight in the eye, holding any other emotions I might have at bay. "Yes, let's move forward, Kyvox Young." I take his hand and shake it.

V

LIVI: EMERGENCY MEETING

"**N**OT EVEN A FULL DAY as our Kyvox and he's already calling an emergency meeting? I wonder what's going on?"

Haven rubs the sleep from his eyes, and Keria yawns loudly next to him. The rest of Team Horizon is even less awake. It's four in the morning, and Rox slumps in his chair, the rim of his cap covering his eyes. Song snores softly on my left, her head resting on the table, and Jia and Remeni slouch against each other on the other side of me.

Keria replies, "Well, whatever it is, it better be important. And what does he mean to keep us waiting for nearly an hour? A girl needs her beauty sleep you know."

"Yes, dear sister, especially you." Haven laughs as his twin sister throws mock daggers at him with her eyes.

"Shh." She elbows her brother hard in the side as she sits up straight. "Here he comes." Keria's eyes dart past my shoulder, and I quickly nudge Jia and Song awake next to me.

"Sorry to keep you waiting, cadets." Kyvox Keenon Young comes strolling into our ops room. Even at four in the morning, the Kyvox looks perfectly sharp in his crisp black uniform. Clean-shaven. Dark eyes alert. It is *unfair* how good he looks.

Now, I'm not usually one to be vain, but suddenly, a small part of me wishes I had taken some time to at least comb my hair before dragging myself over here. Across from me, Keria tucks a loose strand of hair behind her ear.

The Kyvox steps easily to the head of the table and clears his throat. "I've just been given a thorough debriefing by Galactic Central about some critical intel. One of our important satellites was downed by the Quadrati less than three star hours ago, and Galactic Central believes the wreckage may be in the Saltlands. They want us to find it before the Droids do." Kyvox Young's arms sweep across the navigational screen, his movements confident and sure. "Team Horizon has been ordered to search the Saltlands, and you are to split into three hovercrafts. Cadets Finch, Ong, and Park will cover the Fielands. Cadets Singh, Cathay, Dylton will search the Yves Plains. Cadets Vivila, Kao, and the Rochens will search the Yinlin straits."

The Kyvox's voice demands attention, and his gaze could hold a hostage. He commands the podium like he was born to be there. *Is this really the same boy I knew back in Traxos?* I find myself strangely annoyed at the way none too few of the female cadets in my group look up dreamily at him, even Jia for crying out loud.

Oblivious to the attention, he continues. "I will be your eyes and ears at Galactic Central. Anything significant or even remotely out of place, report back to me immediately. The Quadrati threat has been increasing exponentially of late. So even though Galactic Central has given the all clear for Droid activity in those areas, you still need to be extremely careful." He casts his hard gaze across the group, finally landing on mine. "Understood?"

A deluge of inner dialogue floods through me. *Stay confident. Keep your head up. Meet his gaze, darn it.* "Understood," I bark out with the rest of Team Horizon.

"Very well. Be back by sundown. The hovercrafts are waiting for you. Dismissed."

VI

LIVI: THE EXCURSION

"**N**OT SO FAST, REMENI! Some of us want to make it back to the Choosing Ceremony in one piece you know."

Jia grips the dash of the open-top hovercraft next to me. Her chocolate-brown hair whips wildly behind her. In the distance, dawn breaks along the coast, a shimmering dance of light on water as day meets night.

"Well, you don't want to let Keria, Haven, and Rox find the satellite first, do you?" With both hands on the dual roller balls, Remeni still manages to steer the hovercraft while turning to tease Jia from the seat in front of me. "Plus, I've got a reputation to maintain."

Despite what he says, the speed of the hovercraft eases ever so slightly. Now that we've reached the southernmost border of the Saltlands, the terrain grows progressively more treacherous and rocky as we get closer to the coast. The way Remeni weaves in and out between the jutting crags of rocks makes my stomach sway. Good thing I didn't eat anything for breakfast.

"You really think this satellite is that important?" Jia asks.

"You heard what the Kyvox said. Galactic wants to find it. Badly."

Jia turns to look at me. "Speaking of our new Kyvox, what's the deal between the two of you, Livi? You were nearly at each other's throats the other day. Is there something I should know about?"

I shift away from her so she can't see the heat creeping into my face. A part of me wants to tell Jia everything. How the Kyvox and I basically grew up together. How he was like a brother to me—and maybe something else too. But a bigger part of me just wants a fresh start. So even though Jia is my best friend, all I say is, "We just got off on the wrong foot. That's all. I talked to him after our little tiff, straightened things out."

"Well, in that case, good. You don't want to hurt your chances of becoming a Beacon next year, do you?"

"You're absolutely right. I don't," I say as I shake my head. But Jia is still looking at me. I know her well enough by now to see the way her eyebrows are just slightly furrowed. *She's not finished grilling me.*

She opens her mouth about to speak when Remeni calls back to us, "Hey! I think I see something! There along the beach."

Thank you, Remeni, for your impeccable timing. My shoulders drop in relief as Jia's discerning gaze spins away from me. Remeni points to the edge of the ocean about a hundred meters out, the sunlight catching on a flash of metal.

Quickly, I whip out my oculars and look in that direction. Beside me, Jia does the same.

25

"Yea, I see it too!" Jia calls out. Her brown eyes squint into the digitally enhanced visual device.

And as I look into my own ocular, I can make out what looks to be a shiny metallic sphere with the telltale axial poles protruding from one end. "Well, Remeni, looks like your reputation as Galactic's best hovercraft pilot will remain intact after all. Nice work!"

But just as I say this, Jia jerks beside me and screams, "Remeni, watch out!"

A blinding flash of hurtling flame strikes, followed by a deafening boom.

I barely feel the heat before I find myself airborne.

VII

LIVI: THE HOVERCRAFT ACCIDENT

THE ANGLED EDGE OF LIGHT creeps in as I open my eyes.

The world around me untilts as I push myself slowly upright, palms braced against warm sand and the grittiness clinging to my bare arms. A lingering breeze that speaks of Cerulean citrus and wild ocean fills my first breath. I take another deeper breath in, only to stop short as a sharp pain knifes my side. Clutching at the pain reflexively, I look down to find myself covered in soot and ash, a gash on my thigh where blood seeps through the dark maroon of my uniform.

But the raucous quarreling of birds draws my attention away from the pain, up towards the half-blinding light. Circling above is a family of seafaeries. Their pearly wings spread against a canvas of azurean sky and gauzy pink clouds. I squint against the three suns pitched up high. Altheria, Thea, and Calani. The Gliese Sisters, we like to call them. I blink and rub at my eyes. *It must be midday already.*

A soft moaning comes from behind, and I twist reflexively. Jia. She lies prone against the rocky sand. Sodden tendrils of hair mat down the back of her neck, and her once-spotless cadet uniform is torn and charred. But I can recognize my friend anywhere. Though my head throbs and my leg still bleeds, I heave myself up and hobble towards her. I kneel down next to her and turn her gently onto her back.

"Jia, are you okay?" My stomach churns at the sight of dark blood trickling down her forehead, weaving a spindly trail along her left temple and pooling at her hairline. But her eyes flutter open, and I heave a small sigh of relief.

"Aside from having the worst headache in my life, I think I'm okay." She wheezes, her whisper barely audible over the roiling waters. "What happened?"

Yes. What in all hellas just happened? I look up, my eyes zeroing in on a patchy mound a couple of meters away. Cintian metal and rubber tangle under wisps of steaming smoke. *The hovercraft.* I can't tell where the crags of Cerulean rock end and the crushed pylons of what used to be our hovercraft begin. My heart trips haphazardly in my chest as I remember. Quickly scanning the area beyond the remains of the hovercraft, my eyes catch on a lifeless form, half buried behind the crooked rocks and crystalline sand, legs bent at odd angles. *Oh no. No. No. No.* I shake my head, trying to undo the image. It can't be. *Not Remeni.*

"Livi?" Jia starts to sit up.

"Wait here, Jia." I put a firm hand on her shoulder, easing her back onto the sand. "I have to go check something out. I promise I'll be right back." I keep my voice steady for her sake and force myself up. Pushing my heavy boots forward into a half run, my calves protest with each step. *Please let him be alive.* I chant to myself. *Please. Please let him be alive.*

As I get closer, the smell of burning rubber sears through my lungs even more, and the blackened smoke stings like acid in my eyes. I slow to pick my way through the mangled mass of what was the hovercraft, its broken remains strewn amongst the rocks and sand.

"R-Remeni?" His name clatters to the ground like falling gravel, and I cough on the acrid air. I recognize his curly copper hair rustling in the coastal wind before I see his face. His eyes are half closed and his ashen lips match the color of the grey Cerulean stone around him. I drop down next to him, ignoring the burning of my knees on the hot sand. I reach out to feel his neck and almost draw back at the first touch, so unnaturally cool. Pressing my fingers there, I will myself to feel something, anything. No pulse. *Stars, this can't be happening.* With my own heart thumping up into my throat, I press my ear to his chest, not caring that the sandy granules that cling to his torn uniform scratch at my face. And I sit there listening, just listening.

But all I can hear is a cold, hollow silence. I grit my teeth and swallow hard. A tightening grips my chest, threatening to strangle me.

"Everything okay?" Jia calls out to me.

Hold it together. I choke in an uneven breath and stand up unsteadily, dragging myself through the hot sand back to Jia.

"Livi?" Jia's deep brown eyes flicker to mine as I drop down by her side. Despite the intense heat, she is shivering. "Where's Remeni?"

How am I going to tell her? That our friend who was always so strong didn't make it. The bloody gash on Jia's forehead is still oozing at a steady pace. Her face looks pale. *Too pale.* No, I can't tell her now. *It would be too much.*

I shrug out of the torn remains of my cadet jacket and use it to cover her. "Shhh. You're hurt, Jia. Just rest, okay?" I kneel down and gently stroke her hair until her eyes drift closed. I've got to get her help first. But we're nowhere near Galactic's campus, nor any Cerulean outposts for that matter.

As I look towards the ocean, my heart thumps a beat out of sync. I must have missed it earlier. The haze of clouds in the distance has thinned somewhat, and now I can see it clearly—Tusela's Arch, a graceful stone archway carved out high above the distant ocean waters. This area was all under water once, a millennium ago. But more importantly, of all the places to get stranded in, this is probably the worst. With Tusela's Arch to the west past Altheria, that can only mean we're already in the Fielands, where Quadrati sightings have been growing more frequent despite the protection the Bionics offer. But as I look towards the bleeding horizon, my gaze stops short as something else catches my attention closer to shore. *There.* A glistening at the edge of the ocean.

Getting up carefully so as not to jostle Jia, I scramble across the beach towards the rolling waters and manage to grab hold of the haloed ring. Though the turbulent waters threaten to bowl me over, somehow I manage to stay upright. I drag the dead weight through the cresting waves and wet sand, not caring as the cold water sloshes up onto my legs and into my boots. Finally, one last heaving pull and I have it out of the crashing waters, safe from the ocean's grasp. Through panting breaths, I take a good look. The haloed metallic sphere is spiked at both ends, covered in sludge and seaweed. The downed satellite.

The irony of the situation hits me all at once. *Remeni gave up his life to find this hulking piece of metal? Is it really worth it?* Somehow it doesn't seem quite so important anymore. I fight off the bitterness rising up in the back of my throat and take a swigging breath in of the pungent air.

But I have no time to dwell on the twisted nature of things, for a low whirring sound draws my attention past Tusela's Arch. My heart lifts. Perhaps it's Keria and Haven's hovercraft. I scan the horizon. Then freeze. A piercing bullet shape mars the horizon, its metallic casing glaring back like fire in the sunlight. Though still quite a distance away, even a first year cadet would recognize what this is. A Quadrati Tracker. My innards drop. It's just like the one I saw the night my father disappeared. Can the unfeeling universe be any more cruel?

Quickly, I scan the area and spy what looks to be a cave entrance about a dozen meters behind us. I run back towards my best friend. "Jia." I squeeze her hand. Her eyes peel open. "We've got to take cover. Do you think you can move at all?"

"Wh-why?" Her words come out thick, slurred. Dirty blood continues to trickle down her forehead.

The whirring of engines is getting louder. I glance back over my shoulder. *They're getting closer.* What if they've already detected the heat signature of the still-smoldering hovercraft? "It's the Quadrati."

Jia's eyes widen and her body stiffens. She's more awake now, and her pale face nearly matches the whites of her eyes. She knows, perhaps more than me, how much cruddling we're in. "Oh stars, Livi. What are we going to do?" Her teeth chatter and her fingers tremble.

I put a hand on her shoulder. "We made it through those stinking Luthati drills, right?" Jia's head bobs slightly. "Well, we're going to get through this too. And we're going to get you back in time for the Choosing Ceremony. Just hang in there, okay? But we've got to get out of the open space and move. *Now.*"

"All right," she mumbles weakly.

I hook my hands underneath her arms and haul her up, steering her towards the cave entrance. We shuffle haphazardly across the sand. Halfway there, Jia misses a step and we tumble forward, hands and knees pitching into flying sand. Jia crumples on the spot, lying there, her eyes squeezed shut. Her face contorts. "Too much pain," she groans tightly.

I scramble up again, dragging at her arm. "Just a bit farther, Jia. Come on, you can do it. Hurry!" But to my horror, her body goes completely limp, eyes rolling to the back of her head. "Jia!" I shake her shoulders. Not Jia too.

Luckily, she's still breathing, rapid shallow breaths, but still breathing. I hope to the heavens that she has merely passed out from the pain, but I have no time to figure that out now. Mustering every last bit of energy, I drag her limp form the rest of the way, finally collapsing at the mouth of the cave. I gently push her further in, deep enough so that her heat signature hopefully will be undetectable from the entrance.

Heaving the air in and out of my lungs, each breath burns. When I look back towards the cave entrance to see how far away the Quadrati are, my eyes catch on something flashing in the sand. Ignoring the searing pain across my chest, I move closer and grab hold of it. It's Jia's spartok, a reminder of her keen interest in primitive survival gear. It must have fallen out of her holster when I moved her. And it gives me an idea.

I don't have much time. The Quadrati Tracker ship is clearly in sight now, perhaps even close enough to get a visual on me. But I have to do this. I have to take the chance. As quickly as my aching legs will allow, I stagger back over to the remains of the hovercraft. My eyes home in on the metal bottle I spotted earlier, and I swipe it up. The metal casing has a few dents in it, but based on the hefty weight in my hands, it's still full. Quickly, I wrench the cap open and douse its contents amongst the remains of the hovercraft and along its perimeter. I wish I had more, but this will have to do.

After I'm done, I haul myself back to the cave and crouch down, hidden from view behind some pockmarked boulders. If I'm lucky, this Tracker will be no different from the rest, commandeered by a single Droid. All I need to do is take out that Droid. But I'll have to time it just right. One false move and I'll blow myself to Altheria and back.

The blood pumps furiously in my chest as the Tracker ship lands less than a hundred meters away, right on the sandy beach where I stood a few moments ago. The ground shudders violently underneath. Bits of dust and

33

terra rain down from the cave walls. I hold my breath as a hidden door peels open from the side of the Tracker. A metal beast made of nightmares steps out.

I've never seen one of these things up close, and the Droid looks even more menacing in person. Its hulking metal encasement looms several feet taller than me and is framed in lethal edges that gleam under the harsh rays of the suns. Arm and leg joints cut sharp angles, no doubt designed to render deadly blows with ease and efficiency. It is said that the Quadrati are as vicious as the Dark Skythes of Charon and stronger than any human. And at this moment, I believe it.

The ground reverberates in time with the beating in my own chest as the Droid stomps heavily through the sand. Its long strides carry it swiftly across the beach, to the satellite. Its pulsatile eyes send out a laser-like beam, which briefly wraps the metal sphere in an angry red light.

Maybe it will just take the satellite and go.

But I have no such luck. For in the next moment, the metal beast spins *and heads directly for us.*

As it tracks closer, I can see its red laser eyes shift and pulsate. I ready the spartok in my hands and hold my breath. One chance. *That's all I'll have.*

The Quadrati Droid pauses at the edge of the hovercraft, bending slightly as it telescopes its metallic arm and spears a piece of debris with its claw-like fingers. Metal on metal scratches the air. Jia lets out a soft whimper behind me.

I freeze.

The Droid's inhuman eyes shoot up, locking onto mine. Crimeny. I have no choice now. This will just have to be close enough.

In one swift motion, I snap the spartok and hurl it towards the Droid, a trail of crackling sparks spewing in its wake as it hits the ground. Before I can even blink, all hellfire breaks loose. Hot air blasts across my face as the hovercraft erupts in screaming blue flames, swallowing the Droid whole. The air around it blazes, and the Droid starts sweating metal, the tinny skin of its face and arms peeling. But to my horror the Droid jerks upright, stalking rapidly towards me.

I stagger back, balancing my weight between bent knees, preparing to defend myself and Jia with my bare hands. But as the Droid reaches the edge of the flames, he starts to falter, listing to the side. The next moment the whole of its hulking body comes crashing down, the ground beneath jolting violently. I stand there, not even daring to breathe, my heart thumping in my chest.

His limbs and torso slowly liquefy into a shimmery pool, but somehow his laser-red eyes are still locked on mine. Despite the heat, a chill runs through me. Then the Droid's eyes flicker once, twice, and finally—dead. And for a few moments, there is only the sound of crackling flame.

Soft whimpering comes from behind me and snaps me back into motion. "We're okay, Jia. I'm just going to make sure everything's clear, and I'll be right back." My voice comes out shaky, not my own. I step gingerly towards the wreckage and the remains of the Quadrati. The blue flames are dying down now that the kestanol I spread earlier has all but burned off. But I can still feel the smoldering heat through the thick soles of my boots.

What is left of the Droid is a shapeless blob of metal. What is left of the hovercraft is even more indeterminate.

I'm lucky kestanol burns even hotter than the carbon subnitride coals of Cryon. Who knew cooking oil could be so useful?

Slowly, I creep towards the Tracker ship.

VIII

LIVI: DRAMATIC RETURNS

THANK THE STARS I didn't shirk my training on Quadrati vessel technology.

The Fielands are a dead zone. No comms link. No nothing. It is no wonder the Quadrati have been able to infiltrate this area. The only way out of here is to fly us out. If I can fly a Buggard, then by the light of the triple suns, I am going to fly this Tracker ship too, even if it kills me. And in truth there's a good chance that it will. Kill me, that is. But I have no other choice. I can't very well drag Jia across the Fielands all the way back to Galactic. That would take several weeks at best, and that's if the Quadrati don't get us first.

My hands grip the sides of the Tracker's hatch, the hard edges smooth but cold under my grasp. I try to reassure myself that if there was another Droid inside, I would likely already have been blown to bits by now. Still, ignoring the pain in my chest, I pull myself in through the open entrance with one fluid motion.

My eyes quickly scan the cockpit. It's empty. I heave a sigh of relief. But I can't let my guard down just yet. No doubt, other Droids will be on their way soon. For they are all linked. One collective brain. One neural network of free-flowing thought. Who controls them, I don't know. But what I do know is that I don't have much time before the other metal beasts come to find out what has happened here.

I have only once ever been in Tracker mock-ups before. No Quadrati Tracker has ever been taken intact like this. The inside of this vessel is much fancier than the mock-ups, but the control panel at least looks familiar. I should be able to fly this thing. *Sure, right.*

Boy am I going to give the gang back at Galactic a big surprise. That is if they don't shoot me down first. But I can worry about that later. Right now, I have to get Jia on board and out of the Fielands.

I heave myself back out of the ship onto the coarse sand, my boots sinking deep with each step, though my thoughts feel lighter. As I get closer to the cave entrance, I see Jia lying with her arms outstretched at its opening, dusted with a light layer of Cerulean sand. She must have crawled there herself while I was in the ship. I quicken my steps.

"Jia?"

Her head lifts up, brown eyes squinting at me, then widening. "Livi!" She struggles to a sitting position just as I reach her, her arms quickly wrapping around me like a vise as I lean down.

"Thank goodness you're okay." Jia squeezes so hard my chest aches. "I saw what happened with the Droid.

Stars, Livi. Do you realize that you just took out a Droid single-handedly?"

"Well, I can't take all the credit you know. I did use your spartok." Jia still looks pale, but the bleeding has actually stopped at the gash on her forehead. "Look, I've got a plan to get us back to Galactic. Do you think you can walk at all?"

Jia nods slightly. "I'll try. Sorry I was no help before, but I feel a little better now. I must have passed out from the pain. Crimeny, I hate feeling like such a wimp." She pauses, then her gaze lifts up past my shoulder, looking. "But Livi, where's Remeni?"

Oh no. I was hoping she wouldn't ask me that. Not now, when I should be getting us out of this deathtrap. But I owe her the truth sooner rather than later. The Quadrati can go rot in their high Riolian towers, and I'll just have to deal with them if they show up before then.

My throat closes up as the memory of Remeni's broken body flashes like a lightning strike across the dendrites in my mind. I look away, trying to control the emotions I forced down earlier, but they bubble back up to the surface. Why? Why is life such a struggle sometimes? Why do we try so hard to be the best, only to end up like this? I clench my hands, nails digging hard into skin. I can feel Jia studying me, her brows furrowing. There's no choice but to tell her straight.

I turn back to face her and clear my throat once, twice. "Jia—" My voice cracks.

Jia's face crumples, hands flying to her half-open mouth, her eyes already begging me not to say more.

I know she's already read the unspoken words no doubt scrawled in big ugly letters across my face. But still,

I force the awful words past my lips. "Jia, Remeni didn't . . . Remeni didn't make it." There. It's out, sealing reality into stone. There is no bringing Remeni back now, no more avoiding the grim truth.

Jia's body starts shaking, racked in silent spasms. Finally, a strangled sound escapes her, not quite human.

But I have no more words for her either, my own body threatening to give in to the shadowed pits. All we can do is cling to each other.

***

I'm not sure exactly how long we've sat here, holding each other tightly against the dark ebb and flow of the universe. But I know it has been too long.

Altheria and her sisters are trailing well past star center now, and a cold breeze drifts in from its long travels across the ocean, making me shiver. We cannot risk spending any more time in the Fielands. If the Droids don't come for us, then dehydration or the near-freezing temperatures that creep in at night here will. And our tattered uniforms will certainly offer little protection from that.

Jia looks a mess. Her face is stained with bloody tears and dirty sweat. Her lids are swollen, and her temple is marked with an angry gash. I know I'm no better off.

I stand up and tug at her arm. "Jia. We've got to go."

She nods reluctantly, following my lead. At least we're both moving.

"What about Remeni?" Jia hesitates a step, pulling back at my arm where the sleeve has already torn.

I look back at my best friend. The one who helped me move in my first day at Galactic. The one who has always been there to help me out of the trenches when I was down. The one whose face is now etched in acute suffering of the worst kind. "I'll get him." I give her hand a squeeze. "Wait for me in the Tracker ship, okay?"

Jia nods numbly. "Thank you, Livi. I don't think I could bear to see him right now."

I direct Jia into the cockpit of the Tracker ship. After settling her into the straps of a seat, I head back out to face the task I've been avoiding. Remeni.

His body is the same as when I left him, a broken shard amongst the unyielding boulders, his life-force ripped away. I touch his forehead gently and then brush his eyes closed, whispering a silent goodbye that drifts away with the sighing winds. It takes me far too long to move him into the gulley of the Tracker. But I can't just leave him behind.

After I'm done, I go back for the satellite, dragging it through wet sand and my own bitterness, until it too is safely secured on the Tracker. I try to convince myself that maybe something worthwhile can come out of this awful tragedy.

My heavy boots clank like lead as I force myself forward into the cockpit. Every part of my body aches now, and I don't know how I can ever move another muscle. But I sit myself down in front of the control panel into the seat next to Jia.

Jia looks at me, pain still clear in her eyes. "Done?"

"Done." I nod grimly. "Now it's time to get us out of here."

Jia angles towards me, eyebrows unsure. "I know you're Galactic's best pilot, Livi, but are you sure you can fly this mammoth?"

Quickly, I examine the sleek control panel, the gauges and meters slightly foreign, yet at its core the same. Yes, I can do this. I have to do this. Like I said, I've flown Buggards before, the Quadrati stealth vessels, and this Tracker shouldn't be much different, though perhaps just a wee bit bigger. Okay, maybe five times the size is more like it. I look over at Jia, her brows now deeply furrowed. "Do you want to have a go at it?"

"No thanks," Jia replies, shaking her head.

"You sure?"

"You beat Team Lunai almost single-handedly during the Luthati drills. I'm sure, Livi."

"All right then, here goes nothing."

I disable the homing device that otherwise would give away our location to every other Tracker ship within a thousand kilometers of us. My hands then quickly fly over the control panels. Really, I could do this in my sleep. Flying is like some innate thing I was born to do. I can't really explain it, except that it's like playing a fine instrument, knowing exactly where to push and pull through instinct and feeling, rather than any actual thinking. A natural reflex. I sense the shift of the craft, how it lists just slightly right wing downward as we lift, and my muscle memory kicks in to even us out.

The sleek metal floor underneath my feet vibrates subtly as we drift upwards. I can see the reach of Tusela's Arch now, through the wide spread of the window before me, and steadily turn the craft in the opposite direction. *Galactic is in for a big surprise.*

The Tracker ship slices into the sky as I rev it into high gear with my bare hands. We shoot up along the rocky cliff face that walls off the beach. Jia grips the edges of her seat as we slip between the mean edges of a gaping crevice, but I have it all under control. The ship careens through the hollows of a narrow and winding glen, but for me, it all may as well be a walk in the park. Frankly, the feeling of flying is soothing, lifting away layers of pain, even if it is an enemy ship.

Jia's groan next to me brings me back to reality, and I glance over at her. She holds her head between her knees, and her skin has morphed into a putrid green. "Are you okay, Jia?" I ask.

"Don't worry about me." She grumbles, turning towards me but keeping her head down just the same. But she looks as if she's about to hurl her guts out. A sickly grimace contorts her face.

I guess I *was* getting a bit carried away. Flying does that to me though, the freedom of movement, the feel of being unbound and limitless. "Okay, sorry about that, Jia. Things should get better from here on out. It's a straight shot back to Galactic now." We've made it past the rocky outer rim of the Fielands and are heading over the flat Plains of Charon. No more cliff faces or sunken valleys to deal with.

We fly along in silence, each of us lost in our own thoughts or perhaps trying not to think at all. I know *I'm* trying not to think about the destroyed remains of the stars-knows-how-expensive hovercraft. And I'm also trying not to think about the splintering pain in my chest every time I move. But most of all, I'm desperately trying not to think about Remeni. Looking over at Jia, I know she's doing the same.

We are so close to Galactic base now. Seeing the familiar terrain eases some of the tension that had built up in my shoulders.

Without our communicator, it's going to be tricky, but I plan to land us just outside of Galactic's outermost post. Close enough to walk on foot to the Galactic perimeter patrols for help, but far enough away so they don't mistakenly shoot us down.

As the details of this plan tumble around like rough stones in my head, Jia groans in the seat next to me. "Stars, Livi, if I'm being honest right now, I feel like the Dark Skythe is pounding on my head from the inside out." Her speech slurs slightly.

I looked over at her, and my chest tightens. She really does not look well. Sweat trickles down her face now despite the fact that it's actually a little cold in the Tracker ship. She groans again, hands coming up to her temples. Then to my horror, her eyes roll back and her head droops to the side like a hanging duck.

"Jia!" I reach out and shake her gently, but there's no response. Crimeny. I put my bare hand close to her nose and mouth. I feel more than hear a soft intake of breath. She *is* breathing, but they are rapid and shallow. I feel for her pulse next, which is barely there, thready. She clearly needs help sooner rather than later. There is no way I can risk taking her back the long and scenic route.

That leaves only one option. Fly us directly to the Galactic base in the enemy ship. Sounds crazy because it is crazy, because there is one big gaping mother-of-all-black-holes in that plan. We don't have a way to communicate with Galactic. Once they see us, Galactic will assume we're the Quadrati. And they will shoot to kill first, and ask questions later.

How am I going to signal them? I rack my brain, trying to come up with something, anything. I look around the sparsely arrayed cockpit. The comms link on the Tracker isn't compatible with Galactic's communication system. There isn't even a darn spartok. There is absolutely nothing I can use. *Think, Livi. Think.* I have to get Jia back to Galactic, fast.

Then an idea strikes me. Admittedly, it's not a great idea, because it involves probably getting shot at first. The plan also requires me being able to fly this hulking bastard of a Tracker ship like I did with the lightweight Buggards during the Luthati drills. Can I pull this off without getting both Jia and me outright killed? I've always been a risk taker, but even I know that the chances of making it out in one piece are pretty miserable.

But Jia needs the few precious hours that my new plan could save us if it works. I look over at Jia, her face even more pale than before. I have no choice. I have to do this. I have to choose the option that is *less* worse.

I let the new idea jigsaw in my brain, trying to fit the pieces together as I fly us closer. It occurs to me that much of my life has always been like this, a choosing between options to find the least worst. There has to be something theoretically wrong with that. Even chance should have given me a good hand at some point, right? But I don't have time to dwell on that now. As we near Galactic's outer perimeter, I see familiar pools of cobalt-blue below, the lake reservoirs that surround the base. We're close now.

Through the window, Galactic towers come into view next, a subtle shifting towards us at their tops catches my eyes. Sensorcam. We've gotten their attention. *It is time.* I take a deep breath in and blow warmth onto my hands. I'm going to need them very steady in a few moments.

Suddenly a fireball arcs towards us from the ground up into the sky. Without even thinking, I slam the left cabin wing downward and it narrowly misses torching us, booming immediately to our right. The seams of the ship shake violently, rattling clear through into my teeth. "Crimeny!" I curse, not taking my eyes off the control panel.

Yes, it's really too bad we have no way to communicate with Galactic. But I have their attention now. And I'm going to use it.

My hands fly into autopilot. I know what I have to do, a certain maneuver I used to do with my drone during a Scrimt run, and I hope a certain someone at Galactic Central will recognize it.

Quickly I shoot us straight up, spiraling up through hazy wisps of clouds in a zigzagging pattern, barely missing the balls of fire that flash and boom so closely that I can feel my heart quake. Higher and higher we fly, continuing the spiraling zigzag until I feel dizzy in the head, my stomach lurching to my throat. But the gosh-darn fireballs keep coming.

Stars, when will they get the message? I can't do this much longer. Not only am I already fighting to stay conscious, but we're also quickly approaching terminal altitude. I zigzag again and spiral across the sky this time. Then suddenly everything quiets around me. The fireballs have stopped. I continue my well-honed maneuvers for a few more runs until I'm sure they have truly stopped their assault. A few breathless moments pass. Nothing.

Thank the stars, I chant to myself, throwing my gaze upwards to the skies. They have finally gotten my message. It's time to land this hulking brute.

***

"What in the name of Altheria and her two sisters are you doing in a Quadrati Tracker ship, Cadet Park? Do you realize we almost shot you down?" Kyvox Young bounds towards me, elbowing past several heavily armed cadets, his dark brown eyes bladed in cintian metal and the muscles in his angular jaw clenched tightly. "If I hadn't recognized your to-hell-and-back maneuvers at the last second, you'd be deader than dead right now." He stops abruptly in front of me, his young face pinched hard, chest heaving up and down in deep breaths. The Kyvox might as well be spewing fire out of his nose. He is beyond mad.

"Yes, the shooting down part was fairly obvious," I retort. I must be out of my mind speaking to a Kyvox like that, but I'm truly beyond exhausted now, barely holding myself upright. "Sorry, sir. It's a long story. Really, really long."

His eyes widen as his gaze runs from my head down to my toes and back up again, lingering at my face. I must look as awful as I feel because normally, a Kyvox would have tasked me with midnight Tracker patrol runs by now and given me much more flame, but to my surprise, though his eyebrows knit together, he just lets it go at that.

47

"Okay, let's just get you and Cadet Ong to the infirmary."

As I look at him more closely, he seems oddly shaken too, and he almost never loses his cool.

Kyvox Young yells sharply over his shoulder, motioning to a group of junior cadets with a jerking sweep of his arm. "You four. Priority Level Red. Get Cadets Park and Ong to the infirmary right now. Tell Dr. Kang what happened, and that they both need a full MedScan stat. I want the results reported back to me immediately."

The cadets nod dutifully, and before I can protest, to tell him about Remeni and the satellite, strong arms lift me up onto a stretcher. There's a gentle rocking motion as they haul me off, my head lolling from side to side against the smooth canvas. My harried thoughts pitch and yaw along the undulating waves until I cannot fight it anymore and let the dark sheeba collect me into a dreamless sleep.

IX

TRITON: TOO LATE

I WATCH NUMBLY as the jagged cut that runs the length of my femur deep into the raw strands of fibered muscle knits together in front of my eyes.

Even with my enhanced vision, I cannot see them, the nanobots that chart a different course for my life away from otherwise certain death. The blood has just barely congealed, not even crusted, before all that is left underneath is a faint scar that even a Bionic would be hard-pressed to find. The skin on my chest and arms tingles and pricks, and I know that the third-degree burns there are being repaired just as quickly. This last run-in with the Quadrati Trackers nearly got me killed. *Good thing I'm nearly indestructible.*

This time I went too far. Breaking protocol. The tenth Quadrati Tracker ship slipped through my watch in the meantime. After I realized what happened, it took me half a star day to track it down here to Cerulea, to the sunforsaken Fielands no less.

A smoky haze catches my eye past Tusela's Arch. I follow its wispy trail along the softly glowing horizon, and my eyes hitch on a reflective flash of vermilion in the sand. I rev my azar into high gear, speeding over the sun-bleached beach, leaving a raging storm of flying sand in my wake.

As I get closer, curling tendrils of smoke leak up from the battered ground, hinting at a bygone blaze. But the tawny burnt metal littering the sand is not of a Quadrati Tracker ship. The only metal that turns that fiery orange when exposed to high temperatures is cintian metal, and that only comes from one place, Cerulea. I know it's a Galactic hovercraft.

Triple eclipses, I'm too late. The tenth Quadrati Tracker must have attacked the unsuspecting Galactic craft. *No one could have survived that kind of attack.* Quickly I search amongst the burnt rubble. But everything is too far decimated, not even a trace of any bodies.

My hands ball up into fists. Today is one of those days when I can hardly bear this life. To the burning blazes of Hespron with responsibility. *Immortality is killing me.* What's clear is that I messed up. *Badly.* Whatever happened here was my fault. This wouldn't have happened if I hadn't broken the rules. How will I face the Domseis when I get back to Atlas? How will I face my own darn self? *You will just have to accept the consequences.*

I force myself up.

Then something strange catches my eye. *There*—at the edge of the burnt rubble. A shimmery pool of liquid. But as I get closer I realize something else. It's not liquid, but metal. Tinston in fact, from its telltale dark sheen. And the only possible source of tinston in these parts? A Droid. Or at least what's left of one.

What in the dark infinites happened here?

That's when I notice. *Boot prints. Two sets. Undoubtedly injured—specks of dried blood, tracking away from the wreckage.* Could someone have actually survived? I follow the trail of blood. It leads to a cave entrance. "Hello?" I call out. Only an empty silence answers me. And when I step inside and do a quick search—no one. Not a single darn soul. My heart lifts a notch. Could whoever was in the hovercraft actually have survived? Escaped even?

I trace my way back to the hovercraft site and, per protocol, take several samples of the dried blood and place them into the collection kits for our Upper Council.

Now the next question is—where on Cerulea is the tenth Tracker ship? What if there was more than one Droid? I've got to find that blasted thing before anyone else gets hurt. I swipe at the sweat that trickles down my forehead. In the dying light of the Gliese Sisters, I quickly scan along the beach and into the long and drifting shadows of the hanging cliffs. But there's no sign of the Tracker ship. I check the nav device strapped to my side. A weak signal flashes about two thousand kilometers— east. And that means . . . *infinite black holes.*

My legs are already scrambling in the direction of my azar before my mind catches up. *I'll think things through later*, I tell myself. Right now, I have to get to Galactic. Because if the Quadrati Tracker ship makes it there before I do, there's no telling how much more destruction there will be, how many more lives will be lost. If anyone else gets harmed because of my neglect of protocol, I will never forgive myself. I won't even wait for the Domseis to Nullify me—I'll do it myself.

***

Any other day, I would have enjoyed the lush and boundless views of Cerulea's landscape—the blooming wildflowers scattered across Charon's windy plains, the clear blue of the crystalline lakes. Any other day, I would have reveled in the open air.

Today is not one of those days.

I turn on the azar's deflector and cloaking devices that will shield me from detection by Galactic's radar and also keep me hidden from view. I try to relax my shoulders as I approach the campus. I'll be of no use if I'm too strung up.

As my azar hovers high over campus, I brace myself for what I might find. To my surprise, all seems strangely quiet at Galactic.

Slowly, I begin to descend. The tension in my shoulders eases somewhat as I scan the campus. Cadets mill about the popular caffea shops. Students cluster in small hordes around the dormitories, laughing and smiling. And most importantly, there are no sirens, no breach alarms.

I check my nav device, and my heart nearly leaps into my throat from what I see. The Tracker signal blinks madly. I'm dead on. Quickly, I scan the campus again. Then I see it. To my amazement, the Tracker sits in open view in the midst of the Tullies just past Gregum's Hill. Just like one of the pack.

Then it dawns on me. Whoever was in that Galactic hovercraft must have managed to overcome the Droid and take control of the Tracker ship. A tremendous sense of relief flows through me. But I wonder who on Cerulea was able to take out a Droid? A feat that's difficult even for some Bionics.

I would like to find out more, but I remind myself that I have no more time to investigate. I've already been away from Finlan's Point too long. It's time to return to Atlas and face the Domseis.

X

LIVI: MORNING AFTER

I WAKE UP TO a tremendous pounding, as if the Dark Skythes of Charon are trying to bludgeon their way out of my head.

Undiluted light assaults my retinas from my open dormitory window, and I blink rapidly, trying to focus. Crimeny it's late, for Altheria already leads her sisters up into the sky. But I cannot bring myself to get up yet. I never realized it's possible for every single cell in my body to ache. Even my toenails feel sore.

Today is definitely worse, now that the natural endorphin rush from yesterday's accident is gone. The rest of the day went by in a blur. A few of my scattered neurons vaguely remember getting moved into the MedScan unit, and that's only because my chest hurt like heck when they shoved me into that ridiculously tiny capsule. Turns out I have a hairline rib fracture and a mild concussion. Otherwise, after a few blood tests, six forehead and ten thigh stitches, and a proper cleanup—antiseptic shower and newly pressed uniform included—

Dr. Kang released me back to the dormitories. The doc put my chest in a binder with strict orders to get a good night's rest and to stay in bed for a few days.

I pestered Dr. Kang about Jia, but the only answer he would give me was that she was still in surgery, and it was too soon to tell. As for Remeni, Kyvox Young saw to it that his relatives were notified. As far as I know, Remeni was an only child. To say that I feel awful for his parents and more is an understatement. Kyvox Young also told me that the Galactic flag was flown at half-staff in his honor.

Needless to say, I am completely exhausted this morning, my head feeling like a block of Andurian cement, too heavy to lift off the soft nest of my pillow. But I desperately need to find out how Jia is doing.

I push myself upright with my elbows and nearly bite my tongue off. Burning black holes. Who said it was only a hairline rib fracture? There is nothing hairline about the lancing pain that slashes across my chest, forcing me back down with a wheezing whoosh out of my lungs. Trying to catch my breath as the pain slowly subsides, I stare up at the walls of my room until I can think again.

Granted there's nothing much to look at. I tend to live simply, just an old holograph of Grandpa Wren and me hanging on the far grey wall. But it feels comforting just the same, just me, the empty walls, and the air. No bruhaha. No screeching metal. No burnt rubber. And no Quadrati. I lie there savoring the quiet calm of my own breath, no matter how much my ribs complain.

Jia, who has stuffed chitterrings lining her shelves and holographs of pupobears and her family covering every inch of her walls, often teases me that I must have been a

Droid in another life because of how sparsely decorated my room is. And I suppose perhaps there is some truth to it, for I never really was the nostalgic type. I just can't afford to be. Perhaps my most prized possession is my digitek, which lies untouched on my desk. The last time I treated myself to a good reading on it was several star days ago. I've just been too busy lately. But I promised myself I would read one of my favorite books from Ianthia Yen once the Choosing was over.

And that reminds me. The Choosing. It's *today*, the day when all senior cadets will be assigned to their stations in life, whether that be in the Engineering unit, Weaponries, Intelligence, or Combat. The day when three of our best senior cadets are supposed to be chosen to become Beacons and work with the most elite Galactics helping to protect Cerulea, something that just about everyone at the academy dreams of.

I still have one more year to go before my own Choosing. But this year, both Remeni and Jia were *supposed* to have been up for the honors. In fact they were both front runners for the Beaconship positions this year. And they were so looking forward to it too, especially Remeni. *Now he will never have that chance.*

With that thought weighing on my mind, I force myself up again, albeit more slowly this time. Yes, it still hurts, but I can manage the pain if I'm careful. I drift into the bathroom, fighting the sluggishness that is a big puffy cloud in my head. Sidling up to the watering spout, I splash my face with cool water, trying to wash away the tiredness from around my eyes but avoiding the now angry-looking stitches running along a crease in my upper forehead down to my right temple. I brush through the thick tangles of my dark brown hair. Usually, I pull it back in a simple ponytail, but since I can barely lift my elbows past my shoulders, I leave it loose down my back for once. There will be no training today anyway. And my ribs could use a break—not literally, that is.

My academy uniform, with the school emblem of swirling golds emblazoned at its left shoulder, awaits me in my clothes receptacle. I slide the jumpsuit off the slim prongs and slip it on gingerly. My fair skin contrasts against the dark maroon of the uniform, and I appreciate its comfortable fit.

Now it's time to find Jia. I'm anxious to find out how she's doing. I head out.

The long halls are alive with other cadets bustling about, no doubt in preparation for the Choosing Ceremony later today. Despite everything, their high energy is contagious. Just as I hurry around the corner, I crash headfirst into what feels like a solid wall. I nearly fall backwards, squeaking from the sharp pain that shoots across my chest, but firm hands grip my sides, keeping me upright.

"Livi? What in the name of Altheria are you doing up?"

I cringe. I know that voice without even looking. But I look up in surprise anyway, because the Kyvox hasn't called me anything besides *Cadet this*, or *Cadet that* ever since our *reunion* at Tullies Field.

"Just getting some fresh air," I reply lightly, trying to defuse some of the tension.

Kyvox Young is not amused. "I was under the impression that Dr. Kang gave you strict orders to stay in bed and get some rest."

I find myself looking into intensely dark eyes that are nearly as familiar as my own. At least the frigid iciness has melted somewhat. His hands linger at my sides, as if he's afraid I might tip over at any minute. But then he abruptly drops them.

An uncomfortable warmth creeps up into my cheeks. He smells of hard metal and sweat. I haven't stood so close to him in a long time. I take a step back and clear my throat, trying not to wince. "Sorry, Kyvox, actually I was just going to find out how Jia is doing."

I must be imagining it, but his gaze seems to soften ever so slightly. "I was just coming to tell you that Cadet Ong will be fine. She is still in the Intensive Care Unit, but she's awake and talking."

Is Keenon actually being sort of nice to me? Wow. He really must have thought I was heading down Plank's pipe. He continues when I don't say anything. "Dr. Kang said that you got Jia back to Galactic just in time. Apparently, Jia had a slow bleed in her head, what the doc called an epidural hematoma, and if she hadn't gotten the surgery when she did, she wouldn't have made it."

I stand there a few moments absorbing the news, the stone weights of Juthri lifting off of my chest. Jia is going to be fine. Thank the stars. I don't know what I would have done if things had been otherwise. I look over at Kyvox Young but keep my chin up, trying to maintain the formality that he expects from me. "Thank you, Kyvox. I appreciate your coming to tell me the good news."

"It's what a Kyvox is for." He shrugs, briefly glancing away. "To look out for—my troop."

I nod silently, for I'm too surprised by his unexpected kindness to say anything else. Since seeing him again, things between us have been a junction of straight lines and perpendicular angles. No funny arcs. No softly meandering edges. But now I feel strangely awkward, especially since I can't even think of a thing to say. I stand there shifting uncomfortably until I can't take it anymore. "Well, thank you again, Kyvox." I give him a reluctant smile and turn to walk away.

"Livi, wait."

I feel a hand on my arm and am suddenly aware of the warmth of his palm through my sleeve. When I look back at him, I find him staring at me with the cutting edge of a blade. *And I can't look away.*

"What happened to you yesterday—you, you scared the living starlight out of me." He pauses and clears his throat. "It made me realize that I really—what I'm trying to say is that I know I said before that I've moved—" He fumbles his words, glancing down at the concrete floors.

I have never seen him like this. My own face ignites, burning hotter than even Altheria's flame.

But then he straightens, and his gaze squares back on mine. "I just want you to know that if you ever need anything, Livi, I'm here for you." His last words tumble out of his mouth like an avalanche, leaving me in billowing dust.

A wisp of his dark, wavy hair drifts over his eyes as he looks back at me. I'm not really sure what to say. The old history between us does nothing to negate the awkwardness that I suddenly feel. Perhaps it has made it worse. My hands sweat, and my heart is pumping at breakneck speed inside my chest. *Just say something, Livi. But what am I supposed to say?* "Thank you, Kyvox. I really appreciate it." *That's it? That's all you can say? Stars, I stink at this.*

For a moment he just looks at me, and I think he's going to say something else, but then his eyes fall to his hand that still rests on my arm, and his eyes cloud over. Abruptly his grip on my arm drops away, the warmth there evaporating just as quickly into the cool air. Clearing his throat, he straightens. "Okay. Good. Well then, Cadet Park, let's get you back to your room. Doc's orders." Looks like we're back to formalities.

For some reason I feel an odd combination of relief and disappointment, but mostly relief. I'm used to straight lines. I *can do* straight lines. I regain my composure. "But the Choosing Ceremony is this afternoon, sir." Dr. Kang mentioned to me earlier that Galactic Central was going to hold a remembrance there for Remeni. I want to go. *I need to go*, broken ribs and all, *for Remeni and for Jia.*

The Kyvox's eyes briefly shoot skyward as he shakes his head. "All these years, Cadet Park, and you're still the same headstrong girl. Not only did you single-handedly destroy a Droid, rescue one of your fellow cadets, retrieve our satellite, and fly a Tracker ship like no other Galactic has ever done before, but you still want to go to this ceremony despite having a broken rib and a nasty gash on your head. Can nothing stop you?" He looks me up and down as if trying to see if I'm truly sane. Finally, Kyvox Young shakes his head but smiles genuinely at me, flashing his perfectly straight teeth. "Fine. You can go. But if Dr. Kang catches you, you're on your own."

And I can't help but to offer a grateful smile back.

XI

TRITON: SOLITUDE

"YOU KNOW PEOPLE have been looking for you, Triton."

A familiar voice startles me from my stupor. I've been up since the nadir with my bum planted solidly against the only Psyla tree in the whole of the flora chamber. My nightmare was a tangled mess of torn bodies and Droids, spooking sleep away to the ethers.

The immense chamber, with its plethora of pearly fronds and climbing vines, is the only place on Atlas that I've found that gives me any amount of solace. I was hoping that the Psyla's wide canopy would hide me from view. I suppose I should have known better.

"I just needed some time for myself," I grumble, surrendering my moment of solitude. I look up into light hazel eyes that have kept me sane the last few years on Atlas Station I. Fila. She can predict my actions like her own shadow. Though she's the closest thing I have to family here on this hurtling piece of tin in space, it still doesn't mean I want to tell her what's troubling me. But of course, Fila ignores what I say and sits down next to me anyway without even asking. For Fila is persistent, as she always has been ever since she took me under her wing when I was a Young Blood.

"You've been skulking around like a Petronian wildebeast ever since your last watch. What's gotten into you lately, Triton?"

I work to keep my expression doggedly blank. "It's not something I want to talk about." I clamp my mouth shut before she coaxes any more cursed words out of it. Even a hespera's stone-sharpened claws couldn't pry my mouth open right now. Speaking means bringing back to life the grim events I've been trying to forget these last few hours. I've had missteps before, but this time I've really gone into the gulch. I look away, purposefully avoiding her ever-knowing gaze.

Though perhaps a little rough around the edges, Fila is like empathy incarnate, as in tune with and dedicated to the alleviation of human suffering as they come. I really don't deserve a friend like her.

She continues to sit quietly by my side through the interminable silence, the artificial mist of the flora chamber's humidification system slowly collecting on the rough hairs of my arms like a moist blanket. It's so quiet, I can even hear the soft burbling of water through the tiny irrigation pipes that crisscross underneath the imported Cerulean dirt that I sit on.

After many long moments, I'm beginning to think Fila's just going to abandon me to my surly silence, but then she takes a deep breath and lets loose. "Triton, I don't know what you've been through, but you've got to accept the fact that sometimes things just *happen*, tragedies and mishaps that only the universe and the stars control." She pauses a moment as we both watch a butterfly flit before us, its bright coral wings a delicate dance of color through air. She takes my hand with a softly reassuring pressure. "Triton, there's no need to throw yourself to the Infinite Darkness for one small blunder." She's facing me now, a strange mixture of concern and stubbornness on her face.

Though I don't want to, as a friend I owe her an explanation. "It was hardly a small blunder." I let my life's breath out slowly and shake my head. The disaster of today quickly replays in my mind as the words spill out. "I broke protocol, and one of the Quadrati got by on my watch."

Fila looks at me sharply, letting out a rapid whoosh through her nose. She doesn't say it aloud, but I can read the words sandwiched between her raised eyebrows and crinkled forehead. *Breaking protocol again?* "For the love of the stars, Triton. You may be as near invincible as any Bionic can be, but you know how strict the Domseis are about *that*."

I rip my hand out from under hers, and she jerks in surprise. "Don't you think I know that?" I lash out, regretting the harsh words as soon as they come out.

A flash of hurt splays across her face. I'm being a Dark Skythe's behind, and I know it. Really, I'm just angry with myself. I take a breath in.

"I'm sorry, Fila, but I've just been under a lot of stress lately. The Quadrati are up to something big. *I just know it.* I left Finlan's Point unguarded to try to find out. But then a Cerulean hovercraft was attacked because of *my* mistake. Ceruleans were injured, maybe even killed for all I know."

63

I shake my head and slump back against the gnarled trunk of the Psyla tree. "I'm sorry. I just don't know how much longer I can bear it. The burden of one life. The burden of a million lives. It's too much. Bionic or not."

Before I can wallow into the weeds any deeper, Fila twists towards me and grabs me by the shoulder. "Triton Travler. Do I need to remind you of how many lives you *have* saved? The millions of Ceruleans who would have perished had it not been for your bravery and dedication over the last five years as Comstadt? There's a reason the Domseis picked you above all of the others as first in command of all Magnars. Who was the one who staved off the total annihilation of Cerulea's southern hemisphere less than a star year ago? Who prevented the Quadrati from discovering Hurako? The whole of the Gateways might have already fallen prey to the Quadrati had it not been for you."

I look away. I don't want to hear this. But she comes to kneel in front of me, planting her beautiful face directly before mine, tendrils of her honey-colored hair grazing the skin on my arms. Her hazel eyes gleam with sparks of fire.

"Triton, you have single-handedly saved more Ceruleans than one hundred Bionics put together. Pull yourself together. Tell the Domseis what you told me. They will—"

Before Fila can finish her diatribe, racing footsteps clatter from above, drawing our gazes upwards. Fila takes a step away from me, and we both look up through the stray light between the leaves to find Magnar Juki skidding to a stop on the flora chamber's starboard platform, only millimeters away from toppling over the edge. His head pivots back and forth, scanning the grounds below. He stands at least a few dozen meters above where I sit, but before I can even think to duck, his eyes home in on mine. Darn that freakishly good Bionic vision.

"Pardon me, Comstadt." His voice tumbles down towards me in rapid succession, anxiety echoing off the high ceilings of the chamber. "But I've been trying to contact you on your comms unit." His gaze flicks to my side, noticing Fila for the first time and undoubtedly misreading the situation. Even from here, I can see his face flush. What he doesn't know is that I would never think of Fila like *that*. She's practically a sister to me. Juki takes a moment to collect himself and clears his throat. "The Domseis summoned you to the Upper Chamber over an hour ago."

Fila looks at me, silently giving me her *better not do what I wouldn't do* look. Despite my frustrations, I quickly stand up to go. No one keeps the Domseis waiting.

XII

TRITON: MEETING WITH THE

DOMSEIS

"**Y**OU SUMMONED, Domsei Shen?" I touch my right hand to my heart, a customary sign of respect to the Domsei, who stands at the far wall of the Upper Chamber. His eyes ponder the starry depths through the observation windows. The other Domseis must still be resting, their pods hovering high above my head.

"Yes, Comstadt Travler." The Domsei's voice echoes through the ornate chamber that seems so out of place here on Atlas Station I. It's filled with glittering relics from various civilizations, collected over the millennium that the Bionics have been protecting the Gateways. Holographic projections of Cerulea and the other worlds spin along the perimeter of the chamber. I pull my attention away from the encasement of Fojardian jewels that sits nearby as the Domsei approaches. The metallic blue cape that drapes down his back flows around him like the shimmering waves of a distant ocean.

I meet Domsei Shen's gaze as he comes near. Though he is over a millennium older than me, he could easily pass for my own brother. The results of a few failing melanocytes speckle his otherwise bronze hair, but nary an ancient wrinkle mars his youthful face. "Comstadt, I wanted to talk to you about the details of the last Quadrati attack."

I knew this was coming. Frankly, I deserve it. Though this situation is perhaps more serious than my previous misadventures, I've been under the barge before. I should own up from the start. I clear my throat and square my shoulders. "Yes, I wanted to talk to you about that too. You have received my report?"

"Yes, Comstadt."

Having ruminated over the Quadrati breach ad infinitum, my thoughts are already posited on the tip of my tongue. "Then please know that I take full responsibility for the mishap at Finlan's Point. Because of my failure, I accept whatever disciplinary action you deem appropriate."

The Domsei's dark eyebrows rise ever so slightly. My shoulders tighten as I wait to hear his verdict. But the Domsei casually adjusts the wings of his cape, brushing at some minuscule dust mote that even I cannot see.

I suppose when one has lived a millennium, seconds and minutes are hardly worth notice. Barely beyond a Young Blood myself, I wouldn't know. The pressure of impatience builds underneath my skin. Finally he looks up at me, his words like careful steps through sinking sand.

"Comstadt. You directly disobeyed orders and pursued the Tracker ships past the Brakeline. This left Finlan's Point completely unguarded, which allowed a Quadrati Tracker to slip through our defense into the Gateways, something that has only happened once before."

"I can't deny it. What you say is true." I look past his shoulders, the horrific events replaying in my head.

"Triton."

The tone of his voice makes me look back at him, almost like a father to a son. I'm surprised to see the expression of the Domsei's rigid face somewhat softened.

"You are our most talented Bionic, and you single-handedly subdued the other Tracker ships you pursued, but that does not negate the fact that you ignored protocol. Your punishment today is not about the Quadrati that slipped through our defenses, nor is it about what happened to the Cerulean hovercraft. This is, however, about you disobeying the rules—not just once, but many times now." He shakes his head ever so slightly. "I'm afraid you must learn to stay the line. One cannot just amend the rules and disobey orders to suit whim and convenience." He takes a drawn-out breath. "The Upper Council has already discussed the situation. As much as I hate to do this, I hereby restrict you from the Gateways for one month."

I make a conscious effort not to let my jaw drop. I didn't expect to be stripped of my Gateway privileges. Perhaps extra dropdead training runs along the breach lines, but not *this*. I take a moment to collect myself before clearing my throat. "But what about Finlan's Point? Who's going to protect the Gate?"

"Magnar Kreon will be given that point duty in your absence."

"Magnar Kreon?" I fight to keep my voice down, but I don't withhold the disbelief. Though no one ever counters the Domseis, I've got to say something. "A thousand pardons, Domsei Shen, but Magnar Kreon barely even passed the NAD simulator last year. The Quadrati will make mincemeat out of him. The Quadrati threat doubles at Finlan's Point every day. I've witnessed it firsthand. I've been suspecting that they are trying to build a power source nearby. That's why I pursued the Quadrati past the Brakeline after the initial attack and left Finlan's Point unguarded. Please, Domsei, give Magnar Kreon rank over me at Finlan's Point, but at least let me stay at the Gateways and assist him. I promise to stay the line."

"I'm sorry, Comstadt, the Upper Council has already made our decision. You are off Gateway duty. However, given your immense concern about a possible buildup of Quadrati forces there, I will advise Magnar Kreon of your concerns."

I want to argue further, to tell him not to wait, to go ahead and post more Bionics at Finlan's Point. But I'm already toeing the line. If they're taking away my Gateway privileges, perhaps I'm not too far from Nullification. I sag back. "What do you propose I do in the meantime?"

"You will be relegated to civilian duty."

What? Civilian duty? Only the Eaddies, the sub-standard Bionics do that. Boring pavement-pounding work. I may be young, but I've saved more Ceruleans than half of the Bionics put together. Surely they could put me to better use than that. My insides roil. It takes all of my concentration to keep my voice flat. "I respectfully request, Domsei Shen, that you reconsider. There must be another alternative."

"Comstadt Travler, until you can demonstrate a proper respect for the natural order of things, I'm afraid we cannot risk having you out in the Gateways. Too many lives are at risk. And despite what you might think, civilian duty is not without its merits and importance. In fact we already have your first assignment."

"Wonderful," I say flatly. Despite my efforts, I can't withhold the sarcasm from my voice. I know I'm being disrespectful, but I can't believe this is happening to me. For the last several star years since Comstadt Falk disappeared, I've been considered the lead Bionic. The best. Now, not only are the Domseis taking me off Gateway duty, I'm being relegated to watch over the civs—basically no better than a babysitter.

But the Domsei has dealt with his share of impertinence before and moves smoothly forward, ignoring my sarcasm.

"Do you remember the blood samples you collected down in the Fielands?"

"Yes." I make an effort to pull my thoughts back together. If I want to earn back my Gateway privileges, I'll need to show more resilience than that.

"Well, Comstadt, those blood samples have proven to be remarkably interesting."

"What do you mean?" I manage with a tinge more enthusiasm.

"It seems that you have uncovered a new Mark of Dresden."

My eyes snap to his, all thoughts momentarily commandeered by this new development. "But that's impossible." Or so I've been told.

Fila once mentioned that in the ancient times before The Great Dispersion, the Mark of Dresden mutation occurred almost as frequently as the wild moon. But since then, this mutation, which defines us Bionics, became more and more rare over the years, made worse by the fact that those with the Mark of Dresden cannot bear children. And though we may be near immortal, we are not quite. Based on their extrapolative calculations, our mathematicians have long predicted the end of the Bionic line. Though we number over a thousand total now, it has been twenty-three star years to this day since the last Mark of Dresden was born. And until now, most of us assumed that event to be the last. And once our numbers truly die out, that would leave no one to protect the Gateways. Well, who said math was absolute?

But something doesn't quite make sense. "Why has this new Mark of Dresden not shown up in the Gens Pool before?" Atlas carries a genetic database linked to all births in the Gateway system. Every new Mark of Dresden is identified at birth and immediately brought to Atlas.

"That's something we can't explain right now either. Rest assured that we've repeated the tests, and the results are the same. Whoever was in that Galactic hovercraft has the Mark of Dresden."

My mind flashes with an image of boot prints in the sand. The possibilities whirl in my head. "But there were multiple people on that hovercraft."

Domsei Shen nods. "You're absolutely right. The test results showed that the samples you collected were from three different individuals. Two matches were found in the Gens Pool. However, the third does not match *any* of our records."

"How can that be?"

"We don't know. But we've taken extra precautions to make sure this information doesn't get leaked to the Quadrati. We can't risk them getting to the new Mark first." The Domsei scrubs at his chin for several moments before continuing. "Which brings me to your new assignment."

"What do you propose?"

"Go down to Cerulea and find this new Mark of Dresden. Perhaps she is the missing link we have been searching for."

"*She?*"

"Yes, the new Mark of Dresden is a female. From the genetic analysis, that much we do know."

My eyes quirk up. Even more interesting. As the numbers would have it, only one in every ten Marks of Dresden is a female. Another reason Fila is so popular.

"Tracking this new Mark of Dresden may be difficult. We'll give clearance for you to go undercover. You will leave on the next star date. Understood, Comstadt?"

For a Comstadt, doing civilian duty for a month is normally considered almost worse than being Nullified. But a small part of me is intrigued by the thought of finding this new Mark of Dresden. The importance of such a find could change the course of the Gateways. Perhaps if I successfully retrieve this new Mark of Dresden the Domseis will rescind my one-month suspension from the Gateways. "As you wish. I will begin preparations."

"Very good, and by the way, happy twenty-third birthday, Comstadt Travler."

"Thank you, Domsei Shen." I fist my hand to my heart and turn to go.

XIII

LIVI: THE CHOOSING CEREMONY

WHEN THE ANCIENT clock tower bongs loudly, vibrating the late afternoon air, I quicken my pace, my regulation boots clicking double time against the paved stone. I don't want to be late.

The solid cintian metal spire of a tower looms high overhead, one of the few remnants left over from an era when the first colonists came to Cerulea many eons ago, and a solemn reminder of the struggles of our past. Above it, the softest of blues drapes lightly across the sky, and the suns glow orange-pink through a gossamer of clouds. The breezy air feels good against my flushed face as I take a breath in and notice a single fairlot perched on a short branch of a whippleseed tree just ahead of me. Its translucent sunlit wings slow its rotation and retract into its head as I approach. Curious blue orbs track me.

There is an old Cerulean saying that the songs of the fairlot are so beautiful, it's as if the stars themselves are singing. And if you're lucky enough to hear a fairlot sing, then that means the universe is looking out for you. I hold my breath and listen as I pass, but am met with only complete and utter silence. *That figures.*

After finding out that Jia is—thank the stars—going to be fine, I did in fact decide after all to drag myself back to my dormitory room for another few hours of resting my sorry bones before the Choosing Ceremony. That turned out to be a darn good thing because Dr. Kang actually stopped by not long after I got back, to make sure I was doing okay and had indeed followed his instructions. He also practically coerced me into taking a blue pain pill and some hecka-bad-smelling ointment to rub on my bruised ribs and stitched forehead. To my surprise, I did feel much better. Who knew stink could actually heal? I can even move my arms now without yelping in pain. I'll have to remember to give Dr. Kang my Tram Tram tickets from our Luthati drill win as a token of my appreciation.

Now feeling much better, I make my way along the smooth pathway of Andurian cement, melding in with the other cadets in their crisp maroon uniforms. When I get to Quellum Auditorium where the Choosing Ceremony is to be held, I have little time to appreciate the intricate latticework of the enormous geodesic dome. The wave of other cadets rushes me inside, and I'm quickly enveloped by the hum of excited chatter buzzing overhead.

"Seniors this way," Dr. Shen calls out meekly. One of the visiting quantum physics professors that I sometimes take classes from flails his thin, insect-like arms in sync. His meager and thinning hair scatters across his narrow forehead, and he struggles to direct the rowdy seniors towards the front seats. With sunken cheeks and the dusky grey of sagging skin, he looks barely able to tread even life's shallow waters.

As the throngs disperse, my thoughts can't help but go to Jia. Of all the cadets, she has studied the hardest to become one of the Beacons. One could always find Jia by heading to Chenong Library, where she would inevitably be tucked into the farthest corner near the ancient texts, where no one else would bother her while she studied. I cross my fingers that she will get chosen today.

My legs complain sharply as I climb the long steps of the auditorium stairs. I ascend higher and higher nevertheless. Patches of warm sunlight pitch onto me through the latticework of icosahedral glass that lines the domed ceiling. I let the warmth soak through and lift me. I catch a few curious glances thrown my way. With my hair draped loosely, I hope nobody notices the unsightly stretch of stitches on my forehead. But I hold my head up and keep going. I make it past several rowdy cadets, when I hear my name.

"Livi! Over here!"

I turn in surprise as I spot Haven and Keria, the twins from my troop. I've known Keria and Haven since we were grouped together on Team Horizon as freshmen.

I head over to them, and before I can even plant myself down, Keria bounces up and nearly knocks me over in a hug.

"Stars, it's good to see you, Livi. We've all been a mess after we heard what happened to Remeni and Jia. Team Horizon's practically been falling apart without you guys."

Finally, Keria releases me. Her eyes dart to the stitches on my forehead. "And are you okay? You know we've been so anxious to talk to you, but that Kyvox Young wouldn't let anyone visit you after what happened. He said you needed your rest and barked at us every time we came near your door."

Despite the pain in my side, I give her a reassuring smile, not wanting to worry them any more. "Yes. I'm managing, Keria. Thanks. And no need to be so dramatic."

"Who's being dramatic? Remember I'm not the one who came roaring back to campus in a hijacked Tracker ship all beaten up and bloodied."

Even Haven pipes up behind his sister. His spiky blond hair juts out at odd angles and is just as pale as his twin sister's. "No really, Livi, it's true. Keria may not have a single unobtrusive cell in her body, but the Kyvox really did plant himself right outside your door the first night after the accident. He wouldn't let any one of us go near you."

The cockeyed glare that Keria gives Haven makes me chuckle, but the idea of the Kyvox looking after me is unsettling for some reason.

"That's odd," I mutter, but then a thought comes to me. *Of course.* "He's just looking out for his troop. He would do the same for you too."

Keria raises an eyebrow at me. "Well then, if that's the case, he must be the most dedicated Kyvox in the history of Galactic."

I can feel the redness creeping into my cheeks. I need to change the subject before my face catches on fire. "So who do you think will be the Beacons this year?"

"With our Remeni gone, unfortunately that leaves Jacek Wilkie. After all, he won the Juniper competition this year," Haven replies.

Keria shakes her head. "But we all know that draggart cheats."

"Try telling that to Galactic Central. His father is one of their main contributors." Haven scoffs, though he is far too young to be so cynical.

Not to be outjockeyed by her twin, Keria adds, "Well, I'm betting on Kyvox Young. Being the Head Kyvox from Polaria has got to be worth something, not to mention that he also is the most handsome." She quirks a small smile at me before aiming her gaze down towards the front of the auditorium.

As Keria and Haven continue debating, I follow the line of Keria's rolling eyes down to the large mass of senior cadets near the stage, before being ensnared by a familiar dash of coal-black hair.

Kyvox Young sits in the very front row with the rest of the senior cadets, looking calm and seemingly unaffected by the hand wringing and knee jiggling around him. So much for changing the subject. But I have to agree with Keria. As Head Kyvox, I have no doubt he will be one of the Beacons this year. And from the way he holds his head high and back straight, I know he has no doubts either. A senior girl that I've seen around the dorms sits purposefully next to the Head Kyvox, flashing him a flirty smile. I don't know why, but I have to look away.

I distract myself by watching the other seniors. They all seem so excited to be finishing up at Galactic. Will I feel the same way next year? Galactic has become like a second family to me.

Glancing around the rest of the auditorium, though I desperately wish Jia and Remeni were here, I let the energy around me fill some of the aching hollows. It's clear from the spirited laughter and cheer of my fellow cadets, they are eager to ascend to their new stations in life within Galactic, to protect Cerulea, to explore space. And I realize that despite everything that has happened, I'm still glad to be here, to be at Galactic, living the dreams I held as a child, no matter what the risk.

I'm wrapped up in my own ruminations until a slight movement catches my attention out of the corner of my eye. I glance back over my shoulder.

All thoughts immediately scatter out of my head like holliberry leaves adrift in the Andurian winds. As much as I try, I can't help but open-face stare at who sits a few seats behind me almost hidden in the shadows of an overarching beam. His body is built like a mountain, but what strikes me is the fierceness of his gaze as he looks towards the stage and the subtle flexing of well-honed muscles brimming with some otherworldly power. He faces forward, and his angled jaws clench tightly. Though he wears the Galactic cap and uniform of an officer, I'm sure I have never seen him around campus before. And he is not someone I would miss.

Fighting the urge to keep staring, I turn my head back before he notices. Luckily, Professor Hensly, the director of the academy for as long as I can remember, takes to the stage, pulling our attention to him.

Professor Hensly is an elderly man. His balding head perfectly matched with his beaked nose, pinpoint chin, and hunched back have earned him the nickname The Vulture. But despite the nickname, most consider him to be mild mannered. Holographic reproductions of his image project throughout the auditorium, and one such image appears like a floating deity less than an arm's length away. I restrain the urge to reach out and touch it. This close up, I can see that Professor Hensly's eyes are rimmed in dark shadows. I'm not the only one who needs more rest. Professor Hensly clears his throat, his voice pelting the microphone like rough gravel.

"Cadets. Today marks the 200th anniversary of the Choosing at Galactic's International Space Academy. This day will be a new starting point for our seniors as they begin their new stations within the Galactic society to not only protect Cerulea but also to expand humankind's reach into the universe. Every year we select three of our best and most promising seniors across all of our campuses to join the Beacons, our most elite team based in Polaria, who will serve on the most challenging and dangerous of Galactic's missions. The remaining seniors will be assigned to land-based units, which are critical to the everyday functions within the Galactic society. As you know, everyone goes through a rigorous set of exams at the year's end to help us determine where you fit best within Galactic."

Professor Hensly pauses a moment to take an audible breath. "But first, I would like to take a moment of silence for Cadet Remeni Finch. As many of you already know, he was killed yesterday in a terrible hovercraft accident while on a mission in the Fielands. Cadet Finch was one of our most promising senior cadets, and we feel his loss greatly."

A solemn silence blankets the room as Professor Hensly bows his head and brings his right hand up to his chest, palm to the left, in a salute of remembrance. The whole of the auditorium follows in suit. My chest tightens, and I fight to keep my breaths even. I can feel a couple of glances thrown in my direction, but I keep my head down. *Keep it together, Livi. Do it for Remeni. Just breathe.* Next to me, Keria takes my hand and gives it a comforting squeeze.

"And so today's Choosing Ceremony will be dedicated to Cadet Remeni Finch and all of the other heroes like him who have lost their lives to protect our beloved Cerulea. May our actions as Galactics from this day forth continue to be bold and brave just as they had been." Several more long moments of silence pass before Professor Hensly finally continues, his thin lips angled up ever so slightly. "Now, with the indomitable spirit of our past heroes to guide us, we must forge ahead into the future. Let's proceed with the Choosing."

The stage explodes in a multicolored dance of bright lights. The words "The Beacons" project in shimmering gold in the background. A cheer rises from the cadets in the crowd as the seniors sit, nervously looking from one to the other. The tightness in my chest eases ever so slightly.

"Being selected as a Beacon is in itself an honor, but being the Head Beacon is the greatest honor that can be bestowed on any Galactic. This year, that honor goes to—Kyvox Keenon Young."

Cheers erupt from the crowd as all eyes train on Kyvox Young, who surges forward towards the stage. Keria was right. There is no surprise here. One doesn't get to be Head Kyvox by being a slackerhead. The insecurities of the boy I used to know are nowhere to be found. His fluid movements embody strength and inevitability, a study of momentum in nature carrying him perpetually forward. He is no trickling stream, but instead moves

81

with the force of a crashing wave. As he gets on the stage, he turns and nods to Professor Hensly with a confident smile.

"Jacek Wilkie." This time our nemesis from Team Lunai fist-bumps his friends before jogging up on stage with a placid smile.

I sit here rigidly, fingers digging into the hard edge of my seat. There's only one more Beacon spot left.

"And Jia Ong, who could not be here this afternoon, but who I am told will make a speedy recovery in time for her Beaconship training."

I cannot believe what I hear. Despite everything that has happened and ignoring my protesting ribs, I jump up cheering for my friend. I just wish she could have been here to enjoy this moment.

Professor Hensly steps forward, then motions for everyone to take our seats as quiet reacquires the room. "Now, I'd like to make a special announcement. In light of the recently escalating Quadrati attacks, Galactic has decided to create a second pathway to Beaconship, a new class of Beacons to be selected from the junior cadets. They will train alongside the Beacons at Polaria in an accelerated program to help shore up our defense systems there. We will begin by selecting one cadet for the inaugural Junior Beacon class."

A collective gasp issues forth from the crowd. The cadets murmur excitedly to each other. Whoever heard of having a Junior Beacon? Either the Quadrati threat really is growing dire, or—

Before I can ponder more on this, Professor Hensly clears his throat and announces, "The Junior Beacon this year will be Cadet Livinthea Park. Please come forward."

What in the name of Altheria? Did I hear that right?

I sit momentarily stunned, solid and heavy like a stone. Time stretches out. The roaring of an ocean wave fills my head, and I am carried away. It must have been several seconds before I realize that Keria is shaking my shoulders and trying to get my attention.

"Livi! You'd better get down there. They're waiting for you."

Breaking out of my daze, I swallow hard and stand up. I nod to Haven as I slide past him. *Whatever this is about, I can show no fear*, I remind myself. Though I feel as if I'm about to leap off of some ungodly high precipice with no foreseeable bottom, I keep my posture straight as I make my way down the auditorium stairs. I know all eyes are on me.

When I finally make it on stage, Professor Hensly takes a step towards me and offers a handshake. I take it gratefully and try to keep my hands from trembling as I whisper to him. "Surely this must be some mistake, Professor Hensly. You know I haven't even taken astrodynamics yet."

Professor Hensly squeezes my hand. "There is no mistake, Cadet Park. Galactic's choice has been made. Congratulations." But on his face is a grimness I can't quite figure out.

I'm too stunned to speak and simply nod. I find myself standing next to Kyvox Young. To my surprise he gives me a wide reassuring smile before turning back towards the crowd. I know I should be happy, and I force myself to turn and smile at the cheering crowd as well. But underneath it all, my thoughts are swirling.

Am I really ready?

XIV

LIVI: THE STRIKING STRANGER

THOUGH IN A DAZE, somehow I manage to find my way back from the stage to my seat next to Keria and Haven. They smile gleefully at me the minute I get back.

The rest of the Choosing progresses uneventfully. But it strikes me how one single decision by the higher-ups can completely alter the trajectory of one's life. In any case, the seniors seem ecstatic all around. And though I'm still stunned being chosen as a Beacon, I also can't wait to go find Jia after the ceremonies and tell her the good news. Finally, Professor Hensly makes his last announcements, and the other students eagerly start to file out of the auditorium.

Keria stands up, jumping up and down as she hugs me. "Congratulations, Livi! How about we go celebrate your new Beaconship at the Tram Tram finals? You know who's going to be playing in it, don't you?" Her eyes trip down in the direction of Kyvox Young, and I just have to giggle at her funny expression.

"You guys go ahead. I'm going to stop by and see Jia first. I want to tell her the good news."

Haven stands up too. "I'll go with you, Livi."

"It's okay, Haven. I'm a big girl. I wouldn't want you to miss the finals game." Gently, I shove him after Keria. He practically lives for those Tram Tram games.

Haven throws me a peevish smile. "All right, *Beacon* Livi, but if you need anything, just call." He taps at the comms link braced on his forearm.

"Will do, Captain Safety." I give him a mock salute. "Now get going before all the good seats are taken." Haven and Keria don't need any more encouragement and jog down the stairs two at a time. I can't help but to smile after them.

I stand up to go, when a slight movement catches my eye. I glance back over my shoulder.

The striking stranger.

I almost forgot about him through the excitement of the Choosing Ceremony. He appears deep in thought and fingers something shiny hanging at the collar of his cadet uniform. When I look more closely at what hangs there, my mind grinds to a halt.

It looks alive. A gloriously charged orb holding captive a lightning storm of multicolored sparks underneath its smooth surface. And in this moment, I find myself flung into the vast and gaping crevices of space-time, with all things long forgotten. The dusty floorboard of the old cellar, hastily nailed shut, creaks open in my mind. Not even the swirling sands of Dresden are enough to pull me back. The pendant looks exactly like the one my father wore when I was a child.

I play in my room, when my father walks in. Normally, he's impeccably dressed, but today streaks of dirt mar his handsome face, his dark hair lies disheveled, and the top button of his shirt is torn open. But what grabs the attention of my young eyes the most is the brilliant pendant he wears at his neck. I have never seen it before. It's as if the pendant is bursting forth with all the suns and the stars of the universe all at once.

"Papa, could I have a pretty pendant just like the one you are wearing?"

At first he says nothing, looking down at the pendant and fingering it gently. And then I become frightened because I notice a single tear trailing down his cheek. But perhaps it's my imagination, for then he looks up at me with his familiar smile and explains to me in his always calm voice that the pendant is an important family treasure and ". . . someday when you're older and the right time comes, I will pass mine on to you, my Comet."

I nod back to him, satisfied and eager for that day to come.

But after that day, I never saw my father again. Almost everything I've worked for since then stems from the horrific events following that day. And now the reminder of that memory reopens a jagged hole deep within, the edges raw even though I've tried to smooth them down for so many years.

My eyes clamp onto the pendant that the stranger wears. I don't want to let go. The emptying bleachers and the clip-clop of hundreds of regulation boots slowly fade away. Even the shock of my new Beaconship status dulls, and I find my feet slowly sidling towards the stranger of their own accord. I've got to find out more. Where did the striking stranger get that pendant? Suddenly the stranger's eyes pivot up, knowledge and knowing locking onto mine, and I stutter to a halt.

"Congratulations," a booming voice calls up to me from behind.

I whirl around startled, almost losing my footing off the narrow bleacher, to find Kyvox Young looking up at me from the lower tiers of the auditorium. What's he still doing here? I'm surprised he hasn't already left to warm up for his finals game tonight. It takes me a moment to collect my thoughts.

"Th-thank you, Kyvox."

The Kyvox's dark eyebrows furrow. "Everything okay, Livi?"

"Um . . . yes. I mean . . . yes, sir. Kyvox, sir." *Stars, why am I being such a ninny?* I clear my throat. "I just saw something that reminded me of—" Steadying myself, I pivot slightly, only to find—no one. I twist around fully, but the stranger is nowhere in sight. *What in the name of Altheria?* When I turn back towards Kyvox Young, I find him looking at me with a puzzled expression lining his face.

"What were you going to say?" he asks.

"That's strange. He was just here a minute ago."

Kyvox Young follows my gaze as I continue scanning the empty benches and scaffolding. *How very strange.*

"Are you feeling all right, Livi? I know there's been quite a bit of excitement for you. Perhaps we should have Dr. Kang see you again."

What? Great. Now the Kyvox thinks I've lost it. "No really, there was a guy in a Galactic officer's uniform, and he was wearing something that looked just like—" I stumble for an explanation. I certainly do not want to see

87

Dr. Kang or the insides of his ridiculously cramped MedScan unit again. "—and I feel fine. *Really*." I stand up straight, trying to wipe the confusion off my face. But my insides are still roiled up. How did the stranger disappear so quickly? Why did he have a pendant like the one my father had?

Before I can say anything else, the Kyvox advances without hesitation the rest of the way up towards me, until we are face to face. Actually, face to chest, since the Kyvox is easily a foot taller than me. I have to tilt my head back when he speaks. He eyes me with concern. "Remember what I said before. If you need anything, just let me know. I mean it."

When he looks at me, I feel myself getting lost in the funny arcs and softly meandering edges again. An uncomfortable fluttering pickets my chest, and questions about the phantom stranger and the Beaconship get shoved aside. *Get a grip, Livi. He said the past was over. As your Kyvox, he just wants to make sure you're okay.*

"Thank you, Kyvox. I really appreciate your offer, but—"

"You know you shouldn't call me that anymore, don't you?" Kyvox Young interrupts me abruptly.

"What?" Oh what an idiot I am. I can feel my face flushing. "Sorry, I mean, Beacon Young."

To my surprise the corners of his lips quirk up, and I can see the smallest of dimples gracing his left cheek. I've never noticed it before.

"No. Just Keenon. We're both Beacons now, remember?"

"Oh right."

"You sure you're okay?"

"I'm sure. Thanks."

The Kyvox turns to leave. "Just promise me you'll get some rest tonight. I'll see you tomorrow at the celebration festival?"

"Will do, Kyvox. I mean, Keenon." I muster a response and start to leave as well. I throw one last glance around the empty auditorium. A shiver slivers down my spine. Maybe the Kyvox is right. I really do need to get some rest.

XV

TRITON: FOUND HER

FINALLY. I'M ON THE RIGHT TRACK. When I spot her walking through that auditorium door, I know that this time, she's the one.

Yesterday was a different story, a day of false leads and dead ends. I even swiped a blood sample from the med unit, apparently from a girl badly injured in the hovercraft accident. As the jinxes would have it—wrong girl.

But today I will not make that same mistake.

Now that I see her, it's obvious.

I can even pick her out from a thousand cadets clear across the auditorium. And it's not just because my Bionic eyes can detect the telltale injuries suggesting recovery from a recent accident. And it's also not because the genetic analysis told me I would be looking for someone of slight build, with deep brown hair and eyes to match. It's just *her*.

Despite her injuries, she holds her head up as if nothing could get her down. Her movements flow decisively and sure. People can't help but turn and watch as she climbs up the auditorium stairs, and she doesn't even seem to notice.

Her long, straight, dark hair frames her gamine face, her features blending delicately, *except for those eyes*. And the quiet determination in her eyes makes me drawn to her even more.

Yes, I'm certain of it. *She's the one who took down that Droid.*

I'd bet my Hemlock points on it.

I stalk along the shadowed perimeter of the auditorium, drawing closer without even thinking. Some of her friends call out to her, and she goes to greet them. I haven't decided how I'm going to approach her yet, so I keep my head down under my Galactic cap, hunch my shoulders, and head up the back bleachers until I find a seat close to her but within the shadows of an overarching beam.

She speaks with her friends, and the sound trickles back to me like the floating bubbles of Chef Aton's Stars Day drink. Intoxicating. There is an invincibility about her, and something else important: She looks like she belongs here. She looks content.

And now I am to take that life away from her.

In that instant, I find myself feeling an unexpected sense of—loss. Regret. And it hits me hard. *I could have been like her,* living the carefree life of a cadet, a Cerulean, without the weight of the whole universe nearly crushing me. And in that moment, as her eyes sparkle with the light of a thousand stars, so brightly that I have a hard time looking away, I also realize something else.

I can't do it.
I won't do it.

I won't be the one responsible for taking away that carefree life the way mine was stolen. I take one last look at her. She reminds me of the strength of the human spirit that I have dedicated my life to protect.

I force my gaze away and make my decision. I will go back to the Domseis and tell them the lab result was a mistake. The Quadrati haven't discovered her yet, so she's still safe in that respect.

The Ceremony begins and ends almost in the same breath. But it's useful in confirming her identity. Livinthea Park—a Beacon, no less.

Just as I'm about to go, I feel a sudden burning at the notch of my neck, my hands reaching reflexively for the orling there.

Something is wrong with the Gateways.

I mustn't take it out in plain view, but I'm still hidden in the shadows. The cadets around me are already starting to disperse and are too caught up in their own conversations to notice me. I take the risk.

I sneak out the orling and look at it. With my Bionic vision, I can make out the miniature map and mercatorian lines of the Gateways that glow as usual. However, a spark lights up at Finlan's Point. That could only mean one thing: another breach. I've got to go help.

But when I take another quick glance around, I suddenly find myself staring—straight into her eyes. *Livinthea Park. Double jinx.*

But just at that moment, someone calls to her from behind, distracting her.

Now's my chance, and luckily I have my modified darkwing suit on underneath the Galactic uniform the Domseis gave me. I reach down and activate it.

XVI

LIVI: SNEAKING IN

"ONLY A FEW MINUTES, got it? Your friend has got to get some rest if you want her to get better."

The medicus levels me with a stern look while plucking the tickets from my hands.

"Of course," I reply assuredly, swinging my backpack over my shoulder and slipping through the door before he changes his mind.

As soon as I step into the room, I'm assaulted by the pungent smell of antiseptic. The small medical chamber is darkened, and I have to blink a few times before my eyes adjust. But when they do, my insides sink like the cold stones of Juthri. I find myself unable to speak. She looks so broken.

"Livi? Is that you?" Jia's voice sounds small and shattered. Her head is wrapped like a mummy's, eyes barely peeking out from underneath the heavy bandages. Several wires splay out from her chest to a bedside monitor, which pings in a rhythmic cadence. When she struggles to sit up, her face contorts in pain.

My chest tightens. Quickly, I take the last few steps towards her and place my hand on hers.

"Shh. Yes, Jia. It's me. Don't try to get up, okay? You're still recovering from surgery." My voice grates in my throat.

Jia manages a weak smile. "Stars, Livi, it's so good to see you. I don't know how much more of this place I can take." Her eyes grow somber. "But I suppose I have no right to complain. Not after what happened to Remeni."

"It's okay, Jia. You've been through a lot, and according to Dr. Kang, you just barely survived an epidural hematoma. I don't think anyone could fault you for complaining just a little bit."

"But poor Remeni, I wish I could have gone to his remembrance." Jia's eyes well up at the corners, and her heart rate on the monitor blips rapidly upwards.

Truth be told, I want to cry too. Seeing her brings back all the awful recent events to the forefront of my mind. And I'm tired of putting up a strong facade. But I can't cry in front of Jia, not now when she is still so fragile. I've got to get her mind off of things.

I give her hand a squeeze. "Here, look what I brought you." I pull out the red tablet from my pack and hand it to her.

Her face lights up. "My digitek. Thank you, Livi. At least now I'll have all the time in the world to catch up on my reading." She turns on the tablet and gives me a grateful smile through her sniffles. "You know I still haven't had a chance to read Ianthia Yen's latest thriller?"

"Well, now's your chance," I reply as I pat her hand gently, glad to see her tears subside. I have the strange sensation of wanting to laugh, but at the same time still fighting the lump that has gotten me in the gizzard.

Jia slumps back in her bed with a grunt. "By the way, how did you get in? They haven't been letting me have any visitors."

"Let's just say a few Tram Tram tickets go a long way."

"What?" Jia's eyebrows shoot up. "Oh no, Livi. You didn't give up your seats to the finals game, did you?"

I nod my head slightly. "Don't worry about that, okay? Everyone knows Kyvox Young's team is going to win anyway."

"But Livi, you didn't need to do that. I know how much you wanted to see that game. You used up your last month's allowance for those tickets, remember?"

"It's no big deal, Jia. I just wanted to make sure you were doing okay. And for your information, I didn't use up my allowance on just those tickets." I bring out the two cans of sparkling apple cider and the box of holliberries covered in Svetlian chocolate that I had hidden in my backpack. They're Jia's favorites.

"Wow, Livi, what's all this for?" Jia reaches for the chocolates eagerly.

"How else are we going to celebrate the good news?"

"What good news?"

"You mean they haven't told you?"

"What *good news*? Spill it already, will you, Livi?" Jia looks ready to pummel me, even in her weakened state.

"You're one of the Beacons this year."

Jia's eyes go wide, and her mouth drops open. "You're just throwing me around the Yentian belt."

"No. It's true. You know I would never pull a trick like that on you, especially since you're only steps away from death's door already. Really, Jia, I'm telling you the truth. I just came from the Choosing Ceremony to tell you. You're one of them." I pause a moment. Maybe this is already too much to tell her since she's just recovering. *Oh what the heck.* "And guess what? I'm a Beacon too."

Jia looks at me speechless for several moments like I've lost all the nuggins in my head. "You too? But you're not even a senior yet."

"I know, it's crazy." I'm the one babbling now. "But Galactic made some adjustments to the program. We're going to be Beacons *together.*"

Jia squeals so loudly that I have to cover her mouth with my hand to shush her. Maybe letting her know now wasn't the best idea. "Keep it down, Jia, or that mean old medicus is going to come back and stick you with some strong sedatives for sure."

Jia stills, and I hold my breath thinking I hear footsteps running down the hallway.

We sit there tensely for a few moments, but no one bursts through the door. Finally, I let myself relax. Opening a can of apple cider, I carefully hand it over to Jia. "Congratulations, Jia. You totally deserve it."

"Thanks, Livi. That really means a lot to me." Jia looks down at the cider and takes it, the corners of her eyes glistening. She's worked harder for this than anyone I know. Her voice quivers. "I just wish Remeni were here."

"Me too," I say, my throat tightening. "You know Remeni would have been proud of you, Jia."

"And you as well," Jia replies.

"To Remeni." I hold my can of cider up to Jia's.

"To Remeni," she repeats, clinking her can against mine. We both take a drawn-out swig of our cider, then sit there silently for a long moment. Neither one of us is brave enough to talk, lest we start blubbering.

But finally Jia breaks the silence, her voice more steady. "I can't believe we're going to be Beacons together."

Though I may one of Galactic's best pilots, the uncertainty about the whole Beaconship thing still lingers. "I know I should be happy, Jia, but—but what if I'm not ready? I haven't even gone through senior training yet."

Now it's Jia's turn to put her hand over mine. "You're hands down the most talented cadet I know, Livi, even if you do wear plaid shorts with striped shirts on hot summer days. But luckily I think Galactic can overlook that deficiency."

"Thanks, Jia, for reminding me what's important in life." I can't help but chuckle. "Now, how wrong is it that you're the one giving me a shot of confidence when you're the one in the sick bed?"

"Job security you know. Best friend's gotta do what she's gotta do, even if it does sap the last of the life-force out of me." Jia flails a hand to her bandaged forehead while slumping back in her bed. She has always had a flair for dramatics. But in the next moment she perks back up. "Who else was chosen?"

"Kyvox Young of course. And that draggart Cadet Wilkie."

"Oh stars, Livi. Kyvox Young? You sure you can bear to be around him? You know there will be no escaping him on the tiny Polaria campus."

I hesitate a moment, though I know I can tell Jia anything. "The funny thing is, he's been acting kind of strange lately."

"Strange? What do you mean strange?"

"I mean nicer. I'm not sure how else to put it. Like he's not just out to run me into the ground anymore."

"Well, I'll believe it when I see it," Jia says with a huff. She grabs one of the chocolates and pops it in her mouth. "Stars, Livi, you *are* the best friend ever. You sure I'm supposed to have these?" Her voice is muffled as she chews noisily. "One day, after I retire from Galactic, I'm going to go visit Svetlia and learn how to make these chocolates myself."

I laugh. That's what I love about Jia—her indomitable spirit—and why we've been best friends at Galactic. "Take me with you, okay?"

"Always."

XVII

LIVI: QUADRATI ATTACK

O NLY MY REGULATION BOOTS sound on the cobbled walkway as I trek back through the south end of campus to my dormitory, my pack swinging lightly at my shoulder.

Though the dark buildings loom like specters against the lamplights and the night air runs chilled, somehow I feel heartened now that I've seen Jia on the mend. I waited until she was snoring soundly, before slipping out of the infirmary.

An unnatural quietness breathes through the deserted campus hub. Usually, Union Square is filled with the raucous laughter and chatter of cadets during their downtime. But even the caffea shop is shuttered tonight. I suppose most are attending the Tram Tram finals on the far side of campus. Part of me wishes I hadn't bartered off my tickets, but it was worth seeing Jia just the same.

Suddenly the breach alarm sounds, screeching through the evening air like a wounded Skythe and slicing a direct path straight down to my nerves. *Crimeny, I hate that sound.*

Every time I hear it, it catapults me back me to that terrible day over ten years ago. But then I take a few calming breaths through my nose and remind myself that we've had these drills many times before, almost as frequently as the Altherian eclipses. Anyone out of doors should get immediately inside. At this time of night though, most of the campus buildings are locked, including the infirmary. My best bet is just to head back to the dormitory bunkers, though they're on the other side of campus. *Well, better get going then.* I pick up my pace to a steady jog.

Just as I round the corner of Union Square, warning flares streak up from the three perimeter towers of Galactic campus, electrifying the slumbering clouds in bright flashes of crimson, and bringing me to a halt. My insides quiver in time with the echoing shots as I glance quickly around, my eyes darting to the suddenly creeping shadows.

This is not a drill.

And it can only mean one thing.

Quadrati attack.

Crimeny. But the Quadrati have never been so bold as to attack the international campus before. I don't know if I can handle running into a Droid again so soon. Being so far from any lockdown bunkers, I'm too exposed here. *Keep it together, Livi. Just do what you have to do.* Various scenarios and probabilities whirl in my head. And it only takes me a moment to realize that there's only one real option.

My muscles bunch and release into a sprint in the opposite direction of where I was going. It's several kilometers to the nearest dormitory bunker, but only half a kilometer to Southanger, where what remains of our Tularian ships will be out on the launchpad in preparation for standard drills tomorrow morning. I may not be able to get into the hangar, but I can get into a Tully. And I'm safe from anything in a ship.

My legs churn over hard pavement, patchy grass, crunching gravel, and back to hard pavement again. The shortest distance between any two points is a straight line, and I am not concerned with staying on the sidewalks and roads at this point. Tendrils of hair fly across my face, and I drop my pack, but I'm far from caring. I don't want to be out in the open when the Quadrati get here.

The breach alarm continues to blare, and the night sky flashes with more warning flares. Normally, I could sprint this distance no problem, but with my recent rib injury, I find myself quickly winded. Still I push myself harder. If I can just get to the ships, I can hide there. Worst case scenario, I fly.

As I crest Gregum's Hill, our Tularian ships come into view below. I pause in relief, my breaths heaving in and out in rapid succession. I've made it.

Suddenly, high-pitched buzzing saws through the air, drawing my attention to the skies. I swear under my breath. *A Tracker ship.*

The sleek bullet shape of the Quadrati ambush ship streaks from the south, a barely visible slash across the moonlit sky. I stare as it abruptly freezes in a hover *above the fleet of Tullies.* Keeping an eye on the Tracker, I drop to a dead crouch next to the gnarled trunk of a cyprian tree, sidling up so close that its rough bark digs into my side.

How is this happening to me *again?* Somehow, I've managed to put myself right in the middle of the Quadrati attack. Just my luck. I've got to let Galactic Central know where I've spotted them. I reach down for my comms link, only to remember that I left it in my backpack, which I dropped who knows where. Double drat.

Within moments, the belly of the ship yawns open. To my horror, not one but four Droids hatch from its underside into the midst of our Tullies fleet. What in the name of Altheria? Why are they here?

One by one, the Droids disappear into the Tullies as the Tracker ship hurtles away. *They're going to steal the last of our ships.* I briefly entertain the idea of running back to let Galactic Central know what's happening, but probably by that time, the Quadrati will be long gone with our few remaining Tullies.

But the two Tullies closest to me haven't yet been boarded. Perhaps I can get myself into one of the ships and use the comms device to alert Galactic Central. The thick brush and trees should provide me enough cover. There's no time to waste. Any minute now, they're likely to take off.

Ignoring the pain in my side, I pick my way down the edge of the embankment, staying low to the ground out of sight. My feet skid on the loose gravel, but I manage to remain unscathed save for a few scrapes on my hands. I reach the bottom and crouch behind an outcropping of thick bushes. One of the empty Tullies is only a few steps away.

Suddenly the ground in front of me erupts, a shocking jolt clear through the base of my brain. Chunks of terra spew in every direction and barely miss knocking me out from amongst the living and into long-forgotten eternity. Stars alive. I turn to find a Droid coming at me, a pulsating device in his hand. How could he have even spotted me? This Quadrati Droid looks different from the others. Taller. A dark golden tinge to its metal. A Sensate Droid. The most dangerous kind.

And I don't even have my sikkar.

With every ounce of energy I have left, I leap over the gaping hole. I just need to get myself inside that Tully. But as soon as I wrench open the hatch, cool metal clamps down on my collar, and I'm flung back. My spine cracks against hard dirt, and the air rushes out of my lungs. A small part of me vaguely wonders if I'll ever breathe again. My ears ring, and for a moment I lie there in a daze, just the stars and me. *Get up, Livi. Get up. Get up.* I struggle to gain my bearings, pushing myself up to a sitting position with my bloodied hands. My head whirls violently, but what's worse is that I find myself staring right up into the red pulsating pupils of a Droid.

I'm such a goner.

My thoughts don't even have time to scream. The Quadrati arches back his lethal metallic arm, and I squeeze my eyes shut, whispering a silent goodbye to my Grandpa Wren. I hope he can forgive me.

A rush of air comes at me, then the clashing sound of metal against—metal? I open my eyes, only to be greeted by a blinding flash of light.

When my eyes adjust, I don't see the Quadrati anywhere. Instead I find myself staring into startling grey eyes rimmed in the dark ebony of night. An unusual shimmering plays at the familiar edges, emphasizing an angular jaw and a powerful frame. Stars.

It's the Striking Stranger.

Is this what death is like? Could this be why he disappeared earlier, because I was seeing a ghost?

But then in a voice as deep and barreling as Pan's Ocean, he speaks to me. "Are you all right, Cadet Park?"

And only then, as I glance down at myself, do I realize that though every aching surface on me is dirt-encrusted and my cadet uniform looks like hellas, I am all right. I'm still *alive*.

I nod my head silently, too stunned to speak. A powerful roar bursts around us, and I vaguely register that the other Droids are taking off with our Tullies. When I struggle to get up, strong arms help me to my feet.

"Good. Then I suggest, Cadet Park, that you get to the bunkers. Now." He motions in the direction of the dormitories, a lock of white brushing at his temple. Before I can say anything, he vaults through the Tully's open hatch several feet off the ground as if it takes no effort at all. Within seconds, his Tully takes off, shooting after the stolen ships.

For a moment, a part of me considers heading back to the safety of the bunkers. But how can I leave the Striking Stranger alone to fight the four Quadrati Droids himself? After all, there's still one Tully left.

I scramble towards the last remaining Tully, drag open its hatch, and with some effort pull myself up with the handholds. Once inside, I launch myself at the pilot's seat, ignoring the pain in my chest as I strap myself in.

"Galactic Central. This is Cadet Park. I've spotted the Quadrati near Southanger. They've taken off with our Tullies."

"Any idea where they went?"

"They headed due south, and the Striking—I mean, I saw one of our own go after them."

"Well done, Cadet. Bunker down, and we will send reinforcements after them."

"With all due respect, sir, by the time reinforcements arrive, the Tullies will be long gone. Request permission to go after them." There's a slight pause, static humming thickly through the air.

"Very well, Cadet, permission granted."

The engines come alive as my hands take over, and I can feel myself relaxing. Instinct kicks in, a synaptic reflex that bypasses the normal cognitive chain-linked pathway required in the overrated process of thinking.

But the moment the Tully lifts, I realize something is wrong. The ship lists sharply to the right, almost careening into the embankment that is Gregum's Hill. The blast from before must have damaged its wing. I would have been thrown from my seat had it not been for my restraints. Immediately, I shut down the thrusters, and the Tully sinks to the ground with a resounding thud. Of all the worst possible timing.

But as I stare out the cockpit window at the Tullies, what I see amazes me. Perhaps we won't need reinforcements after all. For the Striking Stranger has already taken down three of the four stolen ships. He pilots like no one I've seen before, not even close. That is, except perhaps one person—me. He spirals up, arcs down, shoots sideways after the last stolen Tully. While watching his aerial acrobatics, one thought pushes forward through the chaos of my mind.

Who is he?

The dance continues, and I strain my eyes until the Tullies are mere flecks of light, intermingling amongst the hanging stars. Though I have no idea who the Striking Stranger is, I throw a silent plea to the universe just the same. *Please let him be okay.*

The breach alarm finally subsides, and I sit there for a few moments staring after them until a flurry of activity outside catches my attention. Galactic patrols swarm the area like ants. *Well, it's about time.* No doubt I should head out to give the higher-ups a debriefing.

I climb back down slowly out of the Tully, the night's events replaying in my head. With one leg dangling midair, another question stops me short. How did the Striking Stranger know my name?

XVIII

LIVI: BIONICS

THE BROKEN TULLIES AND COLD EYES of the Quadrati seem a world away now that I step inside the training center for Senior Celebrations.

The training center, where we normally push our bodies to their utmost limits, has been transformed into something otherworldly. Holographic images of Erlion's twenty constellations pulsate and glow in the misted air above. Live music and raucous laughter echo loudly off the far walls. Close to the entrance, Professor Hensly's balding head stands out despite being engulfed within a throng of cadets who linger there. He nods towards me as I pass.

The last star day has gone by in a blur, a deluge of meetings with Galactic Central regarding the Quadrati attack. And forget about any preparations for my Beaconship. With all the chaos lately, I'm surprised these celebrations haven't been cancelled. I suppose, though, that it is a much needed break to keep up cadet morale.

Personally, I would have preferred a nice quiet evening visiting Jia in the med unit, then catching up on sleep. But regrettably for me, I promised Keria and Haven I would be here tonight.

As I move deeper into the crowd, I tug uncomfortably at my light blue dress, adjusting the annoying strap that keeps slipping down my right shoulder every time I move. Even worse, it itches in all the wrong places. Unfortunately, I had no other choice. It's the only dress I own. Despite the dress, perhaps I can enjoy this party. But then again, my feet also hurt like all hellas, stuffed into heeled sandals like an oversized lobster into an undersized shell. Give me my regulation boots any day.

Earlier, I just stepped out the door wearing my usual cadet uniform, when I ran into Keria all glammed up. She made me do an immediate about-face right back into my dorm room and instructed me to "for once in your life" put something nice on, and "quit hiding the fact that you're a girl." While she pulled my hair out of my ponytail, brushing it until it fanned out in soft waves down my back, I proceeded to remind her that we were all cadets here at Galactic, and that there was no need to be fancy. Keria proceeded to promise me that if I insisted on dressing in my usual tomboy fatigues to a once-a-year fancy party, she would personally strip me down and change me into her most frilly, over-the-top dress if I was not going to choose a nicer one for myself. That was all the encouragement I needed. Keria always kept her word. I suppose it doesn't hurt to try to look at least a little bit nice.

To my relief, I spot the twins hovering over the buffet of assorted foods. Scrumptious meats and pastry desserts overflow on the long table, a stark contrast to the usual fare of day-old potatoes and beans we eat at the dorms. Only once a year does Galactic hold a celebration like this, a final send-off for the senior cadets on their way to their new assignments. Keria and Haven are not alone in taking full advantage of that.

I sneak up to them, but Keria's senses are like that of no other. She spins around just as I'm about to surprise her. "There you are, Livi!" She looks me up and down. "I knew you could do it. Stars, you look great. Doesn't she, Haven?" She embraces me as if it were my last day on Cerulea.

Haven turns and his eyes widen when he sees me. "You really do look beautiful, Livi." Then he winks at me. "But you know I think you're beautiful no matter what, frilly dress or fatigues, makes no difference to me."

"Thank you, Haven." I wink back.

Keria will not be deterred. "Well, I think she looks especially lovely tonight, and I'm so glad you made it. Here, you've got to try this chocolate mousse. It's delish." She shoves a goblet filled with dark brown goo at me.

Haven rolls his eyes at his twin. "For star's sake, Keria, food and fancy clothing aside, aren't there more important things to talk about? Livi hasn't even had a chance to tell us about the Quadrati attack."

I smile at Haven. "No. It's fine, really. In fact, I could use something to eat right now since I missed dinner. Everyone at Galactic Central has been going crazy since that last Quadrati breach. I don't know how many more debriefings I can take." I spoon a bit of the mousse into my mouth. "Mmmmm, the dinner of champions. Just what I needed." Despite its appearance, the mousse really does taste good.

"I don't know how you got so lucky, Livi," Haven mumbles between bites of food. "Two Quadrati sightings in less than two weeks, and you were there for both of them. I have yet to lay eyes on a single real-life Droid."

"I wouldn't necessarily call it lucky," I reply. "In fact, if that's what you consider luck, I'm more than happy to share."

Keria chimes in after her brother, "Well, you know we were stuck in the dormitory bunkers for hours until the Kyvoxes gave the all clear. No, for once I agree with Haven, I'd much rather be where the action is." Keria is about to say something further, but then her posture straightens, and she waggles her eyebrows at me. "I think someone is looking for you." She nudges me to turn around, at the same time grabbing Haven's arm and tugging him away.

"Wait, Keria, where are you—"

"Livi?"

I spin around, forgetting I'm in these darned heels and almost lose my balance.

It's Kyvox—I mean *Keenon* Young, and his arm shoots out to my elbow just in time, then drops immediately to his side. He's dressed to the tee, in a formal Galactic suit with a high open collar that emphasizes the defined angles of his jaw. "Thank goodness I finally found you. Your dormmate told me I'd find you here." Then he looks me up and down, his eyebrows arched. "Well, I suppose that answers one of my questions. Looks like you're more than all right."

The way he says it makes the warmth creep up into my face. Thank goodness for the dim lighting. "Yes, I'm just fine. Why?"

"I heard what happened to you after the Choosing Ceremony, and I've been meaning to come by and see you, but Galactic Central has all the Kyvoxes doing double duty, trying to figure out how the Quadrati breached our defenses."

Luckily he doesn't seem to notice my embarrassment. "What did you find?"

"Not much. But what's odd is that we did find one of our Tullies just past the southern border of the Fielands. Abandoned."

"Abandoned?"

"Yes, abandoned and completely intact. And we still haven't been able to identify the Galactic officer who helped you during the Quadrati attack. No one has stepped forward, and your description of him doesn't fit anyone on our rosters, even from our Polaria and Wynlee campuses."

"That *is* strange." A shiver runs up my spine. But on some level, I'm not entirely surprised. Though the Striking Stranger wore the distinct black-and-gold uniform of a Galactic officer, I know I've never seen him before, and he's certainly not someone I would forget. But who could he be then? And why did he help me?

Keenon pauses a moment, shifting on his feet. "Livi, there's something else too, something I wanted to talk to you about. And perhaps this is not the best time, but after these recent events, I just can't let things that I've been feeling go unsaid any longer." He hesitates, taking a slow breath in. "I know we said some hurtful things to each other four years ago. And I know I told you that I've moved on. But now that we're both Beacons and going to Polaria together, maybe things could be different. Maybe we could try star—"

Suddenly, the side door to the training center bangs open, interrupting Keenon midsentence. The music peters to a stop, and the entire room quiets as the sound of heavy boots thunders through the entrance. Around me, heads weave like a field of blooming holliflowers caught in the swirling Andurian winds. Everyone is trying to get a better look. Half-stolen murmurings and whispers litter the air.

"What's that *thing* doing here?" Keenon rasps out under his breath.

I lob my head with the others, following the raw line of Keenon's gaze, and can't help but open-face stare at what has strode in.

The Striking Stranger.

But this time, I have a full-on view. I might as well be seeing him for the first time, for I don't know how I missed it before. And like the others in the room, now I see him for what he really is.

A Bionic. Undoubtedly Bionic. More muscular and taller than a human. But what sets it apart, as is true of all Bionics, is the snowy comet streaking through its otherwise jet-black hair. The Mark of Dresden they call it, for that is the name of the genetic mutation that causes a flash of white hair to appear on its sixteenth birthday. A mutation that marked the beginning of a new branch from human beings. Beings whose immune systems accept the nanotechnology that allows for almost indefinite self-repair and gives them something that makes them, in many eyes, no longer human: near immortality.

With the nanotechnology coursing through their arteries and veins, their organs can reknit and rebuild around any sustained injury within a matter of seconds. Not only that, the nanobots give their hosts new inhuman abilities. They can hear barely uttered words from across a Tram Tram field, and also spring across that same field within a few easy bounding steps. But I suppose it's unfair to call the Bionic a *thing* or an *it* since they still technically share 99.99999% of the same DNA as those of us who are more like our mortally challenged predecessors.

Though rarely seen these days, of course every Cerulean has heard the many stories of the Bionics. In the dusty recesses of my mind, I'm hurled back into the fables Grandpa Wren used to tell me about beautiful beings created during the Great Dispersion who were part human, part machine, molded for not only power and indestructibility, but stealth and cunning as well. Beings who were storied to have existed when Cerulea was barely habitable, sent from the old world to tame and terraform Cerulea's harsh environment so that humans and life from the old world could have a chance.

Bionics and Ceruleans worked side by side until fortune and plenty nurtured the ill side of human nature. When life was no longer a common united struggle for food and shelter, it became a struggle for power. Jealously and fear of the Bionics led some Ceruleans to lash out, and soon Cerulea entered a dark period in its thousand-year-old history. Though the Bionics were stronger than we were, sheer numbers were on our side. A bloodbath ensued, costing many lives on both sides.

And perhaps the clash between Ceruleans and Bionics would have continued to consume us, had it not been for the appearance one day of a common enemy. The Quadrati. A greater external threat that united the two adversaries, hence the Treaty of Dresden. Now in return for control of Atlas Station I, Cerulea's only space outpost, the Bionics also serve as Cerulea's first line of defense against the Quadrati.

So what is this Bionic doing here? They rarely come down to Cerulea unless it's for something important. I watch with an odd combination of fascination and dread as the Bionic stands at the entrance, scanning the room.

His raw strength is obvious under his fitted, dark metallic uniform, a swirling crest of gold at his chest. He *looks* young, perhaps early twenties at the most, but one can never really know for sure. Wrinkle-reversing technology is certainly one of the perks of having self-repairing nanobots coursing through one's vessels. And I notice that there are none too few heavy sighs coming from a few cadets of the female persuasion. Admittedly, this Bionic is handsome, in a chiseled and muscled sort of way, but I can't help but inwardly roll my eyes. Bionics are said to be as emotionless and unfeeling as the cintian metal flowing through their veins. And this one looks to be no different.

My mind sifts haphazardly through everything I can recall about the Treaty of Dresden, hitching on a lesser known detail: any person born with the Mark of Dresden is to be given up to the Bionics to further the Bionic line, since they themselves cannot bear any children. As the mysterious forces of natural selection would have it, the Mark of Dresden has become progressively scarce with each successive generation of Ceruleans. And so luckily this sacrifice of a Cerulean infant to the Bionics is rarely made these days. In fact, the last time Grandpa Wren said a Cerulean infant was given up to the Bionics was apparently well over twenty years ago.

Despite the treaty, the Bionics' defense of Cerulea has not been flawless, hence the continued sporadic attacks we experience, but I don't even want to think about how many more Ceruleans would have died were it not for the Bionics' efforts on Atlas.

I watch as the Bionic scans the crowd, his power and ire rolling off of him in waves. His gaze is fierce and glinting, promising broken fingers and bruises if anyone stands in his way. Everyone in the training room has quieted, and all eyes are on him. I feel some relief that at the age of twenty, every single strand of my own hair is still as dark as the midnight sands of Dresden.

But that relief doesn't last long. Subconsciously, I hold my breath as his gaze shifts to the area where Keenon and I are standing. It is said that a Bionic can see farther and more precisely than even a Warfian telescope. His gaze passes directly over to me, and freezes there.

With one swift motion, the Bionic is moving again, propelling himself through the crowd of cadets like an unstoppable boulder. The Bionic's boots click purposefully as he makes his way across the room. Cadets step back, whether consciously or unconsciously I'm not sure, clearing a path for him nonetheless. Even Cadet Wilkie stumbles back a pace, eyes wide as the Bionic steps past him.

My breath hitches as I realize—

He's heading straight towards me.

I stand there like a cyprian tree rooted to the unforgiving ground. And before I can even suck in a startled breath, his hulking frame stands *towering* over me. I'm so close to him now that I can see the ring of ebony rimming the dark grey irises of his eyes. Yes, he saved me during the Quadrati breach, but even that memory does not soften the menacing lines before me.

Beside me, Keenon steps forward, wedging himself between the Bionic and me.

But the Bionic keeps his gaze solidly focused on me. "Livinthea Park." *Not a question.* The Bionic's voice echoes off the walls. "I hereby invoke the Treaty of Dresden to escort you to Atlas Station I. You will follow me."

Boiling suns above. Is this for real? But my heart pounds in my chest, and I can't make my mouth move.

To my relief, Professor Hensly, who must have followed in the Bionic's wake, steps out from behind him and speaks up. "Surely there must be some mistake, Bionic. As you can see, Beacon Park does not have the Mark of Dresden." His arm gestures towards the top of my head.

The Bionic's gaze flicks over to Professor Hensly, but his stance remains rigid, unbending. "Her blood tells a different story. You see, based on the results of the genetic testing that we have recently acquired, we believe she harbors the mutation."

Finally, I find my voice. "Wh-what are you talking about? What blood sample?"

116

His gaze flicks to mine, unblinking. "The one you left at the hovercraft accident a few days ago."

My mouth sags open. How is that possible? But I think about the bloody gashes that were sure to have left plenty of blood at the accident site.

I bob my head ever so slightly but keep my chin firm. "Perhaps the genetic testing was incorrect. As Professor Hensly pointed out, I'm not *skunked* like you." I will not let him rail me.

But the Bionic doesn't even blink. "There was no error. That blood test showed that you have what we consider a new variant of the Mark of Dresden, which could explain your atypical phenotype. So unless you would like to spark an intergalactic incident, you will abide by the terms of the Treaty of Dresden and come with me to Atlas Station I." He narrows his eyes. "You do realize that this is considered an honor, Beacon Park, do you not?"

Sure, some cadets might consider it an honor. But I am not one of them. "Anything that is forced upon the will of another person in my mind is called *coercion*, not honor, Bionic." These words fly out of my mouth before I can stop them. But underneath, my thoughts are frantic. Do I really have no choice in this?

I look to Professor Hensly, who casts his eyes downwards, shaking his head. "I'm sorry, Beacon Park. If what he says is true, we truly have no choice." He is not going to risk an intergalactic incident and the safety of the whole of Cerulea by going against the several-hundred-year-old Treaty of Dresden. I really can't blame him. He's no match for this Bionic.

"Come with me, Park." The Bionic turns to go. A firm hand clamps down on my shoulder, forcing me with him. It is not a request, but a command.

At that moment, Keenon springs forward, his arm shoving me behind him, out of the Bionic's grasp. "She's not going anywhere with you, *Bionic*." He practically spits out the last word.

A low gasp issues from the other cadets.

The Bionic barely condescends a brief glance at Keenon, but his eyebrows arch up. "Perhaps you don't realize that every additional minute she spends here, out of the protection of the Bionics, puts not only her life but everyone else's life at risk here at Galactic."

My head whips in his direction. "What do you mean by that?"

"The Quadrati. Somehow, they have acquired the same information we have. The second attack on your life confirms it. The Quadrati will continue to seek you out and destroy whomever and whatever is in their way until they have you. If you don't come with me, the accident you had a week ago will only be the first of such tragedies to come."

Double boiling suns. Is what he is saying true? My mind stumbles over the recent sequence of events. Perhaps the hovercraft accident wasn't an accident at all? And then a second Quadrati breach in a matter of days? It *is* odd, considering the fact that the last Quadrati attack on all of Cerulea was at least several weeks ago, and the one common element between the two events—me.

Stars help me.

Remeni.

Jia.

It was my fault.
Remeni died because of me.

My gaze falters, and I can't look anywhere but the ground. What am I going to do?

But Keenon's voice breaks me from my daze. "Those attacks were just coincidence, Bionic. You have no proof of that."

But even I know the unlikely odds of two back-to-back Quadrati attacks. Who knows if I really have this Mark of Dresden mutation, but I can't risk putting my friends in further danger. I couldn't bear the thought of letting anyone else get hurt or, even worse, die because of me.

I push firmly past Keenon's protective arm. "It's okay, Keenon. I'll be *fine*. I can take care of myself." I say these last words as steadily as I can.

The Bionic's gaze pivots between the two of us. "Very wise decision, Beacon Park. Please follow me."

The hulking mass of muscle and stone then turns and strides towards the exit, not even bothering to look back to see if I follow. Expecting—assuming—complete obedience. *Arrogant snob.* Crimeny. I'm in trouble for sure.

With as much confidence as I can muster, I turn to follow the Bionic. The whole training center is silent except for our footsteps, which ricochet off the far walls like an odd mixture of pebbles and stone.

I look back over my shoulder just as I pass through the exit, only to see Keenon's strained face. His mouth is set in a tight line, eyebrows deeply furrowed. Silently, he mouths the words *be careful* before the large doors slam shut behind me.

XIX

LIVI: LAUNCH TO ATLAS

ONLY THE POUNDING in my chest disturbs the eerie quiet that has descended upon the Galactic campus as I struggle to keep up with the Bionic's long strides.

In the distance, the vermilion glow from the Gliese Sisters sinks below the eastern horizon as dark remnants of endlessly wandering clouds scatter across the aging sky. The flowing winds of evening seep in through the seams of my too-thin dress, sending a chill up my arms as I follow a few paces behind the Bionic.

Bionics always seemed such ethereal beings, rarely seen and hardly known. I feel as though I'm following in the wake of some phantom shadow come to life. Only the pain from my damnable heels reminds me that I'm not dreaming.

Up close now, the Bionic's towering figure is even more imposing. He strides forward like a Dark Skythe, his movements long and powerful, his jaw rigid as if clamped down onto some wild prey.

I consider making a run for it. Damn the consequences. But as my eyes shift to the Bionic's taut and braided form, bound in herculean muscles, I know one thing—there is no outrunning a Bionic. But I promise myself—*I'll figure something out.*

The Bionic thrusts his arm to his side, pressing a flashing red button on a metal bracelet at his wrist. A burst of light surges forth from it. I shield my eyes and have to blink several times before my eyes adjust, not quite sure of what I'm seeing. A large halo of light appears before the Bionic, its shimmering edges expanding and contracting ever so slightly. And then, just as the light dissipates, what is left in its place makes me stagger back. A starship.

The sleekly winged bird of dark metal rests on a tripod of arched haunches, its tapered nose sniffing the sky. Now I am not one of those people who has nothing but free-flowing gems spilling out of her mouth, but I certainly am more talkative than the vacuum of silence standing in front of me. It's clear that the Bionic is not even the least bit inclined to explain what's going on.

Finally, I blurt out, "Where in the name of Altheria and all her sisters did that come from?" So much for making polite conversation, but he certainly isn't trying, so why should I?

"Cloaking device," he grunts. Yes grunts. Not even looking at me as his fingers manipulate a device holstered at his side.

"And may I ask what *that* is for?" My finger points shakily at the goliath looming before me.

His gaze finally lifts up grudgingly. "*That* is going to take *us* to Atlas Station I."

"You're not serious, are you?" Stars, I didn't realize the Bionic was literally just going to whisk me away to Atlas. I feel as if I am on a cyber loop veering dangerously off course, in a stars-forsaken and hellas uncomfortable dress no less.

"A Bionic is always serious." He looks back down to continue working at his gadget.

I struggle at the realization. *I've got to see my Grandpa Wren and Jia first.* "What about my family? My friends?"

"We do not have the luxury of time. As I pointed out earlier, every moment on Cerulea leaves you exposed to further attacks, including those on your family and friends should you insist on visiting them. You will be given access to a comms device when you arrive on Atlas."

My stomach sinks. But he's right. I can't risk putting them in danger. "At the very least, could I retrieve some of my belongings first?"

He scans me from head to toe, perhaps really looking at me for the first time. Darn that Keria for making me wear this ridiculously thin-as-threads and completely useless scrap of a dress. Though the Bionic's eyes give away no emotion, in the next instant he takes off his jacket and tosses it to me. "You will be provided with everything that you need once we arrive on Atlas. In the meantime, this should tide you over."

I barely catch the jacket, mumbling a gee-thanks-a-lot under my breath.

Grudgingly I put it on, but I have to admit that it provides some much-needed warmth. Meanwhile, the Bionic dutifully busies himself with the gadget at his side. It flashes periodically in alternating red and blue lights.

What appears to be an entrance into the starship materializes on the side of the ship.

Without so much as waiting for my response, he clamps his hand on my shoulder and pushes me towards the entrance of the starship. "Watch your head," he advises.

Before I can even protest or be afraid, he shoves me in.

***

Having thousands of hours of piloting experience under my belt, I anticipated the triple-digit g-force of the steep ascent. Still, my body feels like pure Andurian cement latched in by the five-point restraints of the cockpit seat that the Bionic has not-so-gently strapped me into. And there is a lot more rumbling and brain-numbing jostling than I thought there would be. Even with the launch helmet on that the Bionic has given me, the noise is practically deafening as we climb higher and higher beyond the confines of Cerulea's atmosphere. The shaking is the worst part. Everything around me seems to be vibrating at the quantum level, with such force that I truly wonder if the seams of the starship will hold together.

I happen to catch sight of a grotesquely distorted face on a small reflective surface slightly above me. It takes me a moment to realize that what I'm in fact seeing is me. My nose is flattened. The skin around my eyes and mouth wobbles back and forth. And my twenty-year-old jowls— yes, jowls—flap back like the wings of a seafaerie taking off in wondrous flight. *This sure isn't as smooth as my ride on that Quadrati Tracker.*

Out of the corner of my eye, I can see the Bionic. And from what I can tell, he might as well be taking a stroll through a field of blooming holliflowers. Not even a single furrowed brow mars his perfect and placid face. How is that even possible?

It seems as if now that the Bionic is back in his own environment, even if it is a rattling hunk of tin hurtling into space, he's visibly more relaxed. For the briefest of moments, I can see his eyes flick to me, and the angle of his mouth quirks ever so slightly upwards. I twist my head away, oddly self-conscious all of a sudden.

Well, at least one of us enjoys this ride. I grip the armrests, gritting my teeth hard trying to keep them contained within my head. The violence stretches on and on, reaching deep into the marrow of my bones. Just when I think the ship, along with all of the marbles in my noggin, are certain to disintegrate, everything goes abruptly still. I have the strange sensation of disembodied weightlessness, internal organs floating and carefree, but intact. Thank the stars. We made it.

To my surprise, the Bionic actually makes an effort to glance over at me, eyeing me for a moment before he speaks. "I must commend you, Park. Only one Bionic has made it through their first launch without either passing out or screaming by now. Perhaps you are Atlas material after all."

"Well, that's encouraging," I reply, not withholding the sarcasm from my voice.

Before I can say more, a loud voice rumbles over some hidden speaker. "*Cassiopia*, report your status."

"Mission complete. Objective acquired. Preparing for docking, starside port," the Bionic responds, not missing a beat.

Objective? I certainly hope he's not referring to me. But his eyes shift to a far window and his hands start flying over the control panel. Even I have enough sense not to interrupt him now. I throw my gaze alongside his.

At first, all I see is the inky blackness of empty space. But as our starship's angle continues to rotate and propel forward, I blink and can't help but gasp at what comes into view. All other thoughts flit from my head. *Atlas Station I.*

The space station looks very different from the many holographs I pored over as a child. It's not a mere spare wheel, but seemingly alive. It pulsates and spins in the empty void of space, a living and breathing force unto itself. Dark green lights flash around the edges of the goliath, an enormous, central rotating sphere surrounded by four smaller spinning spheres in perfectly aligned orbit. Intricate scaffolding interconnects all the spheres in a complex yet graceful interplay of lines and arcs.

It's like some mysterious and never before seen creature roaming the dark ocean depths, a pirouette of lighted orbs and gracefully revolving arcs bringing energy and substance to the void around it. And this behemoth is soon to be my new home.

Despite everything that has happened, I can't help but be in awe. "It's even more spectacular than what I imagined."

The Bionic turns to me. "And I assure you, Beacon Park, soon you will find there are many more things on

Atlas that will far exceed your imagination. This is only the beginning."

XX

LIVI: REVELATION

THE BIONIC *IS* RIGHT. Even my wildest imagination dulls compared to this reality.

The Bionic steps off the starship as I stand frozen at the threshold of what can only be a dream. I'm not sure what I was expecting, but certainly not what lies before me. I heard many of the usual stories about the Bionics, and in my mind imagined a small paltry group of superhumans who stationed themselves on a lonely outpost. Never could I have dreamt Atlas could be like *this*.

My eyes are riveted on what lies before me within the immense spherical chamber—a floating *city*, and *hundreds* of people. Glowing orbs cast an ethereal light down onto an impossible number of people and bots as they zoom past on moving walkways in seemingly all possible variations of lines connecting two points—up, down, sideways, parabolic arc, spiral, zigzag. Flying drones navigate the space between like single-minded wasps.

Sleek glass encases the chamber, affording a view of twinkling stars and the infinite void of space beyond.

And I have never seen anything more beautiful.

The Bionic's voice breaks me from my reverie, his eyebrows notched up. "Coming, Beacon Park?" He stands atop one of the crystalline platforms. Only a sheet of glass and the air of one's breath suspends his powerful frame over the dizzying height.

I clear my throat and swallow. "Of course," I reply in the most nonchalant voice I can muster and take a step forward. Admittedly, I've never been one for heights, but I'll be a Dark Skythe's behind before letting *him* know that.

"You may not want to look down the first time," the Bionic advises, matter-of-fact. He presses a panel at his side.

To my relief, protective railings spring up around the edges of the platform. Then smooth as a gentle stream, the platform detaches from the hold as we float up and across the chamber.

The chamber is even more impressive from our new vantage point. I take a quick glance down, immediately gulping not only at the altitude but also at the sheer number of people I see. *Are they all Bionics?* "If I may ask, how many people actually live up here on Atlas?"

"Five thousand three hundred and ten, give or take a few Bionics who are offsite."

"I had no idea operations here on Atlas were so"—I struggle for the right word—"extensive." Letting a breath out, I'm overcome with the surreal sensation of being on a never before seen alien world.

The Bionic's gaze is unwavering. "Yes. For security purposes, we tend to keep our activities up on Atlas shielded from outsiders. As I said, coming to Atlas is an honor that only a select few Ceruleans have the privilege of."

"And what *activities* are you referring to?"

"Of course you know about our endeavors against the Quadrati. But there are many other things you will learn of soon enough, Park. First, however, you must meet the Domseis."

"Domseis?"

"Yes, they make up the Upper Council in charge of operations here on Atlas."

As we climb higher and higher into the sphere, a drone zings by my head so closely that I have to duck. "Crimeny!"

The Bionic waves an arm and calls out after it, "Pascal! You'll get a chance to meet her later. Not so close next time." Then he turns to me. "Don't worry. They are just curious about you. They always do that to any new Mark of Dresden."

"You mean those things are actually sentient?"

"To a significant extent, yes."

"Oh," I say, before I realize we've already made it completely across the chamber. The platform docks with a barely audible click at the threshold of another entrance.

As we enter a circular corridor built within the walls of the sphere, the clatter of boots draws my attention down the hallway. A person clad in a fitted wolf-grey uniform and cap suddenly emerges from around the curve, almost knocking me over. Luckily for me, the Bionic's quick reflexes keep me from getting bowled over.

"Whoa. Sorry about that." The words tumble out of the stranger's mouth. Frankly, he looks as startled as I am. Then he turns to the Bionic with a look of disbelief on his face. "Triton! What are you doing here?"

Triton. I turn this word over in my head, getting a feel for the hard edges and smooth curves as I observe the way the two interact.

The Bionic—or should I say *Triton*—claps the stranger on the back as if he's seeing a long-lost friend. And he actually *smiles*—not a stingy, closed-mouth smile, but a full-on grin, flashing a set of perfect teeth. "Well, it's good to see you too, Eppel."

It strikes me that suddenly the Bionic looks much less daunting. It's as if the Bionic I've been with for the last few hours is a completely different person—more animated and engaged, *warm even.*

The stranger scans Triton from head to toe. "I heard about what happened at Finlan's Point. Are you all right?" The newcomer is like the embodiment of pure motion. Everything about him flows, from his long wavy locks to his lithe and slender arms.

"I'll have to tell you about Finlan's Point later. I only got back a star week ago, and the Domseis sent me to retrieve this new Mark of Dresden."

The newcomer's eyes flash to mine, then back to Triton. "Retrieval duty? As Comstadt?" Eppel's eyebrows arch skyward. "You must have really dug yourself into the dark infinites this time. I thought that would have been beneath you."

Triton only shrugs. "Special assignment. In fact, I was just on my way to deliver her to the Upper Chamber."

"Well?" Eppel casts another curious glance towards me.

"Well, what?"

"Well, aren't you even going to introduce me to this new Mark of Dresden, or have you lost all of your good manners now that you are the esteemed Comstadt?"

Triton looks miffed, but his gaze reluctantly travels towards me. "As you wish. Beacon Livinthea Park, this is Sar Eppelian Linteh, Second Officer of the Upper Council."

"Yes, and only outranked by your Comstadt here." He flashes me a smile while shaking my hand. "Very pleased to meet the newest Mark of Dresden. I've heard a lot about you."

Before I can respond, Triton clears his throat and gives Eppel an annoyed look as if to silence him. "Well, it was good to see you, Eppel, but we must get going. As you know, the Domseis do not like to be kept waiting."

Eppel flashes me an easy smile. "Very well then, Beacon Park. Welcome to Atlas, and if this humorless brute gives you too much grief, you can always come and find me."

Despite everything, I can't help but stifle a chuckle as Triton gives Eppel a stern look.

Eppel turns to leave, flashing his own set of perfectly straight teeth. "Don't forget who trained you, Comstadt Travler."

"And don't forget who your superiors are, Sar Eppel," Triton says with a mock growl and motions for us to go.

I continue after Triton through the circular and tubed hallways of Atlas Station I's perimeter, leaving Eppel staring after us. Though Triton has returned to his stony self, our encounter with the other Bionic is like a sliver of light in the dark. A new thought occurs to me. Perhaps the Bionics are not made of pure Andurian cement as I was led to believe. They have feelings just like us, even the hulking mass walking before me.

XXI

LIVI: DOMSEIS

T HOUGH THE CORRIDORS are teeming with people and bots, Triton cuts through them like an unstoppable boulder through blades of grass.

While I'm met with a few curious glances, the others stutter and part from Triton's path, as if he were the blazing sun.

I thank my lucky stars that Atlas's engineers believe in artificial gravity, otherwise there is no doubt I would have been careening headfirst into the walls consisting mostly of too-fragile-to-be-in-space glass and clearly-not-enough metal framing. As far as I can tell, we're still located in the station's main sphere. I have to admit that though the views are spectacular, it's also most disconcerting to be looking through the glass under my feet to see nothing but empty space and the blue-green orb of Cerulea far below.

After turning down a few more nondescript hallways, I nearly bump into the Bionic as he abruptly stops. For all I can tell, we're in the middle of a long hallway with no doors or entrances. He presses his hand on a lighted panel, and the wall in front of us dematerializes revealing an inner chamber beyond. "Speak only when spoken to," he orders, and leads the way in.

***

As soon as I step into the dim light just past the entrance to the immense chamber, I take in the disjointed sight before me: an encasement of sparkling jewels spanning the full spectrum of colors, a lethal display of weapons the likes of which I have never seen before, and holographic projections of Cerulea and her three suns spinning along the perimeter. But what really catches my attention are three brightly lit metallic pods floating high in the air above our heads.

I continue forward after Triton as he steps atop a platform of shimmering gold levitating in the center of the room. As I scan my surroundings more closely, I start to get that uneasy, wrench-in-the-gut feeling. Several individuals clad in midnight stand sentry in the faded dark of the chamber's far wall. I'm not sure what I expected, but it's not this.

Firmly, Triton prods me forward, then brings his right hand to his chest. "Upper Council, I present to you Livinthea Park."

A voice booms from above. "Well done, *Comstadt*. Of course we did not expect anything less from you."

Silently, one of the floating orbs begins to descend. My eyes track it as it gently comes to rest on the ground a few paces in front of me. I brace myself as the pod opens up and out steps a heavily cloaked figure. Though his face is hidden behind the drooping of an oversized cowl, his rickety movements and posture are oddly familiar. With skeletal hands, he slowly peels the hood away. I suck in a breath, for underneath is the thinning hair and gaunt face that I know. What in the name of Altheria?

"Dr. Shen? Wh-what are you doing here?"

My old quantum physics professor looks directly at me, and I could swear his jade-green eyes are giving off their own strange light.

"My apologies for the secrecy, Beacon Park, but the nature of things requires that oftentimes we keep our identities hidden while on Cerulea."

And without another word, Dr. Shen's face and body begin to shift and transform into one of the most handsome people I have ever seen. His bent back straightens. His insect-like arms bulk and strengthen. The skin on his face stretches smooth and the hollows fill in. My eyes drift to the top of his head and freeze there. Not only has he managed to sprout a full head of dark brown hair, but a streak of white runs through it, just like the Comstadt. Things have gone from out of control to seriously and irrevocably out of control. My mouth jacks open as I choke on my own breath. "H-how did you do that?"

"Morphosis. It's a little-known talent of a few of us Bionics. Very useful when we do undercover civilian work."

My eyes are riveted to his now flawless face. *Hold it together, Livi.* "May I ask—is every single person on Atlas a Bionic?" I search the faces of those around me. Wordlessly, Dr. Shen nods to the sentries around him, who take off their caps in unison, each revealing a streak of white underneath.

Bionics. All of them.

"And the sooner we perform the transformative process on you as well, Beacon Park, the safer. In fact, perhaps we should do it now." He pivots towards Triton. "What do you think, Comstadt, is she ready?"

I'm about to laugh, thinking it a joke until I take in Dr. Shen's unbending and humorless expression. *He's not joking.* Boiling suns above. Do the transformation now? Of course I'm not *ready*. "Look," I say, "I just got here. How do you even know if I truly have this Mark of Dresden mutation? As I pointed out to your Comstadt here, I'm not skunked like the rest of you," I quip.

But the Domsei does not look amused. "There is no mistaking it, Beacon Park, you have the Mark of Dresden mutation like the rest of us Bionics. It's true that normally we discover the new Marks of Dresden at an *earlier* stage. However, in your case, we came across a sample of your blood at the hovercraft accident site only a few days ago. How you slipped by our screening protocols admittedly is a mystery to us. And though your phenotype may suggest otherwise, blood tests don't lie. You have the special mutation which allows your immune system to accept the nanotechnology that will give your body infinite capacity to self-repair. In other words, you have the chance at near immortality."

The air seems suddenly heavy. That queasy feeling in my stomach bellows. I scrabble for the edges, the hard planes that I'm used to. But as I lean in closer, I realize that perhaps all along I've been leaning on water, and I'm finally falling through.

I force myself to breathe.

These people are serious. *But I'm not ready yet.* I stumble back away from the Domsei, only to come up against the unmoving wall that is the *Comstadt.*

Triton grumbles and steps forward around me. He's been silent until now. "A thousand pardons, Domsei Shen, but perhaps we could give this new Mark of Dresden some time to acclimate to the idea."

The Domsei turns to Triton. "Unfortunately, Comstadt, we do not have the luxury of time for culling Young Bloods as we traditionally did, as we did for you. The Quadrati forces have been increasing exponentially of late, and every day that goes by, they encroach closer and closer to Cerulea, to the Gateways. She must understand who she is. She must be prepared as soon as possible. There is no time to waste." And with that he tilts his head up and calls out, "Domsei Kristof and Domsei Ping, please commence preparations for the nanobot infusion." And before my eyes, the other two pods begin to descend.

I'm in such longhorn's cud. But there is no way I'm going to let them touch me. Everything is coming at me too fast. I need time to think. And wasn't that one of the golden rules we always learned as first year cadets? Always have an exit plan. I have no idea what I'm going to do, but I do know that I better get the hellas out of here. While they argue, I start to back up until I'm only inches from the exit.

Triton's voice echoes into the chamber. "Perhaps we would have been better off retrieving the other Mark of Dresden. At least he was further along in his training."

"No, our choice is the correct one. Did you see the results of the genetic testing? The analysis is clear. She is the one we have been looking for."

I have no idea what they're talking about, but what I do know is that everyone's eyes are on the Domsei and the Comstadt as they move towards a holographic projection that suddenly appears between them.

This is the distraction I need.

XXII

LIVI: NOT READY

BEHIND TRITON'S BACK, I slip out the door and break into a sprint, dodging flying bots and Bionics who litter the corridors.

My eyes dart for somewhere to hide until I can figure things out more clearly. Before long, steps clatter behind me. I push myself even faster, hurtling through the passages, not a clue of where I'm going. As I sprint around a corner, I take a quick look back to see if anyone is following me, and then suddenly, I find myself—falling. Not just a tumbling-down-a-grassy-knoll-on-a-light-summer's-day kind of falling, but a stomach-lurching free fall into an undiluted void. I scrabble at the air, trying to find purchase on anything, but there is—nothing.

No amount of training can keep me from screaming at the top of my lungs.

Aaaaaaaaaaaaaaaaah.

Then out of nowhere something slams into my body from above, and I find myself suddenly tangled and tumbling head over feet. Needles scratch at my arms, my face, and I squeeze my eyes shut just before—smashing hard into the ground.

The wind whooshes out of me, and I feel as if I've fallen onto a block of genuine Andurian cement. But by some miracle, I'm alive.

I gulp down several breaths trying to get air back into my collapsed lungs. And when I open my eyes again, I realize it's not hard ground that I've smashed into, but the Comstadt. Somehow, he managed to break my fall. For a few seconds, I look down at him dazed, his arms still tight around me.

He has a grimace on his face, but his eyes are closed and his skin is blanched in shades of pale. But to my amazement, the color soon returns to Triton's face, and his eyelids flutter open, revealing dark charcoal greys ringed in ebony. How both he and I are not deader than dead, I can't even fathom.

"Unless you have a death wish, Park, you will refrain from wandering around Atlas by yourself until you are more familiar with its layout." His eyes lock hard onto mine. "Is that clear?"

His words break me out of my daze. I struggle and twist. "Let. Go. Of. Me."

His arms drop immediately to his sides, and I shrug off unceremoniously onto the rough ground. And I find that I'm lying in the midst of a—jungle? My fingers have splayed out not onto hard cement, but in fact moss-covered dirt. As my gaze crawls upwards, I see pearly fronds draped overhead in the misted air. And past these broad leaves I barely make out the platform that I must have fallen from. Stars, *it's so high*. The only possible way I could have survived that is . . . My breath hitches in my throat. I stare at him in wonder. "You *saved* me?"

Triton scans me from head to toe, his eyebrows raised. "As Domsei Shen was trying to explain to you before you *wandered* off, becoming a Bionic has its *advantages*."

Footsteps draw our attention past the pearly fronds. We simultaneously launch ourselves up, and I fight a wave of dizziness. Domsei Shen and several of his sentries step into the clearing. "Everything all right, Comstadt?"

The Comstadt clears his throat, a flicker of a glance towards me. "Yes, Domsei."

"Very well, then let us return directly to the Upper Chamber and proceed with the infusion before any other mishaps. Domseis Kristof and Ping are waiting."

To my surprise, Triton actually steps forward in front me, as if shielding me. "Domsei Shen, as I alluded to earlier, I believe the new Mark of Dresden is not yet ready for the transformative process. In her defense, she has only just learned of her mutation several hours ago and is just beginning to understand the implications of becoming a Bionic. Unlike the rest of us who have been transitioned from birth, the process may not be as easy for her. Perhaps we should wait until she has had time to come to a full understanding of what it means to be a Bionic?"

I can't believe what I'm hearing. Triton is actually *defending* me?

But Domsei Shen shakes his head. "As you say, Comstadt, the situation is unique, one that we have not encountered before. She is clearly past the stage when we normally retrieve Young Bloods. And while I note your concern, *I* am concerned that leaving her without the transformation leaves her exposed should the Quadrati attack."

Triton stands unwavering. "But she is safe on Atlas and its surrounding perimeter. The Quadrati would not dare attack her here."

"Then what do you suggest we do, Comstadt?"

"Give her one year. One year to understand what the life of a Bionic would be like. Let her decide for herself whether to become a Bionic or not."

My eyes flash to Triton. So he *was* listening to me after all. And again, it's like a sliver of light in the dark.

The Domsei remarks, "You realize that would be unprecedented, do you not? To let her *choose* for herself?"

"I do," the Comstadt concedes, but does not back down. "However, as you cannot deny, her situation is *also* unprecedented. Aside from the time before the Great Dispersion, all transformations until now have occurred during infancy, when personal choice was not a possibility."

The Domsei and Comstadt argue back and forth, and by the looks the sentries are giving each other, I suspect not many have challenged the will of the Domsei before.

"And what if at the end of one year she refuses the infusion?"

Triton turns to me, holding my gaze while answering the Domsei. "Then she returns to Cerulea at her own risk."

Domsei Shen is silent as the shifting of time becomes a slowly flowing wind, and I can almost hear the mist as it drifts over the pearly fronds. Finally the Domsei breaks the silence. "Very well, Livinthea Park, you will be given one *month* to decide whether or not to undergo the transformation that would render you a Bionic like the rest of us."

My eyes snap to the Domsei's, and though Triton starts to open his mouth, I've kept silent for too long. This is really my fight. "One *month*, but that's hardly enough time to decide something that has the potential to change the trajectory of my entire life." I struggle to keep my voice steady.

But the Domsei shakes his head. "I hope you will find, Livinthea Park, that we are reasonable and honorable people. However, as much as I would like to afford you as much time as you need to make an informed decision, I'm afraid we do not have that luxury. Despite what the Comstadt here believes, every minute you wait for transformation puts the whole of Atlas at risk from the Quadrati." He pauses, holding my gaze, his jade-green eyes piercing, unwavering. "No, the sooner you make your decision to become a Bionic, the safer it will be for all of us. If it were up to me, you would already be undergoing the transformation. But I have too much respect for the Comstadt's opinion. So I will give you one month, during which time you will be under the Comstadt's tutelage and protection."

Now it's Triton's gaze that snaps to the Domsei, muscles feathering at the angles of his jaw. "A thousand pardons, Domsei Shen, but I've got to get back to the Gateways, to Finlan's Point. Surely another Bionic can be found to train the new Mark of Dresden."

"Yes, and you will return to your duties, Comstadt, *accompanied by* the new Mark of Dresden. What better way to show her the life of a Bionic than to travel the

143

Gateways, so she can truly learn what it is that Bionics do."

"But the Gateways are too dangerous for her. Surely you do not want to risk the first new Mark of Dresden we have seen in over twenty years?"

The Domsei has a ready answer. "Then who better to protect her than our very best." He pauses, looking sternly at Triton. "I need *you*, Comstadt, to show her the Gateways and the realm of the Bionics so that she can fully understand our way of life here on the fringes of the void. Of course with the recent Quadrati attacks there, Finlan's Point will be out of the question. However, you may return to duties at the outskirts of the Gateways." The Domsei's gaze turns to the Comstadt. "As I recall, this explorative period was your idea in the first place, was it not?"

Triton holds his gaze for a long moment, a silent battle between two strong wills. Triton's hand clenches and unfurls at his side while the corners of the Domsei's mouth twitch ever so slightly. But finally, Triton breaks. "As you wish, Domsei." He dips his head.

"Then it is agreed." The Domsei nods back to the Comstadt, and then his gaze flicks to mine. "Until we meet again, Livinthea Park. May the Gateways reveal their many wonders to you." The feather of a smile touches the corners of his mouth, and then he turns to go, his sentries following not far behind.

And now, my fate is to be decided.

In one month.

XXIII

LIVI: REGRETS

I FOLLOW TRITON NUMBLY through the winding corridors, utter disbelief of what is happening to me enveloping me in a hazy fog.

Do I really have the Mark of Dresden mutation? If so, *could* I really become a Bionic? More importantly, do I really *want* to be one of them?

My mind floats, an unattached observer as my body follows the Bionic's stalking form through the busy corridors. He's even more wound up than before, clearly less than happy that he'll be babysitting me for a whole month. I can't say I really blame him. And yet earlier, the Bionic not only saved my hard noggin but also spoke up for me. Perhaps there is more to the fables portraying the Bionics as just unfeeling beasts. And if I'm truly stuck here for one month, perhaps it's time to make an effort.

I lengthen my strides so that I walk apace the Comstadt. A sideways glance tells me what I know already. He's as happy as a stone wall, but I clear my throat anyway. "Thank you."

The Comstadt's bouldering stride breaks ever so slightly, a loosened breath before he answers through gritted teeth. "For what?"

I keep my gaze forward. "For saving me—and for giving me a choice." At first, the only answer in the air is our continued steps resounding through the corridors. But slowly, his clipped pace eases somewhat, and when I steal a glance at him, the clenching in his jaw has softened. "If I may ask. Why did you help me?"

He keeps his eyes fixed on the busy corridors ahead, but his eyebrows furrow ever so slightly. We plod forward a few more steps before he lets out a lengthy exhalation. "Perhaps I am giving you the choice I would have liked for myself. Being a Bionic is not an easy thing."

"What do you mean?"

"Immortality is not an easy path. We carry a heavy and sometimes overwhelming burden. Though many may regard immortality as this wonderful thing, to me it is like swimming solo in an ocean of stars. We experience the beauty of the universe but have few to share it with." He clears his throat and finally looks over at me. "You see, as Bionics, we have no families. The Treaty of Dresden forbids communication with our Cerulean relatives, for our own good of course. When one lives a near-immortal life, having attachments to mortal ones can be—" he hesitates before continuing, "—emotionally debilitating. Not only that, Bionics are barren. It's an unfortunate side effect of the nanobot technology, which will destroy any cells not recognized as self, including an embryo. That is the reason we rely on Ceruleans to continue the Bionic line."

I ruminate on his words as we weave between robots of all shapes and sizes. Sneaking a sidelong glance at him, I take in his grim and somber face, and another thought occurs to me. I don't know if I should ask, but I do anyway. "Do you regret becoming a Bionic?"

We walk together in silence for several minutes, his face stony. I wonder if I have offended him. But finally he clears his throat and replies, "Unlike you, I had no choice of whether to become a Bionic or not, so to some extent, that question is irrelevant to me. A Bionic's life is all that I know. However, what I do know is that I have led a remarkable life, one in which imagination meets reality, seen and done things that no mortal could have done."

As he finishes talking, I find that we have slowed to a stop near an intersection of corridors.

He turns to me. "We're here."

"Where?"

"Your new quarters."

This time I recognize the small luminescent patch on the wall and am not surprised when a section of the wall dissolves when he puts his hand there.

"You may take the rest of the day to rest and get settled. But tomorrow, I will come to retrieve you promptly at 0700 as dictated by the Domseis. In the meantime, Jasella will see to your needs." He nods stiffly to me and turns as if about to go, but then looks back over his shoulder, holding my gaze. "And to answer your question," he hesitates only a split second "—no, I do not regret becoming a Bionic. But unlike you, I have never known any other life." Then, without so much as a farewell or measly goodbye, he spins away.

XXIV

LIVI: MEETING JASELLA

I T TAKES ME A MOMENT to think to ask, "Who's Jasella?"

But Triton's footsteps are already fading away. I turn to the open entranceway, his answer to my question percolating through my mind as I step inside. So much for a full orientation to things around here.

The wall reappears behind me with a vibrating hum, and I halt at the first sight of my new quarters. Brightly lit, I blink at the hovering bed splashed with tangerine sheets, soft pillows piled high in layers of marigold and bluebonnets. I blink again at the lime-green chair, which actually levitates by itself in the far corner. The gently curved walls in contrast whisper back in muted grey, but crystals embedded within it make the whole room seem like it is sparkling. This is not what I expected.

I walk over to the chair and sink down onto its plush surface. The room is far more fancy than my quarters back at Galactic. But despite the luxury, I suddenly feel very tired and—alone. There's no more need to put on a hard exterior, and I take a deep breath in and sigh, letting my shoulders slump. An empty ache hollows my insides. I miss my Grandpa Wren. I miss Jia and my friends. I hope they're not worrying about me.

Suddenly, a rustling startles me, and I spin towards it.

From behind the wall emerges a shiny ivory robot, similar to the one that had nearly run over my toes earlier. It looks like an overgrown seafaerie egg, only without the powdery yellow speckles. The top of its oblong head and body barely reach past my hips. Jointed arms jut out rigidly from both sides, tapering into three-pronged, rounded fingertips the shape and size of a child's toy marbles. Almost imperceptibly, it twitches back and forth balancing on a single large spherical wheel. I hear a small whirring and clicking as its large lens of an eye swivels and focuses in on me.

"Welcome. I am Jasella, your bot helper. Is there anything that you require of me?" So this is Jasella. Her voice is feminine and undulating like a rolling wave, not the monotonous droning of the few maintenance robots we have back on Cerulea.

One thing stands at the forefront of my mind. Perhaps this bot will be able to help me. I clear my throat. "Yes. I need to holomessage my Grandpa Wren and my friends at Galactic."

"That can be arranged. However, optimal transmission to Cerulea best occurs at 26:00, when Altheria is past star-center. What else can I do for you until then?" For a robot, she is pure motion, constantly whirring, clicking. If she were human, I would almost call it fidgeting.

There are so many things I need to do. So many things I need to think about. But after the events of today, my lids flounder, my ribs have started aching again, and I feel ready to drop. "I'm just tired, that's all."

"In that case, perhaps you would like to retire for the evening." Jasella's robotic lens pivots as it propels itself towards the side wall. Its lanky arms shoot out, and a side door slides open. "You will be able to refresh yourself in the lavatory."

"Thank you." I sidle past Jasella towards the open door and step inside. As soon as I pass the threshold, a blast of warm steam greets me. A shower starts running in the far corner. It seems like too long since I've bathed, and I'm still in the stars-forsaken dress. The door zips closed behind me. I catch a glimpse of my reflection in a sleek mirror, and I can hardly recognize myself. My eyes are red and sunken, rimmed with dark smudges. I turn my head slightly and see the angry red gash on my temple. It throbs dully but looks even worse now than before. My dark, brown hair hangs lifelessly and matted around my face.

I've seen better days.

With some relief, I quickly shed the Comstadt's jacket and the dress, gingerly stepping into the shower. The hot water and steam eases some of the tension out of my shoulders. I'm pleasantly surprised when the sweet fragrance of holliflowers fills the air. And as I close my eyes, I can almost imagine being back on Cerulea.

When I step out of the shower, I find that a fresh towel and change of clothes have magically materialized in an alcove recessed within the wall. I even find a tube of medicated ointment next to them.

Feeling somewhat better now after the shower, I quickly dress in the soft white sleeping pants and shirt that have been left for me, and apply the ointment to the angry gash on my forehead. Cautiously, I place my hand on the door just as I saw Jasella do, and it swishes open. Jasella waits behind the door exactly where I left it.

"I will prepare your quarters for respite time." Jasella spins towards the room.

The lights dim and the bed levitates up. The mauve-colored walls darken to shades of midnight. But what makes my jaw sag open is what becomes of the entirety of the far wall. I rub at my eyes as the wall begins to shimmer, granules of light and dark intermingling with space and air, and then becomes completely transparent, a broad and clear view to the deep space beyond. It's as if the room has transformed into its own observatory, just like the ones I would go to visit with Grandpa Wren as a child. Never in a millennium could I have dreamed of living in a place like this. What greets me from beyond the windows are the constellations I know so well.

Starlock, my birth constellation, raises his fiery arm in greeting and glows brighter and clearer than I've ever seen him before. He's like an old childhood friend, who comforted me during the dark hours after I lost my parents and who listened night after night as I wondered about the vast unknown mysteries of the night sky as I grew older. I cross the room to the transparent wall, raising my fingers to trace Starlock's familiar edges; gently though, for I'm afraid that the only thing I know here will disappear. Perhaps I imagine it, but he seems to twinkle in response, and somehow I feel less alone.

"If there is anything else you need, you need only call my name." Jasella's almost motherly voice breaks me out of my reverie.

I turn towards the bot. "Thank you, Jasella."

Jasella silently returns to her cubby in the wall. I pad over to the levitating bed and lie down, my cheeks sinking into the smooth rayanesse of the soft pillow. I turn to face the familiar stars, and I lie there for many moments, just looking.

My mind replays the events of the day. Despite all of the stories about how unfeeling these Bionics are, so far they've shown me some degree of kindness. And I cling to one thought, one thought that gives me a glimmer of hope. They promised me a *choice*. And I remind myself, didn't I always dream of being in space? Isn't that the reason I joined Galactic in the first place? Maybe I should give the Bionics and their way of life a chance. Keep my mind open, and perhaps things here for the next month won't be so bad. Maybe this is one of those lucky turns in life disguised as pain and misfortune, and perhaps not so unlucky after all.

The calming strength of Grandpa Wren's voice edges into my thoughts, the words he used to tell me when things were tough. *Just keep moving forward, Livi. Keep moving forward, and you will be fine.*

With this in mind, I drift off into a dreamless sleep.

XXV

TRITON: FUMING

I KICK AT THE TRASH RECEPTACLE, sending it skittering across the floor. But I don't care. Babysitting duty? *I'd rather dive headfirst into a black hole.*

I've got more important things to attend to.

I'm still seething after my meeting with the Domseis. It was all I could do to keep it together while I showed the new Mark of Dresden to her new quarters.

Somehow she managed to distract me as I escorted her to her new quarters, but now that I'm back in the privacy of my own rooms, the frustration has returned full force.

I'm wasting my time. I need to get back to the escalating attacks on Finlan's Point, not get stuck babysitting some Young Blood. Who knows what the Quadrati have been able to accomplish while I was on Cerulea? It's also critical that I continue my efforts to locate the Quadrati home base. Perhaps we would have a chance at stemming the ever-increasing attacks from those slipshots if we can figure out where they are coming from.

But Domsei Shen's wishes were clear. I will be stuck protecting and training the new Mark of Dresden for the next month.

I suppose I walked right into it. I kick myself now. Wasn't I the one who suggested that the girl be allowed some extra time to learn about a Bionic's life? I'm not sure what came over me, but I actually started to feel sorry for her. That she was terrified was clear. Who could blame her? The girl's life was about to change even more drastically than she could possibly imagine. And in some way, she reminds me too much of myself. The same misdirected fire. The same naive drive. Perhaps I would have grown up like her had I not been given up by my own parents over twenty years ago.

I also couldn't really blame the Domseis for feeling desperate too, for wanting to protect the new Mark as if she were our last hope in the universe. For we Bionics are a dying race. With the Quadrati picking off our numbers at an ever-increasing pace lately, it's only a matter of time before the mathematical predictions about the Bionic line come true.

Nanobots or not, we are headed towards oblivion.

Still, one whole month protecting *and training* the Young Blood? It is almost worse than being Nullified.

But I practically did it to myself, and now I can do nothing about it.

I throw off my torn clothes and head for the shower. It is time to cool off.

XXVI

LIVI: DAY ONE

A VERMILION GLOW burns through my lids, and I peel my eyes open.

It takes me a moment to understand what I'm seeing: a fiery crescent that is near blinding, set against the pitch-black darkness of space.

Altheria.

It peeks around the blue orb of Cerulea.

I have never seen a sunrise like this.

These thoughts stutter through my head when a whirring and clicking draws my attention to the far corner away from the expansive window. Jasella.

"Livinthea Park. You are to meet with Comstadt Travler at 0700. It is time to wake." Her familiar voice is an odd comfort to me, though I've only been here less than a star day.

"Thank you, Jasella," I say as I jump out of bed, feeling surprisingly well rested, more so than I have in the last few days. I don't want to be late for my meeting with the Comstadt.

***

I clean up, donning a fresh white jumpsuit that Jasella has set out for me and wonder how it can fit me so perfectly. As it is, I feel better today as I follow Jasella through the winding corridors. My ribs don't throb at all against the fitted suit, and the gash on my forehead feels less swollen.

Whereas yesterday was haze in mist, I feel clearheaded this morning. I find myself able to start picking out patterns in the maze. Every few meters, distinctly colored orbs mark different passageways. I try to memorize as much as I can.

We pass through the vast open chamber again via a floating platform, and it's just as amazing as I remember—hundreds of Bionics on levitating walkways and even more bots navigating the air between. I could spend hours perched up here just taking it all in, but Jasella plows forward off the platform and leaves me no choice but to follow.

Before long, we're back in the social hub I passed through yesterday. Again, Bionics and robots intermingle. On the far side, I immediately spy Triton speaking with a group of Bionics looking—different. He smiles widely and laughs, his broad shoulders and posture—relaxed. If it weren't for the signature crested gold emblem the Comstadt wears at his chest, I would hardly have recognized him. The others look up at him with admiring glances, and seeing him as he is now, I can understand why. Even amongst other Bionics, he shines like the sun.

He turns and spots me. Instantly, his whole demeanor changes. Gone is the laughing smile, and in its place is a face pitched into a storm, nostrils flaring, brows knit tightly. Clearly written across his brows is the fact that he is still less than pleased about being stuck supervising me and would rather be elsewhere. The rest of his group quiets as their eyes follow his gaze to me as well.

My insides clench, but I hold myself as tall as possible, looking straight ahead, and approach them. I will not be intimidated.

He clears his throat as I near. "Beacon Park, I must say I am pleasantly surprised at your punctuality today. I was expecting you to have a difficult time adjusting to Atlas's thirty-hour star day." Despite his words, nothing in his grim face seems remotely pleased. His gaze is hard, jaw tight. "You're just in time to accompany us on a patrol run."

"You sure don't waste time around here," I reply.

"If you would rather not go, I will inform the Domseis that perhaps it would be better to wait until you are acquainted with things around Atlas." His right eyebrow arches up ever so slightly.

It's a challenge. I hold his penetrating gaze and remind myself of Grandpa Wren's advice. "No, in fact a patrol run sounds very interesting indeed." And in truth, I realize that I really *do* want to see what these Bionics actually do, how they work. To see their power in action. They were always such a mystery to us Ceruleans.

"Good." He pauses, and for once his face concedes a satisfied smile. "Then let me introduce you to your team." Triton turns towards the other Bionics. "These are Magnars Juki, Halo, and Phlynnt."

157

I turn to the three Bionics standing by Triton's side and nod to each one in turn. Juki and Halo, with their brassy brown locks streaked with white, dark brown eyes, slender builds, and fair skin look so similar they could be brother and sister. Phlynnt, on the other hand, is a mop of flaming red hair and comet's tail overlaying sweat and muscle.

"They will be your trinam," Triton adds.

"Trinam?"

"Yes. In addition to myself, they will accompany and protect you on any missions outside of Atlas."

"I'm a Galactic Beacon." I tilt my chin up. "I don't *need* protection."

Triton shakes his head. "I don't care what kind of training you have had at Galactic. Do not underestimate the Quadrati. As Domsei Shen pointed out—from this point on, you are a living target."

A chill runs down my arms. "Why? What are they after?"

"We're not entirely certain. But lately, the Quadrati seem to be targeting those with the Mark of Dresden mutation. We've lost three of our most talented Bionics to the Quadrati over the last year alone. Without the nanobot transfusion, you are particularly vulnerable. You will be the weak link on every outing we have."

The Comstadt continues. "But you asked to be given a choice, so the Domseis are giving it to you. And now is your chance to see what a Bionic's life is like before you make the decision yourself. However, as I have been commissioned to protect you, you will play by my rules: every outing we have outside of Atlas requires you to be with myself and your trinam. Do not underestimate the danger that lies out there. If you fail to follow this rule, you will never make it back to Atlas, or to your beloved Cerulea. Is that understood?"

From the way his jaw is set rigidly, I know that Triton really means what he's saying. I've never been one to shy from danger, but I'll go along with what he says if only to get a chance to see the Bionics in action. I bite back a smart-lipped retort and nod back silently.

"Very well. Then let's get going." With that, he spins to go.

XXVII

LIVI: THE WARP SHIP

"**W**ELL, THROW ME AROUND the Yentian belt," I mutter under my breath as I slip past Phlynnt through the wide entrance into the cavernous hangar.

I can't help but stop short. Row after row of gleaming birdlike crafts fill the enormous chamber. I feel as if I've taken a step into the future. With their nearly clear exterior and sleek frames, the crafts are far more dazzling than our Tullies.

"Is there a problem, Park?" Triton's hulking form materializes right next to me, so closely that one inch more and our arms would be touching. It takes every ounce of effort I have not to flinch. The comet of white in his hair flashes particularly starkly under the bright lights as he turns to face me, a sparkle of amusement in his eyes. But to my relief, he boulders past me into the room without waiting for my answer.

I turn to Phlynnt, who still stands beside me. "What are those exactly?"

"Hawwk scouting crafts," he replies with a look of pride. "They can go faster and farther than any known Cerulean ship."

"How many types of crafts do you have? It looks nothing like the one that brought me here from Cerulea."

"Oh, you must be talking about our Talons. Those old birds are used purely for local travel." Phlynnt lowers his voice to barely a whisper. "We heard about your first ride up here. Not bad for a Young Blood. Didn't even hurl I heard. You know the Comstadt deactivated the Talon's atmospheric stabilizers when you launched off of Cerulea."

"Why would he do that?" My eyes track over to the Comstadt inspecting one of the beautiful Hawwks. He presses his hand to a panel, and the entrance to the Hawwk slides soundlessly open. The whole craft lights up. The Comstadt turns back in our direction.

"To test your mettle," Phlynnt replies hurriedly, his voice still low. "But no worries"—he winks conspiratorially at me—"you passed with flying colors. But I promise you'll like our Hawwks much better. They can go warp speed without even a twitch."

Warp speed? I knew the Bionics possessed technology far more advanced than on Cerulea. I just didn't realize by how much. Up until today, the mere existence of these warp ships was the stuff of cadet folklore and happenstance rumors. Never did I imagine it was actually real. "And where exactly are we planning to go on this patrol run?"

"Hurako." The Comstadt's voice startles me. His long strides have taken him quickly back to my side.

"H-Hurako?" I stutter, not sure I'm hearing him right.

161

"Yes. We have an outpost there that needs to be checked on. Given that Hurako is far from any known recent Quadrati activity, it is also the perfect destination for your first patrol run."

"You can't be serious." I look towards Phlynnt and the other Bionics, but their faces remain perfectly straight.

"What's not to be serious about?"

"But that's within the Starlock system, well over four light-years away," I say, though my eyes remain riveted on the now-glowing craft.

The Comstadt leads the way towards the Hawwk. He presses a few buttons on a control panel next to the entrance of the craft. "Then we had better get going. Isn't that right, Magnar Juki?"

"Yes, sir," Juki replies with a wide smile as he heads over to a second craft. "You know I hate to miss dinner, especially today. Chef Aton is cooking mullet fish stew."

"In fact, Beacon Park"—Triton turns back to me—"if we leave now, you may even make it back to Atlas for lunch."

Did the Comstadt just make a joke? Phlynnt and Halo chuckle, but now it's my turn to be serious. "How is that possible?"

"You'll see soon enough." His eyes spark with a familiar glint. "You afraid, Park?" *Again, a challenge.* He rests his hands against his powerful thighs, waiting for my answer, and I can feel the curious gazes of the other Bionics on me as well.

No matter how much I want to say yes—that I'm scared out of my wits, that all of this is coming at me too fast—I can't back down. Besides, how different could traveling on a warp ship be compared to the Tullies we have back at home? So I tilt my chin up and shake my head. "Not at all, Comstadt. Hurako sounds just perfect." And it really does hold more meaning to me than the Comstadt could ever have guessed.

"All right then. You and I will take the first Hawwk out." Triton turns to my trinam, who have thus far been watching our exchange with bemused expressions. "The rest of you, flank formation until we land on Hurako."

The other Bionics nod knowingly.

XXVIII

LIVI: BEYOND IMAGINATION

OH STARS. *What have I gotten myself into?*

"You sure you want to do this, Beacon Park? No one would think less of you if you wanted to back out. After all, it is only your first week on Atlas." Triton's gaze hardly strays from the control panel in front of him, yet somehow he perceives my fraying nerves.

Damn those Bionic senses.

And I know the Comstadt is testing me. I clamp my jaw tight against the pounding in my chest but am unable to quell the trembling in my double-crossing fingers as I readjust the straps holding me into the co-pilot seat next to him. *Keep it together, Livi. You're Galactic's best pilot, for star's sake. How different could flying at warp speed be anyway?* I force my hands down by my sides and answer as steadily as I can. "Yes, I'm sure."

But to my surprise instead of taunting me, the Bionic actually nods over with a look akin to sympathy. "Don't worry, the first time is always the worst. After that it's actually kind of fun. Just think of it as a cybercoaster on steroids."

"Cybercoaster?"

"Oh, I forgot. That was before your time. Anyway, just think of it as a joyride. Fast, but perfectly safe."

"Well, in that case, I feel *much* better," I say, not withholding the sarcasm in my voice.

As we pull away from Atlas, the void of space opens up before us, and I stare into the vast infinite, a dark emptiness that feels endless, that feels like *forever*. Soon the craft makes a wide arced turn, and the blue orb of Cerulea comes into view. Though I feel as if I could just reach out and touch it, I know it's well beyond my reach. Thoughts of Jia and Grandpa Wren, even Keenon, flit through my head.

"You miss them, don't you?"

"Pardon me?"

"You miss your friends and family back on Cerulea." This time he states it as fact, not even a question.

Was it that clearly written on my face, or can Bionics read minds too? I fight the painful tightening in my throat. "I wouldn't be human if I didn't miss anyone." For some reason, I feel defensive. But why should I feel guilty about something that is so basic to human emotion?

And a thought occurs to me. "Do Bionics and Ceruleans ever"—I try to find the most tactful word— "mix?"

The Bionic doesn't answer me right away, but his fingers pause ever so slightly in their rapid-fire motion over the control panel. "We don't have the luxury of forming deep attachments with Ceruleans—if that is what you are asking. In fact, it is prohibited by the Treaty of Dresden. As you can imagine, the end results are almost always pain and mental suffering on *both* sides."

"But surely one's heart cannot always comply with rules and regulations, no matter how law-abiding you are. Has a Bionic never gone against the edict of the treaty?"

He hesitates a split second before answering. "Not *never*, but so rarely that in the thousand-year history of the Bionics' line of existence, such an event has occurred only a handful of times. You see, the consequences of forming such an attachment are very severe and would merit Nullification."

"Nullification?"

"Yes, the reversal of the nanotechnology transfusion and the stripping of a Bionic's powers and immortality."

"But why? Why go to such an extreme? Just because one falls in love, it shouldn't be considered a crime."

"Because attachments of the heart not only jeopardize a Bionic's focus, but also the safety of the Gateways."

"Then how—oh!" I gasp. Something catches my eye from outside, cutting off all thoughts. Cerulea has fallen from view, and instead what appears is a brilliant halo of lights, a shimmering aurora of colors with bolts of electricity dancing and swirling, converging like a whirlpool towards its center. *Alive.*

And we're heading straight towards it.

"What in the name of Altheria is that?" The words spill out of my mouth before I can stop them.

"*That* is going to be our shortcut to Hurako and will get us back to Atlas in time for dinner. I believe you call it a wormhole. Here on Atlas we call it a gateway."

Wormhole. Dr. Shen taught us about wormholes in quantum physics class, theoretical shortcuts between two far away points. *Of course they would be reality here.* "Any other surprises I should know about?" I say as I tug nervously at the harnesses of my five-point restraint.

"You'll see." Triton smiles ever so slightly while his hands fly over the control panel. I feel myself being firmly pushed back into my seat as we accelerate towards the halo.

We continue to accelerate faster and faster until the cabin lights start to flicker, and a deep rumbling creeps in through the floor up to my bones. It's a low hum at first, but as the lights start to flash even more, the ship begins to shake violently. I hope to the stars that the seams of the ship hold. My heart leaps in my chest as electrical bolts of light zing and crackle just beyond the craft's exterior.

"Brace yourself, Park. This will be the worst part."

Worse? How can it get any worse? I'm Galactic's best pilot, and yet I squeeze my eyes shut and grasp at the armrests with all my might. I don't care if he sees me now. This is not your typical flyby.

Suddenly the shuttle rocks and lists, and my eyes fly open. Were I not strapped down, I would surely be splattered on the pristine metallic walls of the Hawwk's innards by now. The craft hurtles faster and faster. It's all I can do to keep myself from yelling. I grit down hard on my teeth. We snake in all possible directions of three-dimensional space and then some, violently jostling. I start to feel light-headed as dark shadows creep into my peripheral vision, and I fight to stay conscious.

167

Then abruptly, everything slows, and despite the artificial gravity, I feel myself lifting off the seat, my feet losing contact with the floor. I'm overcome with the odd sensation of being underwater, everything petering at quarter speed, distorted, floating. I glance out of the control windows, not quite comprehending what I'm seeing. Gone is the blackness of space. Instead, spirals of brilliant colors whirl past. And ahead is the most shockingly bright light of all, getting closer by the millisecond.

And there is no way in hellas we will survive going through that.

I open my mouth to call out to the Comstadt, to warn him, but find that no words come out of my mouth, just a garbled distortion of incoherency.

We spiral closer and closer to the blinding light. Now I'm certain we're going to meet a fiery death. I clamp my hands to my ears as the screeching sound of rust on rust rends the air, as if the very fabric of space-time were ripping open. The ground beneath me shifts like a rolling wave. A strange feeling of disembodiment overcomes me, as I become one with the light.

***

Time comes crashing back in the next instant, and I find Triton's angular face hovering mere inches from mine, the corners of his eyes crinkled, his breath brushing mine. "You all right, Park?"

I glance down at my arms and legs and am surprised to see that every body part seems to be in its proper place. I can only manage a weak nod, my voice comes out hoarse.

"Stars alive. What just happened? And don't tell me that was just a joyride."

Perhaps I'm imagining it in my disoriented state, but for just a split second, a look of relief seems to pass over the Comstadt's face, and he huffs out, "My congratulations, Beacon Park, you just survived your first trip through a wormhole. For a minute there, I wasn't sure you were going to make it."

"Well, then I guess we agree for once. I didn't think I was going to make it either," I admit. I don't care about pretending to be the tough Galactic Beacon anymore. I'm just thankful to be alive.

Triton actually laughs, the sound of it deep like the rumble of rough boulders on stone. "First time through the wormhole is always a little disconcerting. But you will get used to it. Next time will be easier." He eases back into his seat.

Next time? I'm about to ask, but as I take in the new scene before me, all reasonable thought escapes, my question quickly forgotten. For outside my window is a view that I didn't even know I was waiting for all of my life, until now.

Three red dwarfs intertwine with two curving nebulas, outlining the five points of a perfectly drawn star, a view so new, yet so familiar.

Starlock.

Of Erlion's Galaxy.

But the constellation is so close now that it is more than the distant specks in the night sky from my childhood gazing, but rather titans of the void bursting with fire and power. I can hardly breathe. This *is* beyond my imagination.

XXIX

LIVI: HURAKO

"**I** CAN'T BELIEVE IT," I mutter under my breath. "We're actually here, aren't we?"

Triton surprises me with a broad smile as he gazes out of the cockpit window. "Yes, the Starlock system is beautiful, isn't it? I don't know how many times I've been here, but the view never disappoints. You ready to proceed to Hurako?"

"Since we've already come this far, you know, a mere four light-years out, why the hellas not?" And I can't help but smile back in return. My nerves have calmed somewhat, replaced by the infectious thrill and wonder of traveling through the wormhole. As a child, I spent many a night admiring the deep forest-green hue of Hurako from afar through Grandpa Wren's homemade starscope. Never in a millennium did I ever think I would one day get to visit it. *Maybe the life of a Bionic isn't so bad after all.*

Triton speaks into his comms line. "Everyone else through?"

"Affirmative, Comstadt." Phlynnt's voice crackles over the line.

"Smoothest ride ever." Halo chuckles.

"Can't leave me behind no matter how hard you try." Juki's voice pitches into the air between us, making me laugh, while Triton groans next to me.

"All right then, cloaks on and flanking formation until we land at the outpost," the Comstadt orders into his microphone. Though the others may joke, there is no question who's in command here.

As we approach what can only be the light green-blue orb of Hurako, I marvel at the smooth agility with which the Comstadt navigates the craft through the thick atmosphere. I may be an excellent pilot, but not even my skills come close to his. The way the Hawwk's metal heats and glows orange at the wings' edges outside my window, I know we must be going at near Mach speed, and yet the Comstadt's fingers blur over the control panel with the ease of playing a fine musical instrument. When we break through, I'm not quite prepared for what I see.

"So amazing," I whisper under my breath as I'm met with the majestic peaks of an endless mountain range, reigning like a powerful grey giant over the distant horizon. The sky glows in soft wispy layers of orange on pink, patches of sunlight filtering down through perfectly tufted clouds. As we dive further, a crystalline lake stretches clear as far as I can see, its waters lapping gently against bald patches of rocky beach. The whole of the lake is surrounded by the dusky purple of overarching trees, the likes of which I have never seen before.

We dive and dip, careening past mountaintops and gangly trees, cutting them so close that I could probably reach out and touch them. But never once am I afraid. The Comstadt has things under control. Being in the air like this, the familiar itch crawls back under my skin. I look down at the control panel in front of me. Though most of it is foreign, the basics of it are familiar. Perhaps I could do this. Never hurts to ask, my Grandpa Wren would always tell me.

"Mind if I give it a go?"

"Pardon me?" Triton throws a raised brow at me.

"Mind if I pilot this thing for a few minutes? I'm a good pilot you know."

Triton eyes me for a long second as if I asked him the most ridiculous question in the universe, then shakes his head. "I do not have a death wish and neither should you."

"What's to lose? You Bionics can't die off anyway right?"

"I'm worried for *your* safety, Park, not mine. Anyway, the Domseis would be none too happy if one of their precious Hawwks came back damaged. But perhaps"—he pauses midsentence as if considering something—"an alternative can be arranged later."

Before I can ask him what it is, something catches my eye in the far distance. I watch in amazement as seafaerie-like creatures soar and dive, careening over the peaceful waters. But when we approach the far shoreline, something else stops me short, makes me blink, and blink again: pattern within chaos, coordinated movement.

Squinting against the light, I look closer, and the realization of what I'm seeing sends a shivering shock down my spine. I spin towards the Comstadt. "There, there are people here," I stammer, for I'm still gulping down the sight of a small dock overlying the sleepy waters, a group of two men and a woman launching the red sliver of a boat out onto it. *People. Living within the Starlock constellation.* All those years I looked up into the night sky and *wondered*, I never even knew—never ever dreamed, that perhaps there were *people* wondering *right back at me.*

The Comstadt looks at me sidelong. "Yes, very keen observation, Park. Hurako is, in fact, inhabited."

"But where did they come from?"

"Their predecessors came from the same mother world as your very own ancestors during the time of the Great Dispersion."

My jaw sags. He might as well have told me he's discovered a new dimension. His words are like a gust of wind into the small room that is my world, blowing the windows and flimsy doors suddenly wide open. Stories and tall tales come whirling back inside, the ones Grandpa Wren used to tell me about the Great Dispersion. It was said that the Great Dispersion was a period of terrible upheaval when our ancestors fled the World of Origins in search of another habitable world. As the stories go, Cerulea was that habitable world. In all of the teachings at Galactic, never once was there a suggestion that humans had successfully terraformed another planet besides our own tiny blue orb. As far as I knew, we were the *only* survivors from the World of Origins after the Great Dispersion. "H-how is that possible?"

"As with many things, Park, there is much yet for you to learn. Suffice it to say that your understanding of the world is going to change more than even your wildest dreams."

So many questions swirl in my head, but one stands out. "Why keep us Ceruleans in the dark?"

The Comstadt's gaze remains focused on the distant horizon, his full brows furrowed, cryptic. "The reason is as complicated as the history of the Great Dispersion. The simplest explanation is that Cerulea's ignorance of Hurako was deliberately orchestrated by our forefounders to help ensure the survival of the human race. They took their lessons from the history of the mother world, where humankind was in constant upheaval and disharmony. A history where humans of every race were greedy and unable to coexist. Ceruleans and the people of Hurako were each deliberately led to believe they were the only survivors so that they would not become greedy and try to conquer the other."

"Then why bring *me* here?"

The Comstadt finally looks at me, his gaze penetrating. "The Domseis wanted you to begin to understand and appreciate the role and importance of Bionics, to convince you that becoming a Bionic is a worthy cause. They wanted you to see that our roles encompass not only the protection of Cerulea, but of all three human colonies which have survived the Great Dispersion."

All three colonies? "You mean there's another one?" I can't keep the incredulity out of my voice.

"Yes, there is yet another surviving human colony on the Solarian planet of Axos." Triton remains serious. "We Bionics have been commissioned to protect all the colonies which survived the Great Dispersion, to promote what the founding group had worked so hard to achieve, the survival of humankind."

His words are awe inspiring, frightening even. Yet at some primal level, at the very core of my being, I want to believe him. I want to believe that humans thrive on other worlds, that many more people exist elsewhere. That we were not the only ones to have made it through the Great Dispersion. And I *desperately* want to believe that we are far from being alone in the universe, that we as the human race have extended our reach farther than I ever imagined possible.

My mind feels as if it will burst with all of this new information, but I can't help but want to know more. "But how do you manage to oversee all three planets?" My mind reaches for the minute dregs from my astronomy class. "I mean, Axos is even further away from Cerulea than Hurako. It's over thirty light-years away."

"I see you know your astronomy, Park." Triton nods approvingly. "As with travel between Hurako and Cerulea, we utilize a series of local wormhole networks that survived the destruction of the original artificial gateway that was used during the Great Dispersion. Unlike the original wormhole network which destabilized long ago, these shorter branch segments are naturally occurring wormholes that have existed even before the Great Dispersion."

The original artificial gateways. A moment passes as the cogs and wheels churn in my head, finally snagging on the implications of what he's saying. Amongst the stories Grandpa Wren told about the Great Dispersion, he often spoke of the Ritarian Gateways, an ancient human-made wormhole network that supposedly connected the World of Origins to hundreds of possible habitable planets all across the universe, the thoroughfare by which humans ultimately first came to be on Cerulea. But because of the natural instability of this artificial wormhole network, it only lasted long enough for people to escape the dying world before it collapsed. "You mean the fabled Ritarian Gateways?"

The Comstadt nods. "You'd be surprised how many fables in history stem from elements of truth."

Stars alive. *The Ritarian Gateways are real.*

As I try to make sense of what the Comstadt has just told me, outside the Hawwk's broad windows, we barrel closer and closer to the lake's rocky shoreline. Just beyond, majestic grey mountains slide along the horizon. By now, several more groups of people have come out from under the gangly purpling of trees and gathered along the shore. Others bear their own sleek watercrafts on broad backs. Colorful banners in greens and golds hail along the shore's edges with children darting merrily underneath them. We are so close that I can even see individual faces, individual features. A man with a burly beard open-face laughs at his comrade, hardily slapping his friend's shoulder. A woman with long flowing black hair, launches a giggling child skyward, and then back down into her waiting arms. They truly are no different from me. "Can they see us?"

The Comstadt glances down to the shoreline where my own gaze falls. "Our Bionic code prevents us from revealing ourselves unless necessary. For the most part, our presence is kept hidden. Even now, this ship is heavily cloaked. The villagers don't know that we're here."

"Unless necessary?" I ask.

"Perhaps once every few decades we will recruit a rare new Mark of Dresden in secret, from Hurako or Axos. Luckily, the Quadrati have not posed a threat to these populations yet, so we have not had to interfere in that respect at least. So far our roles here and on Axos have been primarily to patrol and monitor." The Comstadt tilts his head ever so slightly, the sunlight glancing off the comet of white in his hair. "Though Bionics originally helped to establish these colonies, after our help was no longer needed, we destroyed any records of our existence and left the people alone to develop on their own, to have a fresh start. It was so long ago now, that just like the Ritarian Gateways, we exist for the most part only in their tall tales, in the fables told around campfires and at bedtimes. We would have done the same for Cerulea too, but the Quadrati attacks there necessitated our public interference."

I have the satisfaction of knowing that at least we Ceruleans aren't completely ignorant. But I also think about how lonely that kind of life would be for a Bionic, like a ghost in the wind. The Hawwk hovers just above the group of people and their boats. Below, men, women, and children laugh and smile, completely oblivious to our presence. "Will Ceruleans ever be allowed knowledge of the other inhabited planets, and vice versa?"

"Perhaps eventually the civilizations will prove themselves capable of coexisting peacefully, but until then the more that the knowledge of the surviving colonies is kept safe, the less likely it will wind up in the wrong hands."

I sit here for a few minutes absorbing all that Triton has told me. What I have seen and done today is already enough to short-circuit my brain. I don't know what I expected on my first outing with the Bionics. But learning about the enormity of the Bionics' role in protecting the human race was not one of them. I look over at the Comstadt now, who reigns over the craft like a force unto himself, with power, strength, perfection rolling off of him in waves. Could I become one of them? Even if I could, do I want the responsibility and life of a Bionic?

There would be so much I'd have to give up. My friends, my family. Could I do that? Or should I be selfish? Should I run back home to Cerulea and live out my life, ignoring the greater issues and threats that lie out there.

I'm lost in my thoughts when suddenly below, all the sails of the water crafts unfurl at the same instant, sending the crafts racing across the lake. It's like watching a rainbow of ribbons dancing over the waters. Some crafts even launch into the air. Jets of water propel them from behind, airborne for several moments before splashing back down. Fists pump, men and women cheering into the wind. I can't help but grin at the excitement below. And suddenly, I see what life as a Bionic could be like— exploring new worlds, expanding my understanding of all that is out there. In that instant I know why Domsei Shen insisted that the Comstadt take me around. Who could say no to this life?

But I still have one month to decide. There's no rush to make a decision that will forever change my life. *Slow down. Take it all in. Learn as much as you can. Then decide.*

XXX

LIVI: MULLET FISH STEW

"YOU'RE RIGHT, JUKI. The mullet fish *is* to die for."

I scoop up another spoonful of the stew. The juicy, tender fillet practically melts in my mouth. I have to admit, I never had anything this good at Galactic. As I sit with my trinam at Atlas's cantina, other Bionics throw curious glances our way, but no one else moves to sit with us.

Swallowing noisily, Juki replies, "Yes, Chef Aton is amazing. He can cook almost anything. He can even cook you food from the time of the Ancients."

"Like what?" I ask in between mouthfuls. As promised, Triton did in fact get us back to Atlas by dinnertime, though he himself couldn't join us as he had "important business to attend to." And apparently we would have made it back for lunch too, but Phlynnt had to make an unexpected pit stop when his Hawwk's excrement receptacle malfunctioned.

Now it's Phlynnt's turn to reply. "Spaghetti and meatballs. Chow mein. Pizza. French fries. Garlic naan. You should really give them a try. Of course the carbohydrate loading was terrible during the old days, absolutely decadent in fact. So Chef Aton only cooks those dishes once a star-rotation."

An odd thought occurs to me. "Do you have to watch your waistline?"

Phlynnt takes a slug from his water jug, his slender form at odds with the large volume of food he's been shoveling into his mouth. "Though the nanobots help maintain a healthy metabolic rate, even us Bionics need to watch what we eat. Living until eternity means there's *plenty* of time to build up belly fat."

I look over at Halo, her youthful face and perfect skin. She doesn't look a day over twenty-five. "If you don't mind me asking, just how old are you all?"

Halo's reply nearly knocks me off my chair. "Two hundred and eighteen, and my brother Juki is two hundred and sixteen. But our toddler over here"—she slaps Phlynnt on the back, practically making him spew out a mouthful of stew—"is only seventy years old."

"Hey. Who you calling a toddler? Need I remind you that our esteemed Comstadt is the youngest of us all?"

"Really?" I ask while scraping up every last drop of the stew.

"Yes, he's just a few years over twenty. He was the last Mark of Dresden that came to Atlas, right before you in fact."

This information surprises me. "Then how did he climb the ranks so quickly?"

Phlynnt chuckles. "You know those youngsters. Give them a fancy gadget, and they learn it lickety-split. Whereas you take one of these old-timers"—now it's Phlynnt's turn to slap Halo hard on the back, earning him a scowl from her—"well, you know the saying. It's hard to teach an old dog new tricks. Even with the help of the nanobots."

Juki chuckles at his sister's contorted face. "I have to agree with Phlynnt. There's nothing like growing up with the technology. Comstadt has had the advantage of growing up with the latest and greatest. Piloting the Hawwks, using the NAD simulators, firing a hazar, navigating the wormholes—for him it's all like breathing. Second nature. And it doesn't hurt that he's built like a mountain carthea. He's tops in hand-to-hand combat too."

Halo chimes in. "And can you believe that as a Young Blood the Comstadt passed those Hawwk simulators in ten sessions straight? Didn't sleep a wink for ten whole star days. His stamina is legendary."

"I can believe it." I laugh. Somehow, it's a relief to know that I'm not the only one who feels intimidated by him. "Does he ever take a break?"

Someone clears his throat loudly. "All right, troops—"

I nearly fall off my seat as I spin around to find the Comstadt standing right behind me, clean-shaven and with a fresh Bionic uniform on. Halo's lips lock up tightly, and Phlynnt almost spills his mug of water but recovers and salutes the Comstadt. The others, including myself, quickly follow suit.

The Comstadt continues with a perfectly straight face. "Get to Hemlock. Last one to one hundred goes with Sar

Eppel to Finlan's Point tomorrow. Park, you're coming with me."

The others bolt immediately up. Halo offers me a consoling smile before running off.

How much of the conversation did the Comstadt hear? Warmth is creeping up into my face, but I try to keep my voice even. "Where are we going?"

"*Break's* over." The Comstadt's steel-grey eyes twinkle even in the dim light as he turns to me. "You wanted to learn how to fly a Hawwk right?"

Drat that impeccable Bionic hearing. "Right."

XXXI

LIVI: SIMULATOR

THE BREAK CERTAINLY *IS* OVER.
When the Comstadt asked me if I still wanted to learn how to fly the Hawwk, of course I nodded eagerly. Now, I'm not so sure. Especially since I sit sealed inside a crystalline sphere with no obvious exit. The Comstadt called it a Neuromodulation Augmentation Device, or NAD for short, explaining to me that it was a Hawwk reality simulator. But at this moment, it feels more like a cage to me. But the Comstadt also said that if I wanted to fly a real Hawwk, I would have to pass the simulator tests first, *all one hundred of them.*

I peer over to my right in the circular room and spot the Comstadt as he readies himself for the simulator. Without any hesitation, he slips inside his own glass encasement in the center of the room, his seal suit molding over taut muscle and the confident arch of his back. As soon as the clear glass slides shut in front of him, the walls come alive in flowing rivulets of white currents as the wireless transmitters activate.

"We will go through basic maneuvers first so that you can get the hang of the controls." The Comstadt's voice courses evenly through my earpiece. His dark grey gaze travels across the room to mine. "Ready, Park?"

I'm not sure that I'm ready, but I give the go signal anyway, fisting my left hand a few inches into the air. The walls of the sphere opacify and darken. And in the next instant, a tingling begins at the top of my scalp, spreading gradually until every inch of my skin seems to come alive. Around me the electrical currents intensify and brighten, the heat palpable. Soon, the light grows so bright that I'm forced to close my eyes. A few moments pass. When I'm able to open them again, what I see makes my jaw drop.

XXXII

LIVI: NAD

NO GALLIMIMUS WAY.
The inside of a Hawwk cockpit. Gone is the crystalline sphere. Gone are the annoying pings and beeping monitors of the suit. The simulation looks, smells, and feels exactly like the Hawwk that the Comstadt shuttled me around in this morning, down to the faint coolness of metal of the pilot's seat that I now sit on. Outside my window crouches a fleet of Hawwks within the cavernous hollows of Atlas's hangar. Triton's voice flows through my head.

"Park, are you engaged in the simulation?"

"How in stars name is this possible?" I bring up a hand, flexing and extending my fingers in front of my virtual face. Though just a shade lighter than my real skin, it looks exactly like my hand. Not even the hint of a pixel.

"I'll take that as a yes." Triton chuckles.

"Everything seems so real." I finger the thick armrests at my side, the smooth surface of the orb-like control fob.

There's even a gentle vibration where the soles of my feet rest on the cockpit floor.

"You can thank Magnar Juki's engineering prowess for the special effects. Only downside is that you may get a headache and a little nauseous afterwards." Triton adds, "Especially since this is your first time through."

Great. Now he tells me.

In the next instant, Triton materializes right next to me in the co-pilot's seat, making my virtual self jump. And I have to admit his virtual image does him justice. He wears the fitted black uniform that outlines his powerful frame. His charcoal-grey eyes are just as deep and penetrating as in real life. There's even the feather of a dimple that graces his chin. His virtual self quirks an eyebrow when he sees me looking at him.

"The Hawwks are controlled in similar fashion to your Tullies, but about a hundred times more powerful, and a thousand times faster. Any small movement you make will be magnified. Let's get the basics down first, and we'll go over its special capabilities later. Ready?"

I have to remind myself that all of this is just a simulation. Nothing is real. When I examine the flight instruments, though the three-dimensional displays are fancier than in the Tullies, I recognize almost everything—the altimeter, airspeed indicators, X-meter, hailing beacon, shielding frequency, Mach indicator. I settle my fingers around the control fob. "Sure, why not?"

"Okay, like I said, just like the Tully, but more calculated moves. If the controls of your Tullies were like a fork and a spoon, consider the controls of the Hawwk like fine microsurgical instruments. Nothing too drastic, all right?"

"Microsurgical instruments. Got it." I flick my virtual chin up. I am no newbie. I was Galactic's best cadet pilot after all. Surely I can handle a Hawwk, and just a simulator at that.

"Good. Let's disembark and take orbit around Cerulea," the Comstadt instructs.

***

Triton spends the whole morning with me in the NAD. I never thought I would admit it, but I'm glad for the Bionic's presence beside me, even if it is virtual. He exudes a no-nonsense confidence, which I find reassuring, especially as I fail time and time again at what would have been the most basic maneuver in my Tully. Triton wasn't kidding when he warned me that the Hawwk is *much* more responsive than the Galactic crafts I'm used to. It's kind of like relearning how to balance on a bicycle again, except this time with one wheel—that's motorized—and can fly. Admittedly, perhaps I was a little too cocky coming into this thing. For even as I try *over and over* again just to fly this crazy turbocharged hulk of metal out of Atlas's hangar, I thank the stars that the Hawwk is merely a simulator. Otherwise I surely would have crashed, burned, and met my maker a million lives over by now. It seems as if even the slightest twitch of my fingers on the control fob sends the virtual Hawwk spinning one eighty.

To his credit, the Comstadt is as steady as Juthri's stone. Not once does he raise his voice. "Okay, try again,

Park. This time a little less wrist, easy on the aft thrusters."

Easy for him to say.

Finally, by the end of the morning, with sweat drenching the back of my virtual self, I'm starting to get a feel for it. So far I've mastered not getting myself virtually killed straight away while pulling out of Atlas's hull and capturing Cerulea's orbit at its highest apogee.

"Okay, Park, you've got the basics down now. Show me you can pass the simulation tests, and you earn yourself controls to a real Hawwk." And without another word, Triton's handsome visage disappears from the simulation.

XXXIII

LIVI: A FRIEND

THE COMSTADT WAS RIGHT. Not only does the Hawwk flay me alive, but my first evening after the simulator run was plagued with one heck of a headache. I could barely even stomach my favorite meal thus far on Atlas of phylla berries and longhorn soup. Luckily, I haven't had to put on a stoic face. For since that first day, Triton has left me alone to my own devices, and my trinam have their own busy schedules. I have not seen them at all for the last several star days. I suppose the Comstadt thinks the Hawwk simulator will keep me plenty occupied.

And it does. Time passes like a gusting wind. I've been plowing through the simulator, struggling to stay afloat, to master not only the controls but also the formations and attack drills the Hawwk throws my way. Did Triton say I would have to pass all hundred simulations? I shake my head. I've only completed ten, and I've already been at this for three long star days. *Sigh.*

This afternoon was particularly tough. No matter how many times I tried to learn the black hole formation, tweaking the fore and aft thruster this way and that, adjusting my airspeed and capture angles, the only thing I managed to accomplish was putting my Hawwk in a deadly tailspin, *every single darn time*. It was like learning how to use chopsticks when one had grown up using only forks. I understood what needed to be done, but my brain was so used to flying a Tully, it was not calibrated to fly the Hawwk. So needless to say, my headache this evening is particularly bad.

To top it off, slogging away at the simulations has also somehow triggered some unexpected feelings of— longing—for my life at Galactic. Team Horizon. Jia, Remeni, Keria, Haven, even good old Rox. I miss all the times we trained *together*, whether it was running flight drills over the Fielands, or navigating the Nebulands. Sure, it was tough, but never once did I feel *lonely*. I wonder about things back on Cerulea. Is Jia out of the med unit yet? How did Keria and Haven fare in the last Luthati drills? And stars, my Grandpa Wren. Keenon. Will I ever get to see them again?

Life here on Atlas is *so* different. And though I may not be the most socially engaged person that ever lived, even I am starting to feel abandoned in the rows of empty simulators of Atlas's NAD unit. I can't help but feel as if I'm being swallowed by the dismal hollows. The tightness in my throat, which has built up all day, now threatens to strangle me. *I've got to fight it*, I scold myself. Grandpa Wren taught me to be stronger than this, didn't he?

But being holed up in my quarters alone where it's much too easy to feel sorry for myself doesn't help. So despite being a little green in the face and my head feeling as if it will split in two, I force myself to head out to the cantina. Even if I don't have an appetite and no Bionic besides my trinam deigns to sit with me, at least I can listen to some music while I'm there and get my mind off of things.

Jasella perks up as I near the exit of my quarters. Seeing her reminds me that I'm not quite all alone, even if she is just a bot. For through it all, Jasella attends to my every need. Every day, she dutifully wakes me up at 0700, making sure I'm thoroughly bathed and properly clothed in a crisp uniform. Jasella shuttles me around Atlas to the simulator for practice. She accompanies me to the cantina for breakfast, lunch, and dinner. She's even more chatty than the first day I met her, and certainly nothing like the monotonous robots we have on Cerulea.

"Cadet Park, shall I inform the cantina of your arrival so that they may have your table and meal ready?"

"Thank you, Jasella, I would appreciate that very much."

"Your usual phylla berries and longhorn stew?"

"Maybe I'll try something different today. What do you recommend?"

"Sar Eppel and Magnar Phlynnt both swear by the holliflower soup and roasted mullet fish egg. Perhaps you would like to try those?"

Hmm. The queasiness still sits in my stomach like a block of Andurian cement. But I should eat something, especially if I plan to go back for extra practice in the simulator tonight. "Thank you, Jasella, just the holliflower soup will be fine."

"Very good choice," she answers.

Through whatever magical communication line Jasella possesses built into her fancy wires, she's already ordering up a cup of soup for me. It will be ready by the time we make the five-minute trek to the cantina. I guess living on Atlas does have a few perks.

As we start along the halls filled with Bionics and bots, I'm desperate to get my mind off things. "How old are you, Jasella?"

Jasella's robot eye pivots towards me, while her spherical wheel whirs smoothly along the glossy floor through the curved corridors. "My Boot date was just at the turn of the millennium."

Turn of the millennium? And I thought my Grandpa Wren was old. But looking at her, there is not a single rusted bolt or loose wire to be seen. Her sleek white, lightly speckled surface still has the sheen of a brand-new Tully. "But you look like you were just built yesterday."

"I've had hundreds of different versions over the years, but my neurochip has always been preserved."

Oh. That explains it. "And how long have you known the Comstadt?"

"I've been the Comstadt's personal bot for the last five years, but I've known the Comstadt since he first came to Atlas twenty-three years ago."

"So if you've lived over a millennium, and you've only been with the Comstadt for five years, what did you do before that?"

"I served the prior Comstadt before the current one."

That's strange. I thought Bionics were immortal. "What happened to the previous Comstadt?"

"The former Comstadt Falk was irretrievably lost to the Quadrati."

"Oh." It's hard to imagine these powerful Bionics as being vulnerable to anyone or anything. Another thought bothers me. "Jasella, if you are the Comstadt's personal bot, then why are you helping me?"

"Comstadt Travler thought that I would be of more use to you than him. So until you make your own transformation and have a new bot formally assigned to you, I will continue to assist you," Jasella states, no nonsense and matter-of-fact.

I didn't realize the Comstadt gave up his own personal helper for me. I did not want anyone to baby me. I turn towards Jasella as we near the end of the gently curved corridor. Despite my reluctance to give up the only companion I've had for the last few days, I know I shouldn't keep her. "You've been of great assistance and company over the last few days Jasella, but you may return to the Comstadt. You've shown me enough of Atlas, and I think I can manage on my own now."

Jasella doesn't even budge. "Comstadt's direct orders were to help you until your transformation. Only the Domseis have the authority to override the Comstadt's orders."

I want to argue further, but by now we've reached the cantina. The dim lights and jazzy music trickling through the air remind me more of Galactic's swanky officer lounge than a cafeteria. A few Bionics look my way as we step into the large room with wall-to-wall windows, but offer no more than a curious glance before returning to their own conversations. *Well, looks like it will be table for one.*

Jasella leads me to a small side table next to the expansive window, where a bowl of steaming soup and some basic utensils already wait. "I will station myself in the Reserve until you have further need for me."

I look over to where she indicates to find that a row of bots wait along the cantina wall. "Thank you, Jasella, but—" Before I can say anything else, to ask her if she would like to join me, Jasella spins away and heads towards the other bots. *I guess that would have been silly anyway. Bots don't eat.*

To my surprise, my stomach growls as I near the table, my appetite apparently returning when the savory aroma of holliflower soup wafts towards me. This time, I'm not taken by surprise when a bench materializes out of thin air just behind me, and I ease myself carefully onto it. Even now, my face heats at the memory of being catapulted face first into a bowl of longhorn stew one of my first meals in the cantina, when that bench took me by surprise. Needless to say, I'm not going to let *that* happen again. And I can now understand why no one is willing to sit with me.

I take a sip of the clear broth flecked with bits of tart red-and-yellow petals and gaze out the window. Stars, if Grandpa Wren could see me now. All my big talk when I was younger about exploring space, joining Galactic so I could learn how to pilot a Tully.

He never once discouraged me though. *Go after your dreams, Livi, and never give up. Your reality is what you make of it.*

Though Atlas isn't Galactic, it is perhaps beyond what I ever thought possible to experience in my lifetime. And yet somehow, I can't help but feel a nameless something missing right at my core. Sure, Atlas is exciting, and one can't deny the amazing views. But the ache in my chest is still painfully there, an emptiness that even a bowl of hot holliflower soup can't fill. Too quickly, I gulp down the scalding liquid past the lump in my throat.

"Mind if I sit here?"

I make a hasty swipe at my eyes before I look up, blinking back the stinging. My gaze is met with a kind, smiling face. It takes me only a moment to recognize him. What did the Comstadt call him? I remember just before things get awkward. "Of course not, Sar Eppel."

The Comstadt's old mentor positions himself across from me and sits down on the seat that materializes there. Like all Bionics, Sar Eppel Linteh looks far from being old. The youthful skin on his face is unwrinkled, his skunked brown hair dangles over his smooth forehead. He's just as forward as the first time I met him. "So how is our famed new Mark of Dresden doing? Not eating alone, I hope?"

I breathe past the ache in my chest, attempting to force out a chuckle, but unfortunately comes out more like a feeble whimper. "I'm afraid I'm not particularly popular with you Bionics."

"Nonsense," he exclaims, then leans towards me ever so slightly, his voice lowered. "The truth of it is—is that the other Bionics are volleying to see who gets to meet our new Mark of Dresden first. It's not every day that a Young Blood shows up on our doorstep. Take Drake for instance, the one over there with the shaggy blond hair?" Sar Eppel nods towards the group of Bionics sitting at a table behind me. "He's been wanting to come introduce himself to you over the last few days since you arrived on Atlas, but still hasn't built up the nerve." And to my surprise, when I peer over my shoulder at the group of

Bionics nearby, the blond that Eppel refers to meets my gaze with a shy smile.

Sar Eppel scoffs at them in amusement. "Unfortunately, they are all too afraid to get in the Comstadt's way. After all, you are his charge for now. But you and I both know that I have no such qualms." He winks sideways at me, making me laugh. "And shame on the Comstadt for leaving our new Mark of Dresden to fend for herself."

"Well, it's really not like that." After all the Comstadt has done for me, I feel the strange need to defend him. "The Comstadt has taken me to see Hurako and shown me how to work the Hawwk simulator. In fact that's where I'll be heading after I have a quick dinner. So you see, I have plenty to keep me occupied."

His eyebrows quirk up ever so slightly, his voice gentle. "Then why are you sitting by yourself, looking like the loneliest being in the universe?"

It used to be that only my mother could pull that trick. One little tweak with her words, in precisely the right spot that was just enough to break the dams that I had so arduously built up, and the whole of Lake Polaria would come crashing through. Perhaps it's his kind brown eyes. Or perhaps Atlas has made me into a soft, sniffling, crybaby. Either way, I curse myself and turn away as large, wet, embarrassing tears tumble down my cheeks. *And I can do nothing to stop them. Great.*

The Comstadt's old mentor fishes out a handkerchief and hands it to me. He has the kindness to do it discreetly. "I'm sorry if I have upset you. I can see things have been—difficult for you."

I start to shake my head, to tell him, *no I'm just tired from too many hours spent in that blasted simulator, and I will surely be fine in just a few minutes*, but I can't quite get the words past the gizzard in my throat.

Sar Eppel continues in a gentle voice. "Perhaps it would make you feel better if you knew that you've lasted longer than most under the Comstadt's direction. Only last year, five of our prospective Magnars gave up on their officer training because of the Comstadt. He's not known to be particularly touchy feely. But perhaps that is also why he so rapidly climbed the ranks to become our esteemed Comstadt."

My eyes flash to his. Though his demeanor is light-hearted, his eyes show genuine concern. And somehow, his words help soothe the raw edges, a salve to the blistering cracks. "Thank you for that bit of information. But I can't really blame my sorry state of being on the Comstadt. I suppose I'm just a little homesick for my friends and family."

"And who can really blame you?" He shifts in his seat, his eyes serious. "You didn't hear this from me, but sometimes I think the Treaty of Dresden is utterly backwards, barbaric even."

"Then why not change it?" I make one last dab at the few straggling tears.

"Because we cannot survive otherwise. Even Bionics need to be repopulated, and we cannot do it without the new Marks of Dresden. And without Bionics, Cerulea and the Gateways would be left unprotected from the Quadrati."

A bot brings Sar Eppel a meal of mullet fish egg and holliflower soup, which he eats while I mull over what he's told me. We continue talking about the Gateways and my life back on Cerulea. By the end of the conversation, somehow I find myself feeling *whole* again.

As we finish, Sar Eppel asks me, "You say you've been working on the Hawwk simulators?"

"Yes, for the last several days, and it's been kicking my behind."

He chuckles and smiles broadly. "Well, I used to be quite an expert on it myself, though I haven't been in one of those in many years now. How about I join you when you go tonight?"

Something in my heart lightens, and somehow things feel a little less dismal. "Sure, that would be great."

XXXIV

TRITON: TURNING POINT

IT MUST BE CLOSE TO THE NADIR of night.
Only a few Bionics patrol the hangar at this time.
Even Bionics require sleep, but I'm still too wound up from my meeting with the Domseis earlier today. I need something to take my mind off of things.

I head for the NAD.

Reaching the long rows of Hawwk simulators where we sometimes come for extra practice on the various flight scenarios, I notice that one of the crystalline spheres is activated. Who's pulling extra hours? Usually, I'm the only one to come here and practice late at night when I can't sleep. Granted I've missed the last several days because of my meetings with the Domseis.

I move to the control room, which displays all the various flight simulators. The moment I step into the darkened room, I recognize a familiar profile manning the station. "What in the dark infinites are you doing here at this hour, Sar Eppel?"

"I suppose I could ask you the same thing, Comstadt." My old tutor turns towards me with an air of feigned innocence.

"You know very well that I come here to practice. I haven't seen you set foot in here since we lost Tomas during the Battle of the Arches, so I know that can't be your excuse."

Eppel blinks once, the only sign that I've affected him. I know I shouldn't mention his best friend's name, but my old mentor always seems so unflappable—and I'm still mad at him from our meeting with the Domseis earlier today. He told the Domseis that everything was fine at Finlan's Point and didn't need my return to post there, saying this even though he knew how badly I wanted to get back to the Gateways.

My old mentor, in usual fashion, recovers quickly. "Well, when one comes by skills out of natural talent, one doesn't need to practice so much." Eppel throws his chin up in the air. "I'm here because the new Mark of Dresden asked me to help her."

My gaze jerks to his. "The new Mark of—you mean *she's* the one practicing at this hour?" I can't help but remark in surprise. Though I haven't seen her at all this week, I was keeping tabs on her safety and whereabouts through Jasella. My most trusted bot would notify me instantaneously if she thought the new Mark of Dresden was in danger, but of course not for something like this. And somehow, while being so caught up trying to figure out what the Quadrati are up to at Finlan's Point when everyone else is too blind to see, I overlooked the fact that the new Mark of Dresden was up training at all hours.

Just last week the new Mark asked if she could try piloting the Hawwk. Of course I told her it was completely out of the question, *at first.* The Domseis would most assuredly have Nullified me, Comstadt or not, if I really allowed her to fly that death machine before she made her transformation. But I had to give her a bone, give her a taste of what we Bionics do day in and day out. And could anyone blame me if that something also happened to mean that I didn't have to babysit her every second of the day, and freed me to look into what was happening at Finlan's Point before things got out of hand there?

So I struck a bargain with her. If she could pass all of the flight simulator tests on the Hawwks, then I would give her a chance to take out a real one. But I was not worried. There are well over a hundred tests she'll have to pass before that happens. And some of these tests are real rattlers. Even Phlynnt, one of our best pilots, spent several months in the NAD before managing to pass all the various scenarios the simulator threw his way. I predicted it would be at least several months before this new Mark of Dresden would manage to get through even the first few simulations, well after her transformation. So I had no qualms then about making that bargain.

I'm not so certain now. For while Eppel and I were chatting, I was also watching the display screen monitoring each simulator's progress. I lean in closer to the only one currently operational, not quite believing what I am seeing.

Not only is the new Mark of Dresden completing the simulator tests, she is knocking them out like no one I have seen before. And she hasn't even received her nanobot infusion yet. She completes the jack knife simulation in less than a minute. The black hole formation in less than thirty seconds. The gravitas test with a full solar cell to spare. Where in the world did she learn to fly like that?

I turn to Eppel. "How in the dark infinites is this possible?"

His gaze travels to where mine rests, and he shakes his head. "I was wondering the same thing myself. I wouldn't have believed it, maybe attributed it to beginner's luck, but she's been kicking those simulations just like the black hole formation every night for the last five nights in a row. Hasn't missed a single one yet. The funny thing is, she thinks she is having a hard time of it."

"You're rattling me, right? You mean she's been at this for five nights straight already?" I had no idea the new Mark of Dresden would take the bargain so seriously.

"Yeah, comes and gets me straight from the cantina every day. The first few days, I gave her some tips about the takeoffs, landings, the usual Young Blood difficulties. But since then, she's been managing well enough on her own. Now, mostly I'm here to keep her company. I can't say I've ever seen any new Mark as talented and hardworking. Not even you." He smirks.

"You're here just to keep the girl company?" I can't keep the skepticism from my voice. Never before has my old mentor been one for social niceties. I'm not quite sure what has gotten into him. One other thing bothers me. "And why would she ask *you* to help?"

"You did introduce us, if you recall. But perhaps she would have approached you instead, if you were not always so busy, Comstadt. So logically, Livi sought out the next best thing, the former, esteemed tutor of the holier-than-thou Comstadt, otherwise known as me."

Livi? "I was not aware you were on a first-name basis with the new Mark of Dresden."

Eppel slaps me on the shoulder, a mischievous grin lighting his face. "Is that a hint of jealousy I detect, Comstadt?"

Being several hundred years older and currently lower rank than me does not prevent my old tutor from teasing me like a school kid. Some people never grow out of that prepubescent mentality I suppose. Even Bionics.

I shrug. "All I meant was that I had not realized she had been able to cultivate some friendships already, given her short time here on Atlas."

Eppel shakes his head ever so slightly. "Well, then perhaps *you* should *pay more attention* to your new Mark."

I hate it when my mentor is right, but still I won't admit it. "Of course I've been keeping an eye on her. I am in continuous contact with Jasella about the new Mark of Dresden's whereabouts and her safety. You and I both know that Jasella would notify me right away if anything were amiss." And double jinxes on me, I even know that her favorite item to order at the cantina is longhorn stew, but I'm certainly not going to admit that to my old mentor.

Eppel actually rolls his eyes at me. "You may be the most brilliant and powerful Bionic that we have, but you still have much to learn when it comes to human nature."

"What are you talking about?"

"What I'm trying to get you to see is that the new Mark of Dresden doesn't just need someone to keep an eye on her and keep her safe. She needs someone to guide her, to understand what she is going through. Did you never notice that the poor girl is lonely? And who can blame her? She's left all of her friends and family back on Cerulea. How do you expect her to want to be a Bionic if she is so lonely?"

My eyes go wide. *This* coming from the one who so vehemently denied me contact with my family back on Cerulea during my own training? "As I recall," I growl back as old emotions come rioting back, "*someone* taught me long ago that the privilege of being a Bionic and exploring the universe like no mortal should be enough incentive."

My old mentor actually has the good sense to look guilty, eyes cast downwards and avoiding my gaze, his mouth drawn tight. "I've changed, Triton. Despite all the nanotechnology coursing through our veins, even Bionics need more to life than just the Gateways. And sometimes things happen that make you realize what really is important."

And I know very well what *thing* he is referring to.

Several years ago, Eppel lost his best friend, Tomas, the last Comstadt before me. Since then my old mentor has never been the same. Fila once told me that Tomas and Eppel were like brothers. They arrived on Atlas almost at the same time, shortly after the turn of the millennium, and were Young Bloods together, training, going through the challenges and pitfalls of being Bionics together. They climbed the ranks of the Bionics until Tomas was chosen to be the Comstadt, and Eppel went on to be the Sar, or head trainer of the Magnars. Together they were unbeatable, fighting many successful battles against the Quadrati.

But the Battle of the Arches changed that. As Fila tells it, Tomas for some reason refused to go on the Quadrati run that day. No one understood why, least of all Eppel, who was all about guts and glory. After an argument between the two ensued where unkind words were exchanged, the Comstadt disappeared for several hours. No one could find him. So finally Eppel left for the Quadrati sighting without him.

But when the orlings flared, indicating that the Gateways were compromised, of course the Comstadt came back. He couldn't ignore that his best friend was in trouble. So the Comstadt took off for the Battle of the Arches, saved Eppel's behind, but in the process was captured by the Quadrati. Tomas has never been seen or heard from since. The Upper Council's intel suggested that he was executed by the Quadrati. Since then, Eppel has never been the same. I know that underneath his unflappable exterior, my old mentor carries that terrible guilt with him every day.

Seeing the dragging pain in my mentor's eyes makes me regret bringing up Tomas's name. I feel like such a Dark Skythe's behind. How could I do this to the one person on Atlas who has been like a father to me even if he is the most irritating buzzard that ever became a Bionic? Now it's my turn to feel ashamed. "I'm sorry, Eppel. You are right about the girl. It's just that I've been so caught up in trying to figure out what the Quadrati are up to at Finlan's Point that I haven't paid proper attention to the new Mark of Dresden. I'll try to do better."

"If you really want to try to do better, then help the new Mark, *really* help her, not just go through the motions. You have so much more to offer her than just your bot helper. The Domseis assigned you to be her mentor and protector for a reason." And with that, he picks up his things and walks right out of the control room, leaving me alone to deal with the new Mark of Dresden.

XXXV

LIVI: UNEXPECTED VISITOR

FOR THE LAST SEVERAL NIGHTS, even in my dreams I soar over the snow-capped mountaintops, diving at the last second before the Quadrati attack, but the Hellion ship comes out of nowhere, *and I am dead.*

But this time, dreams and virtual reality merge. I can hardly tell the difference as I sit in the cockpit of the Hawwk simulator. That wretched Hellion with its claw-like wings blasts the daylights out of me, and I am dead *again*. And no matter how closely I pay attention to the radar, how carefully I check the argon perimeters, the Hellion manages to sneak up on me *every single darn time*.

Who knows how many hours I've been at this. But what I do know is that even my thick skull feels ready to crack, to splinter open and let the little mushy pieces fall out. This is the final hurdle on the Hawwk simulation, the last test before the Comstadt promised he would let me fly a Hawwk for real. All the other tests I completed in no time. I'd even venture to say that some were kind of easy.

But the Hellion simulation has eluded me so far, *by a long shot*. I let my head drop wearily into my hands and knead my knuckles hard into my temples.

A noise beside me, like someone politely clearing his throat, makes me jerk up. My heart practically seizes in my chest when I realize that someone's big and powerful visage is sitting in the virtual seat next to me.

"C-Comstadt?" I tense, swiping at a lock of hair that has strayed from my virtual ponytail into my eyes. Suddenly the cockpit of the Hawwk simulator feels too small, the air too thick.

To my surprise, the usually imperturbable Comstadt seems rather uncomfortable too. He shifts in his seat and clears his throat. "Apologies, Park, I didn't mean to surprise you."

"N-no, I wasn't s-surprised," I stammer. Great. Now *that's* believable. Might as well announce to him that I was just about ready to pee in my pants. Finally, I manage to explain in a rush of words. "It's just that I didn't expect to see you here. That's all." I force my shoulders to relax and even try to smile. Clearing my throat, I ask as evenly as I can, "Where did Eppel go? Is everything all right?"

The Comstadt's thick eyebrows arch up for some strange reason, but he replies smoothly, "*Sar* Eppel had some business to take care of, and it looked like you could use a few pointers."

"*You* were watching?" Stars alive. Now I *really am* embarrassed. How many times did he see my Hawwk crash and burn in a hot flaming mess? Just fantastic. Now he'll never let me at the real thing.

But instead of berating me, to my surprise, the Comstadt replies, "Perhaps I underestimated your abilities, Park."

Is the Comstadt actually complimenting me? "But I've been at this Hellion simulation for the twentieth time now, and I still end up the biggest exploding star this side of the Erlion System."

"Well, then you don't know that even Phlynnt, who is one of our best pilots, failed a hundred times over before he passed this Hellion simulation. And most others take at least a thousand tries. So you see, you still have some room to go." And to my surprise, his virtual self actually smiles back. And I catch myself wondering if his teeth are really that nice and perfect in real life. "These simulations are meant to challenge and train you for every type of scenario you could possibly encounter. Only one person in the history of Bionics has made it this far in as short of time as you."

"Well, I suppose that does make me feel *a little* better. Because I swear on Juthri's stone, if I do one more Hellion run, my head's going to split open for sure."

Maybe the virtual reality image is playing tricks on me, for the Comstadt actually *laughs*. "Then how about we take a break?"

I look at him uncertainly for a few moments. I really want to pass this stars-forsaken simulator so I can try out the Hawwk for real. But I suppose taking a short break wouldn't hurt. Finally, I shrug. "Very well. What do you suggest then, Comstadt?"

"How about a late dinner? Chef Aton keeps the cantina open round the clock."

I shake my head. "Maybe later, the loop-de-loop on the Hellion run hasn't been terribly good for my appetite. Honestly, I just need to let off some steam."

Triton thinks for a long moment, then looks at me with a twinkle his eye. "In that case, I know the perfect place."

XXXVI

LIVI: LETTING OFF STEAM

WELL I'LL BE a Dark Skythe's behind.
And I thought I had seen everything.
We stand on a flattened tripod overhanging a darkened chamber below. Laser fire splits the air between. Bionics leap on and off of rapidly moving and impossibly thin ledges below us. They twirl and somersault onto floating platforms and geometric islands overrun by attacking, attacking—*Droids?*

Burning black holes. Am I seeing things? What are Droids doing on Atlas?

"Look out!" I yell at the Comstadt. From above, a Droid descends from seemingly nowhere, right at the Comstadt's back.

In one smooth move, the Comstadt spins. His arm arcs through the air, striking the Droid in the center of its back, and in the next moment does a low sweep with his legs. The Droid comes crashing down at my feet. I stumble back, my heart pounding in my chest.

The Comstadt's eyes flash to mine as he rights himself, not a hair out of place. "Well, that's a new one. Domseis must have planted that one when they upgraded the program yesterday. They like to switch things up now and then."

"Program?" I'm still trying to calm my runaway pulse.

"Yes. Welcome to Hemlock, our training center. All of this"—his arms gesture widely—"is a carefully choreographed, holographic program, designed by the Domseis no less."

"But it seems so real." I put a hand on the fallen Droid before me. *Yes. Solid as Juthri's stone.*

"You can thank Domsei Shen for that. He invented a way to configure electromagnetic fields combined with holographic overlays to simulate the substance of matter. It may feel real, but it's nothing more than the complex interplay of magnetic fields, much as two magnets repelling each other."

In the next moment, the Droid at my feet disintegrates, right before my eyes. Not even a dust mote remains in its place.

Whoa.

I peer over the edge of the bridge elevated a dozen meters up in the air. Triton stands next to me also assessing the scene below. The training center is like a cadet wonderland on steroids. If only Keenon could see this now.

As I look more closely amongst the dozens of Bionics below, a twirling flash of red catches my eye. Phlynnt. Vaulting right beside him are Juki and Sar Eppel. Phlynnt narrowly misses getting pummeled by two Droids before Juki and Eppel take them down. "*This* is your way of letting off some steam? And in the middle of the night too? Remind me never to ask what you Bionics do for fun."

"As Bionics, we only require a fraction of the amount of sleep as you. Hemlock is a useful way to fill our downtime. Whether you ultimately decide to become a Bionic or not, knowing how to take down a Droid is a good skill to have. Anyway, it's not as hard as it looks." Triton throws me a broad smile. "You wanted to get your mind off of things, right?"

He's trying to be nice to me? "Well, I also did not particularly want to die in the process. I said I wanted to let off some steam, not to end up in the med unit again."

"As I said, none of this is actually real. The electromagnetic matrix holograms simulate matter but are mostly harmless. They are designed to deactivate at fifty newtons of force, enough to give you a good workout, a few bruises, maybe a concussion at the most. But you certainly can't die from it, even with your non-Bionic constitution."

"Well, that's reassuring. But forget the Droids, those sky-high ledges alone seem treacherous enough."

"If it makes you feel any better, there is also an antigravity device built into the chamber floor. Get too close to the bottom, and it will automatically activate."

"Your Domseis have thought of everything, haven't they?"

Down on a ledge below, a Droid suddenly charges at Halo, sending her toppling over the edge. *Look out!* I'm about to yell. But just as the Comstadt explained, the moment before she hits the floor, an invisible force kicks in, preventing certain impact. Unscathed and unperturbed, Halo brushes herself off and steps into a clear tube that reaches up the vertical height of the chamber.

A moment later, she's standing right next to us.

Halo flashes the Comstadt a perfect smile while fisting her hand to her chest. "Late night workout, Comstadt?"

The Comstadt smiles back and nods. "The new Mark of Dresden here wanted to let off some steam."

"Well, sorry I can't stay and chat. I made a bet with Juki and Phlynnt. First one to one hundred points gets the others' servings of Chef Aton's tartleberry pie. He just got a fresh batch sent in from Hurako." Her gaze goes to a far wall where mine follows. "For star's sake. That Phlynnt is ahead of me by ten already."

On the wall is a scoreboard of sorts, boldly displaying a few names I recognize, but most I don't. The numbers blinking next to them I presume are their current scores.

Halo smiles at me. "Nice to see you here, Young Blood, and hope you rattle some Droids!" She gives the Comstadt another salute, and in the next instant leaps onto one of the moving ledges below, her brassy brown ponytail with its streak of white whipping wildly behind her.

The Comstadt's eyes follow her only briefly before he turns to me. "As you may have guessed, the goal is to get to the end of the course without getting hazarded. Disable as many Droids as you can."

"And how exactly does one disable a Droid?"

"You mean Galactic didn't teach the cadets this? Disgraceful." The Comstadt shakes his head but proceeds to demonstrate. "Remember. Their shells are made out of tinston, the hardest metal known in the universe. They only have one vulnerable point, right in the notch between the shoulder blades. Their main power source is located just a few millimeters below the surface there. But you have to get it just right. A centimeter too far to the left or right, and you will miss it. It's not even the size of a holliberry."

He holds a shiny metal device towards me. "Use this mock hazar to help you. Left button activates the laser, right button unsheathes the dagger." He promptly passes the weapon over to me. "And because the cores of a Droid's legs are solid tinston, their center of gravity sits remarkably low. You've got to swipe them below their knees to even have a chance at toppling them. Otherwise, they're almost impossible to knock down."

"Anything else?"

"Bonus points for disabling a Dogger bot."

"Dogger bot?"

"Yes." The Comstadt directs my attention to the bottom of the chamber. Strange animal-like robots skitter around on four legs, and as fast as all hellas. "The Quadrati sent those to the last attack on us, and the Domseis have just recently incorporated them into these programs. We're still trying to figure out the best way to disable them. A single bite from their jaws delivers as much electrical voltage as a bolt of lightning."

"Sounds painful."

"Unfortunately, Magnar Juki found that out the hard way. So remember, avoid their jaws as much as possible. Also keep your arms tucked when you get into the holoport, otherwise you'll find yourself with an ugly friction burn at the top. Oh, and there's one other thing you need to know."

"What's that?"

"Watch out for the Saucers." And with a quick shove, he pushes me aside—right before a flying disc whizzes past my head, nearly grazing my left ear.

"Please tell me I'm not just in some virtual video game," I mumble as I right myself.

"Video game?" the Comstadt asks, eyebrows raised.

"Uhh yeah. Never mind."

"Okay then." The Comstadt actually smiles. "Ready to rattle some Droids?"

XXXVII

LIVI: HEMLOCK

NOTE TO SELF, NEVER SUCCUMB to peer pressure ever again. *Ever.*
Left. Right. Left again. *Get to the first ledge.* Leap. *The second.* Vault and duck. *Now aim for the island.* Catapult across the void. Miss—and fall. Scream like a ninny right before the impact of certain death that never comes. Open my eyes to find my face floating an arm's length from the very solid chamber floor. Get back up, my face undoubtedly holliberry-red. *Try again.*

This is not letting off steam. This is pure, unadulterated torture. Second note to self, *never let the Comstadt be nice to you ever again.*

But I won't give up. Not with the Comstadt and all the other Bionics in the chamber side-eyeing me as I fumble my way through Hemlock.

Despite everything, at this moment I'm thankful—thankful for my Galactic cadet training. Thankful for the solid strength in my legs built up from the many long hours spent running up and down Guilan's Peak for the umpteenth time over the last three years. Thankful for the hundreds of pushups that Kyvox Scott made me do every day, four times a day. Thankful for the thousands of times I made myself cycle through Ferret drills—climbing ropes, scaling barriers, crawling through mazes of electrical currents—to get to the end of Galactic's ninja-like obstacle course. Even I have to admit—*I didn't get chosen to be one of Galactic's Beacons for nothing.*

For surely if I hadn't been run through the gamut of Galactic's cadet training, I certainly wouldn't have the remotest of chances right now. I would have already been knocked out or fainted dead away. Just leaping from ledge to ledge while dodging the dozens of flying Saucers is difficult enough. Forget about getting any bonus points.

The holoport propels me upwards in a rush, and just in time I remember to keep my arms tucked. It spits me back out at the overlook of Hemlock.

At the top again, I can easily pick out the Comstadt in the vast arena below. He's a whirlwind of perpetual motion, disabling Droid after Droid, vaulting from one moving ledge to another, dodging Saucers with ease. The long graceful lines of his powerful form slice through the air. Unerringly precise. Lethal by nature. I can't help but admire him. Even the other Bionics stop and watch. His numbers on the scoreboard blink rapidly up. Fifty. Sixty. Seventy. A quick hazaring shot to a Dogger bot below. One hundred.

Well, there's no use being a wallflower—my Grandpa Wren used to say. I take a deep breath in. *Here I go again.*

I catapult back down to one of the moving ledges. My foot skids to a stop only a hairsbreadth from the edge. *Too close.* When a platform below lines up just right, I take another calculated running jump down and across. *At least I stick the landing.* Even further below me, a flurry of activity—Bionics and Droids tangle on the pyramid-shaped island. The Droids may be virtual, but their pulsatile glowing eyes and hard metal faces still scare the hellas out of me. Suddenly, a flash of tinston comes rushing at me. *Where did that come from?*

But I've had enough of free-falling. I'm not willing to get back in that holoport again so soon. I'm more prepared this time. Just before the Droid rams into me, I dodge to the side. It goes careening over the edge all the way to the chamber floor, then disintegrates moments later.

I can't celebrate just yet. Another Droid quickly takes its place. But now, I'm backed up to the platform's corner. And it's still too far for me to jump to the next landing.

"Get down low, Park! Use your size to your advantage!" The Comstadt's voice pummels me from somewhere I cannot see.

I drop to a low crouch just as the Droid rushes at me, sending the Droid sprawling over me and down to a platform below.

When the platform comes within jumping distance, I leap down after the Droid. But the Droid has already recovered and rushes at me again. I spin and sweep out my leg, just as the Comstadt did. *Right below the knees.* The line of my leg connects with hard metal, but I don't even feel the pain. The Droid hits the platform with a satisfying clang. For once, the universe is with me.

I've got to hand it to the Domseis, the special effects are pretty darn realistic.

"Now get it right in the notch between the shoulder blades!" Again the Comstadt's voice rings out.

Adrenaline sends me back up. But too late. The Droid is already back on its feet, charging towards me. I turn and try to do a graceful leap for the platform below, but its long metal arm whacks me on the back, sending me sprawling onto it instead. My forehead hits the platform hard enough for me to see stars, and my left leg dangles halfway off of the edge, over a precipitous drop. I roll away from the edge onto my back. But the Droid is too quick. In a single leap the Droid lands on my platform, his metal form looming over me. Before I can even move, his metal arm arcs down, hazar in hand. I squeeze my eyes shut and brace my arms in front of my face.

A long moment passes.

"You can get up now, Park."

I crack my eyes open and see not the pulsatile red eyes of the Droid, but the Comstadt's towering form and mildly amused face.

"Had enough?" The corner of his mouth twitches ever so slightly. His chin wobbles.

I almost want to say yes. That this is not really my idea of letting off steam. But in truth, in that moment, I realize that I have never felt more alive than I do now. Pushing myself beyond my limits, the thrill of it all still pumps through my veins. And the way the Comstadt is looking at me, I can't help but feel that this is another test, to test my mettle. I'll be a Dark Skythe's behind before I show any weakness.

My feet feel a little shaky, but I force myself up. "Are you kidding? I'm just starting to get the hang of things," I say and grin as widely as I can. Just before another Saucer nearly takes off my right ear.

XXXVIII

LIVI: TARTLEBERRY PIE

EVERY NIGHT MY BODY ACHES, and fresh bruises cover my shins and elbows.

But each night, I'm just a little less sore, my mind feels a little more—free. Even without the nanobot infusion, I'm achieving more than I ever thought possible. Today, I managed to disable five Droids on my own. And so what if they're not actually real. It still feels darn good.

The days and weeks on Atlas start to blend together, progressing in some variation of the usual fashion— Hemlock, Hawwk simulator, Hemlock again, cantina, eat, sleep, eat again. And through all the nail-biting training runs, the Comstadt's hulking presence is by my side, whether I like it or not. I don't really understand his new-found attentiveness, but I have neither the time nor the energy to question it.

Now, I've never been one to snack between meals, but with all the training, I've built up a voracious appetite. This evening, I had a particularly hard run through

Hemlock, and I find myself in the cantina late at night *again*.

"I've got one more slice left of that tartleberry pie when you finish that one, Livi." Chef Aton knows me by name now. The rest of the tables in the cantina are empty this late. Chef Aton places a mug of steaming hot chocolate in front of me, makes one for himself as well, and then sits down across from me.

"Thanks, Chef, but I'd better not. I'm supposed to meet the Comstadt early in the morning for another run on the Hawwk simulators. I think we're going to do the Hellion run again, and I don't want to be cleaning half-digested tartleberries off the inside of the simulator if I can help it," I say, between mouthfuls of the syrupy berries that are sweet and tangy at the same time. "But this is delicious. If you don't mind me asking, how did you end up becoming chef of this place?"

Chef Aton chuckles low as he sips on his hot chocolate. The streak of white in his hair barely contrasts with the blond. "As you can imagine, Livi, not everyone with the Mark of Dresden mutation is cut out for life in the fray. The few of us Bionics who happen to enjoy the quieter life serve roles on Atlas that cannot be fulfilled by our various bots. And I just happen to have the talent for satisfying the palate. On Atlas, we also have Bionic barbers, musicians, artists, inventors. As you can imagine, with so much time to perfect our trade, most of us get to be very good at what we do."

"So if it turned out that I became a Bionic and decided to lead a 'quieter life' as you say, I could?"

"You certainly could. But from what I've heard from Sar Eppel about your piloting skills and penchant for living life on the edge, I think you would get bored very quickly, especially when one has a millennium of time to kill."

He eyes me for a moment, as if pondering something, and shakes his head. "No, definitely not the quiet life for you, but don't worry. I think you will fit in with the more adventurous Bionics just fine. Just make sure the Comstadt doesn't run you into the ground the way he does to himself. That man will work himself to a five-hundred-year early grave if he's not careful." He takes one last sip of his hot chocolate before setting the mug down. "Now if you'll excuse me, I've got to get back to my holliberry muffins. I promised everyone a fresh batch in the morning. Give me a holler if you change your mind about that last slice of tartleberry pie."

"I will, Chef. Thank you." I smile.

Chef Aton gives me a kindly smile back and heads into the kitchen.

As I finish up my hot cocoa and tartleberry pie, it suddenly strikes me how wrong I was about the Bionics only four weeks ago. Bionics are not the unfeeling beasts as portrayed in all of those Cerulean childhood fables. So what if cintian metal flows through their veins? So what if they're ten times stronger than regular folks and near immortal? The Bionics—like the chef, Sar Eppel, my trinam, hellas, even the Comstadt—are just as kind and honorable as people on Cerulea. With that thought in mind, I head back to my chamber for the night, navigating the nearly empty halls save for a few bots.

When I get back to my chambers, Jasella has already prepared my bed for sleep, and clean pajamas hang neatly by the bathroom door. In no time I take a quick shower and slip between the soft tangerine-colored sheets of the hovering bed.

But tonight, despite the coziness of the bed, I can't sleep. It's hard to believe that tomorrow will mark the end of my first star month on Atlas. I lie there restlessly for almost an hour before I finally force myself back up. *What will I decide tomorrow?*

Starlock, my birth constellation, greets me from the broad window of my room, his fiery arm and broad shoulders, a familiar friend from my lonely childhood nights. I can't help but to be thrown into memories from bygone times.

"Will you tell me the story of the Great Dispersion again, Grandpa Wren?" I ask sleepily. My head rests on his lap as he strokes my forehead gently and gazes up at the stars.

"Of course, my little seafaerie. Look there." He points his long, bent finger up into the starlit sky just to the north of Solaria, just past where Starlock resides and where one star twinkles brighter than the rest. "There, Livi. There beyond Starlock was a planet called the World of Origins, where humans came from, a once lush planet where thousands upon thousands of different living creatures sang in the trees and frolicked in the grasslands; until one day the humans forgot how to take care of it, and the land which once grew the most beautiful flowers now only grew dust. And that's when the Great Dispersion began. The strongest of us built powerful ships and reached across the stars to find another home. And that is how we came to be on Cerulea."

"And what of the others? The others who were not as strong?" I ask anxiously, though in my heart I already know the answer.

Grandpa Wren's face grows cloudy. Sadness further creases the wizened lines of his face. "We can only hope that they found their way to the end in peace."

Grandpa Wren is far away now, and only Starlock is left to hold my hand. I reach up with my fingertips, tracing the edges of Starlock, as if that reaching will somehow give me the understanding that I have always craved and needed.

Until now, life somehow always felt limited, restricted to what was possible within a mortal life. The decision I make tomorrow could potentially change that. It strikes me that perhaps now I have the opportunity to go beyond. Now that I understand what the Bionics really stand for, what they do, what their roles have been in protecting the people of Cerulea and Hurako, perhaps I can do better with my life. Be better. Reach higher and farther. For what other meaning is there in life aside from bringing the dreams and wishes that one sees in the mind into reality?

And in that moment of contemplation, I slip back in bed and let the starlit night caress and fill the hollows of my soul until I fall soundly asleep. I know what I will choose.

XXXIX

LIVI: EMERGENCY AT POLARIA

I T SEEMS FITTING that today we would make an
outing to Hurako.

My first patrol run on Atlas will also mark the end
of my month with the Bionics. Tonight, I will announce
my decision to the Domseis, one that could change the
storyline of my life.

I spent half the morning in the Comstadt's office trying
to persuade him to please let me try to pilot the Hawwk.
In hindsight, perhaps it would have been easier to roll a
square boulder through Anduria's mud swamps. But I
promptly reminded him that a deal was a deal, and that I
passed all one hundred of the Hawwk simulator tests fair
and square, even the Hellion one. By some miracle, I
managed to extract the slightest of nods from him. Before
the Comstadt could change his mind, I reached out and
gave him a big hug—and promptly jettisoned out of his
office, not daring to look back.

Later this morning as we went through the flight
simulators and the Hawwk's controls for the umpteenth

time, he warned me that if *his* Hawwk came back with even the tiniest scratch, he would personally have to hang me out to dry by my toenails from the very top of the flora chamber. He further explained that this was especially necessary since the Domseis would exact their punishment on him instead of their precious new Mark of Dresden. I promised him that it would certainly not come to that.

Now Triton fans his gaze towards me. "Okay, Park. First thing is to take us around Cerulea's orbit. You think you can handle that?"

"Don't worry, I'm a fast learner. And as my Grandpa Wren used to say—try until you fail, and then try again."

"Your Grandpa Wren sounds like a very wise if not stubborn person. Perhaps he would have done well on Atlas."

"Of that I have no doubt." But with my thoughts on Grandpa Wren, I feel a painful squeeze, right in the gizzard. I wonder how he's doing. But I push past the ache in my throat. *You have to be strong, Livi. Keep moving forward. I'm doing this for him.*

"She's all yours."

I turn on the jets that fire on the underbelly of the Hawwk, easing on the rear thrusters just enough to peel out and away from Atlas's hangar. Soon we clear the Atlas perimeter. The blue orb of Cerulea comes into view.

"Very nicely done." Triton raises his eyebrows, as if surprised.

Time to test out the controls. Bank left. Veer right. Climb. Dive. It's like being home after a long journey away. Though the fancy toggles and brightly lit panels may look different, the basic elements are the same.

Having trained in the simulators, it doesn't take long for me to get the hang of the real deal. I guide the Hawwk closer to the blue orb of Cerulea, getting a feel for the controls.

"Ease into orbit. Maintenance velocity when we reach five hundred kilometers."

"Got it." I throw a few more switches, decelerating just enough to capture Cerulea's gravitational pull at its apogee.

"Well done, Park. Perhaps I won't have to string you up by your toenails after all."

"Too bad, Comstadt. And I was so looking forward to spending a night in the flora chamber too."

As the Hawwk settles into orbit, I peer out the window and get swallowed by my thoughts. Beyond Cerulea, the endless black universe beckons to me, and I'm overcome with the strangest sensation—a speck of dust between the stars, wandering the great unknowns of space. In the distance I can make out a tiny shimmering twinkle—Hurako—and it dawns on me that my very existence in the vast stretches of nothingness is truly a miracle.

"Beautiful, isn't it?" Triton's voice startles me, and I flush when a quick glance at him tells me that he's been watching me.

I turn my gaze abruptly back to the window. "Yes, it truly is."

"One go around, then we head to Hurako. You remember what I said about star jump?"

"Of course," I say as confidently as I can.

"Good. Same protocol we practiced in the simulator. Keep your eyes focused on the end point."

"Eyes on the end point. Got it." With our high speeds, it doesn't take long for us to complete our orbit, and moments later I'm flying us towards it, the ring of electrical wildfire. The wormhole is still daunting even though I've been through it twice already.

"Straight shot right down the middle. Don't let the Hawwk wings get too close to the edges."

"Understood." My hand grips the toggle firmly. I certainly do not want to be burnt to a crisp.

To my amazement, this time, Star Jump is in fact more tolerable. It's still not quite a walk in the park, but tolerable nonetheless. My head doesn't spin quite so much, and I manage to maintain consciousness.

"Not bad, Park. Not bad at all." Triton gives me an approving nod once we're completely through. Starlock's five stars hail brightly in the distance.

"Fast learner, remember?" I tap at my temple for emphasis, and Triton lets out a low rumbling laugh.

We pass over the whites of Hurako's southern pole in silence, when suddenly Triton tenses. His head jerks to the side, fingers reaching for the comms link in his ear. "Burning black holes," he mutters. The pendant I noticed the first time I met Triton glows in the notch below his neck. He barks into the comms line. "Juki, Phlynnt, Halo. Return to Atlas immediately. The Quadrati got past Finlan's Point again and are heading for Cerulea. A whole rattling fleet of them. The Domseis are readying a counterattack. We launch at oh nine hundred. Drop off Park first though."

Quadrati attack on Cerulea? *Burning black holes indeed.* "Where are they headed?" My words tumble out in a rush.

"Polaria." Triton's face is grim. Eyes narrowed. "I'm taking back controls. Prepare for Star Jump."

I tighten my straps as my insides sink. Stars no. Keenon and Jia. They're both stationed at Polaria now. "Let me go too."

"Out of the question, Park." I'm forced back into my seat as the Comstadt's fingers fly over the control panel, and we pull away from Hurako's orbit.

"But my friends are stationed there." I know I can help, Bionic or not.

"I'm sorry, but without the nanobot transfusion, you'll be a wide-open target for the Quadrati." He shakes his head. "No, Park. Domseis' orders. You'll be safer on Atlas." He continues to face forward, brows furrowed in concentration on his navigational equipment.

"I *can* help. Though I may be new to the Hawwk, I'm one of Galactic's best pilots. Please, Comstadt." I'm begging now.

"You've barely just completed the Hawwk *simulators*. And while they are good training tools, they're still far different from the real beast." The Comstadt concentrates rigidly on the control panel in front of him.

"You forget, I've flown Buggards and Tracker ships before, and I don't think I need to tell you that those *are* the real beasts." I grab at Triton's arm, forcing his eyes on mine, and the Hawwk lurches. "Let me help. Please. They're my friends out there. You know you would do the same if it were your friends."

Triton looks at me for a hard moment, processing what I'm saying, the grey especially steely in the dim light of the Hawwk. A long moment passes, the air tense between us.

Just when I think he's going to give in, he looks away, busying himself at the controls again. "I'm sorry, Park. I just can't risk it." His jaw sets into a rigid line. He's not going to change his mind. What I wouldn't give to be a Bionic right now.

When we land back on Atlas, the hangar is a flurry of activity. The clatter of boots and bots echo off the far walls.

The Comstadt calls out, "Cassiopia unit. Head out as soon as the Hawwks are recharged. Meet back here in ten."

I try again. "Please, Comstadt. Give me a chance. I need to go help my friends."

He pivots towards me. "Sorry, Park, this is your stop. Go to the cantina. Get yourself something to eat. It's been a long day." He's about to go, when he pauses and turns back to me. "I'll do my best to see that your friends are okay. Keenon, right? Tall one with the jet-black hair?"

How does he remember him? "And my friend Jia," I blurt out. "Brunette with puppy dog eyes and funny as all hellas."

He nods and, before I can blink, disappears around the corner.

What he doesn't know is that I'm not particularly hungry.

XL

LIVI: BREAKING THE RULES

NOW I'M THANKFUL to have spent the extra nights in the Hawwk simulator room practicing, using the controls, going over its defense and weapon capabilities, learning various tactical formations, even after the Comstadt drilled everything into me earlier for the umpteenth time for several days straight.

Just like this morning, I fire up the jets of the Hawwk's underbelly. Using the cover of chaos, no one noticed when I slipped aboard a Hawwk idling unproductively on the sidelines. I figure they had plenty of spare Hawwks—might as well make them useful.

In any case, no one is going to leave me behind. Especially since they are *my* friends at stake. I position the Hawwk on the launching pad right behind the lines of others. Just as I reach the front, a flash of fiery red catches my eye. Phlynnt. His Hawwk taxis alongside my craft. His eyes widen, and he waves his arms frantically at me.

I smile as sweetly as I can.

Wave right back.

And with a push of a button, fire the thrusters. I'm off. Following the dizzying line of other Hawwks shooting out of Atlas at Mach speed, heading for Cerulea.

Within minutes the comms link crackles to life. "Livinthea Park. Turn your Hawwk around immediately. You have not been authorized for this mission." The Comstadt's voice is like steel and ice, slashing through the air right into my ears.

But I remind myself what I'm fighting for. "I will do no such thing, Comstadt. As I told you earlier, my friends are out there. I will not sit idly by when they need my help."

"Do you realize the amount of danger you will put yourself and the other Bionics in? Now instead of focusing on fighting the Quadrati and protecting the citizens of Cerulea, we have to look out for you as well." His voice growls through the comms link.

"I never asked you or any of the other Bionics to protect me, Comstadt. And I'm just doing what I would be expected to do as a Bionic anyway. Save and protect others."

"Then let me remind you that without the nanobot transfusion, you are no Bionic. And I guarantee you that if you don't turn your ship around, as a mere shell of flesh and bone, you will be nothing but a casualty."

"Well, try telling that to my friends who *are out there*. Who don't have the benefit of having cintian metal coursing through their veins. Though I may not be a Bionic yet, I'm Galactic's best pilot. I should be down there fighting with them *anyway*. And no matter what you might think, I can still help my friends. And if I die trying in the process, so be it. Find yourself another Mark of Dresden. I will not be a coward. Shoot me down yourself if you have to, but I guarantee *you,* Comstadt, that nothing is going to make me turn this ship around."

Moments of silence tick by. He is so mad, I wonder if he really is preparing to shoot me down himself. I can almost picture his grim face, brows furrowed in a scowl.

"*Triple eclipses.* You're as stubborn as a Dark Skythe's behind. So be it then, Park. But if you get into trouble, you're on your own. Now put your electromagnetic shields up like I taught you, and go help your friends." His voice flickers out, leaving a dull silence.

I can't dwell too long on the anger in his voice, I'm already in viewing range of Cerulea's northern pole. I knit my eyebrows, blinking at what I see. A fleet of Galactic Tullies already shooting into the skies above Polaria. I can even make out the red-tipped wings of the special Polarian unit. And I recognize the curved gold wings of the lead Tully flown by the head Beacon. It has to be Keenon.

Another bit of movement catches my eye, just rounding the curve of Cerulea's northern pole into the light of Calani and Thea, and I stop short. The Comstadt wasn't kidding when he said there was a whole fleet of Quadrati coming. What he didn't mention was that the swarm is ten times larger than the Tullies fleet. Just beyond the halo of Cerulea's sister suns, they fly like daggers, slashes of dark through the light, heading straight for our fleet of Tullies. *And I have never seen so many Buggards in my life.*

When I look back at the Tullies, the realization hits me. I shudder in my seat. They're still in scout formation. To them, it's still just a training run. The Tullies fleet is completely unaware of the approaching enemy. *Keenon has no idea.*

And why would he when the Quadrati are completely hidden from their direct view, and the enemy signals are no doubt cloaked from their primitive radar detection? Otherwise, with an enemy fleet that large, the Tullies would have taken evasive combat maneuvers by now. And our Bionics are still too far away to help.

It's going to be a massacre.

Think, Livi. Think. There must be some way to warn them. I try the Hawwk's comms link. Nothing. No doubt the Tullies are on Scout mode now, their communication frequencies encrypted. The Hawwk line won't be able to get through. Unless, unless—

The universal link. The Comstadt showed me how to manually patch into another ship yesterday. But I have to get closer, then find the right frequency. I toggle my thrusters, peeling away from the line of Hawwks, and race ahead, getting pinned back in my seat as I fumble for the accessory line.

I'm not sure how close I have to be, but I start to punch in the various frequencies we have used in the past at Galactic, all ten of them. *Mu 221, Lambda 32.* Nothing. *Rho 113, Alpha 1115.* Darn red light again. As quickly as I can, I run through the next six codes. The comms link still flashes red. Dagnabit. And the Quadrati are getting closer. Two more codes left. *Delta 1030, Beta 1220. Come on. Work. Please work.* Red light. My hands are shaking now. The Quadrati are almost on top of the Tullies. Last chance. *Keep it together, Livi. Kappa 121, Iiota 1118.* I hold my breath. The comms link flashes green. *Thank the stars.*

"Keenon, get yourself out of there! The Quadrati are straight ahead. Circle back and evasive measures now!" I pound my voice into my comms unit wishing I could squeeze myself through the ethers.

"What—stars above, Livi, is that you? What are you doing out here?" Keenon's clear and familiar voice cuts through the gravel.

Despite the cursing, hearing it makes my chest squeeze. But I fight through it. There's no time for that.

"I'll explain later. Right now you're headed straight for an ugly nest of Buggards. Evasive maneuvers now!"

"What are you talking about, our sensors don't—"

"Darn it, Keenon. For once in your life just listen to me. Retreat. Evasive maneuvers or you're dog's meat." My voice rises higher, the Quadrati are almost on top of them.

"All right, all right, Livi. Gold Team, retreat. Seafaerie formation until I call it. Eyes open for those nasty Buggards."

In the distance, the Tullies fleet splinters apart in threes, like the splaying of fireworks, circling back. *Good. Good.* I exhale, releasing a small bit of the tension taut in my shoulders. At least that will buy them some time until we can reach them.

A few moment later, a Hawwk nudges next to me, black fins the shade of midnight. Oh no. It's the Comstadt. But instead of herding me back towards Atlas, he pushes ahead. A crackle in my ear. "What are you waiting for, Park? Full throttle already. We don't have all day you know." Then he barks to the rest, "All units. Code Red. Full thrusters until we reach firing range of the

Quadrati fleet, then black hole formation. Park, follow my tail."

I don't know if I should be frightened or relieved that the Comstadt takes Pole position. But I have no time to question it as his thrusters engage full throttle. And I'm forced to do the same.

My Hawwk slingshots forward. I fight to stay conscious as my craft accelerates faster than I've ever gone before.

XLI

LIVI: BATTLE OF A LIFETIME

I T TAKES EVERY OUNCE of my concentration to stay on the Comstadt's tail as he hurtles towards the blue orb of Cerulea and the impending melee. My fingers fly desperately over the control panel in an effort to keep up. Stars he's a good pilot. Now I know for sure that he must have been holding back during our runs to Hurako.

"You were right, Livi. We're picking up on those darn Buggards now." Keenon's voice cuts through my concentration, making my fingers falter ever so slightly.

"No time to talk, Keenon. Just get yourselves outta there. Let the Bionics take care of it."

"But what about you?"

"Like I said, the Bionics will take care of them. Get back to Galactic base. There's too many of them." As we approach, the Buggards splinter, a few diving for Cerulea's Ferrion satellite, but the lion's share barrel straight for us.

"Then it sounds like Bionics or not, we're going to need to help each other. We'll go after the divers." The universal link cackles out.

"Wait, Keenon, those Buggard ships are too strong, they'll—Keenon!" But the line hangs limp, silent. Blasted, *stubborn mule. Just like when we were younger.* And to my dismay, the Tullies scrap evasive maneuvers, lining themselves up like the whetted tip of an arrow. Attack formation, chasing after the breakaway Buggards. Crimeny.

But I have no time to argue with him.

"Ready for black hole." The Comstadt's voice grinds out through the comms line. "Pummel the larger group first, we'll worry about the stragglers later. Shields up. We're almost within shooting range."

A red laser light slices directly at me, and I bank left, narrowly missing getting shot. *Too close.* My eyes track back, the Buggard's already spinning away. *Oh no you don't.* I fire up my rear lasers and let loose. The Buggard ship lights up in a fiery ball of flames. I could get to like these Hawwks.

"Not bad for a newbie." Juki chuckles, his Hawwk flanking mine.

"Black hole formation now!" the Comstadt growls. "Supernovas form the perimeter. Round those Buggards up. Juki and Halo, flank formation around Park. Keep her out of range. The rest of you run bait. As soon as they are in the hole, I'll unleash the dark matter. Everyone else, EMG shields up hundred percent. When I say scatter, clear the dark infinites out."

Fiery balls explode and red laser slashes the void around me, but the Hawwk smoothly obeys my every impulse—bank left, veer right, swoon to a dive through the whirlpool of Hawwks that's already forming. Juki and Halo follow in my wake, protecting my tail. The other Bionics run bait immediately behind them. Buggards swarm after us. But little do they know, they've flown right into the Comstadt's trap. Other Buggards careen in and out through the vortex but are quickly taken out by the perimeter runners. And I realize, to my amazement, that the Comstadt's plan is working. Despite the fact that the Quadrati forces outnumbers us, the Bionics more than make up for it with speed, agility, and tactical precision. The Hawwks swirl, a living tornado, and the remaining Buggards who were pursuing us are caught in the treacherous depths of the funnel.

"Pull free now!" the Comstadt orders.

Full throttle, I peel up and away from the eye of the whirlpool, the other Hawwks behind me pulling away as well. Just as the last Bionic clears, the Comstadt's Hawwk, with its shadowed wings, comes barreling through the center behind the Quadrati. "Black Hole scatter!" The whirlpool of Hawwks splinters, but before the Quadrati forces can break free, the Comstadt's Hawwk hurls a pulse of midnight through the center of the funnel. *Dark matter.* It blows through like an endless night, obliterating everything in its wake. Buggard ships get swallowed into the vacuum, evaporating into nothingness.

The comms link explodes with frank celebration.

But as I swing my Hawwk around and look towards the Ferrion satellite where I last saw our Tullies, my hand stills at the control panel. Mangled and torn metal, debris scatters across what once was a void. No crafts in sight except for one gold-winged Tully.

"Keenon! Come in. Are you okay?" I yell into the universal comms link.

Nothing but silence greets me. And I watch in horror as Keenon's ship struggles forward, wobbles, then lists on its side. Something is wrong. *Very wrong.* A strange buzzing starts to niggle at the base of my brain. Then I see it.

Right behind Keenon's Tully, what looks like a world-ending monster of a creature materializes out of the void—a Hellion ship, the most mysterious of all the Quadrati ships. Rarely seen, we barely have any intel about it. Before me now, Keenon's Galactic Tully is dwarfed in comparison.

The Hellion must have snuck up on us cloaked. Now it has Keenon's ship locked within some sort of gravitational beam.

The comms link has quieted, and the Hawwks are curling back around.

Comstadt's voice pierces the air. "All units regroup. Nebula formation and break the gravity beam before the Hellion recloaks and makes star jump."

Halo's voice pipes in. "How about unleashing the dark matter?"

"Can't use the dark matter without hitting the Tully too," the Comstadt replies. "Park, stay behind. If that Quadrati mother ship gets a whiff that you're a new Mark of Dresden, they'll go after you for sure."

Stay behind? But already I can see the edges of both the mother ship and Keenon's Tully shimmering. The Hawwks are going to be too late. I'm the closest by far.

I slam my throttle, blasting my laser fire at the same time, aiming for the mother ship's tail. It's not enough to take out the Hellion. But it's enough to take out the tractor beam.

And enough to get the Quadrati's attention. Vaguely, I hear the Comstadt call my name.

While the edges of Keenon's Tully resolidify, I find my Hawwk engulfed in hazy orange, the misty light flooding the cabin, my controls suddenly nonfunctional. A strange tingling creeps along my skin, and a buzzing sensation nips at the base of my skull. A second gravitational beam.

"Stand down, or your comrade's life is forfeit." A stilted, hard, mechanical voice grates through the air, making my heart jolt inside my chest. The Hellion ship must have commandeered the universal comms link. I've never heard a Quadrati speak before. It's even more ominous than I ever imagined.

Desperately, I try to do a manual override of the control panel, but nothing works. And deep down I know, as my arms and legs suddenly feel as heavy as Andurian cement, that perhaps the Comstadt was right. I will be nothing but a casualty.

XLII

TRITON: DESPERATE MEASURES

TRIPLE ECLIPSES. Now she's gone and done it. Why in the name of Altheria does the new Mark of Dresden have to be so darn bullheaded? "Halo! Fila! Run the omni scan. Pinpoint the last coordinates of that Hellion. See if you can detect any heat shadows."

A split second later, Halo's voice crackles over the comms link. "Last Hellion coordinates chi 122.05, upsilon 103.04, zeta 71.118, tau 681.30. But I'm sorry, Comstadt. There's nothing else. Absolutely no traces of the Hellion or the new Mark's Hawwk."

I slam my fist down hard onto the control panel, cursing under my breath. Dark infinites, where is she? For a few moments, I stare at the exact point in the depthless void of space from where Livi's Hawwk disappeared, disbelief at what has happened coursing through my veins.

For the first time in my Bionic life, I know what it means to feel vulnerable, like something has been ripped right from the center of my soul. How did I let this happen? How did things go so horribly wrong? In my mind I replay the sequence of events. The gold-winged Tully disabled. The Hellion ship appearing out of nowhere. Livi trying to rescue that Tully.

As soon as I realized what was happening I threw my own thrusters, even revving my Hawwk at prismei, almost spinning out of control myself. But I was still just too far away. The Hellion ship had recloaked, taking Livi's Hawwk with it before I could reach her. Despite the nanotechnology running through my veins, I've never felt so helpless before. What confounds me further is why the freed Tully practically threw itself into the Hellion's second tractor beam before they all evaporated into the ethers.

I know now that letting Park come with us to fight the Quadrati was probably the worst decision of my life. But how could I not let her try to help her friends?

It is going to take a miracle to track her down now. There is no telling where that Hellion ship took her. But we might still have one chance—trace the Hawwk's uranium signatures before they decay. Never mind that the process involves pummeling high levels of radiation to delineate the energy disturbance trail. And never mind that the process will take several star days at the best, several star weeks at the worst. There is no telling if Livi will still be alive by then. But still it is my only chance and I have to take it. "Eppel, box the perimeters. I'm going to run Flemming."

"Flemming? But you'll burn yourself to a crisp. Even our nanotechnology can't repair that." The skepticism in Eppel's voice rings clear even through the comms link.

Most other Bionics would bite their own tongue off before talking to the Comstadt like that. But being my old mentor, Eppel has no such reservations. He's seen me at my worst.

"Just do it. You know it's our only chance of finding Park again," I say.

"Very well, *Comstadt*," he grumbles, "but you know, Triton, the Domseis are going to rattle you alive for pulling this stunt when you get back. *If* you get back."

"They're going to rattle me alive anyway for having lost their precious new Mark of Dresden, so I don't really see that as an arguing point."

"As you wish then. But be careful."

XLIII

LIVI: CAPTURED

ALL I KNOW IS THAT I AM COLD. So cold that my whole body rattles ferociously beyond my control. So cold that the tips of my fingers prickle with numbness, and it even hurts to breathe. I crack my eyes open, dragging my cheek up off the hard metal floor.

The jumble in my mind quickly unscrambles as the events at Polaria come rushing back. The Buggards. The Comstadt ordering me back. Keenon's disabled Tully. The Hellion ship. That could only mean

I force myself up, my muscles not quite obeying as I stagger against the wall, nearly collapsing again. My head whirls as I turn. And stop short. A chill runs up my spine as I blink. Blink at the triad of dark solid walls rising up like Goliaths, higher than I can even see. *This is not my Hawwk.*

My breathing picks up, little puffs of air clouding before me. *Keep it together, Livi.*

If the Quadrati wanted me dead, I wouldn't be here. They're keeping me alive for a reason.

But just when I think things couldn't get any worse, I notice a heap of something crumpled unceremoniously on the opposite side of the cell next to a glass wall. As I look closer, a sickening feeling clenches in the pit of my stomach. It is not something, but someone—someone with broad shoulders and jet-black hair.

"Keenon!" I stumble over to him and kneel down, my arms shaking as I roll him onto his back.

He groans, a shudder running though his body. But his eyes peel open. "I'm all right, Livi. Just a little sore, that's all."

"Keenon, what in all hellas are you doing here? I thought—" But as he turns to face me and sits up, the purple swelling that was his left temple keeps me from finishing my sentence.

"Well, I couldn't very well let you have all the fun, could I?" he mumbles weakly. And though his voice is hoarse, he manages a wry smile. "Don't worry, it hurts more than it looks. And you know you've put me through far worse before." He tries to wink at me but fails miserably.

I bite back the retort that normally would have come rolling off my tongue by now—Mr. Tough and Never-Show-Weakness Kyvox is always trying to downplay his own injuries. Instinctively, I reach up towards his temple, but pull back when he winces. Instead, I help him to his feet, and though he sways a little at first, he seems otherwise unhurt. "Stars I'm sorry, Keenon. I thought I disabled their tractor beam."

"You did."

"Then how did you end up here?"

Keenon clears his throat. "Let's just say I hitched a ride."

"You—you followed me here?" I ask incredulously.

Keenon dips his head but holds my gaze. "I wasn't about to make the same mistake *twice*."

"What do you mean the same mista—" I stop midsentence as the revelation dawns on me. *He came here for me. And stars help us, they're going to kills us both now.* I look away, shaking my head furiously, my breath coming faster and faster now. "Keenon Young, that is the most *idiotic* thing you have ever done in the ten long years that I have known you. Even more ridiculous than the time you went belly up for that slice of holliberry pie during the finals quadcopter run. Why didn't you think things through first?"

Keenon throws his gaze skyward and scoffs into the air above. "Will you never *forget* that incident? I was *twelve* years old for Altheria's sake, with nothing but sand and dirt to fill my pitiful stomach. And here I somehow thought you would be *happy* to see me." His voice escalates up the mammoth walls. "Well, I really *must* be an idiot then."

Keenon shakes his head but then brings his gaze back towards me, gripping both of my arms, forcing me to look at him. "One of the worst days in my life was when I let that Bionic take you to stars know where. For weeks I tried to reach you. I didn't know if you were dead or alive. The Bionics wouldn't release even a rat's pellet of information to Galactic about your whereabouts." His eyes scan my face, his voice lowering. "I wasn't sure if I would ever see you again." He swallows, his Adam's apple bobbing ever so slightly. His hands tighten on my arms. "Since that day, I swore that if I found you, I would never make that same mistake again. So believe me when I say, I *have* thought things through—more than you could ever know."

Now it's his turn to narrow his eyes at me. "And what in the name of Altheria were *you* doing? How is it all right that you get to put yourself in danger to save my behind, but I'm not allowed to do the same for you? You think I could live with myself if I let you die because of me?" His eyes search mine as if for an answer to another question left unsaid.

I shake my head. This is *not* how I imagined our reunion would be. He's just as bullheaded as when we were younger, always trying to protect me when I didn't need protecting. "I would have gotten out of here on my own." Admittedly that may not be true, but I say it anyway, because it makes it easier to avoid his questioning gaze. Perhaps I'm a little bullheaded too.

"Well, I have absolutely *no* doubt about *that*, Livi," he remarks sarcastically. And the deep brown eyes that I know so well look back at me intently for a long moment. He gently shakes his head, and I think he's about to continue scolding me, but to my surprise a smile tugs at the corners of his mouth despite the situation we're in. "Would it be so bad to just let me be the hero for once?"

I throw him another exasperated frown.

But as I look past Keenon, I notice something lurking in the shadows beyond the glass wall, and my heart goes suddenly still.

Six pairs of pulsating eyes.

Keenon's brows furrow. "What is—"

250

I bring my hands up to his mouth, quieting him. "Droids." I keep my voice low, nodding in the direction of the metal beasts. Suddenly, the lights begin to shudder, and the ground on which we stand vibrates. I can even feel it through the thick soles of my boots. A prickling sensation roots into the hairs on my arms making them stand on end, as if an electrical charge permeates the air.

"I have a bad feeling about this," Keenon grumbles. "We've got to find a way out of here." Keenon's eyes dart around as mine do the same. Solid metal sheeting stretches as far as I can see. Keenon whirls towards me, pointing to the far wall. "See that vent up there, Livi? Hidden in the shadows?"

I look in the direction he points, at first not seeing anything, but finally making out a small rectangular aperture barely peeking out from under a metal buttress.

Keenon grabs my hand, pulling me with him towards the wall with the vent. "Climb onto my shoulders, Livi. I'm going to try to get you up—" But before he can finish, seemingly out of nowhere, a dark surge of energy flattens both of us onto our backs, forcing the air from my lungs.

Though I can't see anything, I feel an invisible force descend from above, crushing me from all sides. I struggle to breathe as the world suddenly pitches into blades of light and shadows.

Space and time. Rushing through an endless grey tunnel. The jagged slash of lightning. The vacuum of dark nothingness.

One minute I careen above it all, through the stars, the brilliant void of space. The next minute I'm drowning. Drowning in a thousand voices that call out to me. A violent riptide of thoughts claw at my mind, and I'm going to be pulled under. I struggle to break free, break free of the thing swallowing me whole. I feel and see it all—pain, hurt, laughter, a million images that are not my own. Chaos.

I call out. Help! But there is no answer. No help to be had. And I can do nothing to fight it. Soon I will drown.

But in the next moment, a familiar thread. A pinprick of golden light. Starlock.

I clamber after it as it winks in and out, at first weakly, then more steadily. Finally I grab hold of it—with my mind—for I am as formless as the void around me. I hold on with every ounce of concentration that I can. If I don't, I will surely be lost. Forever.

Hanging on as best I can, I fight off the clamor, the maelstrom of intertwined thoughts and voices. Gradually, like the calming waters after a storm, everything quiets. Until all that is left around me is the thread of light I hold onto.

When I open my eyes, I look out atop charred and dry desert sands, twining ribbons of red on black, rolling on for miles on end. Strangled wisps of lazy smoke leak up from dead volcanoes. Bald and blackened terra. Barren. Where in all hellas am I? I make to move, but I have no control.

I have no me.

But then the me that is not me raises a hand. I startle in recognition of it. The skin is not flesh, but laced with a telltale icosahedral pattern of blues and golds. Tinston. The strongest metal known to humans, indestructible except for the heat of the suns. And that's when I understand what I'm looking at. The hand of a Quadrati. I must be having a nightmare.

And when the me that is not me turns, I can do nothing but take it all in.

An army of Quadrati, like a metallic ocean glinting under a dying sun, stretching as far as I can see.

The sheer number makes me quake.

252

But before I can take in any more, I find myself shoved back out into that infinite void of space. The stars hang a mere arm's length away. I wear a feeling of weightless nonbeing. And then I am falling.

XLIV

TRITON: INTERESTING NEWS

"**B**OUT TIME YOU SHOWED UP. Domseis have been asking for you."

Eppel shakes his head as he scans me from head to toe. "For the love of the stars, Triton, you look about as good as a longhorn's cud. Don't tell me you stayed up all night again?"

"Pretty much," I reply coolly. He's been trailing my back for the last few stars days now, nagging me like an old hen. I'm certainly not going to admit to him that I ran Flemming for the third time last night after spending the last ninety hours straight scouring the space grids, looking for any sign of the Hellion ship and Livi's Hawwk. That I haven't slept a wink and even my Bionic nerves are running on neutrinos is beside the point. I'm running out of time.

"Well, you'd better get in there. You know how impatient Domsei Shen can be."

Now I haven't exactly been avoiding the Domseis since the Hellion incident. It's just that I've been too busy looking for *her*. But I'm no closer to finding the new Mark of Dresden now than I was three star days ago. I rub my knuckles hard into my temples. It's time to face my other responsibilities. Of course I knew the Domseis would be asking for me. I knew they would probably strip me of my title as Comstadt. Heck, maybe they were even going to Nullify me. Well, I deserve all of that and more for what I let happen to our new Mark of Dresden. I step past Eppel into the Upper Chamber.

I stop short the moment I enter when I see the three Domseis perched by the large window. It is rare to see all three of them together. *Yes. It's going to be serious. Very serious.*

Domsei Shen turns to me, his wide cape swirling at his feet. "Any progress, Comstadt?"

"I'm afraid not. Uranium trails have led to dead ends so far." I clear my throat, forcing myself to stand tall. "And so now I will bring up the topic to spare you the pain of broaching. I realize that the loss of the Mark of Dresden was my fault, and I hereby offer you my resignation as Comstadt." I must really be living on a knife's edge to speak out of turn, but I can't bear to hear the words from the Domsei. Much better to do it myself.

Domsei Shen's eyebrows rise ever so slightly, and he passes a look to the other two. "Comstadt, I think you misunderstand our reason for summoning you here. We do not wish your resignation."

"You don't?"

"No." Domsei Shen's voice lowers. "We just discovered something about our new Mark of Dresden, something you should know."

My whirling thoughts snap still. "What is it?"

"The new Mark of Dresden is genetically related to our last Comstadt."

It's not like Domsei Shen to be evasive. We all carry common genes with the Ceruleans. Bionic or not, we're still human after all. "What exactly do you mean?" I push for more information.

"Magnar Drune's team in Genetics has finally mapped the new Mark of Dresden's DNA to its full extent. When she ran the relational analysis to compare it to the whole of the Bionics' genetic database, she found something very unexpected." Domsei Shen clears his throat, his eyes gravely serious. "We believe that the late Comstadt Tomasian P. Falk was her father."

It takes me a few moments to process what he is saying. "That's impossible. You know as well as I do that Bionics are a genetic dead end. We can't have children." But even as I say this, the oddly shaped pieces of the puzzle that is Livinthea Park slowly click into place. How she mastered Hemlock so impossibly quickly. How she managed to pass the Hawwk simulators in less than four weeks when it takes most Young Bloods at least a year.

"Agreed, Comstadt. We don't yet quite know how to explain it. But the genetic analysis doesn't lie. Livinthea Park is Tomas's daughter. And that's not all. Dalinthea Song was her mother."

"Dalinthea Song? You mean the former Magnar of Bioengineering? But she disappeared over twenty years ago."

"And now, maybe we know why," Domsei Shen replies.

Dark infinites. "That explains Park's double Mark of Dresden mutation." I never met the Magnar of

Bioengineering, but it was said that she was whip-smart and as stunning as the sun. Her daughter, it seems, is just like her.

"Yes, and her very existence could change the future of the Bionic line of existence."

That is if she's still alive. "Does Park know what her mother and father were?"

"The information only came to light this morning. She has no idea." Domsei Shen clears his throat and looks me square in the eye. "And brings us to the reason we called you here. Comstadt, the Domseis and I hereby authorize the use of as many resources as you need. Use whatever means necessary. But find Livinthea Park and bring her back. *Alive.*"

XLV

LIVI: MASTER SENSATE

A PAINFUL BUZZING THROBS at the base of my brain.

It takes my eyes a minute to adjust to the dim light against the high walls, and I realize I'm still in the Quadrati cell.

The pulsatile eyes of Droids peer out like specters in the night from the deep shadows beyond. A metallic taste singes the tip of my tongue. What in all hellas just happened to me?

As I prop myself up, I realize that Keenon lies unmoving beside me, his lips bloodless, eyes open, but unseeing.

"Keenon!" I lurch towards him, only to crack my head hard and stumble back. What in the name of Altheria? I inch back towards Keenon again, but this time more carefully. And this time I feel it, an invisible barrier separating us that was not there before, reaching across the whole expanse. I fist my hands against the barrier until they hurt, trying to get through. "Keenon—

Keenon!" But only an empty echo answers back from the heights of the ceiling I can't even see. My childhood friend, the one who risked his life to come save me, lies as still as death on the floor. And I can't reach him.

I whip myself towards the Droids, who continue looking back intently at me, their glowing red eyes blank, fathomless. It's their silence and utter lack of emotion that is the most terrifying.

Ignoring the pain in my hands, I bang on the transparent walls even harder. "What have you done to him? Let me out, you draggarts!"

But perhaps I should not have been so eager to get out, for in the next instance, the solidity of the walls dematerializes from underneath my fists, and I barely catch myself from falling face first into the lap of a Droid.

I scramble back, as the Droids flash forward out of the shadows. Before I can even blink, my body is on lockdown. Metal hands restrain every possible moving part of my body. I don't even have a chance to struggle. When I look up, I notice that one Droid stands back from the rest. He looks different from the others, reminds me of the last Droid I spied during the Quadrati attack at Galactic—taller, his movements more fluid, less mechanical, almost—I stutter at the thought—almost human, *almost*. I know what he is. A Sensate Droid. But this one is not just any Sensate Droid, this one has the legendary gleam of dying ash to its metallic hull, a slash of red across its broad chest. This could be no other than the leader of all Droids, the Master Sensate—Gardurak.

Even as first year cadets we learned all about the Sensate Droids at Galactic. These leader Droids have some ability to think for themselves outside of the neural network, and the legendary Master of the Sensates has the ability to control them all. My heart beats double time now. *Hold it together. Don't back down.*

Gardurak's pulsatile eyes laser menacingly into mine. I swallow against the bile rising in my throat. "What have you done to him?" I growl, struggling to keep my voice even.

Before I can react, a flash of movement arcs low as something cracks hard across my shins, the sickening crunch of metal on bone, I can't help but cry out while the edges of my vision blur.

The Droid who struck me grabs me by the neck, his gleaming baton dissolving back into the sheen of tinston that is his arm.

I grit my teeth against the shooting pain crippling my legs, but drag my gaze sideways back up to the taller one. The Master Droid's rigid silence echoes in the hollows, sending a shiver up my spine. Gardurak's laser-red eyes pulse into mine. I will myself not to look away. My mouth unleashes before my mind can stop it. "You draggarts can do better than that."

Out of the corner of my eye, I see the Droid who struck me unleashing his baton again, and I brace myself for another strike.

But in the next moment, Gardurak's head pivots ever so slightly towards the baton Droid. Hesitancy pauses the air around me, as if silent conversation passes between the two.

Then, instead of striking me again, the Droid with the baton releases my neck, twisting my arms hard behind my back. My shoulders scream in pain. I struggle to break free, but the Droids are too strong. They yank me out of the cell through a door that materializes on the far wall, and it's all I can do to keep upright.

I steal one last glance at my childhood friend, who still lies unmoving, unreachable. A lock of hair dangles carelessly across his open but unseeing eyes. *Keenon!* my mind cries out. The weight of Juthri's stone lies heavy within my chest, making it hard to breathe. My insides choke.

The Droids march me away from the cell, my mind spiraling. But despite everything, despite the fear threatening to paralyze my mind, one thought saves me from giving myself up to the dredges, barreling to the forefront of my mind. *I will get Keenon out of here.* Even if it's the last thing I do in my measly little life.

I promise this, because even making nearly impossible promises gives me something to hold onto in the vast and dismal ethers. With that thought in mind, I force myself to pay attention, to gather the loose ends of my wits and try to notice any little thing that may help me stay alive.

XLVI

LIVI: NOWHERE TO RUN

THERE ARE FOUR OF THEM.

The baton Droid prods me from the back. One leads up front. The other two flank me from the sides, my wrists shackled in their icy grips. Their heavy steps resound through dark and dreary tunnels. I have the strange sensation of being underground, in a molerat's burrow, the hollowed passageways snaking this way and that. In the dim light, the Droids look identical. They move in remarkable unison, their measured steps coordinated and clicking in exact time.

As they drag me further along, I get the vague sense of climbing, altitude. Ahead, an eerie red glow emanates from around the curve, and I can't help but pull back. The Droid behind me prods me sharply, right in the tender spot between my shoulder blades, forcing me forward. When we round the bend, a glass tunnel opens up before me, and what I see sears into my mind like a nightmare.

For I look down upon an outside world that is *burning*. Patches of fire blaze from a charred and broken ground. Wisps of shuddering heat leak up from it, melding with layer upon layer of toxic haze. Disfigured crags of jagged rocks claw out, seeking mercy from the dying sky above, not a tree or living thing in sight. *A dead world. How did the Droids end up on this stars-forsaken planet?*

Lightning stabs from above, sending my gaze upwards. But what really catches my eye is the sight of the largest sun I have ever seen, hanging heavily against a crimson sky. Its boiling fingers splay down upon the bald black of igneous. A *single* sun. That fact confirms what I already know—I'm not anywhere near the Erlion System anymore. *Stars help me.*

The baton Droid prods me sharply in the back every few steps until we exit the glass tunnel. We continue on, winding through passageway after passageway, my shoulders and shins throbbing thoroughly now. Finally, the Droids stop as we reach the threshold of an immense chamber.

As I step inside, what I see makes me halt in my tracks, the hairs on my arms standing on end.

An enormous pod sits in the middle of the chamber. Undulating electrical currents of ash and gold spark around it. *It looks alive.*

I have no idea what it is. But what I do know is that I have a *bad* feeling about this. *Really, really bad.* But I don't have many options left.

Just try.

In one quick motion, I twist out of the flanking Droids' grasps. Ramming my shoulder into baton Droid, I manage to send it staggering back.

But before I can take another step, the other Droids surround me in seconds. In less time than it takes to blink, baton Droid rights himself and charges back towards me, his hard metal mask barely a breath away from my face. His metal hand clamps down painfully on my neck, against the wild pulsing of my carotids. His cold fingers dig deeper. The edges of my vision crumble.

Just as I'm about to pass out, the Droid wrenches his hand away from my neck. Before I can protest or struggle, it shoves me straight into the electrical currents and into the open mouth of the pod.

XLVII

ROGUE DROID: EMERGENCE

S OMETIMES I CAN JUST BARELY remember. Glimpses of the fraying threads of a bygone life. Most of the time, I am caught, hands tied within the ordered chaos of the collective. I have the distinct feeling that I tried to fight it once before. Maybe even tried very hard. But now I remember why I never made it. For it is like walking headlong into the heart of a blizzard. Complete disorientation. Where up becomes down, left becomes right, inside becomes outside. A dimensionless realm where thought and being don't intersect, where breath and life are no longer tied together.

Words and thoughts spill out of me that are not my own, but of some amorphous creature crawling from within, eating me out of house and home. Out of my own mind. Stealing my life energy. I'm a slave to my own body.

And I can't get out.

Then in the distance, something pulls at me. Hooks a rope around my waist and tethers me. Slowly pulling me above ground. Giving me a breath of fresh air, when I had forgotten how to breathe for so long.

But the closer I get, the more I know that something is wrong. That something is in trouble too.

The tether strains and pulls, forcing me out of my complacency. And for once in a very long time, I have the inexplicable urge to pull back.

Vaguely, I understand that once upon a time, that life energy was supposed to have been the savior for many. But that was many years ago. Now there is one who overpowers us all. Gardurak.

But something is different about today.

XLVIII

LIVI: QUADRATI NEURAL NETWORK

S OMEONE IS SCREAMING.

And eventually, I vaguely come to understand *that someone is me.* The untouched recesses of my mind are violently pried open. It feels as if needles and pins prod my every nerve, my every neuron. Only unconsciousness saves me from the screaming. But even then, my dreams struggle. Drowning in the dark void of space, an ocean of chaos, there is nothing to hold onto, and only echoes live.

Day bleeds into night, and then into day again, melding together until even reason and logic no longer make sense. Time becomes as amorphous and shapeless as clouds shifting in the sky, measurable only as passing images, the lightning slash of a moment. But I understand this, *I am being hunted.*

Pulsatile red eyes.

Gardurak.

But somehow within the chaos, I catch a fleeting glimpse of gold, a beacon within the dark shadows. *Starlock? Could it be?*

I swim for it as if it were the air above the vast ocean waters, and somehow I'm able to manage one gulp of life-saving air. One gulp, just before the endless ocean of thoughts and voices drag me under.

But there it is again. That golden thread of light. I struggle to reach out and grab hold.

But every moment is the same. A pinprick in time replayed over and over. Until even time tires.

The moments become as endless and infinite as the universe itself. And I have long lost track of when and how the haze crept upon me, until I manage to resurface again. But eventually, even Starlock weakens. And despite the muddle of my mind, I know next time Starlock will not be enough.

But when the next moment comes, something is different. It's the eyes. Glowing like the sun. Beautiful even. Most unfortunate, for it hardly matters now. For this time, I *will* be pulled under. Pulled under the crashing waves, to drown in the chaos where singularity has no meaning.

Strong arms grip me. Heavy and rapid steps. I try to struggle against them, but there is no me left. There is only an empty and discarded shell.

"Fight it!"

A voice I used to know.

"Hold on!"

I must be confused. The cadence is familiar, but the tone is all wrong. Something jabs hard into my chest, but I'm so weak now that I don't even flinch. More rapid steps. Now running. My head jostles uncontrollably. The loud crashing steps slow. Then stop.

And little by little, I begin to feel again. The life-force infuses back into my arms, my legs. My scalp tingles down to each individual hair follicle.

My eyes flutter open. And I gasp at what holds me. What cradles me in his arms like a newborn babe. A Sensate Droid. I can tell by the golden sheen of its metallic face that hovers only a few breaths above mine.

I want to struggle free, but I'm still too weak. Oh stars. So this is it then. I squeeze my eyes shut and brace for whatever will come. And I hope that it will be painless.

But moments pass. Then maybe even a minute. Nothing. More strength returns to my arms and legs. My full senses returning.

The metal of his chest burns cold against my bare skin. I peel my eyes open and take a peek. And find the Droid looking back down at me. And somehow, when I take a closer look at its face, for some inexplicable and completely incomprehensible reason, I don't feel scared.

I must be losing my mind.

But then I realize why. It's the eyes. They're different. Honey gold. Which, despite the hard mask, look back kindly at me, as if such a thing were even possible.

Gently, he stands me on my feet, his cool metal hands supporting me by the arms.

My knees wobble for an instant. But by some miracle, the strength in my legs holds, and I manage to stay upright. I straighten myself cautiously. As the Droid releases his grip on me, logic tells me to run for it. Get away from this strange Droid while I still have the chance. But for some reason, instinct tells me to wait. Wait and see what this Droid is all about.

Stars know I've never been terribly logical. Despite Grandpa Wren's relentless scoldings, I've always ruled with my gut. My legs stubbornly root in place. My mouth blurts out a question, though my mind knows I should keep it shut. "Why are you helping me?"

The Droid's eyes pivot away for a moment, searching for something I cannot see.

But when he looks back down at me, nothing but silence.

"Who are you?" I try again.

A loud bang crashes in the distance, making both our heads pivot back. Realization and awareness slowly frame-shift back into my mind. Only now do I notice where I am. A cavernous hull, housing a single Buggard, its cockpit door ajar.

Another crash, this time louder, rattling the dust off the stony chamber walls.

The Droid rushes me quickly over to the Buggard, practically throwing me into the cockpit seat. *What is he doing?* His metal fingers blur over the control panel then telescope out ever so slightly, engaging with a port next to the cockpit door.

Another loud crash sounds from just outside the chamber, curls of smoke filter in between the seams where door meets wall.

He takes a clanking step back, and before I can react, the cockpit door slams shut between us. The ceiling of the cavern yawns open. An angry red sky glares back at me. I don't even have time to cry out, when the darn Buggard blasts out of the cavern with a will of its own, throwing my head back, pinning my arms back into the seat.

XLIX

LIVI: ESCAPE

CRIIIIMENYYYY!

The Buggard pierces skyward like a quantum missile. I find myself hurtling towards the curved edge of an unfamiliar light, the crescent of a moon dangling against the backdrop of a solitary star. I'm on the verge of falling prey to the shadows again, but just in time the Buggard levels out into the outermost layers of the thin atmosphere, the g-force of the Quadrati ship easing somewhat. The fringes of my vision slowly return, and I can move my arms again.

I'm still in a daze, trying to make sense out of this new reality that is trying its hardest *not* to make sense. *Who was that Droid, and why did he help me?* Even now I question whether it was all just a dream. But as I look outside, nothing can deny the reality of the morphing ring of fire I'm quickly approaching. And nothing can deny the small fleet of Buggards that has just appeared above the Quadrati's northern pole, *heading in my direction, quickly gaining on me.* And my mind has finally cleared enough to remember—*Keenon!* I've got to go back for him.

I scrabble at the Buggard's control panel. *Torque navigator. Reverse thrusters. Override controls and turn this blasted thing around for star's sake.* But nothing I do makes a darn bit of difference. *I'm locked out. No!* That Droid must have preprogrammed this Buggard.

I spring out of my seat and try to wrench open the housing to the electrical circuit board, but I can't get enough purchase. It's sealed tight. Outside, the ring of fire grows larger, closer, so bright that I have to shade my eyes against the light. Then it dawns on me. *A gateway. Just like the one to Hurako.* What's even more clear is that I'm heading straight for it, whether I like it or not.

I scramble back into my seat and strap myself in, *tightly.* If it's anything like the gateway to Hurako, I'm in for quite a ride. The buckle barely clicks when the void around me erupts in laser fire, just missing my Buggard. Crimeny, those Quadrati are fast. They're right on my tail.

But I'm nearly to the ring. *Almost there. Come on. Just a little farther.* I'll worry about where it takes me later. But in the next moment, a lightning flash and my head slams hard against my seat as my Buggard shudders violently. I have barely enough sense to register that outside, my Buggard's right wing blazes brighter than Cerulea's three suns. *So this is it then.*

L

TRITON: SURPRISE

"**W**ELL I THINK that's the best we can do. I'm afraid it's another dead end, Comstadt." Juki's voice crackles over the comms link, the weariness clear in his voice.

I shake my head in exasperation. It just doesn't make sense. How could the uranium signal drop off like that? We finally found a trail, followed it to Finlan's Point in fact, but then suddenly nothing. Not even a single iota of uranium. It is as if Livi's Hawwk just disappeared into thin air.

And for the last forty hours straight, Juki, Halo, Phlynnt, Eppel, and I have been in our Hawwks, scouring the area, even gone as far as Nomad's Line, but we couldn't pick up the trail again anywhere.

It is time to give them a break. Even Bionics need to rest sometime. "All right. Cassiopia unit, head back to Atlas. Meet me back in three hours after respite."

"You're not coming with us?" Juki asks me, his voice incredulous. "A thousand pardons, sir, but you've been

274

going at it far longer than the rest of us. You'll short-circuit your nanobots at this rate."

"I'm just going to look a little bit long—"

Suddenly, a blinding explosion lights up the dark and distant void to my left. It expands then contracts, morphing into a hurtling ball of flames, growing rapidly closer.

"Whoa! What in the dark infinites is that?" Juki's voice pitches into the comms link.

I blink. Even with my Bionic vision, it's still too far away for me to see exactly what it is. But it only takes a few seconds before I realize something that makes even my Bionic heart pause. It's heading straight for Cerulea.

"Red alert! Defensive shields up!" I yell. "Star Sequence! We've got to head it off before it hits Cerulea!"

My body presses hard into the seat as I throw my thrusters, set for a collision course with the rapidly approaching fireball. The others quickly fall into formation behind me. As I lead our pack closer, I begin to see more clearly. *Rattling roids. Not a fireball, but a gosh darned Buggard. Severely crippled. Right wing in flames.*

And there following closely behind are three more Buggards, their laser weapons on open fire.

"Jack knife formation now!" I yell into the comms link while sending my Hawwk into a spiral. "Whoever has a shot. Take it. We can't let these Buggards get past Finlan's Point!"

I fly point position, firing off my argon and picking off the first two of the three live Buggards. But the third Buggard weaves past me. *What? Where's it going?* The shock of realization hits me. It's not targeting us, but going after its own.

"Eppel. Round about! Now!"

Banking sharply from tail position, my old mentor hits the third active Buggard dead center with a single shot. It bursts into flames.

In the meantime, Phlynnt has come within a hairsbreadth of firing range of the flaming Buggard. But in my gut I feel it. Why would the Droids be chasing one of their own? There's something not quite right. Phlynnt angles his laser towards the disabled Buggard, its right wing still burning. He's just about on it.

"Hold your fire, Phlynnt! Repeat, hold your fire!" I shout in exact time with the lasering pulse streaking from Phlynnt's Hawwk.

But Phlynnt veers at the last second, the laser just missing the left wing of the Buggard, which continues to plummet towards Cerulea.

"Pardon the language, Comstadt, but what in all flaming hellas was that?"

"Something about that Buggard is off."

"A thousand pardons, Comstadt, but we can't just let it go. It's a Droid, for star's sake."

"I'm *not* letting it go, Magnar. There's a reason the Droids were after that Buggard. We need to know why. Alert Galactic Central and Atlas. We're going down to retrieve it. Quickly, before there's nothing left to save."

LI

LIVI: SONGS OF THE FAIRLOT

I NEVER THOUGHT THE END would come like this.

There is just so much pain. And air, I cannot seem to get enough air. I gasp and struggle for breath, every effort racking my chest with a splintering pain. That I broke several ribs and then some is certain. My hands fly to my mouth as I cough uncontrollably. A sticky warmth tinged with the taste of metal trickles out the corners of my lips. *Blood.* I cough again, this time harder. A sudden gush of liquid bubbles into my mouth. *Altheria help me. Not just the ribs.* I claw at my neck, but I know I can't clear it. I am drowning in my own blood.

The world tilts and my vision blackens. Through the haze, I hear a sudden rustling of leaves behind me, a thumping of hurried footsteps, a voice—

"I've found it! Dark infinites. Livi? Eppel! Halon extinguisher. Quickly!"

I try to turn towards the voice, but my body won't cooperate. Then, more stampeding footsteps, the crushing of leaves.

"She's injured badly. Get me the medpacks!"

I know that voice. Something thuds down hard at my side. Air rushes past and around me. A finger presses at my neck.

"Stay with me, Livi. Don't you dare leave. You still owe me dinner, remember?"

Hands support my head, propping me up.

"Eppel, grab the infuser. Hurry! We don't have time to waste!"

A frank cacophony of sounds mar the background, then another voice cuts through, loud and clear.

"Comstadt's right. If we don't give her the infusion, she is going to die."

Then that voice again.

"We may already be too late. Connect it up."

But how is it possible? More unintelligible voices in the background.

"I'm not sure it will work. We only have a darn booster dose. But what choice do we have? There's no time to argue, Eppel. For star's sake, inject it now!"

What is he talking about?

Now I'm gagging and retching uncontrollably. Stars, I do not want to leave them all like this. But something tells me it's not up to me this time. Then the strangest thing happens, or perhaps it's the hypoxia finally giving way to hallucinations. My eyes crack open.

Through all the haze and pain, I notice a gorgeous little fairlot. It's as blue as the midday sky, and it lands just a few feet away from where I lie, its light brown orbs looking curiously at me. Then from its tiny little lungs come the most beautiful sounds I have ever heard. The notes dance along the leaves and the wind, and weave their way through the air into the very fabric of space-time towards a distant light. Comforting me. Holding me. And I feel myself floating away with it.

So this is the end, I think. Funny how life plays tricks on you.

I barely feel the pain as I'm pulled into the light.

***

And *this* is what it's like to fly. *Really* fly. I find myself soaring and careening through the clouds, higher and higher, gaining more altitude with each second, not a single shred of metal surrounding me. It's just me, the wind, the sunlight on my face, and the air around me. One by one, the ropes that kept me anchored to the living begin to fray and pop. I should feel scared, and yet there is no pain. The blue sky above is clear and crisp, and not even the universe can hold me down. Higher and higher I fly until soon, even the clouds are a distant memory, and I'm surrounded by the inky blackness of empty space.

Now, only a tenuous wisp of thread tethers me to the world, and this too will soon be stretched too thin and snap. I try to look back, but a familiar pattern of lightness catches my eye up ahead, the childhood friend I know so well. Starlock. I have never been so close to him before.

Countless times I traced his outline in the skies of my lonely childhood nights, wondering about the unknowns of space. Now its brilliance fills me with a sense of awe. I am so close now. I will finally get to hold his hand. I reach out—

Suddenly, I begin to fall, a pulling deep within me that rips me from Starlock's grasp and draws me down, and further down. I yell for Starlock, but I can make no sound. Only the songs of the fairlot persevere. Ambitious trills reach higher and higher, in perfect balance with resounding lows to satisfy the soul.

I never knew sound could shine. But the fairlot's notes are clear, glistening, sparkling fairy dust sprinkled between the rustling of leaves, along the braying of an ancient, unyielding wind.

LII

LIVI: BACK HOME

THE AIR AROUND ME SHIFTS and quivers as I force my eyes open, molecules recalibrating at the quantum level.

What is real, though, is the brightest white light I have ever seen, and it shines down on me. Slowly, I realize that I'm lying on a luminescent table, and that in fact the bright light is streaming out of me, emanating from the very pores of my skin. I try to sit up.

The next instant, someone grasps my hand and gently strokes my forehead. "Shhh. It's okay, Livi. You're just waking up."

Familiar warm brown eyes hover over me. I blink a few times, trying to clear the odd shimmering that taints my vision.

"J-Jia?" My voice comes out gratingly, pebbles on stone.

"Yes, it's me, Livi. I'm here." Her hair is disheveled, as if she hasn't slept for days.

"Stars, it's good to see you. What, what happened?"

"You scared us halfway to Altheria and back. That's what happened. But you were always good at that." Jia gives me a half smile. A smile I haven't seen since the day I was taken up to Atlas. When our positions were reversed. "You're safe now. You're home."

My eyes dart to the large open window. Bands of light stream in, and just beyond, seafaeries glide in formation across the wide blue of Cerulean skies. I have never seen a sight so beautiful. "Home?"

Jia gently pats my arm. "Yes, back at Galactic. Just rest, okay?"

Stiffly, I look down, inspecting myself. The light has since faded away. I feel bare in the thin, canary-yellow infirmary gown, but from what I can tell, aside from a new scar on my right arm, no missing parts, not even a bandage. Was I just imagining things? "How did I get here?"

Jia cracks a smile. "Now, *that* was quite a scene. The whole campus is still buzzing about it, especially the girls. Even Wilkie couldn't stop gaping when that hulk of a Bionic carried you onto campus with his throng of other Bionics and brought you right to the infirmary. Said something about a Quadrati attack and practically ordered Dr. Kang to put you in the MedScan. Paced outside the scanner like a stray cat until Dr. Kang told him that your MedScan looked remarkably perfect. Not a single broken bone or ruptured organ in your body, just a slight concussion and bruised ribs."

So it wasn't just a dream. And is the universe just toying with me? Did I just barely survive being captured by the Quadrati only to now subsequently die of embarrassment? *Carried by a Bionic? For crying out loud and then some.* I sink back into my bed, trying to process things. But Jia's last words also trigger an onslaught of images in my mind. The Quadrati, the Droid with the golden eyes. Keenon.

I bolt upright. Words tumble out in a rush. "Jia, I've got to get back out there. I've got to go back right away."

Jia puts a hand on my shoulder, gently easing me back down. "Easy there, Livi. You're going to set off those pesky monitors again, and so help me if that medicus O'Meilly comes running back in here with another sedating shot."

"No, Jia. I'm f-fine, really," I say, even though I'm suddenly aware of the strange tingling sensation along my ribs, my left temple. "They've got Keenon."

"Slow down, Livi."

"Jia, you've got to listen to me."

Jia's eyes go round.

"I saw things that—that I didn't think were possible."

"What do you mean?"

"Jia. A Droid helped me escape."

"But I thought the Bionics helped you."

"Yes, that too. But when I was trapped on the Quadrati base, a Droid helped me escape. I don't know why, or how it's possible. I can't explain it. But I just know that he helped me. And Keenon"—I force a steadying breath in—"the Quadrati have him trapped. I've got to go back." I grip Jia's hand. "You believe me, don't you?"

Jia looks me over for a long moment, but then gives my hand a squeeze. "A cockamamie story like that from anybody else, Livi, I would have said that something had clearly been knocked irretrievably loose in their noggin.

But a far-out story like that from *you*, well, I suppose anything is believable coming from you."

"Thanks, Jia. *I think*," I say grudgingly. "Now, I've got to speak with the Bionics right away."

"After how they treated you?" Jia asks, her eyebrows arched skyward. "They practically *kidnapped* you, remember?"

Just a few weeks ago, I would have said the same thing as Jia, *felt* the same way. But so much has happened since then. I shake my head. "Jia. The Bionics. We've been wrong about them. They may not be the most warm and fuzzy people in the world, but they're on our side. They're trying to help us. Please I've got to speak with them."

Jia continues to look at me skeptically, but says, "Well, *that* actually won't be too difficult to arrange. That hulk of a Bionic who carried you here has been prowling outside your door for the last five hours straight."

"Really?" My heart *kerthumps* in my chest.

Jia nods. "Yes, says his name is Comstadt Triton Travler, or some ridiculously fancy name like that. Anyway, he's as handsome as hellas, but absolutely *refuses* to leave. Claims he's here to help and needs to see you first thing when you wake up. That Bionic may just very well be the most stubborn and bullnosed person I have ever met. Probably even more so than you. But, you'll be proud of me. I held my ground. I told him there was no way he was allowed near you after what they've done unless you said it was okay."

Jia gives me an apologetic smile. "And Galactic Central wants to talk to you too. You're practically the most popular person on campus right now."

Of course, they just want to talk to me about what happened. *Calm down.* "It's okay, Jia. Please, I really do need to speak with Tri—I mean that Bionic."

"Well, all right." Jia's eyebrows quirk up, and she gives me her what-are-you-not-telling-me and you-better-fess-up-or-else face, but finally only says, "You do look remarkably well considering what you've just been through. You sure you feel up to it?"

"Truly I do."

"Very well then. But if you need anything, just yell. I'll be planted right outside your door. Not eavesdropping of course."

"Thanks, Jia. What would I do without you?"

"I know." Jia smiles as I laugh, and then gives my hand a light squeeze before turning to go.

LIII

LIVI: NO GOING BACK

ALMOST AS SOON AS Jia steps out the door, Comstadt Travler barrels in, his gaze immediately locking onto mine.

For an instant, a look of relief crosses his brow. Ironically, his own appearance rather shocks me. Dark smudges stain his forehead and his usually immaculate uniform is ripped at the elbows. I have never seen him appear so ragged. I didn't even think it was possible for a Bionic to *be* tired. Again I notice that strange shimmering. But this time it outlines the angles of his jawline, the edges of his broad shoulders.

I struggle up, but Triton's long strides take him immediately to my side. "Whoa, not so fast, Park. You know your tyrant of a friend will have me thrown to the Dark Skythes if I let you get out of bed."

In truth, the room heaves back and forth, as if I'm riding the rolling waves of a vast ocean, and reluctantly I acquiesce, lying back down. "Yes, she can be rather protective that way," I mutter. But I also manage to ask him what has been so urgently on my mind. "Comstadt, please, I need one of your Hawwks right away."

"Excuse my language, Park, but why in the dark infinites would you want to do that? You do realize that by the luck of the stars we just barely got you back in one piece? One cannot always count on being so fortunate."

"But I've got to go back for them. Keenon, and—and for the Droid."

The Comstadt startles for a moment. "For a Droid?"

"There was a Droid with honey-gold eyes. He helped me escape." I have the Comstadt's full attention now.

"Tell me exactly what happened."

"I was trapped inside the Quadrati neural network. But somehow this Droid helped to get me out."

An astonished look crosses the Comstadt's face as he mumbles, "Why would a Droid do that?"

"I don't know, but I know he did. Triton. Please, I need one of your Hawwks. I need to go help them—before it's too late."

"Of course we'll try to get Keenon out." He hesitates a moment. "But Park, there's something I need to tell you first. The reason—I have been waiting to speak with you."

The sudden agitation in his voice forces my eyes up to his face—deep shadows haunt his eyes, a muscle feathers in his jaw. He places his hand upon my shoulder, the warmth seeping through the thin fabric there. His demeanor is at once grave, his lips pressed into a tight line. Though he says there is something he *needs* to tell me, clearly he doesn't *want* to.

"Wh-what is it?" I stutter.

The Comstadt's hand drops from my shoulder as he shifts in his seat and clears his throat. "What do you remember of the most recent events?" His eyes search mine, probing.

His words trigger a flood of repressed thoughts back into my consciousness. "I—I remember the Buggard ships on my tail. My right wing going up in flames. The ring of fire. The ground coming up to greet me." I rub at my hands, which have suddenly run cold, and try to continue. "I remember . . ." But my voice drifts off as more recollections churn my insides. *Gardurak. Hurried footsteps. The fear in the Comstadt's voice as he calls my name.*

My hands tremble, and Triton reaches over, warming them. "It's okay, Livi. Take it slowly."

But the images are confusing, scattered, and I can't put the pieces together. "What—what happened to me, Triton?"

He blinks slowly, once, twice. But holds my gaze. "Eppel and I found you after the Buggards shot you down. We brought you back to Galactic."

More images come barreling through, indelible moments of time steeped in thought and feeling. *Pain. Struggling to breathe. Drowning.* Moments pass by in silence as I try to make sense of what replays in my mind. But I just can't.

"Triton, I want to know the—details."

"Livi—" Triton hesitates, looking away as his eyes lose focus on a band of the light streaming in through my window. An internal struggle creases his forehead before he turns back to me. He replies haltingly. "Livi, when we found you, you—*were* hurt. Very badly." He pauses again, his voice coming lower now. "So badly that we thought— *I* thought—we had lost you."

My mind reels. Yes. There was *so* much blood. *Too* much blood. And the songs of the fairlot came to claim me. And yet here I am very much alive. How is it possible? No, it is *impossible*. Unless. *Unless.*

Then it clicks.

Stars above.

"You did it, didn't you?" My voice comes out barely a whisper. I hardly want to say the words, much less hear the answer.

Triton's gaze holds mine, silently reading the question of what is left unsaid in my eyes. Slowly, he nods, his eyes never leaving my face. "Yes, Livi." We sit here in silence for a few moments as he lets the news sink in. "How did you know?"

"I was dying, Triton. No, I *was* dead." I shift slightly, loosening my arms. "And I feel *different*." The room shimmers even more as if in confirmation, my arms and legs suddenly stronger.

"I know that you hadn't made your decision yet." For the first time since I met him, Triton is not able to meet my gaze. He looks down, brows knit tightly together. "It was my call. I'm sorry."

I'm silent for a minute as a jumble of thoughts works its way around in my head. I am no longer just a network of collagen and cells. Cintian metal pumps through the arteries and veins of my body.

I am no longer just human. I am Bionic. And there is no going back.

LIV

LIVI: MOVING FORWARD

NO GOING BACK.
And yet I have to remind myself, when has life ever been about going backwards? As Grandpa Wren would remind me if I ever had a misstep, "Just keep moving forwards, Livi, and you'll be fine." But he had never foreseen a situation like this.

For last the hour, Triton has been filling me in with more details of what happened. I never thought I would be grateful to the Droids. But I'm grateful not only for the Droid who helped me, but also for the marvel that is the engineering masterpiece of the Droid's Buggard ships. Comstadt told me that if the Buggard's main cockpit chamber hadn't been fully lined with that special tinston metal of theirs, I would most certainly have been burned to a crisp, beyond even the nanobots' abilities to repair.

"Livi, there's something else I think you should know."

"More?" I don't think I can take any more surprises. Then again maybe I'm underestimating my new Bionic brain. "What is it?"

Triton turns to me with a strange look in his eyes. Curiosity? Wonderment? Concern? I'm not quite sure. "The Domseis and I were going to tell you the next time we had the chance. The full results of your genetic analysis came back while you were being held captive by the Quadrati. What it revealed was something that shocked us to discover." Triton hesitates a moment before clearing his throat. "Livi, you are the daughter of one of the greatest known Bionics in history—Tomasian Park Falk, the last Comstadt before me."

My father was a Bionic? No, it couldn't be. But as I sift through everything I know about my father, I begin to see that what the Comstadt says is more likely true than not. *The strange necklace my father wore, so similar to the Comstadt's. His extended absences when I was a child. How he disappeared after that Quadrati attack so many years ago. And where else could I have gotten the Mark of Dresden mutation?*

Triton continues. "Not only that, but the genetic analysis revealed that in fact you have a rare double mutation of the Mark of Dresden gene, a homozygous. It explains why you don't have the streak of white in your hair like the rest of us. A search through our genetic database found that, incredibly, your mother was one of our own too, Dalinthea Song, our head bioengineer for many years. She disappeared from Atlas twenty-one years ago. At the time, no one knew what happened to her. But now we can only be left to surmise that she left to have you."

My mother a Bionic as well? Now I'm really being thrown around the Yentian belt. My mother, who was always my rock. Solid and reliable when all else went awry. But she was more too. Her mind extraordinarily quick, resourceful. Despite the newness of the information, in my bones, I can feel the truth of what the Comstadt is saying. And yet my parents never spoke of any of this.

"Why would they keep such important information from me?"

Triton rubs at his chin for a long moment in thought. "Presumably to keep you safe. What you may not realize is that you are an anomaly, Livi, not even a one-in-a-million chance occurrence in our vast universe. *You* are the first."

"What do you mean?"

"Bionics were never meant to have children. Those with the Mark of Dresden mutation are considered barren. Your very existence counters that rule. We are only left to surmise that Tomas and Dalinthea kept your existence strictly hidden, even from other Bionics, to protect you. Over the last few decades, the Quadrati have been targeting those with the Mark of Dresden. Stars only know what they would do with someone like you."

I take a moment to process what Triton has just revealed to me. The thought of everything my parents had to sacrifice for me—life on Atlas, seclusion from their friends—hits me in the gut. And yet something else boils deep within me too, an unexpected feeling of hotblooded anger, resentment. Sure, I was very young when they were both lost from my life and Grandpa Wren took me in. But still, *why didn't my parents tell me? What did Grandpa Wren know? Things could have been so different. All these years I have been in the dark.*

***

"Do you regret it?" Triton's question brings me back to the present amidst my swirling thoughts. We have spent the last hour talking about our childhoods, for me old memories in a new light. I look up to see him staring abjectly at his hands, a pained look in his eyes. In that instant, I see the person underneath the Bionic. I see the vulnerability despite the cintian metal running through his veins, so far from the unfeeling beast that I believed him to be when we first met.

Before I can think to stop myself, I reach over and put my hand on his. "How could I regret what you've done for me, Triton? You *saved* my life. I should *thank* you for that. I would be the most ungrateful Cerulean that ever lived if I were angry with you."

His steel-grey eyes lift up to mine. "But—but I know that being a Bionic is not necessarily what you wanted. I promised you the ability to make that decision for yourself." His voice lowers, and he puts his other hand on top of mine. "For the first time in a long time, I cared about something, *someone*." He shakes his head, a lock of charcoal-black hair falling at his temple. "It nearly broke me to see you lying there so lifeless. I just couldn't bear to let you go." His grip on my hand tightens. "In what once was an eternally lonely and unforgiving world, you gave me hope, Livi, real hope that life could be better. But I was selfish to have given you that nanobot infusion without your consent. I'm sorry."

His words seep past my shock, my confusion. I have something to tell him too. "Triton, I never got a chance to tell you, but the night before the Droids took me, I had already made my decision."

"You did?" Triton's eyebrows arch up.

"Yes, I did. The night before our last trip to Hurako, I had already decided to get the infusion, to become a Bionic. So you see, you gave me what I wanted after all." And deep down, I know I mean what I say. Perhaps I was *always* on this path all along, and just didn't know it.

Triton heaves out a breath, shoulders relaxing. He takes a few moments to compose himself. "Thank you, Livi. That knowledge means more to me than you could ever realize. You don't know the kind of personal black hole I've been living through these past few days wondering if I made the right decision for you, or if I was just being selfish. I never wanted to force my will upon anyone else, especially not you."

In that moment, I'm at a loss for words, overwhelmed. But my hand still in Triton's strong callused grip gives me a sense of connection and belonging, an anchor against a world that is doing its best to spin out of control. And I feel at least that I can move forward, take the next step in this new landscape of my life.

"What should we do now?" I ask.

"That's a very good question, Livi. One that only the stars know the answer to. But I can give you my own humble opinion. Do you want the philosophical version first or the practical one?" Triton's mouth curls up at the corners.

"By all means, go ahead then, philosopher Travler."

Clearing his throat, Triton's face smooths into flat lines, his voice dramatically solemn. "We live up to the potential that was meant to be."

"And your practical answer?"

Triton doesn't answer me right away, but rubs at his chin. "You still want to get your friend back, right?"

"Of course I do," I reply, thoughts of Keenon in the clutches of the Quadrati making my chest squeeze.

Triton's steel-grey eyes flash to mine. "Then, we train."

LV

LIVI: RECOVERY

"I HAD NO IDEA that Bionics had an outpost here on Cerulea. It's just too bad my toes are going to freeze off before we get there."

I try to wiggle some feeling back into my toes, which are stuffed into my old Galactic regulation boots as my breath puffs in clouds of sparkling white crystals before me.

"Yes. We've had this outpost here for over a millennium now, ever since the original colonists came to Cerulea." The Comstadt glances sideways at me as he sweeps a laser beam from side to side, melting an instantaneous path for us through the knee-deep snow. "As you can well imagine, not many would venture here because of the extreme cold, so it's easy to keep hidden. And remember, you're a Bionic now. The nanobots in your system won't let your toes freeze off, one of the perks of being a Bionic you could say. We can survive extremes of temperature despite what you may feel."

"Well, that's reassuring," I reply as we trudge along. In the distance past the towers, a sheer mountainside reaches towards the morning suns. Just minutes ago, I was marveling from above at these same grand snow-covered mountains of Cerulea's arctic pole from within the warm comfort of the Comstadt's Hawwk. I should have guessed my first exodus from the Galactic campus after my recovery was not merely for some holly-jolly sightseeing. Now, I carefully pick my way beside the Comstadt along the frozen path he has created towards the twin arching towers of stone ahead. The Hawwk's landing strip *would* have to be a brutally long trek away in the freezing cold. Lucky my Bionic body can handle it.

It's been about a week since I woke up back on Cerulea, a supposedly new and improved version of myself. My dizziness has since resolved, and I'm starting to get used to my new body.

I'm anxious to get back to the Quadrati base planet, but I know it's not going to be easy. Training with Triton requires much precious time, but I'll need every advantage that my new Bionic body can offer if I want even a chance at getting Keenon back.

Yesterday, I sprinted up to Guilan's Peak with the Comstadt, not even winded. And just this morning I managed to brush my teeth without snapping my toothbrush in half.

Jia was all amazement when I showed her my right arm where the scar had all but disappeared. When I told her that I became a Bionic, she handled it much better than I expected. As a Beacon, Jia is considered one of Galactic's goodwill ambassadors. She was forced to spend some time with the other Bionics that came with Triton to

Galactic while I was recovering. Jia admitted that in fact they weren't so bad after all, *particularly the cute redhead named Phlynnt*, she was quick to point out. Perhaps the fact that they all could pass for ancient Olympian gods didn't hurt their cause either.

Though it has been several days since my transformation, I still marvel at the most minute details around me. High above, a seafaerie glides upon the winds. Still, I can make out the soft, pearled feathers of its underbelly, the lightly speckled blue of its curved beak. And I have gradually gotten used to the underlying vibration of all things, as if I were seeing the energy of every single atom at the quantum level. I asked the Comstadt if all Bionics saw the world this way.

"Yes, in varying degrees," he replied. "But your double mutation may affect things more than usual."

Well, I'm certainly impressed with "more than usual." The mountainside in the distance is awash in glittering sunlight, as if it were glowing from within. And the other day when it rained, it was like seeing the Galactic campus showered in rainbows, each droplet an individual prism of colors. Never had I seen the world so beautiful. I might as well have been blind before.

"How do you not get distracted by all of this beauty?" I marvel as I examine a snowflake that has fallen onto the top of my gloved hand. With just my naked eye, I can appreciate its intricate recursive patterns, stunning with its complexity. When the Comstadt doesn't answer for a few moments, I glance up and find him peering down at me.

"Believe me. It's hard at times." And the way the Comstadt says it as he looks at me throws me off the

Yentian belt, the world suddenly tilting off axis, straight lines bending along new planes.

I have to turn away to hide the sudden flush that I know is creeping up past my neck. Luckily, at that instant, the wind blows the thick hood of my cape forwards covering my face, and by sheer force of will, I keep my feet moving ahead. And for the next few moments, all I can hear beyond the nervous buzzing in my ear is the whooshing wind and the crunching of our boots.

As we near the towers, I finally drum up the courage to break the awkward silence. "So tell me again why we're here in the most frigid part of the world with nothing but snow and ice around us?"

To my relief, the Comstadt is all business again. "Seeing as your strength has returned and you're a hundred and ten percent recovered, I thought it was time to introduce you to one of the special privileges we Bionics have. Flying."

I cough. "Your perfect memory must be failing you, Bionic. Need I remind you that I was one of Galactic's best pilots? I already know how to fly."

"Not like this you don't."

LVI

LIVI: DARKWING SUIT

WHEN WE ARRIVE at the stony outpost, for the life of me, I cannot discern a single entrance or door.

How are we supposed to get in?

But the Comstadt continues approaching a wall that is completely solid as far as I can tell. When we get within an arm's length of it, however, my eyes make out a very slight irregularity, *there near the far left corner.* No doubt my non-Bionic eyes would have missed it. And sure enough, the Comstadt places his hand on it, turns to me, and says, "Just tuck your arms in and make sure to keep your feet first."

"Why do I need to tuck my arms in and keep my—" Before I can finish, the ground opens up underneath me and swallows me whole.

"Ahhhhhhhhhhh!!!" I scream at the top of my lungs. Jia would disown me as a friend if she heard me screaming like this. Luckily she's not here to bear witness. *Of course* I'm going to scream. I may be a Bionic, but I'm still human. And I can only be hurtling down what must be the dark esophagus into hellas.

However, within seconds I get squeezed out not into some Dark Skythe's potbellied stomach, but into an immense underground chamber, where despite my continued screaming at the top of my Bionic lungs, I manage to land on my feet.

By the time I stop screaming, I turn to notice the Comstadt beside me. From his contorted face, I can tell he's trying very hard not to laugh.

"You did that on purpose!" I scowl at him. Stars, I'll *never* live this one down. *At least I landed on my feet.*

"Relax, Park, just trying to keep you on your toes. Could mean the difference between life and death someday."

Could mean the difference between life and death someday? "We're Bionics. We live forever, remember?"

The Comstadt starts to open his mouth to say something, but then seems to think better of it and instead smiles. "Don't worry, no one will ever know what a powerful scream you have."

And I blink to make sure I'm seeing the same person. This may be the one of the few times I've heard the Comstadt be anything less than serious.

Relax. Okay. Well, I *am* still in one piece. I heave a slow breath in and out. I don't know how much more my nerves can take of this day. Slowly, I pry my shoulders away from the nape of my neck, hoping the Comstadt will forget my less-than-stoic behavior, and I promise myself he will never-ever-never hear me scream like *that* again.

The Comstadt leads me into one of the larger tunnels until we arrive in a room filled with multiple strangely formed and odd gadgets. Mostly, they're flashy metal devices with too many wires. I feel like a small child in a toy shop and have to resist the urge to reach out and touch them.

Soon we come to a row of clothing hanging in a recess built into the walls. The Comstadt pauses and eyes me for only a split second, then rifles through the row of clothing. "Here, this should fit you. The seams go in the back." He hands me one of the suits, smooth, black, and a touch—rubbery. It looks like a scuba suit, but quite a bit thicker than normal. I don't ask, and put it on anyway.

Though the material appears loose at first, the minute I put it on, it molds to my skin yet remains remarkably flexible. But what really makes me look twice, and a third time, is the spread of webbing that runs the length of both my arms, fans out along my torso, and stretches down to my ankles. This is not your everyday scuba suit.

I raise up my right arm, wondering at the eccentric design. "What in the name of all the stars above are these for?" Perhaps the answer is obvious, but I ask anyway. Surely it's not what I think.

"Like I said, Park, we're going for some flying lessons."

"In these?"

"We do our best surveillance work in *these*, accessing the awkward places that would otherwise be impractical to reach in our Hawwks. These suits not only have their own propulsion and cloaking system, but they will keep your toes toasty warm even in subzero temperatures." He pauses, pinning me with his intense gaze, his eyebrows raised. "You want to stay back, Park?"

I lift my chin. "I'm game for whatever you throw my way, Comstadt." And in truth, I'm excited to test these puppies out. I didn't become a pilot to keep my two feet firmly on the ground.

"Very well." The Comstadt proceeds to don his own suit. I find myself looking away. The way his suit emphasizes his broad shoulders and hard lines would make any female uneasy, I tell myself.

Next he reaches back into the clothes receptacle and pulls out a helmet from the low shelves. He turns the helmet in his hands, inspecting it. "We have to make sure these seams are airtight, otherwise the air pressure won't hold." The helmet has a hard shell, but with soft seams that mesh with the suit. The Comstadt turns to me, placing the helmet on my head, and despite his gruff and no-nonsense exterior, he has a surprisingly light touch, gentle even. His large hands tuck loose strands of my hair into the helmet before carefully sealing me inside.

Next he helps me into a pair of gloves, again making sure the seams are fully sealed. Now I'm completely covered, not an inch of skin showing. The Comstadt seals the last seams on his own suit.

"Ready to catch some air, Park?" He throws me a grin through his helmet's clear visor, his voice crackling through the comms link built into my helmet.

"I'm always ready, Comstadt." I grin right back. The tingle of excitement pumps headily through my veins. For I feel as if I'm standing at the edge of light, about to see and do things I would never have imagined possible.

He leads me out of the room, and I find myself trekking up a long dimly lit tunnel. While we walk, his voice trickles into my helmet. "We call this our darkwing suit. The inner lining and helmet are pressurized and house a built-in oxygenator and carbon dioxide scrubber. The suit also has its own propulsion system. Microscopic pores direct powerful streams of air throughout the outer lining of this suit. Every subtle movement will be automatically registered and translated into flight. The key to controlling these suits is not to panic. Keep your movements smooth, even, controlled. Place both arms symmetrically out by your side, and your suit with automatically shift to hover mode. Any wild flailing will result in certain injury. Understood, Park?"

"Got it," I say. No wild flailing. I'm a pilot. I can manage that.

When we get to the top of the tunnel, we step into an elevator of sorts. The Comstadt touches some buttons on a blinking panel. I feel myself rising for a few moments. When it stops, the door swishes open. All I see is white on white. We are at the surface.

The Comstadt steps out into the open without hesitation, calling out to me. "Ready to practice?"

"Sure, why the hellas not?" I manage to reply, and step out after him. Despite the obvious cold, I feel completely warm, cozy even. As I walk forward into the open, I marvel at the way the flight suit seems barely there, like a second skin.

"Lucky it's only mildly windy today, perfect for a first run." The Comstadt glances up to the sky before taking a step towards me. "Okay, Park, let's get started. Squeeze your right hand into a fist once to activate the darkwing. When you want to move upwards, slowly reach towards the sky like this."

In one smooth move, the Comstadt guides his long arms out then upwards and, before I can even blink, shoots high into the sky above my head. Stars above. I have to squint against the blazing suns to see him. But with the helmet's built-in comms device, I can still hear him as if he were right next to me.

"Be sure to keep your arms even and symmetric. Any asymmetry will send you listing. When you want to come down, slowly bring your arms back down to your sides. Deactivate the suit by fisting your left hand." And in the next moment, I find him standing just an arm's length in front of me, not even breaking a sweat and with a big grin plastered on his face.

"You really enjoy flying, don't you?"

His eyes look up towards the light of the sky. "Can't say I ever get tired of it even after all these star years. I suppose you could say it is one of the things I enjoy most about my life as a Bionic. The freedom. Feeling untethered. Perhaps in another lifetime I would have been better off as a seafaerie."

He turns to me. "Okay, Park, now it's your turn. Remember what I said, smooth, controlled movements. Stay symmetric unless you want to go flying, no pun intended." The Comstadt quirks his mouth. "Most of all, don't panic."

LVII

LIVI: MAIDEN VOYAGE

"**D**ON'T PANIC. Right. Got it." I run through his instructions one more time.

"First thing we're going to do is go straight up about fifty meters, and then arms out to your side to level off in a hover. The key is to keep your movements small, subtle. Nothing too drastic. Understood?"

"Sure thing," I say. How hard could it be? The Comstadt made it look easy enough. I fist my right hand to activate the suit. Other than a subtle buzzing sensation vibrating the hairs of my skin, things feel no different. *Well, here goes nothing.* I stretch both arms towards the stars.

The next thing I know, I'm hurtling towards what must be the outer limits of space. "Shiiiiiiiiiiiikes!" I scream at the top of my lungs as all snow and land disappear below me. Oh well, so much for empty promises.

The Comstadt's voice barrels into my ear, though I can't comprehend a single word he's saying. The darn suit is starting to heat up. *I'm going too fast, too high.* I jerk my arms down, and suddenly I'm plunging. Stomach in my throat. The white of ground crashing back towards me. At this speed, there's no way I can miss the ground.

Crimennnnny!

The world starts whirling.

Death spin. Now I've done it.

"Arms out, Park! Arms straight out, for crying out loud! Get yourself to a hover!" The Comstadt's voice crackles through my headpiece.

This time I can hear him. *Arms out. Hover.* Fighting the dizzying panic, I force my arms straight to my side. And to my relief, I find myself slowing. *It's working. Thank the stars.* I'm leveling out now.

In the next instant, the Comstadt's form shoots up from nowhere and now hovers just an arm's length away from me. He grabs hold of my elbows, his grip on me firm, reassuring. Even through the slight mist clouding his visor, I can see the thick furrowing of his eyebrows. "You all right, Park?"

I nod very carefully. Who knows what will set off this suit next?

The Comstadt throws an arm around my waist and orders, "Fist your left hand," then more gently, "I'm going to guide us down."

Ignoring the heat creeping into my face, I do as he says. The minute I fist my left hand, I feel a sudden dip, the pull of gravity. But the Comstadt, with whatever inhuman strength he has, manages to bear both of our weights, holding on to me with one arm and guiding us down with the other. The minute our feet crunch down on cold snow he releases me. I resist the sudden urge to fall to my knees and kiss the cold ground. Thank the stars.

Now that I'm no longer on the edge of impending doom, the Comstadt lets me have it. "Park, what part of 'smooth, controlled, movements' and 'whatever you do, don't panic' did you not understand? Do you realize that if you had gone any further you would have become a flaming star? And not in a good way. Perhaps I should mention to you that these suits will blow apart at 0.001 psi of atmospheric pressure."

"That's comforting," I retort. After all, this was my first time trying this crazy flying contraption, and even he has to admit that his own instructions were not particularly detailed. Lousy even. "Well, perhaps if I had a *better* teacher who had properly warned me about something so important *ahead of time* instead of when it's almost *too late*, I would have done better."

The Comstadt continues to shake his head. I can almost see tendrils of steam puffing out from his head. He is beyond furious. "That's it, Park. Out of the suit. Now."

I wince from his painfully loud voice barking into my helmet.

"I thought you would be a quick study at this given your previous pilot training and all, but I guess I was wrong. Wait back inside the southern outpost until I get back."

He's giving up on me already? "Wait. I can do this. I just panicked for a moment. Just let me try one more time."

"No. You had your chance, Park. The Domseis will already be furious at me for letting you try flying so early after the nanobot infusion." His hard expression softens, his voice a little less bladed. "I wanted to give you a chance to experience what it's really like to be a Bionic, see what we really do. But the truth of it is that your equilibrium is still probably off. Your vestibular canal is still adjusting to its enhanced receptors thanks to the nanobots. I'm sorry, I was wrong to have brought you out here so soon after your transformation."

Despite the panic and the chaos, I know one thing. "Comstadt, this may be the craziest thing I have ever done in my life, but it is also the most thrilling, the most eye-opening. And if you really are trying to show me what being a Bionic is like, then doesn't that also include showing me what it's like to be fearless? To keep trying and moving forward no matter what? Please, just let me try one more time. I promise my vestibular thingamajiggies will catch up. *Please.*"

The Comstadt thinks on it for a long hard moment. Silent battle in his eyes. Finally he takes a deep breath and heaves it out.

"All right, Park, I'm going to give you one more chance. Blow this, and we're going to land straight away. Got it?"

"Got it." And this time, I will be more careful.

"Okay then, take my hand."

"What?"

"Take my hand. We're going to try something different this time."

LVIII

LIVI: SECOND CHANCES

"THE GROUND IS ALWAYS going to be there you know."

I drag my gaze away from the tiny houses that dot the snowy plains below to meet the Comstadt's face.

The air is so thin, we must have hit the stratosphere by now. Through the helmet's visor, I can see humor crinkle the corners of his eyes, juxtaposed just above where our hands lock. I do my best to scowl at him without loosening my grip. Being this high up with nothing but whistling wind beneath me, I have to admit, I'm thankful to have something to hold onto.

"Okay, Park, this time try to angle your wrist just a little more like this." He wings back his free right hand, and I do my best to imitate with my left, and almost imperceptibly we rise up as a single unit into the sky, his powerful frame tethering mine. "Remember only small moves are needed to make subtle changes in altitude and direction."

We've been going at it for at least a few hours already, Cerulea's suns at their apices in the sky. I have to give the Comstadt some credit—this really *is* a much easier way to learn, even if it does make me feel like a toddler.

"Now relax your shoulders, let yourself feel the flow of the air around you, through you. Being tense is not going to help. It just makes your balance more unstable."

Relax. Easy for him to say when he's probably done this over a million times. Having nanotechnology coursing through one's veins though, ready to repair any damage even when one free-falls from several kilometers up, is at least *somewhat* reassuring.

I do my best to relax my shoulders, loosening the muscles that are all bunched up there. Feel the air, he says? I think back to my own experience piloting the Tullies back at home. And inherently, I know what he means. But translating that to a situation where one is careening through the sky in a flimsy rubber shell as opposed to a thick layer of metal is easier said than done. A pulse of adrenaline shoots through me as I catch a glimpse of the trees that seem so far below.

"Block it out." The Comstadt's voice rumbles through my head. "Block out your fear of falling. Think about where you want to go, and your body will naturally follow. Don't let the small details throw you off."

In my mind, I imagine myself back in the cockpit of my Tully. Only this time I am the Tully, my wings slicing through the air. And instead of fighting the wind, I use it to propel myself faster, higher.

"That's it, Park. You're getting it." The Comstadt nods approvingly.

We soar over the snow-covered landscape below. We come across a few sparse houses, but nary a person in sight. And now, instead of fearing the height, I'm starting to revel in it.

"Good, Livi. Now I'm going to let go."

My eyes jerk towards his. "What?"

"You're ready, Park. It's time to try on your own now." He holds my gaze for a split second, then to my horror, I feel his grip starting to loosen.

"W-wait, I don't thi—" But before I can finish protesting and remind him that falling from this ridiculous height will result in certain injury, he unceremoniously—lets go of my hand.

Instant panic grips me, and I start to wobble. The smooth webbing that spans the space between my arms and torso flaps and shudders.

"Easy there. Focus. Feel the air around you, Livi. Don't fight it. Head up and keep sight of where you want to go."

I gulp down the acid in my throat. *Keep sight of where I want to go.* Where do I want to go? And suddenly, I remember my childhood dreams. Soaring through the air like a bird. The endless expanse of a Cerulean sky.

I take a deep breath and block out everything but the air in my lungs. I can feel the turbulence calming, stabilizing. Then, I close my eyes and reach. Reach for the light behind the clouds. Reach for the stars that were always too far, twirling my body to feel the air swirl and pump beneath my wings. Space and time rush past me as I gain altitude, the thrill coursing through my veins. And when I open my eyes again a moment later, the stars do seem just a little bit closer, a little more within reach.

But this time, before I get too high, I remember what the Comstadt taught me—to tuck my arms down gently, and I find myself diving, swooping down so close to a mountain peak that I reach out and touch it. I pull my hand back in wonder. *So this is what it's like to be a Bionic.* I marvel at the beauty below me, wisps of cold winter meandering between the mountaintops. Looking for the Comstadt, I see that he's hovering some distance away. The child in me lets go. I race towards him full speed. Closer, and closer. His eyes widen, and he shields his arms up. Just at the last minute I pull to a stop a mere arm's length away from him. This time it's my turn to try to keep from laughing. "Is that what you mean, Comstadt?"

He brings his arms back down while shaking his head and laughs, *out loud.* "Well, I'll be darned, Park. You're a born natural after all, but let's see if you can do this."

And in the next instant, the Comstadt unfurls like the wind, shoots up into the air, and does a perfect loop-de-loop. Upside down.

I can't help but burst out laughing. Perhaps the Comstadt has a sense of humor after all. I can't let him outdo me. I shoot up into the air after him, not doing one, but two loop-de-loops. Upside down.

And for the next several hours, we chase each other over the frozen mountaintops, weaving between boughs of snow-covered cyprian trees, trying our best to one-up and outmaneuver the other. Hours warp to minutes, and I don't remember the last time I have ever had so much fun. For I am either too busy laughing at the crazy stunts the Comstadt pulls, or screaming in terror as I try to pull off my own insane nose dive, to notice that the suns have already come to rest along the distant horizon. But as we careen above a forest of gangly trees, suddenly a strange buzzing niggles at the base of my skull, heat flaring through the tips of my fingers. I start to slow.

The Comstadt is by my side almost instantly. "You all right, Livi?"

"I'm not sure." In the next moment, my vision tunnels. A strange pulling sensation drags at me, from the inside out. "I think—" Before I can finish, my arms and legs seize.

I can't resist.

I am ripped away.

From my own self.

LIX

LIVI: THE SPACE BETWEEN

I 'VE BEEN HERE BEFORE, *the place within space and time that is between, through, under, but not really there. Not really anywhere.*

But this time, no trace of Starlock, only the inescapable surge of something that cannot be seen, only felt, exists. I am pulled through this vortex of nothingness at a speed I can only imagine to be supraluminal. Maybe even faster. The void around me lit up in an electrical dance. Until suddenly.

I am through.

I see from eyes that are not mine. Hold up a hand poised over a trigger from within a cockpit. I know this place too. Sort of. Similar to the insides of a Buggard with its strange icosahedral patterns embedded within its walls. Only the inside of this one is bigger, more spacious. And I'm on the tail of a Hawwk. Another Hawwk veers off farther in the distance. But I have no control. Only the eyes to see the horror of what is about to happen. No! I shout. And for a moment, it's as if I have been heard. The shiny metal hand jerks back. But no. I am mistaken. A force stronger than my own overrides my thoughts, my will, sending a blazing ball of fire hurtling towards the Hawwk that I recognize. The one with the flaming red star on its right wing. The one that belongs to Phlynnt.

The ball of fire clips his tail fin and sends him plummeting down. But not before the me that is not me presses another button, releasing what appears to function as a tractor beam. The Hawwk is trapped now. The hand flicks a few more switches that I do not recognize while the second Hawwk circles back around. I'm expecting a volley of return fire. But the Hawwk careens past without even a second look in our direction. Wait! I want to yell out. But I'm only an ineffectual observer here. The hand manipulates the controls in front of me, the control screen blinking, flashing as the white northern pole of Cerulea rapidly miniaturizes then disappears from my view through the right window. In contrast, Altheria quickly emerges and enlarges up ahead, so closely that I can almost imagine feeling the intense heat. From what I can tell, we are moving fast, very fast. And it finally dawns on me. I know where I am. The innards of a blasted Hellion ship.

But before I can ascertain any more, the hand that is not mine reaches for another toggle and suddenly I am forced out. I find myself plummeting back down into a hole that has no bottom, no end.

LX

LIVI: INSIGHT

IF I THOUGHT my dream was disconcerting, opening my eyes to find myself in the arms of the Comstadt is just about enough to make me think the universe really is playing tricks on me.

I jerk up.

"Easy there, Park. Not so fast." He grips my arm firmly. The dark steel of his eyes drill into mine.

"Wh-what happened?" *I've been saying that a few too many times lately.* My vision spins, and to my embarrassment, I'm forced to lean back against the Comstadt.

"You passed out." He pauses for a moment. "In midair."

Passed out in midair? Of all the most ridiculously cringe-worthy, red-in-the-face moments I have ever experienced in my life (and there have been plenty), this will rate well into the *top ten.*

"And I caught you just in time."

Okay, maybe top five.

But before I can fully wallow in my embarrassment, the Comstadt stands, hoisting me gently up, a steadying hand at my elbow.

"Park, we've got to get back to campus immediately. Atlas has just detected Quadrati in Cerulean space." His hand clasps at something at the V of his neck, sparks of electricity shuddering underneath his palm. *His orling.* "Some of our Bionics are already deployed, but we better get back to Galactic in case they need help."

"Qu-Quadrati?" I sputter, my mind reeling. His words trigger bits of my horrific vision to flash in my head. Hands of tinston metal. Activating a tractor beam. Could I have—I shake my head. No. *It had to be a coincidence.* But what if it wasn't?

"Comstadt—" I chew on my lip, not sure of how to say what I'm going to say without sounding totally crazy. "I think Phlynnt may be in trouble."

"What? What are you talking about, Park?"

"I know this sounds ridiculous, but what happened to me just now, I think—I think somehow I tapped into the Quadrati neural network."

Comstadt looks at me like I've grown another nose, but merely says, "Please explain."

"I saw Phlynnt's Hawwk take a hit. I think a Hellion ship got him. Perhaps it was just a dream, but the same thing happened to me once before, when I was being held captive by the Quadrati." I shake my head. "I don't know how, but I think I can tap into what the Droids are thinking."

The Comstadt scrubs at the dark stubble on his chin. "That certainly would be very unusual. But then again, Park, you and your double Mark of Dresden mutation have already defied the odds more than once. Nothing would surprise me at this point. Let's get back to Galactic and see if they have any more news."

I nod, grateful to the Comstadt for believing in me, especially at a time when I'm not sure I even believe in myself.

LXI

LIVI: CONFIRMATION

WE GET BACK TO the outpost's landing pad in record time.

Flying back to the Hawwk in my darkwing suit alongside the Comstadt sure beats the long, frigid, trek through the snow earlier. And it occurs without incident, except for the brief run-in with a flock of migrating seafaeries that had us dodging drops of nasty yellow-green bird poo. Good thing our darkwing suits are waterproof.

Once we're in the Hawwk, I'm reminded of how the Comstadt pilots like no one I have ever seen. He roars us past the mountaintops at full speed, my stomach draped down well past my toes. Then he weaves us past steep cliff edges and through narrow valleys as if we were out in wide-open air.

And when we get to the main control tower of Galactic Central, I'm not even the least bit surprised when the Comstadt stalks in as if he owns the place, even after only having been at Galactic such a short time.

As we approach, Juki stands up from behind the central control panel, with Professor Hensly following soon after.

"Update, Magnar," the Comstadt demands.

"Four Buggards were spotted in Cerulean space within a hundred kilometers of Finlan's Point, Comstadt. Magnar Phlynnt and Sar Eppel deployed to head them off. However, there has been a complication."

"What *complication*?"

"A Hellion appeared out of nowhere, just above the arctic poles, intercepting our Hawwks. Sar Eppel got away, but"—Juki's voice breaks ever so slightly—"Phlynnt's ship took a direct hit. He's been captured."

The Comstadt's jaw goes rigid, and his eyes flash to mine. "When?"

"Less than fifteen minutes ago, Comstadt."

"Any sign of the Droids now?"

"Unfortunately, Sar Eppel lost visuals when the Hellion ship recloaked, and they've jammed our radars. Eppel's still scouring the area, but with its cloaking device on, that Hellion ship could be anywhere, and we have no way to detect it. I'm afraid we're completely blind, Comstadt."

The Comstadt shakes his head. "My guess is that those draggarts probably made star jump by now. We won't be able to track them." He rubs at his left temple for a few moments, but then stops abruptly. "Unless—" His eyes flick back to mine. "Park, come with me."

My head jerks up. "Where are we going?"

"To track down those darn Droids."

"But how?"

"We're going to test out your new talent."

LXII

LIVI: RECALL

"**T**RY AGAIN, LIVI. You've got to picture exactly what you were doing, what you were thinking when you first made contact with the Quadrati neural network. See if you can establish a connection again," Triton instructs.

I've been holed up in his too-small Hawwk cockpit for the last hour, Finlan's Point a stone's throw away outside my window. Eppel's craft scours the area around us.

What was I thinking? It's already hard enough to concentrate with the Comstadt's hulking form right next to me. Do I honestly want to admit out loud that I was debating which circus trick I was going to perform next in my darkwing suit? I briefly glance over at him, his dark eyes intent on mine. *Definitely not.* So I squeeze my eyes shut, trying to block out the volcanic heat that leaks from him, the steady ebb and flow of his breathing. I search for that tunnel that will take me back to my nightmare, no matter how much I really don't want to. Seconds pass. A long breath of a minute. Then several more dragging moments. But not a thing happens. Not a single darn thing. Finally, I shake my head in exasperation. "I'm sorry, but I don't think it works like that."

To the Comstadt's credit, he doesn't throw his hands up in disgust, doesn't scowl, doesn't even frown, but simply leans back in his seat and says evenly, "Perhaps we're approaching this all wrong."

"I'll say," I mutter, digging my knuckles into my temples. I've been approaching-this-all-wrong so hard my head hurts.

The Comstadt shifts towards me, jaw firm. "Try again. You must take into account all of the variables. You said you've tapped into the Quadrati neural network twice now. Think about the similarities, the common elements."

Common elements? I try to remember that eerie episode when I first tapped into the Quadrati neural network, when I was held captive by the Droids. Were there any similarities between the two situations? I certainly wasn't wearing a darkwing suit at the time. I also wasn't anywhere near Cerulea's freezing arctic poles. But then suddenly, one glaringly obvious fact strikes me in the head like a hazar. My breath stills. It's so simple, why didn't I think of it before? "Sensate Droid," I utter, barely a whisper.

"Sensate Droid?" Triton arches an eyebrow at me.

"Yes, Sensate Droid," I repeat more loudly, feeling the certainty in my bones. My thoughts are spilling out fast now. "First time I mind melded, I was on the Quadrati base. Second time, the Hellion ship was right above the arctic poles where you and I were practicing in the darkwing suits. We all know that only Sensate Droids pilot those Hellions."

The Comstadt rubs at his chin and nods approvingly. "Maybe you're onto something, Park."

I shake my head. "But how is that information going to help us when there's not even a ratty old Droid within a hundred kilometers of us, maybe not even a light-year?" A quick glance at the Comstadt's orling confirms that it's now as dull as stone. "And there's no predicting when they'll show up next."

The Comstadt doesn't answer for several moments, but finally suggests, "If you can't establish a connection with the neural network, let's run through what you do remember of the last mind meld. There may be some clues as to how to track the Droids. Concentrate on even the minutest of details. Don't leave anything out."

It takes some effort for me not to groan. I must have done this a hundred times already. But he is the Comstadt after all, so I humor him. "I remember being on Phlynnt's tail. His right wing damaged—"

"How about right before you lost the connection? Try to picture it *exactly*, Livi." The Comstadt interrupts unapologetically.

"And I remember—" I squeeze my eyes shut, trying to recreate the scene in my mind. "Altheria blazing before me. A metal hand hovering over the control panel."

"What did the navigator show?" the Comstadt presses.

"The numbers were changing rapidly—" I trained on the Galactic Buggard replicas enough to understand the navigational equipment. "Like it was going haywire." Or was it? I replay the scene again in my head. The numbers were churning like mad at first, we were traveling at such high speeds. But at the last minute, right before the metal hand reached for the toggle and I lost contact, the numbers had actually slowed. To a stop.

"4.02, 54.9, 0.034, 120.53, 11.18, 71.14," I say, letting my photographic memory recite for me.

"What did you just say?"

"4.02, 54.9, 0.034, 120.53, 11.18, 71.14," I repeat again, finally opening my eyes. This time, the Comstadt scribbles them down. "The last readings before I lost contact. What do you think they mean?"

The Comstadt puts his hand to his temple for a long moment, his gaze lost on a distant star. "You know, those Quadrati ships are slippery as all hellas, and darn impossible to trace. How the Droids sneak into the Erlion system has eluded us all these years." Triton's dark steel-grey eyes flare to mine. His expression morphs into something I can't quite decipher. "And now, Livi, you may have finally found our answer."

He taps sharply on his comms link, his voice urgent. "Eppel, get Magnar Gucini on comms. I need him to translate some Quadrati coordinates to our star system. Our Young Blood here may very well have just discovered how those blasted Droids have been getting into Erlion."

LXIII

LIVI: WHEN BAD DREAMS ARE

REALITY

"THIS HAS TO BE IT. The dark matter levels are off the charts here." The Comstadt leans forward, his eyes fixed ahead. "What do you make of it, Magnar?"

"Can't say I've ever seen anything like it, Comstadt." Juki shakes his head from the co-pilot's seat. "Those levels shouldn't even be possible."

"And yet it makes perfect sense now," Triton replies. "A Quadrati gateway at Finlan's Point in such close proximity to Altheria would have precluded any of our equipment from detecting it all these miserable years. The perfect camouflage. This *has* to be it." The excitement in the Comstadt's eyes is unmistakable. He turns to Juki, who's in the Hawwk cockpit with us. "Magnar, proceed with the Gravity One probe."

326

"Yes, sir." Juki nods. "Now let's hope Magnar Gucini got his translational calculations right. We'll miss it, and dinner, even if we're just a few meters off." From his co-pilot's seat, the Magnar of Engineering deploys a disc-shaped probe from the Hawwk. The disc spins away in a dizzying array of colors, the live currents lining its perimeter sizzling brighter and brighter as it gains rotational speed.

I grip my armrests as the air stills around me. My eyes rivet on the pulse of the probe growing steadily more distant by the second. Part of me hopes we will finally find the Quadrati gateway, but then again, another part of me hopes that I'm wrong, totally and utterly wrong. That it was all just a bad dream. Because what if I really do have a stars-forsaken connection with the Sensate Droids? What would that mean? My skin crawls at the thought.

The probe spins farther and farther. And the dark void around remains just that—a dark void.

"We should be on it by now." The Comstadt shakes his head. He turns to Juki, his brows furrowed. "Magnar, are you certain the locator coordinates are correct? The sway on Gravity One looks off to me."

Juki scans the multitude of screens and equipment monitoring the Gravity One probe. "I think you're right, Comstadt. Though my locator readings are right on target, visuals suggest that the sway is a few degrees off. Perhaps the pull of dark matter is throwing it?"

"Get Magnar Gucini on comms. Have him recalculate coordinates. Tell him our numbers and to adjust for the dark matter's gravitational field."

Juki rapid fire speaks into the comms link while his hands fly over the equipment before him. ". . . 19.981, 72.74. Got it." He turns to Triton. "Adjustments made. Gravity One reset."

My eyes once again rivet on the Gravity One probe. Its flashing lights are now barely visible even to my Bionic eyes. Several long moments pass. Still nothing. Juki starts to shake his head. Even the Comstadt shifts uncomfortably in his seat.

Well, that's it then. *Only a bad dream.* I guess we missed Chef Aton's mullet fish stew tonight for nothing.

Just when I'm about to apologize to the Comstadt for instigating this frivolous excursion, the empty space before us erupts into a ring of light, practically blinding me.

The Comstadt and Juki swear colorfully from their seats in front. The halo of light yawns rapidly open, expanding to the circumference of a small moon. It swallows Gravity One in a single gulp.

If I blinked, I would have missed it.

***

"It worked!" Juki marvels. "The gateway really is here. But where in the dark infinites did Gravity One go?" His hands flow over the four-dimensional star grid, spinning it, scrolling through it, zooming in and out, then in again.

The Comstadt holds up his hand, his eyes intensely focused, scrutinizing. "Wait!" he orders. "Two scrolls back, Juki. Magnify at lambda 30.9, delta 4001.3, trilon 0.0329, omega 157.33. There! There it is."

"Rattling Droids." Juki shakes his head. "The Hebeda Zone? But why would the Quadrati have a base out there?"

From the back seat, I angle my body so I can get a closer look at the four-dimensional navigational map that the Comstadt and Juki look at. "The Hebeda Zone?" I ask.

Triton wands his hand over the map, further enhancing a relatively bland area of the gridwork. He points out the area surrounding the bright green dot tracking Gravity One's position, then replies, "Yes, the Hebeda Zone. It's over twenty light-years away, a binary star system with only a trio of gas giants, but with certainly nothing that is even remotely habitable, even for Droids."

Rattling Droids indeed.

Suddenly the Comstadt leans forward towards the star grid. "What in all hellas?"

Juki waxes even more animated beside him, practically lurching out of his seat. "It's—it's gone. Disappeared just like that. As if there's . . ." His voice trails off as the numbers spike in front of him. "Another gateway?"

My eyes home in on the blinking green of Gravity One's indicator light, or at least where it *used* to be.

"Quickly, Magnar," the Comstadt orders. "NET algorithm. We can't lose it."

Juki fires up the pulse generator. The four-dimensional map expands threefold, filling the whole of the cockpit window now. Juki jumps from his seat and paces along the map. His hands fly over the gridwork, manipulating it this way and that.

"There! In the Harin System." Triton exclaims as he too bolts up and strides over to another section of the navigational map. "Crimeny—it just made another jump!"

I look to where the Comstadt points. "But I thought wormholes only connected two points in space-time."

"Single Haptonian bridges are the most common, naturally occurring type of wormhole," the Comstadt explains, his eyes never leaving the map. "However, theoretically anything is possible with an *artificial* network. Could be a series of wormholes, connected."

All eyes track the probe's progress on the holographic grid. Juki practically dances before the gridwork, his hands blurring over the four-dimensional map, furiously trying to keep up with Gravity One's location. Each jump takes Gravity One a little farther. Harin, Grisda, Pennet's Bin—over a hundred light-years away. The thought is mind-boggling. But then Gravity One's indicator light blinks out, and doesn't blink on again.

"Dark infinites. Where'd it go now?" Juki swears. His movements are dizzying as he manipulates the gridwork in front of him. Rotating. Zooming in. Out. Scrolling. Rotating again. But Gravity One is nowhere to be found. Finally he shakes his head. "I'm sorry, Comstadt. It's gone. I'm afraid you and I already know what that means."

The Comstadt nods once in grim response.

"What *does* it mean?" I ask.

The Comstadt's brows are furrowed as he turns to me. "Gravity One has supraluminal communication, the most far-reaching probe we have. We should be able to track it anywhere within the Erlion system. Which can only mean that either it was somehow destroyed, or that"—his eyes

grow wide as his gaze pivots back to the void outside—
"Gravity One is no longer within Erlion at all."

LXIV

TRITON: GETTING READY

I TAKE A DEEP BREATH.

Park sits next to me in the co-pilot seat of my Hawwk, trying bravely to hide her nervousness. I know because I've spent almost every waking moment working with the Young Blood over this last star month, and I can read her like a book. And the light tapping of her index finger tells me that she's on edge.

"You sure you want to do this? You can still change your mind. You don't have to go you know. There are plenty of us Bionics going already. Eppel, Juki, and I have volunteered for this mission."

Her finger stops twitching as she looks me hard in the eye, unflinching. "I'm sure."

Perhaps she's stronger than I thought.

And I've got to give the Young Blood some credit. She not only found us the Quadrati gateway but also came up with the rather brilliant idea to send a second probe through the wormhole. And Gravity Two actually returned with some incredibly valuable information. The wormhole is much more extensive than we could have imagined—more like a wormhole network, a multinodal system with twists and turns, several possible destinations, destinations even beyond our own Erlion System. But unfortunately, the probes can only tell us so much. Once the Gravity Probe makes the leap out of Erlion, we are blind. Who knows how far the wormhole will take us. But I do know that if we want a chance at finding out where the Quadrati took Keenon, Phlynnt, and the others, our only option is to go after the darn draggarts ourselves.

And the Young Blood leapt at the chance. In fact she was the first to volunteer. I'm not even sure Juki would have volunteered so readily if he didn't feel the least bit embarrassed that a Young Blood, two hundred years his junior no less, volunteered before him.

But now, as my Hawwk waits at the lip of the gateway, even I feel a tinge of queasiness in the pit of my stomach. This will be nothing like navigating through the Haptonian wormholes connecting the habitable planets of the Erlion System. The gateway from Cerulea to Axos takes nothing more than a single jump through space-time. And from Cerulea to Hurako, an even shorter leap. From the numbers and data points Gravity One and Two spit out, we have never encountered anything as extensive or complex as the gateway before me. And that is only from what we know exists so far within the Erlion system.

One wrong turn, and we may never find our way to the Quadrati base planet. Navigating the wormhole network is going to be like navigating an infinite maze of twists and turns, an endless possibility of outcomes, including the possibility of becoming lost forever.

LXV

LIVI: BRAVE FACE

THE WAY THE COMSTADT is looking at me, I know he's analyzing me with those steel-grey, Bionic eyes of his.

The hard depths of his gaze gauge my every move, my every thought. But I will myself not to break. When the Comstadt asked me if I was sure I wanted to go, my insides sloshed and churned, but there was no way in all hellas I was going to back down. How could I leave Keenon in the hands of the Quadrati? Already I'm anxious to get back. I just hope to the stars that we are not already too late.

I debriefed the Comstadt, the Domseis, and their whole tactical team about everything I could remember about the Quadrati home planet. I was surprised they agreed to my suggestion of sending another Gravity Probe through the wormhole network to gather even more information. And after they gleaned all they could from the probes, we had not just one plan but other contingency plans in case the first one doesn't work. The

Comstadt, Juki, Eppel, and I holed up in the Hawwk simulator for hours on end going through every possible scenario. Through it all, I had to admire the way the Bionics think, the precision with which they prepare. But I hope to the stars that we will only need plan A, because B and C don't necessarily involve making it back.

And if the Quadrati wormhole network is anything like the wormhole to Hurako, I can manage. *I think*. But as I glance over at the Comstadt, even he looks a little uneasy. The Comstadt and I fly together, with Eppel and Juki following our tail in their own Hawwks. This is to be nothing more than a rescue mission. We hope to sneak in without the Quadrati noticing our small band. Get in. Get our people out. Get home. We'll worry about long-term issues later.

***

"Remember, just like we trained, Park." The Comstadt catches my eye, holding my gaze for just a second longer than usual.

Our Hawwk is within a hundred kilometers of the Quadrati's gateway coordinates, and the anticipation of what's to come sends my heart beating to a gallop.

I nod silently and take in a deep breath, trying to quiet the fluttering in my chest. I don't trust my voice at this point.

"Cloaking devices on stealth mode, activate subsonic tracers. And remember, be on your guard. Who knows where the wormhole will spit us out, and where those Droids are lurking. Be prepared to fight your way out," the Comstadt orders into his comms link.

"Affirmative, Comstadt."

"Understood."

Juki and Eppel reply successively.

"Very well. Then subsonic communication lines only. We don't want to give ourselves away." The Comstadt keeps his eyes trained ahead.

With our cloaking devices on, even Eppel and Juki wouldn't know our whereabouts were it not for our encrypted subsonic trackers. So unless the Quadrati are looking for us, we should go undetected. At least that's what the Comstadt assured me. Nevertheless, the Comstadt made me don my darkwing suit, just in case our first plan goes awry.

Perhaps I'm imagining it, but as we steer closer to the Quadrati gateway, I start to feel a strange electric charge vibrating the air. The feeling intensifies as we approach closer, teasing the fine hairs on my arms. *It can't just be my nerves.*

"The Gravity Probes' data was spot on. Dark matter levels are off the charts here." The Comstadt glances over at me. "We're in for quite a ride, Park. Brace yourself." Though there is humor in his voice, his charcoal-grey eyes are all seriousness.

I tighten the straps on my seat harness, yet again.

But this time, I don't even blink when the void before us erupts into a ring of light, yawning rapidly open, though I can barely breathe as the Comstadt guides us forward. For a moment I wonder if we might be entering the mouth into hellas. Even if we are, it's too late. For as soon as the nose of the Hawwk enters the ring, we are accelerating, pulled forward through the bowels of a raging electrical tunnel, pitching left, right, twisting up, down. The Comstadt is shouting something to me, but I can't understand a word he's saying. My head spins, and it's all I can do not to pass out, my insides about ready to spill.

Fortunately, within a matter of seconds, we're through, all movement suddenly still.

"You all right, Park?"

I turn towards where the Comstadt sits, his hands resting lightly on the control panel, not even a hair out of place. How can the Comstadt be so calm after *that*?

I pry my fingers off my armrests. "Yes, I'm fine," I say, though my words come out a little thick, and I feel ready to give up my lunch. At least I'm still able to respond.

The Comstadt gives me a knowing look. "Your newly enhanced Young Blood senses make you particularly prone to the disorienting effects of the wormhole. Things should get better with practice. Next time we jump, remember to keep your eyes focused forward, it will be less disorienting that way."

Oh, was that what he was trying to tell me before?

As I shake off my dizziness, a glance out my window affords a view like I've never seen. Only my recollection of Gravity One's journey helps me orient to where I am. The Hebeda Zone. Nula's unique off-yellow flames burn brighter here compared to its far-off sister sun Hulin in the distance. Before I can dwell on the brilliant shades of Nula's flames, another bright ring yawns open immediately before us. I shield my eyes with my hands against the blazing light. But from the data the Gravity probes sent back, we anticipated this. Another wormhole. And though the Comstadt's hands are nowhere near the control panel, our Hawwk starts drifting towards it.

"What's happening?"

"We are so close to the wormhole, gravity is pulling us in."

"Dark Skythes above," I mutter under my breath. But if this brings us closer to the Quadrati home base, all the better.

The Comstadt's hands fly over the control panel. Again the Hawwk starts vibrating, and the air charges around us through each twist and turn of the tunnel. This time, I try to do as the Comstadt instructed and focus on the tunnel ahead, but still my stomach threatens to empty its contents, and I have to clamp my mouth shut. And just before I think I can't take it anymore, all goes still again. As my vestibulars steady, this time when I peer outside of my window, it's as if a friend is there to greet me. A quiet trio of stars, a young nebula's whirling aurora of reds and golds smack-dab in the middle. The Harin System. Only closer than I've ever seen them before. I could revel in the view forever, but the Comstadt quickly draws my attention away.

"Stars, would you look at that," the Comstadt exclaims.

When I follow the line of the Comstadt's gaze out past his window, what I see takes me a moment to comprehend. Not just one gaping halo of light ready to swallow us whole, but three rapidly enlarging rings of light yawn open before us. The Gravity probes did not help us anticipate *this*. "What in the name of Altheria?"

"Never seen anything like it," Comstadt says, eyeing his instrument panel in puzzlement. "The dark energy levels are ten times what we see compared to Haptonian wormholes. These have got to be artificial. Something like that would be too unstable to occur naturally." He shakes his head. "But how in all hellas did the Quadrati manage to harness all of this dark matter?"

"Which one do we choose?" I ask.

The Comstadt taps at the comms link by his ear. "Magnar, any way to figure out where these things go?"

A few seconds pass before he answers. "I'm afraid not, Comstadt. It was probably just luck that allowed us to track our Gravity Probes as far as we did. We have no way to tell which wormhole the probes took, and even then, who knows if it will takes us to the Quadrati base. I'm afraid we're blind here." Juki's voice crackles over the comms link.

The Comstadt thinks for a long moment. "Then unfortunately we have no choice. I'm calling the mission."

"What?" I whirl towards the Comstadt.

"We can't risk getting lost in deep space, Park. And we can't risk hanging out here just trying to figure out which is the correct tunnel. Sooner or later the Quadrati are going to show up, and we'll be sitting ducks, even with our cloaking devices. No, our only choice is to go back and come up with a different plan."

Go back? "But what about Keenon and Phlynnt? If we go back, we'll waste too much time. Stars only know if we're already too late."

The Comstadt scrubs at his chin but shakes his head. "I'm sorry, Park. We don't know where these will take us. It would be like a shot in the dark. Our best bet is to sneak in unnoticed. If we linger here any longer, we'll be discovered for sure. In which case it won't be just a matter of getting back to Atlas, but getting back to Atlas *alive*, even despite our nanobots. We can't risk it."

I want to argue further, to ask him to just take a chance. But in truth, I know he's right. To proceed without any further information would almost guarantee failure. If only I could remember more from my return trip.

"Juki. Eppel. Abort mission. Clear gateway perimeter. Repeat. Clear gateway perimeter. We do not want to accidentally get pulled in," the Comstadt orders into the comms link as he starts to turn the Hawwk around.

I take one last fleeting look at the three blazing rings, my hopes of finding Keenon evaporating to the ethers. But just then something catches my eye. *There, in the center.* "Whoa, did you see that?"

"What?" The Comstadt cocks his heads towards me.

Before I can answer, a sudden niggling gnaws at the base of my brain. Just like. Just like—*stars it's happening again. That strange pulling sensation. Towards the middle tunnel. An ocean of voices, thoughts, calling. Getting louder, stronger.* I clamp my eyes shut, clutching at the armrests, struggling to hold on.

"Park?" The Comstadt's low baritone is like a boulder against the riptide. With effort, I latch onto its familiar edges.

"It's—It's happening again. The mind meld." I gasp. The words struggle past the tingle of my lips, the numbness creeping into my brain.

"Stay with me, Park." Hands grip hard on my shoulders now, not painful, but firm, unyielding.

"Fight it," he growls, his words an anchor against the strong waves pulling me out.

"Don't let go."

341

Another tether. Something to hold onto as I desperately clamber back, trying to resist the current pulling me out, pulling me under.

"Look at me, Park."

I force my eyes open to find myself looking into the depths of steel-grey eyes. The ring of ebony around the irises clear, familiar. *Focus.*

And slowly, the currents abate. The other-world voices subside. I see the shore. I can tread water again. *I will not drown this time.*

"I'm okay." I breathe out.

A look of relief washes across the Comstadt's face, his jaw unclenches, and I can feel his grip loosen ever so slightly on my arms.

"You sure?"

"Yes, I'm sure. The buzzing sensation is gone."

The Comstadt finally releases his grip on me, brushing back a lock of hair from his forehead. "Then, let's get you back to Atlas." His focus returns to the control panel. He barks into the comms unit. "Juki, Eppel, retreat back to the last wormhole coordinates. Reroute back to Atlas right away. Follow my lead and stay on your guard for Quadrati."

"Wait!" Now it's my turn to grip his arm. "I think I know which is the correct tunnel."

The Comstadt's gaze jerks back to mine. His hands freeze in midair. "What?"

"I think I know which tunnel will lead to the Quadrati home base," I elaborate, not just for him, but for myself as well.

"How?"

I think back on what I experienced, trying to find the right words. "I felt it. I saw a light. No, I heard them. The middle tunnel—that's the correct way." The words feel far from adequate but at least get the message across.

The Comstadt's eyebrows quirk up as he eyes me for several long moments. What he's thinking I can only guess. Finally, he asks, "Are you sure?"

"Positive," I say, infusing all the confidence I can into my reply. For even though it's hard to explain how I know, I really am positive that it's the correct tunnel. And I'm also trying hard not to think of the other possibility—*that I am quickly losing my mind.*

And to my amazement, the Comstadt simply nods his head and speaks into the comms unit. "Juki, Eppel. Change of plans. Park here established some sort of connection with the Quadrati neural network. She thinks the middle tunnel will lead to the Quadrati base planet. It's a risk. She may be wrong. But I for one am willing to take it. I will proceed to the next gateway. You two return to Atlas first."

A long silence pits the air around us.

"A thousand pardons, Comstadt, but that idea really stinks," Eppel replies.

"Excuse me?" the Comstadt volleys back into the comms unit.

Now it's Juki's turn to chime in. "I have to agree with Sar Eppel on this, sir. If you are willing to take the risk, then you can count me in too."

Eppel responds in kind. "Yes. If the Young Blood thinks she knows the right path, then I believe her. She's been right so far. I'm in as well."

343

The Comstadt turns to me. "And you, Park, are you sure you want to go?"

"We've already come this far. If this gives us the chance to get Keenon and Phlynnt out, then I'm willing to take that risk. Anyway, you couldn't leave me behind even if you wanted to," I say, keeping my chin up.

"Well, all right then." A hint of a smile tugs at the corners of his lips. "Let's send a homing signal so that Atlas can track us to this point. And we'd better get going before I change my mind."

LXVI

LIVI: NOT WRONG AFTER ALL

A SMALL PART OF ME WISHES I had been wrong.

Because the scene before me normally, *logically*, would have had me running for the hills by now—a swarm of Buggards by the hundreds dotting the immediate space before us like landmines, bees protecting their hive. And ensconced within the glinting grey stratum of metal, the scarred and disfigured remains of a planet. *An ancient sarcophagus.* There is no doubt in my mind that the middle tunnel did in fact spit us out near the Quadrati home base. *Lucky us.* Even more disturbing, though, is that scattered across the space between are hundreds of other glowing rings, exactly like the gateway we just came through. *Where in all hellas do all of these go?*

"Maybe this wasn't such a great idea after all." I swallow back the bitter taste rising up in my throat. This last run through the middle wormhole was just as turbulent as the others, just as wholly inconsiderate to my stomach. And the living nightmare before us isn't helping to calm the gastric juices burning up my insides either. "What do we do?"

The Comstadt's eyebrows furrow as he takes in the view, fingers thrumming along the rigid line of his jaw. Then his eyes square on mine. "We circle around the perimeter until we can find a safe place through. Fly reconnaissance and try to locate Phlynnt and Keenon in this stars-forsaken place. Odds are they are down on the planet. With our cloaking devices on, as long as we don't get too close, they'll never even suspect that we're here. We'll figure out the rest later."

At least the Comstadt sounds confident. But I'm glad for at least one thing—that despite the hordes of Buggards before us, there is not a single Hellion ship in sight. Because no Hellion ship means no Sensate Droid. And no Sensate Droid means no mind meld. And no mind meld means I can count on staying sane for at least a little while longer.

The Comstadt seems to read my thoughts. "In the meantime, we'll need to figure out how to control your mind meld. If your theory is correct, until then, we can't let you get too close to a Sensate Droid."

"Yes, I can't say that I'm terribly eager to make friends with them at this point. The farther away the better." And I was already wondering, *Why was I able to disentangle myself from the mind meld earlier?* The shift happened with the Comstadt's help. That I'm sure of. Without his voice to focus on, no doubt I would have succumbed to the pull of the Quadrati neural network as I did before. *And why did I have this cursed connection with those Droids in the first place?*

The Comstadt steers our Hawwk away from the nearest Buggard, deftly maintaining some distance as he flies the perimeter—far enough so that we won't risk running into the darn Droids, but close enough to observe.

We've circled for at least a star hour, our Hawwk still cloaked, when I begin to see it. In what I first thought to be chaotic movements, my mind now picks out a pattern. And from my Galactic training I know—*where there's a pattern, there's a way in*. The Buggards patrol the immediate space above the planet in groups, layers—the swarms crisscrossing along diagonal meridians, every space doubly protected. *Except*. Except that every tenth group of sentinel ships drops down and out over the southern pole as a new one takes its place a full minute later. And *there* is the minute-long opening we need.

"We can get in just above the southern pole. *There*." I point.

The Comstadt's gaze follows the line of my finger. And sure enough, just when the tenth sentinel group approaches, the entourage skims downward, disappearing below the thin layer of the planet's dusky red atmosphere, leaving the space wide open for a minute before a new flock flies up to take its place. "Well, I'll be a Dark Skythe's behind." The Comstadt raises an eyebrow in my direction. "How did you manage to see that?"

"Let's just say I'm good at finding patterns. Even before I became a Bionic." I'm not usually one to brag, but hey, doesn't hurt once in a while.

"And I'll bet their home base is not too far from that. Well, Park, you may turn out to be a decent Bionic after all."

"Thanks." *I think.*

The Comstadt taps on his subsonic comms link. "Juki. Eppel. Hole in Quadrati defenses just above the southern pole. A break every tenth squadron. Confirm visuals."

A few moments pass before the comms link crackles with Juki's voice. "Nice catch, Comstadt."

The Comstadt turns to me and winks. "Can't take credit for that. Our Young Blood here did it *again.*"

LXVII

LIVI: SETTLING IN

"J UKI, EPPEL. PREPARE FOR DESCENT. Follow my lead with the subsonic tracers. Park, give the signal," the Comstadt orders into the communicator.

"Okay wait—*wait*." My eyes train on the high arching tails of the Buggards down below. For the last hour we've been hovering just beyond the detectable perimeters, observing and recording the Buggard flight patterns just above the southern pole down to the millisecond, the hole's coordinates down to the exact degrees. The Droids are remarkably precise. But with their precision also comes a weakness—their predictability. From my vantage point within the clear domed underbelly of the Hawwk, the Comstadt asked me to time the descent to maximize our window, while he figured out the best trajectory through the hole past their sentinel ships down to the surface. If we don't get it just right, we'll run into the next wave of Buggards. We've got to slip in at just the right moment. Finally, after an hour of observing and planning, we're going to make our move.

The tenth fleet approaches, the bluish-grey of their tinston shells glinting against the light of the solitary star. One by one, they disappear down through the planet's noxious-looking haze that seconds as the planet's thin atmosphere.

"Almost." I breathe. At last, the subtle grey glint of the last Buggard fades below the haze. "All right, now!" I yell into the subsonic comms link.

The Comstadt pitches our cloaked Hawwk into a rapid descent at a nearly impossible angle, my head thrust back into my seat. I'm hard-pressed to move, despite my new Bionic strength. I can only hope Juki and Eppel are able to follow.

We swerve around the crisscrossing paths of two fleets of Buggards, my insides swirling with the movement. The alarms on the control panels blare. "We've reached maximum descent!" the Comstadt shouts over the frank cacophony of sounds. "Entry on three, two, one—"

The moment our Hawwk slams into the planet's atmosphere, the cabin walls shudder alive. The windows torch with searing heat. And I feel as if every single molecule of my body trembles. "Y-you sure the Hawwk will h-hold?" Even my voice yaws and pitches from the turbulence.

"Let's hope so," the Comstadt shouts over the all of the noise.

Well, that's reassuring.

The heat grows progressively hotter, brighter, the shaking so violent I clench my jaw tightly to keep my teeth from chattering. Just when I'm sure the Hawwk will break up into a thousand—no a million—small pieces, the violence suddenly calms. We're through.

I breathe a sigh of relief.

A very short sigh.

For a peek outside the window reveals the sight I have come to dread in my dreams. Through the murky haze, the planet is just as miserable as I remember—the blackened and charred ruins of a planet, stripped of all life. But a flash of metal-grey in the distance catches my eye. The Buggard squadron streaks towards the horizon. And as my eyes follow the line of their trajectory, what I see there makes me gasp. The towering metal walls of a fortress built into an even more towering mountainside. The Quadrati base. *One of them at least.* "To the right!" I call out into the comms link. "I see them!"

But to my dismay, the Comstadt rapidly steers our Hawwk in exactly the *opposite* direction.

"Wait! Why aren't we following them?"

"We've got to run reconnaissance first, Park. Can't just barge in and expect the Quadrati to hand over your friend." His voice barrels back over the line. "Right now we've got to put some distance between us."

My eyes linger towards the fortress of solid metal, which glints crimson against the dying light. *Is Keenon there? Phlynnt?* But the Comstadt is right. We came into this blind. We need more information first.

When I find my way back up to the cockpit, I find the Comstadt scanning the view outside.

"Dark infinites, what happened here?" He shakes his head. Even the Comstadt seems affected by the barren landscape as we descend below the haze. We careen over desiccated lake beds and bald craters towards a single crimson sun, which hangs low on the horizon. The planet's stark contrast to Cerulea strikes me—even our Andurian deserts are lush compared to this place. The burnt and disfigured rocks, charred land, and ancient metal ruins speak of a past full of violence, total decimation. A chill creeps up my spine that I cannot shake.

The Comstadt continues to fly us over meridiae after meridiae of barren and scarred terrain. He admits he doesn't know where in all hellas we're headed, that in fact he doesn't really even care, as long as it's far away from that base. Far enough away where we can gather information and figure out a plan to find Keenon and Phlynnt, before the Quadrati find us out first.

By my calculations, we travel well over fifty meridiae before the Comstadt finally lands us under a large outcropping of jagged rocks, the overarching slabs broad enough to hide the other Hawwks as well should the cloaking devices fail. The subsonic tracer reassures us that Juki and Eppel follow right behind.

My legs cramp as I follow the Comstadt out of our Hawwk, and I watch in no small amount of amusement as Juki and Eppel climb stiff-legged out of their Hawwks as well, ambling gingerly to where we stand. Just like the Comstadt and me, they donned their darkwing suits. *Until we analyze the planet's atmosphere, better to keep our self-sustaining darkwing suits on*, the Comstadt told me.

As Juki approaches, he rubs at his calf. "Comstadt, next time you volunteer us for an intergalactic mission, I respectfully request you upgrade us to the Hawwks with more legroom. Twenty hours in B-class wings is almost unbearable." He shakes out his leg as if to prove a point. "Even with nanobots scouring our blood."

"Fair enough, Juki," the Comstadt replies. "It has been a far longer trip than we anticipated."

"I'll say," Eppel remarks. "Next time you ask for volunteers, remind me to say no."

"Well, unfortunately for you, my esteemed mentor, it's too late to back out now. So we might as well make ourselves at home in this stars-forsaken place. Eppel, Juki, get the biodome set up while Park and I run the perimeters."

"Already got it right here, Comstadt." Eppel smiles. From his pack, Eppel pulls out a clear-plated triangular panel about as wide as his arm.

"What's a biodome?" I ask.

"You'll see," Eppel says with a wink and a smile. He walks a small distance away from us towards a flat expanse of bald and blackened ground, gritty black sand swirling as he sets the panel gently down. "You might want to step back!" he yells as he backs himself away.

The Comstadt and Juki guide me back several steps, while right before my very eyes, the single panel quadruples in size, and then starts unfolding. *Recursively.* One panel becomes four. Four panels become ten. Ten panels become nineteen, and so on. The geometric shapes ripple out and across, folding and arching back over until it forms a completely sealed and perfect geodesic dome.

This will sure beat sleeping in the cramped cockpit of the Hawwk. "Nice tent!" I shout towards Eppel, and I can't help but grin.

"See, Park, who said being a Bionic didn't have its perks. When we camp, we camp in style," Eppel hollers back. "There's even a special camouflage function. You can thank Domsei Shen for inventing that." Eppel toggles at something at his side, and the next instant the dome seems to magically disappear into the dusky black surroundings.

A smile tugs at even the Comstadt's lips. "Good work, Eppel. Looks like your eons-old nanobots are still functioning after all. Now you and Juki finish setting up the equipment in the biodome while Park and I scout."

"Don't need to ask me twice, Comstadt. Sooner I get out of this darkwing suit, the better," Juki replies, pulling at his helmet.

"Park, with me. Keep your darkwing suit on. Let's make sure you don't sense any Droids."

I've been just about to crawl out of my own skin being cooped up so long. I'm eager to stretch my legs. "Ready to fly whenever you are," I say.

The Comstadt and I make a run in our darkwing suits. And despite the grim surroundings, it feels good to be up in the air. We scour the perimeters at least ten meridiae out in a full circumference—no sign of the Quadrati, and not even a hint of the buzzing niggles at the base of my brain. Once the Comstadt is satisfied that our campsite will be safe from detection, we head back.

I would have been hard-pressed to find our biodome again were it not for Eppel's red pack, which lies out in plain view. The biodome's camouflage makes the dome and everything within blend seamlessly with the charred and blackened terrain surrounding it. Luckily, the Comstadt also has a special device that illuminates the entrance. When we finally get inside, Juki and Eppel not only have set up the biodome fully, but Juki has also prepared a pot full of stew, hot steam rising from where it sits on a makeshift table.

"Find anything?" Juki asks.

The Comstadt steers me into a remarkably comfortable seat at the table. "Not a darn rattling thing." He takes a seat next to mine. "There's not a Droid in sight for at least ten meridiae."

"And that's a good thing," Eppel remarks, his voice muffled. Only his feet stick out from under a panel of instruments that he works at on the far side of the dome.

"Looks like you and Eppel have accomplished quite a bit around here," the Comstadt remarks, his nose sniffing the air. "Let me guess. Mullet fish stew."

"Well, it was the only decent food I could find in our freeze-dried stash, and I'm afraid it won't taste quite as good as when Chef Aton makes it. But it was either mullet fish or keeva beans, and I don't think any of us want to risk eating that tonight since we'll be stuck in the biodome together. Methane buildup in small quarters, not a pleasant situation to be stuck in." Juki places steaming bowls in front of me and the Comstadt.

"Thanks, Juki. I don't think my stomach cares what I shove in there at this point," I reply as I scoop up my first bite, my stomach simultaneously rumbling loudly in agreement, making us all laugh.

"I'm impressed, Magnar." The Comstadt chews and swallows as he nods approvingly. "Mullet fish stew has never really been my thing, but you did a good job with this one."

After the meal, I prepare to settle into the biodome for the night, which to my amazement spans the width of all three Hawwk's put together, far more spacious than the cramped quarters of the cockpit. And I have to admit, the quarters are surprisingly comfortable. Eppel has set up sleeping bunks for us, which hover just slightly off the floor. There's even a small toiletry area sectioned off for privacy. But the best part is that the biodome allows me to shed my darkwing suit, which, after a few hours of sweat and wear, has become annoyingly itchy in all the wrong places.

"Stars, it feels good to get out of that thing," I say as I step out of the makeshift bathroom, more comfortable now in the fitted jumpsuit I changed into after our meal. That's when I notice Juki and Eppel standing by the door to the biodome, suited up with their darkwing helmets in hand.

"Where are you going?" I ask.

"Juki and Eppel will fly reconnaissance first tonight," the Comstadt replies.

Juki and Eppel? Wait a minute. "But I think *I* should go too. I may be able to sense the Quadrati through the neural network." After all, I didn't travel halfway across the universe just to sit on my behind. I start heading back to the makeshift bathroom to change back into my suit.

The Comstadt's firm hand on my shoulder stops me.

"Don't worry, Park. You'll get your chance. But first we need to go over everything you remember about the Quadrati home base, the Sensate Droids, while the others do a preliminary perimeter scout of the structure we saw earlier."

Well, what the Comstadt says certainly does sound reasonable. But I'm still eager to get out there.

The Comstadt drops his hand from my shoulder and turns to Eppel and Juki.

"Map out all possible access points into the Quadrati base. See if you can pick up Phlynnt's tracker, but by no means are you to engage any Droids. I will launch our biodetector sphere and run planetary statistics while you're gone."

Sar Eppel nods. "Understood, Comstadt. Your old tutor isn't as decrepit as you may think. I still have a few old tricks up my sleeve."

"Of that I have no doubt," the Comstadt replies. "Any sign of danger, head back. If you cannot locate any access points by daybreak tomorrow, then I want you and Juki to return to the biodome. No matter what, we need to relay the information about the Quadrati home planet back to the Domseis, and I'd rather not leave this planet without the two of you. Understood?"

"Yes, Comstadt. If all goes well, we should be back before morning."

"Very well then. May the stars guide you." The Comstadt nods solemnly first to Magnar Juki and then to Sar Eppel. Only the slight lingering of the Comstadt's eyes on his old mentor betrays any concern.

"And you as well, Comstadt," Sar Eppel replies.

Without any further commotion, Eppel and Juki put on their darkwing helmets and head out the door.

Some of us are born to be scientists, and others born to be teachers, filonials, musicians, doctors, engineers, pilots, astrophysicists, elematicians, botanists. But all of us, no matter who we are, are also born to be dreamers. To not only live in the current reality but to dream of a new and better reality, of all that is possible. To create and to cultivate. That is what makes us human. That is what makes us special in this vast and unfeeling heap of elements called the universe.

(Excerpt from *The Thoughts and Memoirs of Livinthea Park*, star year 8117)

LXVIII

LIVI: RETURN

"**S**TARS ALIVE. Can this be possible?" The Comstadt's voice startles me from just an arm's length away on his hovering cot, where he has just barely lain down for the last few minutes.

I would never admit it out loud, but his solid presence has been reassuring to me on this strange and foreign world. It's been several hours since Sar Eppel and Magnar Juki left, and the biodome has been our haven amidst the barrenness. The Comstadt and I have spent the time setting up and launching Mistletoe. The biodetector sphere now glows almost imperceptibly as it hovers high above our heads.

The solitary yellow dwarf has since dipped below the horizon, the daytime haze dissipated, leaving a remarkably clear night sky. We finally allowed ourselves a few moments of respite, and lie on our individual cots, staring up at the twinkling of stars that are unfamiliar to me. The clear panels of our portable biodome protect us remarkably well from the cold outside yet give us a full

360-degree unobstructed view of our surroundings. I turn to find Triton propped up by his elbows, neck craned skyward.

His eyes roam the expansive sky above, brows furrowed as he continues to mumble to himself. "Scorpius. Lyra. Andromeda. Equuleus. Stars, even Camelopardalis—" His voice drifts off, and it takes some effort to catch what he's saying.

"What?"

But Triton is too lost in thought to hear me.

I ask again, this time louder. "Triton, what are you talking about?"

He looks back at me, the usually rigid line of his brows arched. "The World of Origins. I never thought we'd find it."

The World of Origins? My mind fumbles for the stories Grandpa Wren used to tell, about the home planet where humans came from over a millennium ago during the Great Dispersion. But from what I remember, knowledge of its location was lost forever.

"Where?" I ask. I shift against the smooth canvas of my floating cot and search the night sky, looking for something I recognize. But my talent for remembering patterns is completely useless with constellations I've never seen before.

"I think we may be on it."

It takes me a moment to process what Comstadt's seemingly simple words mean, what he's implying. My eyes flash first to his face, taking in the wonder written in the charcoal-grey of his eyes, and then out to the deeply shadowed lands beyond our biodome, a place where wind howls against wind with nothing but echoes to hold onto.

"You mean you think *this*"—I struggle in my own disbelief—"this *is* the World of Origins, where we first came from?"

Triton hesitates a moment but then nods solemnly. His gaze pivots back to the constellations above. "I couldn't see the stars at first, through all the haze. And I never would have thought that this"—he sits completely up as he peers outside in wonder, sweeping his arms out widely to encompass the rocky shadows beyond the clear panels of our habitat—"could be the World of Origins. Things are so different from the holograms we studied about the old world. It was said that when humans left the original world a millennium ago, though conditions were dire, the planet was still habitable, there were still at least a few living patches of life. Now there's nothing. Absolutely nothing." He shakes his head. "But the constellations don't lie. They are the same. I memorized the Domseis' ancient star maps as a Young Blood. This has *got* to be the World of Origins."

World of Origins? So many questions barrel into my mind, but one question begs to be answered first. "But if this is the World of Origins, what are the Quadrati doing on it, and what happened to the humans?"

The Comstadt thinks on it for a long while, his face tilted up towards the dim light of a single lonely moon. "It is possible that the Droids are the descendants of the original bots."

"What do you mean?" I ask.

"Based on the stories Eppel and the Domseis have told of the World of Origins, before humans left, robots with artificial intelligence had just been developed. In fact, we had brought some of these bots with us to help terraform

Cerulea. But like your helper bot Jasella, their abilities only reached so far. Neural plasticity, the ability to adapt and change, that's what sets humans apart from the bots. We've never been able to fully develop that ability in our own bots." The Comstadt rubs at the light stubble along his jawline. "Perhaps after humans left the World of Origins, the bots that were left behind found a way to survive. Perhaps they evolved to form a functional— albeit aggressive and brutal—society over the last millennium as the Quadrati."

One of the many instruments the Comstadt set up pings loudly from the far side of the biodome, jarring us from our pondering. The Comstadt heaves himself out of his cot as I join him.

"What's going on?" I peer down at the flashing screen that the Comstadt looks at.

"The receiver for Mistletoe. It's done collecting the first round of planetary data."

Triton glances over the stream of numbers coming through from the biodetector sphere, shaking his head. "Oxygen levels are only 12.8%. The atmosphere here is just barely breathable. Luckily we have the help of our nanobots. Still we will be better off in our darkwing suits outside of the biodome. How this planet even manages to have an iota of oxygen is beyond me. There's not a single green thing in sight."

"Perhaps the Quadrati are generating it somehow."

"Could be," Triton replies, rubbing at his chin. He rambles on. "Nitrogen 9.2%, carbon dioxide 69.76%, argon 1.7%, carbon monoxide .91%, krypton 0.88%, and"—Triton pauses as he presses his face closer to the panel—"solinium 4.75%? That's very strange."

"What do you mean?"

"Solinium is not a natural element, but a byproduct of nuclear fusion. To be found in such large quantities is extremely unusual."

"Maybe on this planet it *is* natural."

"Unlikely. Generating even an ounce of solinium requires vast amounts of energy, more than the power of several suns combined. And as far as I can tell, the only energy source here is that small yellow dwarf of a star."

The screen pings loudly again.

"And more good news," Triton mutters sarcastically as he continues to look over the numbers that the planetary scanner generates. "No detectable surface water, but the ultrasonic sensor shows that deep pools of water exist. Only problem is that they are so far underground that we'd be digging forever before we reached them."

The Comstadt shakes his head again. "Like I said, pretty much uninhabitable. Who knows what might have happened if humans hadn't left this stars-forsaken place during the Great Dispersion."

"Let's hope Eppel and Juki return soon before we find out even more good news. The sooner we get ourselves out of here, the better." I peer out through the biodome's clear panels, once again in awe of the possibility that this is where our ancestors might have come from. It was said that the World of Origins was once like an oasis in the vast emptiness of space-time. A place where life had been born and thrived in so many different shapes and forms. A single birth planet teaming with life, harboring millions of different species, a far greater variety than we have on Cerulea.

But from what I have seen of the planet today, it's almost impossible to believe that now.

LXIX

LIVI: WORLD OF ORIGINS

BEFORE WE TURN IN for the night, the Comstadt and I busy ourselves verifying and double-checking the data from the planetary scanner. Take a run in our darkwing suits to recheck the perimeters. Clean off the solar arrays for our Hawwk generator. Stay busy as much as we can. Because once these tasks are done, there is nothing left to do amidst the barrenness. Nothing to do except worry.

As if sensing my unease, the Comstadt kindly offers me a plate of holliberry biscuits and warm calanthi tea as I rest on my cot.

Grateful for the diversion, I take a bite of the sweet biscuits and look towards Triton, the light still dancing in his eyes after his revelation. "I still can't believe you memorized every single constellation from the old world. What did you call that one again? The one shaped like a person with a belt?"

"Orion, otherwise known as the hunter of the sky. In the old civilizations of the ancient world, hunters and warriors wore skirts."

"How very strange. It seems as if that would be rather limiting and not terribly protective." Glad I didn't live back then. Give me a sturdy pair of pants anytime. Who would want to come face to face with a Droid while wearing a skirt? I'd skin my knees for sure.

The Comstadt laughs and continues describing things he learned about the World of Origins from the Domseis. I didn't realize that most of the Domseis were amongst the original Bionics, chosen as children to undergo the nanobot transfusion because of their Mark of Dresden mutations, then groomed to be elite explorers, colonist of a new world to ensure the habitability of Cerulea well before the arrival of the other colonists. And the tales the Comstadt tells of the World of Origins are nothing short of riveting—aquatic animals that dwarfed my Hawwk, carnivorous plants that ate insects, land animals with necks and proboscises as long as Psyla trees are tall. Some of these species were brought by our ancestors to Cerulea, but many were left behind. His tales are like a peek back into the folds of time, to a place with creatures, customs, and ways of life wholly unfamiliar to me, including a nighttime sky so similar and yet so different from our own. When I look past the panels of the biodome into the shadows beyond, it's hard to believe that humans once came from here. "What made you want to learn about them?"

"Basic curiosity. Have you never wondered about the hows and whys of the world? Where we come from? How we came to be? It's an eternal question that most people have at least once in their lifetime. And being a Bionic means I have a long time to figure things out. To learn not only about our own constellations on Cerulea but also the ancient ones if I want to."

"So you memorized the constellations of an ancient world?"

"It helps that the nanobots enhance our memory. But yes. As Bionics, the questions of the universe are open to us. We have an enormous amount of time to 'figure things out,' if you will. What you'll come to realize, Livi, is that as a Bionic, you are no longer limited to a few goals, a few experiences to be crammed into a single limited lifetime. One can have many purposes, wear many hats, learn an infinite number of things. As a Bionic you will have a lot of time on your hands. Might as well make the most of it."

The Comstadt and I continue philosophizing until our words slowly drift off into the twinkling of stars above, the passage of time and life marked only by the gently shifting points of light in the sky.

LXX

LIVI: DROID ARMY

THE ABRUPT CRACKLING of static startles me from the haze of half asleep. I must have dozed off.

Scrambling out of my cot, I find the Comstadt already hunched over the subtle green glow of the comms unit that he set up earlier along the far wall of the biodome.

". . . connection's patchy, but I can hear you now, Magnar. Go ahead."

Juki's voice sputters in and out over the comms link. ". . . found something, Comstadt. Sar Eppel thinks you should come see this."

"Please elaborate."

"Eppel's gone to take a closer look. We came upon . . . about a kilometer from the Quadrati base near the . . . perimeter. I had no idea they were so . . ." A sharp intake of breath. Juki's suddenly frantic voice pitches out, "Eppel! Behind you! Watch out . . . skyvers!" The sound of running footsteps. The wild flapping of cloth against wind. Juki's voice wanes distantly, but the panic in his voice blares clear as all hellas. "Eppel!" A powerful bang explodes across the line. Then all goes eerily silent.

"Juki?" The Comstadt's hands fly over the comms device in a futile effort to get the link back. "Spitting Skythes." The Comstadt bolts up. His worried eyes flash to mine. "Get your darkwing suit on. We're heading out. Now."

***

"Keep your eyes open, Park." The Comstadt and I perch low behind an outcropping of rocks rimming a wide basin. The planet's solitary sun already sits just above the horizon in the burgeoning crimson sky. It has taken us a good several hours to finally track Juki and Eppel's tracer to just outside the northern perimeter of the base. The goliath that is the Quadrati base looms to the south, a massive perimeter wall surrounding it. A mountainous range towers due west.

The Comstadt sweeps the tracking device through the drizzle of sand swirling around us, first towards the scarred remains of an ancient ruin, arches of rust scraping up towards the sky, then back towards the sandstone slabs rising behind us.

The desiccated land around feels like a thirsty pit. I'm thankful for my helmet, otherwise I'd be drowning in dust and sand by now. Lucky for us, our darkwing suits bear the brunt of the planet's harsh climate.

The Comstadt's gaze dissects the mangled terrain of the deep basin before us. "There's a lot of interference from neutrino particles, but their signal's definitely here." He squints westward against the rays of the lonely sun.

The ground is still so hot it shimmers underneath our feet.

Before I can even blink, the Comstadt pitches up into the crimson sky, the flaps of his darkwing suit flaring behind his powerful frame, and I do my best to keep up. From this vantage point, the basin is a graveyard of colossal proportions—broken metal heaps stretching towards the dwarf sun and megaliths protruding from raw sediment. I really don't want to think about what might have happened to Eppel and Juki, but my mind has never been one to obey my will, and so the thoughts come unbeckoned. "Could be a trap."

The Comstadt nods in agreement as his gaze slices across the ruins. "I don't like it either. Be on the lookout for anything unusual."

From up high, a glimmer amongst the faded sandstone catches my eye, and I swoop down towards it. What I find, partially buried under a layer of silt, makes my breath catch—an orling, the severed ends of an intricately woven Felovian chain straggling limply from it. Gingerly, I pick it up.

"*Dark infinites*, that's Juki's." The Comstadt lands next to me, dusty red billowing up beneath him. His eyebrows notch as he looks down at the orling, its usually fierce electrical storm within dulled to a whimpering sizzle. "He's still alive, but injured. *Badly.*"

"How in Dresden do you know that?"

"A Bionic's orling not only helps us monitor the Ritarian Gateways but also acts as a biosensor, even if separated from its owner. From its nanometrics, I can tell the bots in his system are using a tremendous amount of energy, so much in fact that they may burn out. But I've still got a reading from Eppel's orling." He looks down at his tracker shaking his head. "His nanometrics are going haywire too. My old mentor may have survived a millennium, but even he has his limits. We've got to find them. *Soon.*" The Comstadt sweeps the tracker device in another wide circle. He doesn't show much outward emotion, but from the grim set of his mouth, I know he's worried.

A shudder ripples through me as my eyes follow his, uneasiness sitting in my stomach like a bouldering rock. What happened here eons ago was clearly nothing short of catastrophic. Metal torn from metal. Slabs of what must have been high-reaching walls reduced to rubble. Desperation, calamity, mass extinction clearly written across the dusty ruins. I may as well be walking through a necropolis.

The Comstadt and I scour the hidden crevices between the jagged remains for further clues about what might have happened. But the ages-old sediment and sand surrender nothing else, not even a measly old footprint. I catch some air, scanning the area around the torn and broken edifices, ancient creatures clawing for the surface. From this vantage point, I notice a broadly diagonal pattern faintly etched into a slab of rust along the outer perimeters, something I hadn't noticed up close before. There's something oddly familiar about the pattern. But when I descend towards the metal grate to take a closer look, a sudden niggling sparks at the base of my brain, quickly growing, spreading, clawing its way deep to my very core. *Stars, not now.*

I'm about a hundred meters up, and it's all I can do not to plummet like Juthri's stone the rest of the way down to the basin floor. By the time I land, the buzzing sensation is so strong it makes me falter to the ground hard onto my knees.

The Comstadt is by my side in an instant, a firm grip on my shoulders, his face a hairsbreadth from mine. "Park? You all right?"

I can barely reply. "Th-the Quadrati, I think they're close. It's that strange feeling again."

The Comstadt immediately hauls me to my feet. "You think you can make it to that alcove?" He points towards the steep mountainside to the east, several hundred meters away.

I grapple with the current that's pulling me under, struggling for something to hold onto. *The Comstadt's familiar baritone voice. Focus. Breathe.* "I think I can—" I start to say, but the orphaned words die in my throat as the pull surges. The edges of my vision falter. Voices clamor at me, a parent to a lost child. Urgent. *Livinthea. Livinthea!*

Vaguely, I feel powerful arms encircling my waist, being pressed against a solid form. "Hold on, Livi." The vibration from the Comstadt's chest rumbles close to my ear, but his words travel as if from half a star away. My grasp of the here and now slips like water through a sieve. I'm being swept up into the air. But to my relief, as we pitch higher and higher, the niggling at the base of my brain wanes. The current abates. The deluge of thoughts into my mind slows. Gradually, my thoughts are mine again. But only when we reach the outcropping of rocks does the dust fully clear. Soon I feel solid ground underneath my feet again.

***

"Easy, Park." The Comstadt turns me in his arms until I face him, one hand planted firmly at my back, another solidly gripping my elbow. His brows furrow and his jaw draws rigid lines as he surveys me from head to toe. "That's it. Steady."

I take a shaky breath, though I can't help but grimace at the throbbing blooming at my temples. Vaguely I become aware of the dizzying height of where we've landed, the notched precipice of a mountain, the basin of ruins now far below us.

"That's it." The Comstadt's voice is low, steadying.

One breath in. Another breath out. The trembling in my legs gradually subsides, and I nod at him and straighten. "I-I'm okay now."

Still, several moments pass before he relinquishes his grip at my elbow and turns to survey the ground below. But the scene before us is just as dead as before, completely silent except for the eerie sighing of the wind. Not a Quadrati in sight. *What in all hellas just happened to me? Stars, am I losing my mind?*

My eyes square down upon the deserted ruins. My face heats as I mumble, "Sorry, Comstadt. Perhaps I overreacted."

"It's okay, Park." As he speaks, the Comstadt turns to survey our surroundings. "This stars-forsaken place can get to anyone. As soon as you catch your—" The Comstadt's eyes widen. "Infinite black holes," he breathes.

I turn to follow his gaze past the crags of jutting rocks down the *other* side of the mountain. *Infinite black holes indeed.*

Droids. *A whole army of them.* Stretching across the flat plains below out to the budding dawn like a living nightmare. Galactic and even Atlas would be no match for this army of Droids. This must be what Juki tried to warn us about.

But what is more frightening, what sends slithering snakes down my spine, is that I have seen this before. The image still remains seared like hot coals in my mind—the time I passed out when Keenon and I were captured by the Quadrati. *From that dream.* At least I thought it was a dream. Now I'm not so sure. What could be the meaning of it all? Could this be mere coincidence?

Just as in the dream, the throng of Droids seem oddly frozen in place. "What's wrong with those draggarts? It's like a graveyard down there."

The Comstadt narrows his eyes down at the motionless Droids below, his voice grim. "Or more like a hatching ground."

Before I can ponder his comment further, a flash of movement at the base of the mountain catches my eye, the ground shuddering open there. What emerges in the next moment makes my veins run cold. The telltale flash of tinston against the cutting blades of the morning sun.

"Get down. Quickly," the Comstadt whispers urgently as he pushes me down behind two edges of jutting rock, but not before my mind confirms what I've just seen. Not before my innards sink down to the bottom of Pan's bottomless ocean. Another Droid. But not just any Droid. One taller and darker than all the rest. A slash of red marks his chest. Gardurak. The Master Sensate Droid.

Just what we need.

From the way the Comstadt's eyes widen, he recognizes him too. Peeking between the edges, I can see that the Sensate is not alone. What follows in rapid succession is not just a second Droid, but a third, fourth—tenth. *Ten too many.* Pouring out like angry ants from a hill and carrying strange crossbow-like apparatuses that I've never seen before. But what is clear is that we are sorely outnumbered.

"Boiling suns above. Must be an underground city under there. And pretty extensive from the looks of it," the Comstadt whispers under his breath, then turns to me. "Activate camouflage. We're dead if they catch sight of us." The Comstadt reaches for his own camouflage device as he crouches beside me. "Those skyvers can blast off your toes from several hundred meters away and melt through your skin before you can even blink. Even our nanobots are no match for them."

My pulse accelerates, but I will myself not to hyperventilate. *Keep it together, Livi. You heard the Comstadt, activate your camouflage device. You'll be fine.* I fumble for the camouflage activator—press it once, twice. But not a single thing happens. *Not a single darn thing.* And that's when I notice that the Comstadt is also having trouble with his. The lock of white hair over his furrowed brow and his powerfully built frame right next to me is as clear as day.

"Dark infinites," the Comstadt curses. "Something's jamming our camouflage devices. There's too much electrical interference here." His eyes bore into mine. "We have no choice now, Park. If they sniff us out, be prepared to fight."

LXXI

LIVI: THE UNIVERSE WATCHES

TRAPPED.

That one word stands clear in my mind. With a mountain range stretched at our backs, our camouflage out of commission, there is nowhere to go without revealing ourselves. If the Droids so much as glance in our direction, we're goners. There's just too many of them, and their skyvers could obliterate us in an instant. Still, my wishful thinking tells me that we're high enough. That surely the Droids won't make their way up the jagged edges of the mountain. That they won't find us.

The Droids converge around the Sensate on the rubble below where we were standing only moments before. "What do you think they're doing?" I whisper towards the Comstadt.

The Comstadt's voice is so low I can barely hear what he says even with my Bionic hearing. "We must have triggered a perimeter sensor." His eyes scan back over the ruins, and after a long moment he continues. "There."

The Comstadt points down towards the base of the mountain. "Missed seeing it before because of all the dust."

At first I see nothing, and without my Bionic vision I still would have missed it. But there, a few feet from where we found Juki's orling, glows the dull red of a sensor. "I see it," I whisper. No doubt I triggered it earlier. And where there's one sensor, there's bound to be more. I scan the ruins further. They're easy to pick out now. "Sensors, all along the perimeter."

"Eppel and Juki must have been taken by surprise too." The Comstadt points his tracker device down towards the base of the mountain. "Just as I suspected, signal's stronger there. Eppel and Juki must be underground somewhere." The Comstadt shakes his head but stiffens as he turns back towards the Droids.

My eyes flash down the path of his gaze. The Sensate's ashen gold arm slices through the air in rapid succession, ordering the Droids off in various directions. Two head out to the basin's farthest reach, two towards the tangle of metal arches, two along the array of stony monoliths and four—*four in our direction.*

So much for wishful thinking.

"Get behind me." The Comstadt's voice is low, urgent. "If they get past the ledge, I'll take out as many as I can. You've got to fly like the dark infinites are on your tail. Reactivate your camouflage. There's a good chance it will work once you're past the electromagnetic field surrounding these ruins. Get yourself back to our Hawwk and back to Atlas. Tell them what we've learned."

Wait a minute, my mind protests. "I can't just leave you."

"That's an order, Park."

"What? *No.*"

"*No?*" Triton's head whips towards me. "This is not the time to be stubborn, Park."

"Let's *both* make a run for it," I argue. I don't want to leave him. Suddenly, *he* means *too much* to me. My insides squeeze at the thought of what might happen to him if—

Triton shakes his head. "They're too close already. I'll barely be able to give you enough time to make a run for it as it is."

"But—"

He puts a hand on my shoulder, the solid pressure there making me still. "There's no time to waste, Livi." The Comstadt looks me squarely in the eye with those steel-grey eyes of his. "We Bionics have been searching for the Quadrati home base for too many years now. And Atlas needs to know about that army of Droids. Who knows what those draggarts are planning? One of us needs to make it back to warn Atlas." His gaze softens for a moment. "And that one of us is you. I have a better chance to fend them off. Give you enough time to escape."

Before I can protest further, the rapidly growing sound of clanking metal sends both our gazes down the mountainside.

What I see makes my stomach lurch, bile surging up into my throat. Within the span of a few seconds, the Droids have already ascended halfway past the jagged rocks that litter the mountainside as if they were mere pebbles.

Stars, I can't do it. I don't want to do it. I know Atlas needs to know about the Quadrati home base, but I can't just abandon the Comstadt. He would surely die, Bionic or not.

The Droids are almost upon us now, the rims of their pulsatile eyes close enough to see, their skyvers at the ready. The hairs on my arms stand as an electrical pulse courses through me, sending my thoughts spinning.

"Get ready." The Comstadt's voice rumbles low, his body tense, muscles coiled, a tiger ready to spring.

I fist my hands at my sides to keep them from shaking as I crouch behind the Comstadt. I'm so wound up I can hardly breathe. My insides tick at breakneck speed. My thoughts hurtle and pitch, mind buzzing like a thousand flies. This can't happen. Not like this. *Get back. Get back, you draggarts. Leave us the hellas alone.* I will not abandon the Comstadt. I just won't.

And just as the sheen of tinston peeks above the jagged ledge an arm's breadth away from us, the crunch of their feet on loose rocks palpable, abruptly the Droids stutter to a halt. The air runs still. Time holds its breath. Clenching my fists, I will the Droids to go no further. *That's right. Stop. Go back. There's nothing here for you to see.* In my mind's eye the Droids turn and leave, back down the way they came.

A few long moments pass. My heart pounds so loudly that I'm afraid the Droids will hear. But to my amazement, inexplicably, the Droids slowly pivot back, the metal indentations of their heads glinting against sunlight, then disappearing from sight.

The Comstadt and I hold our positions, my muscles close to cramping as the Droids trail back down the mountainside, just as quickly as they ascended.

"What in the dark infinites?" the Comstadt murmurs beside me. The Comstadt and I exchange looks of disbelief. "Don't tell me that was just a lucky break."

"Or perhaps the universe is looking out for us," I reply, shaking my head in wonder. "Whatever it is, I'll take it."

We sit in silence as the Droids below scour the ruins for a few more minutes. To my relief, not long afterwards, Gardurak heads back into the tunnel with the other Droids following. Soon the flash of tinston from the last Droid is swallowed into the ground they came from. The doors of the tunnel start to slide closed.

Suddenly the Comstadt surges up next to me, uncoiling like a spring. A flash of metal leaves his hand and hurtles down through the air below.

My gaze snaps to his. "What are you doing?"

The Comstadt turns to me with a gleam in his eye. "Getting in."

***

"Head back to the Hawwks and fly yourself back to Atlas," the Comstadt orders.

"What about you?" I ask.

"Juki and Eppel are in serious trouble. I have to go and try to help them." He glances down at Juki's orling. "The dark infinites only know if I'm already too late."

"If you're going in, then I'm going in as well. My friend is in there too, remember?"

The Comstadt shakes his head. "Not only is this dangerous, Livi, but someone also needs to get back to Atlas and warn them about that Droid army. I'll try to find your friend if I can."

"How about I stay here, and you can go back?" I challenge. There is no way in hellas I'm going back now. "I have just as many nanobots running through my veins as you."

"That's completely out of the question. I am certainly not going to leave you here to fend for yourself. You're just a Young Blood, for star's sake." The Comstadt shakes his head. "Were you *born* this stubborn, Park?"

"I guess you just bring out the best in me." I smile sweetly.

The Comstadt throws me an exasperated look. "Well, then I suppose we have no choice. But the moment you feel that strange sensation again, let me know. It may help us steer clear of the Droids, the Sensates at the very least."

The Comstadt looks down towards the basin now bathed in quiet. Even the primal wind has gone to sleep. The dwarf star has sunk below the horizon, and the unfamiliar constellations twinkling in the sky are our sole companions.

The Comstadt looks at me grimly. "Ready?"

"Let's do it." I muster a small nod, though my insides roil and buck.

I follow the Comstadt as he glides through the air down to the metal grate, this time picking our way more carefully to avoid activating the perimeter sensors again.

When we land next to the grate, what I see astonishes me.

The Comstadt's baton wedged between the two sliding doors of the grate, keeping it ever so slightly open.

"H-how'd you do that?"

"That's the beauty of being a Bionic. Strength. Precision. Impeccable reflexes. Anything is possible."

"I'll say." I watch in wonder as he pries the doors open, his powerful arms barely straining.

"After you." He smiles.

LXXII

LIVI: THE MAZE

"**E**PPEL'S SIGNAL is getting stronger, but there's still a crazy amount of interference from the neutrinos."

Triton continues to sweep his tracker device, trying to navigate the maze of tunnels we've found ourselves in. "Any of this look familiar to you, Livi?"

I'm still adjusting to the periodic dim of amber lights and trying not to jump at my own recursive shadow. "I was really only halfway conscious the last time I was here." I shake my head. "I don't remember any of this at all."

"Then we'll just have to go by what we do know." The Comstadt sweeps his tracker in wide arcs in front of him. "Signal's definitely getting stronger down here. This way. Quickly." The Comstadt proceeds down the darkened tunnel. We turn down passage after passage, following Eppel's signal.

At a junction of three tunnels, Triton abruptly stops in front of me, quickly herding me back into an alcove in the tunnel we just came from. A finger presses to his lips. The warning flashes clear in his steel-grey eyes. I don't even dare breathe. Barely a moment later, the synchronized thud of patrolling Droids echoes. Louder. Closer. *Too close.* How many? I can't see with Triton's hulking form pressed in front of me.

Finally, I can feel Triton's taut muscles relax ever so slightly as we cautiously step out of the alcove.

And for the next kilometer or so, this is how it progresses. A few steps forward, several steps back.

But thanks to Triton's well-honed senses, we manage to dodge five more Droids and seven Dogger bots patrolling the tunnels in the process.

And though I could swear by the stars above that I don't recognize any of the passages, as we get deeper into the tunnels, a feeling of foreboding unease creeps into me.

Just as we approach a bend, my stomach and insides squeeze tightly. Something just doesn't feel right, but not like before when we encountered the Sensates. I can't pinpoint it. I hesitate.

"Park?" The Comstadt turns. "You all right?"

"Sorry," I say. "Just the jitters." *Shake it off*, I tell myself.

"Hurry then, we're getting close. Signals practically blaring here." The Comstadt presses forward, and I lose sight of him as his voice echoes back around the bend.

I force my feet forward, but just as I round the corner I smash right into something hard and solid. *The Comstadt's back.* And suddenly he's shoving me backwards. "Get back, Livi! You don't want to see this."

"What? What are you talking about?" I push past the Comstadt, only to halt of my own accord. *Hellas above.*

384

A vast chamber below, with rows upon rows of clear pods as far as my Bionic eyes can see. Electrical currents undulate over and around the pods in wide swathes of flowing colors—each river of electricity a different color. The sight could almost be beautiful, except for the fact that—my heart stutters at the realization—underneath the currents of color, there are *people* in the pods. Hundreds of them. Eyes closed. Nonmoving. As still as death.

And in the pod closest to me, under a river that sizzles dark blue, is a young man with the same jet-black hair and scruffy brows that I've known since childhood.

Keenon.

Stars no.

He looks paler than normal. But I know it's him. I surge forward, only to be yanked swiftly back.

"No, Livi!" Comstadt's firm voice growls low in my ear, his grip on my arm unyielding as I continue struggling forward. "There are Droids stationed along the perimeters."

And only then do I notice the Droid sentries posted underneath the wide metal rafters, their tinston faces halfway hidden under the shadows with only the pulsing of their eyes barely visible.

It takes every ounce of effort to stop myself from bolting down there to save my friend. But Triton is right, there are too many Droids. "What are those draggarts doing to them? Are they still alive?"

"I don't know. I've never seen anything like this before." The Comstadt's grip on me finally loosens as his eyes scan across the chamber. "Where did all these people come from? We've kept track of all the Quadrati attacks on Cerulea, the number of captures and casualties over

385

the last millennium. There can't have been more than a few dozen. How could the Quadrati have taken so many people?" He shakes his head, eyebrows notched as he surveys the chamber below.

It's only after my Bionic eyes home in on the people in the various pods farther out that I realize some of them look *different*. *Really different*. "Perhaps they're not all from Cerulea at all. Look there." I point to a young girl in a pod several rows past Keenon's under a current of pulsing yellow, her long hair cascading in waves of royal purple past her shoulders, the skin on her bare arms speckled with lavender stars. And in the pod next to her bathed under a current of crimson, a young man with pale green skin the shade of polished jade stone.

The Comstadt keeps his voice low. "A few ancient texts described a wormhole network much more extensive than what we know of the Ritarian Gateways." Triton turns to me in wonder. "We assumed they had been destroyed, but perhaps this is proof that they still exist. These other humanoids must come from other worlds we don't even know about."

Stars, could it be true? My hairs stand on end and my mind replays the hazy memories from when I was captured, trying to piece together the various images with what I see before me now. *Keenon and me blacking out. The live wire pod the Droids shoved me into. I could very well have been one of them.* "Maybe that's what they were trying to do to me before I escaped. It could be me in one of those pods." I turn to Triton. "I'm not leaving without him. I've got to get Keenon out—and all of those people. We've got to find a way to get them out too. *All of them*."

"Agreed." Triton nods. "Livi, is there anything else you—"

But before the Comstadt can finish, a sudden movement along the far left chamber catches our attention—a group of Dogger bots flanked by four Droids. The Doggers tow two pods, one clear but unlit, the other opaque. As they round the perimeter closer to us and I'm able to glimpse what's inside, it's all I can do not to curse out loud. *Dark Skythes. We're too late.*

For inside the clear pod is a flawless face topped by a mop of brown hair, a comet of white streaking through it, a face we know so well, *Sar Eppel.* His orling dangles dully at his neck where his darkwing suit hangs half torn. The Comstadt surges forward beside me, and now it's my turn to pull him back. "No, Triton!"

But the Doggers don't drag the pods to the main rows of pods. Instead they haul them towards a group of about fifty pods that seem separate from all the rest.

Though I want to, I can't pull my eyes away from the scene unfolding before me. The Doggers line up Eppel's pod perfectly into place. The Doggers have just barely backed away when a surge of ashen gold charges towards Eppel's pod, encasing it in rivulets of sizzling electricity. Eppel's body within jerks ever so slightly, then lies deathly still again as a blazing current of color ripples forth from his pod towards others in the chamber, bleeding a stream of sizzling magenta into the river of currents where there was none before. Before I can even blink, a second flash of magenta streaks up from Eppel's pod, curling and twisting in the air, then shooting down into the opaque pod beside him. Next to me, Triton is

387

like a taut spring ready to uncoil. It's all I can do to keep him rooted in place.

The opaque pod, which was so dark before, begins to glow; dimly at first, then bright as the midday sun. Just when I think it's going to burst into a flaming ball of fire, the lid cracks open. I suck in a breath at what emerges. A Droid. Blades of magenta light streak out between the joints and gaps of its metal plates and then gradually fade. Within seconds, all that's left is the pulsating flare of its magenta eyes peering out from the ashen gold sheen of its armor. And when it straightens, it becomes obvious that it stands taller than all the rest. This Droid is not just any Droid. This is a Sensate, *newly surged to life*.

Stars above.

LXXIII

LIVI: INVASION

IS THIS HOW THEY DO IT?

Could this be how they power the Droids?

There's an answer lurking here to a very important question, but suddenly I can't think. The niggling at the base of my brain starts again. A maelstrom of voices assails me full force. From down below, the newly born Sensate Droid's head pivots. Dozens of other hard shells turn in unison a split second later. The Sensate's eyes lock onto mine. Then a single voice. Familiar. Resounding in my head. *Run.*

Triton and I scramble back, but suddenly I can't move.

"Triton, I—" I struggle to get the words out as Triton turns to me.

His eyes widen as they find mine. "I'm getting you out of here."

My head lolls against his shoulder as he sweeps me up into his arms, retreating back into the dark passages. *Fight it, for star's sake.* But my arms and legs may as well be made of Andurian cement. I can't lift a single muscle. *Not now.*

But with each bounding step, the maelstrom of voices dissipates. The intense buzzing at my brain wanes to a dull thud. Slowly I become aware of my surroundings again and the fact that our steps reverberate too loudly down the dank passageways. The thunder of metal on stone shudders closely behind us.

And too soon, we stop.

I manage to drag my head up off of Triton's shoulders to see what I already know.

We're surrounded.

Triton lays me gently on the ground. "Stay down," he orders.

My strength is slowly returning, but I'm still so weak. Vaguely, I'm aware of the clashing of metal on metal, the thud of bodies hitting the floor. Triton bears the brunt of over twenty Droids, and I can barely lift my own head. Triton is a whirlwind of movement. He takes down over a dozen Droids in a matter of minutes, but before he can catch his breath, more come barreling down the passageways to take their places. Triton may be the best Bionic Atlas has, but it's clear that we're sorely outnumbered.

Go help him, for crying out loud. Fight it. You're a Bionic now, for star's sake. And slowly, I will feeling back into my arms, legs. *Get up. Get. Up.* I force my legs to a stand. No doubt if it weren't for the nanobots coursing through my veins, I'd still be a pile of noodles right now. But even the nanobots seem to sense the direness of the situation, my energy surging back.

I set my sights on the Droids closest to me. All eyes are on the whirlwind that is Triton, so the Droids' backs are to me. With each step, I take back control of myself. *It's now or never.* I whip my hazar out and charge. *Aim for the notch between their shoulder blades. Hit them where they are most vulnerable.* The many hours I trained in Hemlock kick in. And with a quick jab of my hazar right where it counts, I send the first Droid down with a thud onto the stone floor. *Can't stop now.* Just as quickly, I disable the next one, much the same way. But as I approach the third, it whirls on me, metal hand grabbing my neck. Suddenly, I'm staring into pulsatile green eyes. I swipe and punch but only manage to make the Droid grip my neck even tighter. I struggle to breathe. My eyes water.

"Livi!"

I vaguely register Triton's voice calling out to me. My vision closes in.

Then suddenly, release. The metal grip loosens, and the husk of metal in front of me clangs onto the hard floor. I gulp a breath of life and blink back the stinging in my eyes. Triton appears in front of me in the next instant, quickly retrieving his hazar from the Droid's back. "You okay?"

I nod, but his eyes are already darting past me, and he yells, "Get down!"

I barely have time to duck before he launches one of the downed Droids into the passageway, knocking over a throng of Droids that has just come through.

Triton grabs my hand and pulls me up to a sprint down the tunnels. "Come on. Hurry!"

Left, right. Right again. "I hope—you know—where you're going!" My words come out between ragged breaths.

"Not much choice at this point," Triton calls back as his eyes search the pathways ahead, and we surge farther from the chaos behind us. "We've got to warn Atlas. They need to know what's going on here!"

I've never run so fast in my life. I have my new Bionic body to thank for that. The tunnels ahead twist and turn. But I'm starting to recognize these passages as the ones we first came through. Maybe we have a chance.

Suddenly, three Dogger bots leap from a side tunnel, smashing Triton up against the wall. Their sharp claws tear through his darkwing suit.

"Triton!" I call out as I surge towards him, but another Dogger leaps towards me, knocking me flat onto my back, cold metal fangs digging into my shoulders. "Get off of me, you draggart!" I roll and twist, managing to throw the Dogger off of me. But before I can get up, three Droids descend upon me. Hard metal clamps cold on my arms. One with glowing green eyes squares its knee down hard on my chest. They're too strong for me. I can't budge.

Out of the corner of my eye, I can see Droids wrench Triton's arms behind his back, yet he bucks and kicks and still manages to take down those in front of him. But with each downed Droid, more pour through the tunnel, immediately taking their place. *There's just too many of them.*

A Droid behind Triton raises his baton.

"Watch out!" I scream helplessly as the Droid strikes him with a sickening thud.

Triton's head slumps forward. An ugly gash on his head bleeds profusely.

"Triton!" I yell again. But his body remains unmoving. *No!* I struggle to get free, to get to him, but the pressure on my chest increases, making my head snap to. The Droid's green eyes gleam as his knee digs deeper. It's getting harder to breathe. And just when I think it can't possibly get any worse, the niggling in my brain starts again. Only this time it grows even more quickly than ever before, an electric shock to my dendrites. My limbs go numb. My vision tunnels and wanes. *Stars, not now!* Twisting my body, I try to throw the Droid off of me. But the only thing I manage to do is catch sight of my worst nightmare come to life only a few steps away from me. The Droid with pulsatile red eyes and a slash of red across its chest. The Master of all Sensates. Gardurak.

Stars, this can't be happening. It just can't. But when did the universe ever listen to me?

LXXIV

LIVI: GARDURAK REVISITED

"WELCOME BACK, my little friend."

Am I imagining things? A wheedling voice drills into my brain, though from where I can't tell. The gleam of Gardurak's smoothly plated face lowers towards mine. If I weren't so stone-cold petrified, seeing the intricate weaving pattern of tinston metal so close up might have been fascinating. Is it possible that the Master Droid is communicating with me?

"I was hoping to find you again, my little pet, and you saved me the trouble of having to track you down. How very considerate. Imagine my surprise when you showed up at our very doorstep."

Again that voice. Like a knife piercing my brain. It can't possibly just be my imagination. Gardurak *is* talking to me. But how? I shake my head, trying to block out the voice. But I'm helpless against it as it continues to stab into me.

"You might as well save your energy, little human. Struggling will only make it harder."

"What do you want from me?" I growl against the pain in my chest, the heaviness in my head. "Let us go."

"You are a fascinating little thing, aren't you? I knew you were special the first time we met, and it seems you have grown even more fascinating since. Not only are you resistant to being controlled by our neural network, it appears you can access our network despite that. And I suspect your talents run even deeper. No, I'm sorry, my little pet. You can't very well ask me to give up something that I have been looking for, for such a very long time." He leans down even closer to me, a cold metal hand coming down to grip my chin. I am unable to look away. "No. Especially not you. And you can either cooperate on your own, or with a little *encouragement* from my sisters and brothers here." The Droid's knee on my chest presses deeper. "But if you cooperate, then things will be easier for you and your *friend*."

My heart pounds at breakneck speed. I glance over at Triton. Though he is unconscious, I can detect the subtle rise and fall of his chest. *He's still alive.* I can't let them put him in one of those pods. Having seen what the Quadrati have been doing to the humans, I have never felt so desperate in my life. But instinct tells me that they want something from me. They *need* something from me. And they can't control me like the others. Otherwise I would have been deader than dead by now. "Let him go unharmed, and I will give you what you want."

Gardurak laughs, a strange harsh grating of rust on stone. "And altruistic too? Quite a noble human trait. One that I had almost forgotten about." His pulsatile eyes study me greedily for a moment. "But I'm sorry to inform you that you are not in a position to bargain." Gardurak releases my chin roughly and nods to the Droid immobilizing me. "Brother Heron, take her to the interrogation units." His words continue to resound through my mind, though I could swear my ears still hear nothing. Then he nods towards the other Droids surrounding Triton's slack form. "Red Axis, prepare this other fine specimen for the mind meld. He should prove to be a very strong addition to our Sensates."

"No!" I scream, watching helplessly as a group of Droids drag Triton away. I thrash against the Droids' solid grip on me as they haul me up. "Stop! Stop, you draggarts!" But there's too many of them. I'm helpless. And *where is my so-called mind control power when I need it?* Then something so cold that it burns stabs into my arm, and before I can cry out in pain, I'm forced through what can only be the gates of hellas.

LXXV

LIVI: SURVIVAL

I FIND MYSELF IN A PLACE where the governing laws of space-time are a distant memory.

A streak of light breaks across my brow. Someone is running. *That someone is me.* Fleeing from the onslaught. An electrical storm. Voices, images, a tornado of incoherence, closing in on me. In my bones, I understand—*it's alive.* And it occurs to me—*they put me in one of those pods.* Only this time it's different, different from the last time. If that electrical storm catches me, I will become lost, *forever.* But there's nowhere to run, except further into the dark.

Bolts of sizzling electricity like hellfire strike at me and latch on, sending a shocking jolt of pain coursing through me. I open my mouth to scream, but only a strangled whimper comes out. *Fight it. You did it once before. Pull yourself together and fight, for star's sake.*

"No!" I shout, whether just in my mind or out loud, I don't know. And to my amazement I see a glimpse of it. A flicker of light against the dark. Starlock.

I can feel its pull, its warm energy. Another bolt from the electrical storm charges at me, but this time a pulse surges from my very core, out to my fingertips, and a rainbow of lights arc out, pushing back at the hellfire as I wrench myself free for a moment.

Stars, did I do that? *Don't stop. Do it again. Harder.*

This time I can feel that pulse of energy from within building. When the tentacles of electricity charge at me again, I let go. An arcing rainbow of dazzling currents surges forth from my fingertips, crashing head on with the hellfire in a staggering explosion. Beating it back. The hellfire doesn't quit though, and neither do I. Each time the hellfire attacks, I will that current of energy to surge forth from my fingertips. But the onslaught is endless. The universe is consumed in an electrical storm from all hellas. So all consuming that even time burns. And sooner or later, I know even the universe won't survive.

LXXVI

SAYRIE: HOPE

THE ARTIFICIAL LIGHT of the cell flickers dimly on, and I snap awake despite the sleep concoction that the Droids usually taint our evening gruel with, the gruel I try to eat as little of as possible.

Immediately I scan the room, as is my habit these days. Some of the others still cling restlessly to sleep, and I wish I could do the same. For here, any sleep is far better than the nightmare that is reality. As I blink to accustom myself to the light, I see it. *There.* The newly empty cot. Allara's. *It's her turn today.*

Aside from the mysterious *experiments* the Droids put us through, every day is the same here. And every day I feel I'm losing a piece of myself, losing hope that there will be something better. Even my memories are starting to fail me—memories of Grishen's Gorge where my brother and I would race our twikis, skimming and laughing as we careened over the water without a worry in the world. Without a worry until that one dreadful day when *they* came—monsters of metal wreaking havoc upon the whole of Pantoc. Ever since that day, I've been glad that my parents were already long gone. Safely tucked away within the graces of death to avoid the suffering and misery that was to come.

The only reason I haven't given up already was the hope that I would one day still be able to save Rhyton from this rat's pit we have found ourselves in. To figure out a way to get him out of those dreadful pods and off of this stars-forsaken planet. To get my little brother home and take care of him as I promised my parents before they died.

Only a handful of us were spared. To what end, I know not, except for the fact we all have something in common. The Elder's Brow, they called it back on Pantoc. What significance it holds only the Droids know and won't say. Or perhaps the Droids just want to keep us around to watch us suffer.

Whatever it is, we're at the mercy of the metal beasts. We've been holed up for what feels like weeks, several months. Likely even more, because it has been so long that I've already lost track. So long that days and weeks meld into endless months and the fathomless flowing of time. If not for Rhyton and my promise, I would have given myself up to the black ethers by now.

The artificial light clicks several notches brighter, jarring the others from their restless sleep. Some start to struggle up, the meager white drapes that we are all clothed in barely covering their even more meager bones. And I send up a wish to the stars, *please let Allara be okay.*

Now Allara and I don't always see eye to eye, far from it in fact. And I'll be the first to admit her constant preaching oftentimes gets on my nerves. But she always has my back. And what the Droids do to any one of us is inexcusable. Each day, one of us is taken from the cell, put through whatever twisted experiment the metal beasts have concocted. Most days, that one of us makes it back. But some days, that one of us doesn't. What the Droids are up to, I have no idea. But whatever it is, it can't be good.

Yesterday it was me. The Droids didn't even need to shackle me. The collar was enough. A metal device clamped around my neck since day one that could electrocute the daylights out of me—so excruciatingly painful as to make a person wish she was dead. I found that out the hard way that first day I tried to pry it off, again and again.

Still, yesterday when the Droids led me to the experimentation chamber past the Nesting, it was all I could do not to run up to Rhyton's pod and tear him out. His face looked so wan and pale despite the nourishment they pumped through his body to keep him alive. But I knew rescuing him would not be so simplistic. He had been entrenched in that capsule far too long, his mind somehow held captive by the Droids. I will have to find another way, if such a way even exists. For all I know, the process cannot be reversed. But I will not let myself even entertain that possibility.

But yesterday I was lucky—a few blood draws from my arm, and they sent me right back to the cells. Two weeks ago, it was Brevia. She was not so lucky. The Droids cleared away her cot the very next day.

As I look towards the cell's locked hatch, I notice that Silver Patch is not at his normal post. Even more odd is the fact that the rest of the Droids are changing guards later than usual. Normally, it is right at the Dawning, when the din of their clomping metal feet is enough to jolt everyone awake.

For the first few days, weeks even, the Droids all looked the same. But now I have nicknames for some of them, for the subtle differences we've noticed. Dented Knee. Silver Patch. Needle Nose. Blind Eye. They hardly ever use verbal words, almost always communicating with each other through some form of unspoken advanced technology, something akin to what I imagine to be instantaneous communal thought. We are no match for that.

A rapid shuffling of feet around the corner draws my attention towards the cell hatch. It's Allara, with Needle Nose dragging her roughly by the arm. Her lavender hair is matted down along her sweaty neck, and there are ugly bruises blooming around her wrists, but she's in one piece. *She made it back alive after all.*

The Droid shoves her stumbling backwards into the hatch, and I manage to catch her before she falls. "Pick on someone your own size, you brute!" I yell at them as the hatch slams shut again, and the gleam of Needle Nose's back disappears around the corner along with the thudding of his heavy footsteps.

"Sayrie!" Jin clamps her hand down over my mouth, shushing me. "You want to get yourself trilled?"

I shake my head free of her hand, my earlobes curling as my hot temper flares. "We've got to stand up to those beasts one of these days! We can't just let them walk all over us all the time."

"It's okay, Sayrie." Allara rights herself. She peers back at the hatch door and waits until the thudding of Needle Nose's footsteps fades completely, then turns back to face us. That's when I notice, her eyes are *gleaming*.

"I'm really okay, Sayrie." She puts a hand on my shoulder. "They didn't do anything."

"What? Your wrists are bruised and it looks like you've been struggling against some wild wildebeast. What do you mean they didn't do anything?"

"I mean. They had me pinned in that Geiger unit. It got as hot as all hellas. But just when I thought for sure they were going to buzz me, suddenly they yanked me out of that blasted contraption and hurried me back here."

"What? Why would they do that?"

"I don't know." Allara throws another quick glance towards the cell hatch, her voice lowering to barely above a whisper. "But on the way back, there was a big commotion. Some of the Droids escorting me rushed off in a hurry towards the northern tunnels, leaving me with Needle Nose. You know those Droids hardly speak at all, but what I gathered was there was some sort of breach on the base perimeters. Several hundred Droids downed."

My heart leaps. Could someone from Pantoc be trying to rescue us? Could this be the opportunity we have been hoping for?

"And look!" Allara glances furtively back towards the hatch, making sure it's still clear. "The Droids were so distracted I finally managed to swipe it." She reaches into the seam of her shift, gingerly pulling something out. The gleam of metal flashes in her palm when she opens her hand towards me. *A key*.

All sound hangs suspended for a moment. My heart tumbles in my chest.

One step closer to escape.

Maybe we aren't so doomed after all.

"Good work." We don't always see eye to eye, but today is the exception. I reach out and give her hand a squeeze. It must have taken a lot of courage for her to do such a thing right under the Droids' noses and risk getting trilled. Because of her heightened sensory perception, Allara experiences the excruciating pain of getting trilled tenfold compared to the rest of us. "Now all we need is the key for Telisad's collar." For some reason, the Droids gave the child a collar that is different from all the rest. But there is no way I'm going to leave her behind.

"Yes, we're almost there." Allara nods and squeezes my hand right back.

I turn to the others. "Jin—" I keep my voice low to keep the Droids around the corner from hearing. "Check all the equipment in our hidden stockpile. Make sure they still work. The rest of you, ready yourselves."

Hold on, Rhyton. I'm coming for you.

LXXVII

SAYRIE: GRIM MIRACLES

TONIGHT I SKIPPED the evening gruel, poured it down the excrement drain when the Droids weren't looking.

I needed to make sure I didn't miss anything. Didn't miss any small detail that could even remotely thwart our chance for escape. Because today, when Allara swiped that key, our prospects changed at last.

When Silver Patch's footsteps finally fade dead away, I count to one thousand and then let myself open my eyes. Then I count to two thousand before I allow myself to sit up from the cot while everyone else is dead asleep from the sedatives in our gruel. Finally, when I'm sure Silver Patch is not going to come back, I get up.

Every day in this rat's pit we came a little closer. At least that's what we kept telling ourselves. Telling ourselves that each little piece of information we gathered or random piece of nothingness we could swipe from the experimentation room would bring us that much closer to getting off of this stars-forsaken planet and back to our loved ones. Telling ourselves to keep going when those beasts marched us past the Nesting room where our own kindred lay in some form of twisted hibernation. Forcing ourselves to walk past when all we wanted to do was stop and touch them, grasp their hands, and reassure them that we had not forgotten, that we were still trying—every day, still trying to get them out. Get us all out.

And it would seem, today, that actually might almost be true.

I creep over to the shower area. It is so dark that I can barely find the edges to pull out the false wall we carefully sawed out using Allara's metal combs.

Quietly, I pry open the wall and let out a breath of relief. *Still there*—the assortment of weapons we painstakingly gathered. I dig out the key Allara gave me earlier and wonder briefly how such a small piece of metal could hold so much promise. Today, when Allara whipped out that gnarled sliver of tinston, the one we all know so well, at first I thought I must be imagining things. My brain refused to let my eyes believe that something called hope still existed in this cruel and unfeeling world. For how could a frail, old woman have stolen such a critically important piece of metal from right under the Droids' noses? The illusory key that we have been hoping to acquire for such a long time.

Now it is so close that I can actually touch its strangely mangled edges, so close that it makes my cursed collar feel especially tight around my neck. My hands itch to use the key and take the stars-forsaken thing off *right now*. But I must be patient. After all, I have already waited all day just to add this to our collection. We are almost there. There is no room to make hasty mistakes now. Carefully,

I place the key into the hole in the wall, right next to the hazar.

Each day we were preparing a little bit more, Allara and I made sure of that (though our approaches may have been different—she a little more encouraging and motherly, me not as nicely). We reminded the others to keep their eyes open for makeshift tools, information, *anything* we could get our hands on. Some things we acquired by relentless tenacity—timing the changing of the guards to the second, but others admittedly by pure dumb luck.

And now we are that much closer.

I check through all the equipment we have managed to collect so far. A hazar, two ropes, a baton, even a skyver. Those Droids really have to be more careful. I'm about to check the light on the hazar when suddenly—the familiar tinny clang of approaching footsteps. *Flaming stars.*

Quickly I shove the weapons back, securing the false wall as fast as I can. *What in the name of the stars are they coming back for?* Usually the Droids are so predictable. Blind Eye and Dented Knee never return to our cells until well after the Dim. I dive for my cot, shutting my eyes just in time.

The cell hatch clanks open. I can see the light flooding in through my closed lids. Moments pass in eerie silence, then the creaking of metal on metal.

Steady.

Something thuds heavily to my left. It's all I can do not to twitch. To pretend to be asleep. To pretend to be drugged by the evening's gruel.

Stay calm.

***

It feels like ages before the Droids finally leave. Then again, I suppose it could have been worse. At least I got back into my cot just in time. At least I didn't get trilled. And at least *we still have our key*. But then, there's the extra *gift* the Droids leave behind.

***

Ten black holes. I almost didn't realize it was alive. I almost have to turn away. The burns are so extensive. That can only mean one thing. The Droids put her through the Onterrogation. Just like Brevia. Only Brevia didn't survive. And yet this girl, this girl is *still breathing*. The steady rise and fall of her chest is a miracle in itself considering what she must have been through. But how long she will survive, I don't know. For her sake, I hope it isn't for much longer.

Occasionally there is one amongst the universe who defies the laws of physics. Whose life trajectory cannot be predicted by simple Newtonian motion, but instead leaps and bounds across the undulating planes of space-time. Ungoverned. Unpredictable. Unleashed. Boundless. Defiant.

(Excerpt from *The Thoughts and Memoirs of Livinthea Park*, star year 8117)

LXXVIII

LIVI: AWAKENING

I T'S THE ABRUPT SILENCE that awakens me.

But the whispers start again, and through the haze of my mind, I struggle to reach out. To catch the hushed words. To understand.

"... can't believe she survived the ... Even Brevia didn't ..."

"Yes, those ... cowardly Droids left Brevia for dead. I'll never forgive them for that. But somehow this one's ... just barely."

"Yes, Sayrie. It's all so very strange. Look how fast she's healing. Faster than should be possible. Do you think the Droids know?"

"I doubt it. Otherwise they wouldn't have thrown her down here to rot with the rest of us."

"Where do you think she comes from?"

"Certainly not Pantoc."

"Is it possible that ... the one?"

"Jin, you know I've never been one to put much ... into ancient ... And even if I did, where is her Elder's Brow?"

A momentary pause stills the air, then approaching feet.

"Allara! What do you think you're doing? She could be dangerous."

"Nonsense, Sayrie. Don't be such a nympa. She's as human as the rest of us. Just looks a little different. That's all."

A gentle hand supports the back of my head. The trickle of something cool against my parched lips encourages me to swallow. A light touch brushes across my forehead, my hair, then suddenly stops.

"Look!"

A sharp intake of breath. More hushed words, hard to decipher.

"Yes . . . remarkable indeed."

"See, Allara, even a nonbeliever like you must admit this is no mere coincidence."

"Well, let's hope for all of our sakes that the predictions are . . . Or the Ritarian . . . are truly lost. Stars know there is not much time left."

I want to ask them what they mean, but I don't have the strength to utter a single word.

Hours, possibly days, pass in this manner. Drifting. I try to pull myself out of the quagmire, but I am too weak—forced to exist in the space between the air but still bound within the lines. Not quite lost, not quite present. Through the fog, I only know pain. Every cell of my body aches, but occasionally a gentle hand or softly placed words pierce the haze. And slowly I feel my strength returning.

"She's rousing! Telisad! Quickly! Some water."

"Careful, Allara. We don't yet know what she's about."

"That may be, Sayrie. But may I remind you that you were once in her position too?"

A dribble of something wets my lips.

"Easy, my friend."

Again, these strange voices creep out at me out from the forbidden shadows, accents I don't recognize. A curling of the Rs and a rounding of the Ts. A bottomless dip where the pitch should soar high. As I garner enough strength and wherewithal to crack my eyes open to the dim lighting, I begin to understand why.

A strange face. Dark on light patches of skin and crinkled around the eyes. Ear lobes—pointed? But no, couldn't be. *My mind must be playing tricks on me.*

Slowly, I push myself upright even though every muscle in my body protests. And squint against the light.

A small group of women. Some bent from time's relentless progression, others younger than myself. All clothed in thin white sheets with barely enough skin to cover their meager bones. *How long have they been here?* As my eyes start to focus, I realize that though they look human enough, something tells me they aren't from Cerulea, very far from it in fact. But it's not the lavender hair, green nails, or the strangely spotted skin that makes me look twice and a third time at the group, that makes me blink to make sure I'm seeing clearly. Instead, it's the fact that they all have something else in common. Flashes of white streak like comets through their hair, *each and every one of them.*

The Mark of Dresden.

What I was expecting, I'm not sure. But certainly this is not it.

I try to stand up. A wave of dizziness sweeps over me, and I have to sit down again.

"Slowly, my friend, you're just recovering." Her voice startles me into recognition. It was the gentle one, through the fog.

"Wh-what happened?" Despite putting all of my effort into speaking, my voice barely approaches a whisper.

"The metal beasts. They put you through Onterrogation. It's remarkable that you survived at all."

"Th-thank you for helping me." I hear my own words come out as if from a far distance.

There is a moment's hesitation, then the elderly woman with the kind voice speaks again. "All we did was to keep you watered and fed. Your own body, it seems, managed all the rest. Except, your lips are parched. Telisad, please bring more water."

A young girl who looks to be no more than ten approaches me wide-eyed. She holds a shiny metal cup towards me.

As I lean forward to accept the cup, something squeezes tightly around my neck. My hand flies up reflexively to find something clamped there. *What in all hellas?* I try desperately to tug it off. But my mind still feels thick, my arms responding in slow motion.

"I wouldn't do that if I were you." The next instant, another woman presses towards me and pushes the young girl protectively behind her. She puts a firm hand on my arm and stills it. "I don't know what you're made of or how you heal so quickly, but I don't think even you could tolerate a thousand-joule trill to your system." With her other hand, she points at her own neck collar.

413

I stop struggling. With each passing moment, the clarity returns a little bit more to my head. The woman before me is perhaps just a few years older than me with lightly spotted skin, eyes like jeweled amethyst, and pointed earlobes like the old woman. The way she holds her head high and shoulders thrown back tells me she is one of the leaders of the group.

"Who are you people?" I don't want to sound rude, but this is not the time nor place for niceties.

"I am called Sayrie. And the one who insisted on nursing you back to health even though you had one foot already through the Gates of the Dead, well that's Allara." She nods towards the elderly woman.

These people are like none that I have seen before. Can I trust them? They're certainly not Cerulean. But then I realize I *have* seen them before. Like the *others* in the pods. When I was with Triton—Triton! *How could I forget?* "My"—I struggle to find the right word—"companion. Have you seen him?" I can't speak fast enough.

"You are the only newcomer that we've seen. But as you can imagine"—the leader sweeps her arms to indicate the enclosed chamber surrounding us—"we don't get out much."

Oh stars, I may already be too late. Who knows how long I've been out. What if they've already put Triton in one of those pods? Like Eppel? My pulse races. *Get a grip, Livi. Keep it together. Focus on what needs to be done.* I turn to the leader, forcing my voice to steady. "Please. I have to get out of here, to find my friend. Is there any possible way to escape this place?"

"If there were an easy way out, believe me we would have already tried long ago. These cells are locked tight, and there are at least five Droids at all times patrolling just outside."

She nods towards the cell hatch, where periodic flashes of tinston and beams of laser-like eyes survey us.

"And with these darn collars on, even if we managed to escape, the Droids could incapacitate us regardless of where we were. No, as long as we're collared, we're powerless to escape."

Oh stars. That is not the answer I want to hear. Surely there must be a way. "Is it possible to take the collars off, disable them somehow?"

Sayrie's eyes flash to Allara, who gives her the slightest of nods. Sayrie whispers to me, "The night the Droids so graciously dumped you in our cell, we had actually been planning an escape. Allara managed to swipe one of the keys for the collars from the Droids when they took her for the experiments. The only problem is the child. Her collar is different. We don't have her key."

"Experiments?" *Can this place get any worse?*

"Every night, one of us is taken to a chamber where those Droids perform a number of tests on us. Sometimes they are simple blood tests. Other times—"

"Sayrie!" the elderly woman scolds. "The girl is only just recovering. You want to send her back through the Gates of the Dead?"

Sayrie rolls her eyes. "Allara, you said yourself that we don't have much time. She needs to know what's going on. Besides, if the Droids captured her friend too, likely he is already in Nesting by now. She needs to know these things."

"Nesting?"

"Yes, the hibernation chamber where our fellow comrades are also housed."

They must be talking about the pods.

"If that's where they place most of the captives, then why are you all here? Why am I here?"

"That's a very good question, that we don't know the answer to. We only know that they need a few of us to run experiments on. What the experiments are for is a mystery. We can only speculate that—"

Sayrie stops midsentence as she jerks her head to the rattling sound of heavy footsteps growing rapidly louder until it stops just outside of the cell.

"What in all flaming stars? It's not even the Dim yet, why are the Droids changing guards right now?" Sayrie whispers.

The others' eyes fix towards where the sound came from. Sayrie's and Allara's earlobes curl. It's clear that this is out of their normal routine. And then I feel it, that buzzing at the base of my head. Eating into me. What steps into view the next instant makes my heart go still. Dark tinston with a slash of red. Gardurak.

A voice drills into my head. *Just like before.*

"What a pleasant surprise. Still alive, are we? And so well recovered. Already making new friends, my little pet? I would not have expected any less from you, further proof that my hypothesis about you is correct. Tell me. How are you liking your new quarters?"

"You can go to hellas, Gardurak." Out of the corner of my eye, I can see the way the others' eyes widen.

"Well, that's certainly not very gracious of you. Then again, you humans have always been like that. Luckily your species and your defects will not prevail in this universe much longer. Especially considering what we have planned for you all."

"Let us go, you beast," I growl.

"And demanding little thing too, aren't we? Perhaps next time we can appease you, but today we need your new little friend here. We have a very special experiment lined up for this one." One of the Droids grabs Telisad roughly by the arms and starts to drag her out. Her screams resound through the cell.

"No! She's just a child! Leave her alone!" Sayrie steps forward, only to have another Droid kick her hard in the stomach. She crumples to the ground moaning.

"Stop! You draggart! Pick on someone your own size." Instinct kicks in, and I lunge at Gardurak. Fist connects with hard metal, and to my amazement, I manage to knock him down. But before I can turn towards the other Droids, a life-ending pain sears through my neck and courses down my arms, my legs, the tips of every single hair on my head. I let out a scream as I crumble to the floor and tear uselessly at the collar. Even I didn't know I could scream like that.

Gardurak recovers in a single rebounding leap. The next moment, his cool metal face hovers too closely over mine. "Careful, my sweet pet. Next time will be ten times more painful and twenty times longer. And since you seem so eager to help the child, why delay the inevitable? I had been meaning to test out my new hypothesis a little later, but since you seem so eager to volunteer, we might as well do it now." He motions to the other Droids. "Take her as well."

LXXIX

LIVI: INTO THE MIND OF THE

COLLECTIVE

EFT. RIGHT. LEFT AGAIN.

Gardurak and his Droids drag us through what seems like endless tunnels and chambers. But with my Bionic brain, my enhanced memory, I memorize every single detail I can, down to the jeweled stone embedded every few meters within the tunnel ceilings. It would be an understatement to say that the Quadrati base is enormous. As we pass through what I can only surmise to be the heart of the base, I start to see that the base is more than just a few tunnels and chambers burrowed into the ground. Rather, it's more like an underground city teeming with activity.

We pass Droid after Droid and hundreds of other strangely mechanized creatures. Enormous beetle-like bots, the size of longhorns, skitter through the tunnels bearing large loads upon their backs. Flying discs with curled antennae spin through the corridors, so closely that I'm lucky not to have my head taken off by one of them. And again, there are those vicious-looking Dogger bots.

I shiver as we enter a vast chamber, which can only be what Sayrie referred to as the Nesting, housing all those people in the pods, where Keenon is, where Eppel is. It's all I can do not to yank myself free and try to help them. *Be patient. The time will come,* I tell myself.

"Keep moving." The Droid jabs me in the small of my back, forcing me forward into a smaller room attached to the first. Eerie golden pods line up row after row, similar to the ones in the other chamber but on a smaller scale. Some of the pods glow brightly with rivulets of electricity flowing over them, others dim as brownstone. The chilly, dank air sends shivers down my arms.

"Just so you know, any smart moves, and the little girl will suffer." Gardurak's voice needles into my head.

Telisad trembles violently as one of the Droids uses a key then yanks off her collar, nearly knocking her over.

"You don't have be so rough. She's just a child!" I growl at the Droid. I struggle futilely against the two Droids flanking me, who have me restrained at the elbows.

Gardurak gets in my face, so close that the coolness of tinston wafts against my skin. "You want to know what rough is, my little pet? Rough is when you are left behind to rot on a dying planet, when you are deemed not worthy enough to make the trip to other habitable planets. Rough is when only the most wealthy and fit get chosen to survive, and you are left to die an ugly death. That's what rough is."

"What are you talking about?"

"Oh, you don't know, do you? That your ancestors were such heartless bastards. No, I'm sure your history lessons conveniently left those small details out."

"I don't believe you."

"Then would you believe that we were human once, like you? But your ancestors left us stranded on this dying planet with no other choice but to fend for ourselves, to force evolution to take its next step."

"You're a lying, crazy draggart." Surely Gardurak must be making this up. But even as I say this, a sliver of doubt creeps into my mind. How else could one explain the Quadrati's presence on the World of Origins? That question has bothered me since the day the Comstadt recognized this planet for what it is.

"Am I though?" Gardurak's red eyes pulsate faster, brighter. "Why don't you take a look for yourself? The crimes of your ancestors."

And before I can react, Gardurak surges forward, his cold hand gripping down hard onto my collar. I push back, but with the other two Droids restraining me, I can't tear free. Unwanted images flood into my mind. Thought sequences not my own barrel through a dam I have no ability to control.

A vast starship—propelled by an advanced propulsion system that allows humans to make that final leap, interstellar travel— and something I helped to create. One day I knew human history would recognize the significance of my creation as being on par with the birth of fire, the first automobile, the invention of the internet. But for now, it was about as useful to those of us who watched as a cloud in the sky.

Curls of smoke trail in the starship's wake as it climbs higher and higher into the azurean expanse above and beyond. Out of reach. I sit in a strange metal chair balanced on a single large spherical wheel, surrounded by thousands of people, begging, crying.

I can't move my legs to stand up and beg as the others do. Beg for the last starship to come back. But I refuse be like them. I won't grovel to those who betrayed me, those bastards who had appointed themselves judge, jury, and executioner in the game of life and death.

Anger and rage ripple through the me-that-is-not-me so hard that my head pounds, but I can do nothing more than grit my teeth. But I promise myself that I will never forget the ones who abandoned us. I make a vow from that day on to track them down and to make them pay.

More images.

A workshop. I was clever, once upon a time. Wall after wall of computers line the sides, and in the middle—Droids—odd-looking ones. Almost primitive. Not as sleek and shiny as the ones I am used to. An important-looking man with age under his belt inspects the Droids. His weather-worn skin speaks of years spent under scorching sun and wind. He nods receptively at first as I explain. Yes, of course we would retain the ability to speak. Even I could not let that primitively human habit go.

But his expression grows darker as I explain further. A collective neural network, the ability to draw from each other's experiences.

But what about individuality? the old man questions.

I hedge a little and tell him not to worry. The me-who-is-not-me reminds him that this is our only choice left. Trying to convince him that only my ideas have any chance of saving what's left of humankind.

But the weathered old man scoffs in my face. "Life as a robot? I would rather die than live as a freak."

But I don't give up. Flash forward. Not everyone is as skeptical as the old man who has already lived a full life. Others begin to come around, mostly the younger ones who want a second chance. What are their broken bodies worth to them anyway when they're stranded on a planet near its own extinction?

The first few times were complete disasters, my best volunteers too. Image after image, bodies singed, broken beyond repair. The me-who-is-not-me near despair.

Finally, I would try the experiment on myself, I decided. Even as I grit my teeth to keep from screaming as the mind meld takes place, as the electrical current passes through me and welds my neuronal connections to the machines, I am sure I will not make it. I am sure I will be burned alive. But by some miracle, it works. And as the world turns to ashes and people became more desperate, I gain more and more followers. Freak or not. One by one, my army grows, while the world around me perishes. Until one day, only we are left. The freaks. Not even a single living animal or plant could survive the surface of the harsh planet where temperatures boiled too hot during the day, grew arctically cold at night.

So we built underground. Our Droid bodies survived where our old organic forms would have withered. We created artificial biosphere pods and recycled every single biological thing that we could to keep our hibernating bodies alive, to keep our new collective neural network functioning.

But eventually that was not enough. We were prisoners to our new metal bodies. To keep our neural network healthy, we had to feed it. With more people. To maintain the neural plasticity. That's when we built our own starships. To hunt for those who had left us for dead. Retrace the Ritarian Gateways. And finally seek our revenge.

Just as quickly as the images flooded my mind, they heave out.

I'm shaking uncontrollably now. I can still taste the bitterness in my mouth, feel the hatred, as if it were my very own.

What in all hellas just happened to me? Could it be true? Were Gardurak and the other Droids really one of us so long ago?

"Not so proud of your ancestors now, are you? Not to worry. You will more than make up for their past crimes."

"Even if what you showed me was real, Gardurak, it still doesn't excuse your actions. It doesn't excuse what you and your Droids are doing to the people of Pantoc, of Cerulea. Hurting and controlling others is never right." I twist around so I can look him square in his pulsatile red eyes. "I feel sorry for you, Gardurak. All these years and still not able to let go of the past."

"Careful what you say, my little pet. We'll see how sure of yourself you are after our little experiment here. And you needn't feel sorry for us anymore. Did it ever occur to you that humans are such rudimentary life-forms? So dependent on the world around you? So vulnerable to the elements? What's that old saying you humans like to use? Oh yes, adversity makes the soul stronger. Well, let me tell you this. We embark on the next phase of history. The next phase of Droids, which are stronger, faster, no longer reliant on constant input of humans for the neural network. For you see, you are our solution, you and the rest of those with the Mark of Dresden mutation. You will power our next generation of Droids whether you like it or not. And your newfound friends will help."

The next generation of Droids? Oh stars. He must be referring to that throng of Droids that Triton and I stumbled upon. If Gardurak really does unleash that army of Droids, there's no telling how far the Quadrati will go. *Keep him talking. Find out more information. Self-centered egotists like him always want a chance to brag.* "What are you going to do to us?"

"Even as machines, we need to evolve. To adapt. You and your friends are the key to the next step in our evolution. *Especially you.* Did you know that I have been looking for someone like you for the last millennium? Someone who can power the neural network indefinitely? With your help, the possibilities are endless."

"I would never help someone like you."

"I'm sorry to disappoint you, my pet, but you gave up your right to decide the minute you stepped onto our base. Now enough chitchat." Gardurak turns to the other Droids. "Begin the transformation."

The Droids drag Telisad closer to one of the open pods while simultaneously forcing me towards a metal table at the other end of the chamber. Telisad lets out a strangled cry as she tries desperately to break free of the Droids.

"Leave her alone, you monsters!" I shout as I struggle against the Droids restraining me, but there are too many of them. And with the darn collar around my neck, I don't have many other options.

"I'm afraid you have us confused with your own ancestors, my little pet. Their cruelty is what left us on this dead planet in the first place." Gardurak's cold, red eyes pulsate into mine.

In the next moment the Droids grab me and hoist me onto the cold metallic table. Almost instantaneously, metal restraints curl up around my wrists and elbows, my ankles, my waist. Gardurak approaches me, armed with a long needle. And I'm all but helpless. *Stop. Stop!* Where is my so-called power when I need it?

"Tell me, my little pet, how did you manage to escape our neural network once before? It's quite a feat to be able to extricate yourself from the neural network when the bonding has already started. You couldn't have done it on your own. Tell me. Who helped you?"

My mind flashes to the Droid with the golden eyes. But all I say is, "Perhaps your hold on the neural network isn't so perfect after all."

"Not to worry if you will not share. I know there is a traitor amongst us. I will find out soon enough. And when I do, he will pay dearly. In the meantime, I can't very well let such an exquisite specimen of a human escape again. You and the little girl will be the first to power our next generation of Droids."

I watch in helpless horror as Gardurak stabs into the soft flesh at the crook of my arm in one swift motion. The pain barely registers before he finishes drawing a large syringe of blood.

Gardurak waves the syringe in front of my eyes. "Did you know that the level of nanobots in your system is a thousandfold higher than the few others like yourself? That your very own blood is capable of giving rise to replicating nanobots by itself? We've been trying to develop the technology, but we were unable to. Now you bring the technology to our very doorstep. How very considerate of you, my little pet."

The next instant, he spins and turns towards Telisad, his voice carrying over his shoulder. "Remarkable, isn't it? If my little experiment works, even a small amount of your blood contains enough nanobots to replicate in this child's body. Did you know that we tried with your friend? But unfortunately, he only has the single mutation like all the others. But it was still worth a try. Just too bad it didn't work."

Stars, Triton. *He must be talking about Triton.* "What have you done to him? You're a sick bastard, Gardurak." I curse at him, but he takes no notice.

He positions the needle at Telisad's bony shoulder.

"Stop!" I scream as I twist against the restraints. I may not be a doctor, but even I know that one can't just go injecting incompatible blood into another person without serious consequences. "You're going to kill her!"

Gardurak's metal face rounds on me. His pulsatile eyes lasering into mine.

"No, my pet. You're mistaken. I'm going to save her miserable little life." He turns back towards Telisad, but just as the needle is about to pierce her skin, suddenly he stops. Freezing mid-motion. Perhaps I'm imagining it, but it seems as if his head cocks ever so slightly to the side. He jerks towards me. "Perhaps this is your lucky day after all, my pet. Apparently there is something that requires my immediate attention, so this experiment will just have to wait. How unfortunate, as I was so looking forward to it. Not to worry though, we'll try tomorrow when the magnetic fields of the sun and Asteris align again." He turns to the one of the other Droids. "See these two back to their *quarters*. The rest of you come with me. Quickly."

LXXX

LIVI: ROUND TWO

"TELISAD!"

Allara rushes towards us, with Sayrie close at her heels. Soon all of the others are crowded around us as well.

The little girl collapses into the arms of the elderly woman, who brushes back the tangled hair from her face. "Did they hurt you?"

Telisad's lips tremble, her face holding back tears, but to my surprise, she manages to keep her young voice steady. "No, Allara. I'm okay. They didn't hurt me."

Allara's eyes turn to mine. Her discerning gaze scanning me from head to toe. "And you—are you all right?"

"The Droids did nothing more than draw my blood with a beast of a needle and test my sanity. Other than that, you could say I'm all right. But I agree with what you said earlier. We don't have much time. The Droids are planning something big for all of us, and not in a good way. They only delayed their plans tonight because of a disturbance somewhere on the base."

Sayrie turns to the others, who seem to hang on her every word. "Then we've no other choice. We've prepared long enough. We try our escape. *Tonight.*"

Allara rubs warmth into Telisad's arms, the child's eyelids drooping. She whispers, "But Sayrie, you know as well as I do that without the key for Telisad's collar, we have no way to get it off. I'll go through the Gates of the Dead before I'm willing to leave this child behind."

I bring out the metal pin that I hid in the seam of my shift.

"Is this the key you were looking for?"

Allara claps her hand to her mouth. Excited whispers course through the others before me.

"Well, I'll be a fleefluff's behind." Sayrie chuckles under her breath. Her wide eyes jogging between me and the key. "How in the universe did you get that?"

"I wish I could say it was because of my exceptional stealth and special mind control abilities. But honestly, during all the commotion, the Droids left it on the table. I swiped it when they weren't looking. By the way, what's a fleefluff?"

Sayrie laughs. "It's a very large bird we have on Pantoc, with an even larger behind. And by the way, *you're* going to fit right in."

She throws a nod towards Jin and Wendolyn, who surreptitiously move to obscure the guard Droids' views from the cell hatch. Sayrie then walks over to the sanitation station, a simple excrement drain and shower. She gestures me over and opens a hidden compartment under the shower pipe. I suck in a breath. Two hazars, a rope, one baton, an assortment of other lethal-looking weapons, even a skyver.

"Where'd you get all of these?"

"We're all kleptomaniacs here. Out of pure necessity only of course." Her smile spreads from one curled earlobe to the other. "Told you you'd fit right in."

"Yes, I suppose I will." I grin right back at her. "Tonight then."

LXXXI

LIVI: NOBODY TOUCH THE GRUEL

"**R**EMEMBER, NOBODY TOUCH the gruel. We've got to keep all of our senses tonight," Sayrie whispers to the rest of us.

"But Sayrie, you made us skip lunch too. And I'm so very hungry." Telisad pouts. She's the youngest of them all. Not even ten according to Allara. When her whole family was captured by the Quadrati, only she was spared from the pods. But only to live like this. The others are her only family now.

Sayrie strokes the back of the little girl's head. "I know, my sweet girl. And I promise when we get back to Pantoc I will personally cook you the biggest fen roast you have ever seen."

"Really?" Telisad's face brightens.

"Yes, really." Sayrie smiles at her. "And remember what I said, after we all get our collars off, we've got to be very quiet, so that the Droids don't hear. And when we leave the cell, I want you to stay with Allara no matter what happens. Do you hear?"

Telisad bobs her head.

"That's a good girl." Sayrie pats her hand and then turns to me. "We've been planning for this for what feels like eons now, timing it just right. An hour after the evening gruel, when the cleaner Droid comes to fetch our bowls and cups, they leave the cells unlocked thinking our collars and the sedatives in the gruel are enough to keep us down. There will be five guard Droids stationed a few steps beyond the cell hatch. You've had combat experience, I take it?"

"You could say that." I hold my chin straight.

"Then you and I will head out the hatch door first. Jin, you checked the weapons already?"

"Done, Sayrie."

I'm not sure how much training the others have fighting the Droids. I don't want to take any chances. I look towards the others. "And remember, if push comes to shove, get them right between the shoulder blades. Their power source is located just below the surface there. That's where they are the most vulnerable."

Sayrie nods towards me then faces the others, her voice grim. "Wendolyn and Vipa, take out the cleaner Droid as soon as it enters. Livinthea and I will go for the Droids by the main post. Jin and Chee, I'm counting on you both to charge the flanks. Everyone else, be on the ready. Once we disable them, we've got to run like a flaming fleefluff. I'm guessing only two jaunts before reinforcements pile in. Run for the tunnels and get yourself to Brevia's hidden crafts."

Her last words catch me off guard. "You've got spacecrafts?"

Sayrie turns to me. "I told you we have been planning this for a very long time. The crafts were Brevia's. Several star weeks ago, she had been sent along with other top militia from Pantoc to rescue us from this carrion's pit, but they were thwarted in the process. Brevia was the only one who survived. The Droids threw her in here with us. She told us about the hidden crafts. We had been planning to escape, but we made the mistake of not acting soon enough. The day before our planned escape, the Droids put Brevia through Onterrogation just like you. Only *she* didn't make it. We don't want to make that same mistake again."

"Where are the crafts?"

"Apparently they are hidden just outside the northern tunnels of the base. Brevia left behind a pair of homing devices to help us locate them." She holds out a small round disc in her hand towards me. "I've seen how strong you are. How fast you are. I don't know what you are, but I do know that you're a born soldier, wherever you're from. After getting out of the cell, I would like you to lead the others to the crafts."

"But what about you?"

"I've got to go to Nesting first."

Allara, who was quietly listening to our conversation until now, interrupts. "Nesting, Sayrie? There are too many patrols there. I don't care if you won the title of Eminent Elemature at the engineering academy. You'll get caught for sure."

"Allara, you of all people know I have to try. You yourself wouldn't leave little Telisad behind. Well, I would rather go through the Gates of the Dead before I leave my brother behind on this rat's pit of a planet."

Allara is quiet for a moment but then nods at Sayrie. "As you wish then. What good is life if one cannot fight for what lives in one's heart?"

"I'm going with you," I say. The others look at me in surprise as I explain. "They've got my friends in there as well."

Sayrie spins towards me. "You do realize that going to Nesting is an impossible mission at best, and a doomed mission at worst."

"Then it's the very best kind of mission," I reply, holding her hard gaze.

Sayrie dips her head ever so slightly. "Very well then." Sayrie turns to the others. "Livi and I will meet up with the rest of you when we can. But if we're not there within ten jaunts or if the Droids get a whiff of you, then you must leave without us. Jin, you are responsible for getting everyone onto those crafts and off this rat's pit." She hands Jin one of the homing devices.

Jin takes the disc but shakes her head. "Please, Sayrie. I would rather go through the Gates of the Dead before I left you behind. Don't make me do this. We'll wait for you."

Sayrie puts a hand on Jin's shoulder. "And I would go through the Gates of the Dead for you as well, my friend. But we've waited so long for this opportunity to escape. We've got to save as many of us as we can. We owe it to Pantoc. We owe it to Brevia and all the others who died trying to save us. But I've got to try to get Rhyton out first. That is on me, only me. And Livi here has made her decision as well. I won't jeopardize you or the others' lives for that. As soon as we're out of the cells, you will lead them. Promise me you will get them out."

Jin looks back at Sayrie for a long, hard moment. "Very well, Sayrie. But know that it will crush me to leave you behind after all that we've been through. You have been like a sister to me."

"To me as well." She gives Jin's hand a squeeze.

Sayrie turns to the rest of the group, their faces solemn, worried. "An hour after the Dim commences and the cleaner Droid rumbles in—that's when we'll do it. But we've got to be quick. No more than ten seconds per collar."

The others nod. A mixture of wide eyes and creased brows reflect back at her.

"All right then. Let's get ourselves out of this stars-forsaken place." Sayrie tries to sound confident, but her fingers tremble.

I don't blame her. So many things could go wrong. Terribly wrong.

LXXXII

LIVI: GETTING THE HELLAS OUT

THE LIGHT CLICKS two notches down. This must be what they call the Dim. A little while longer, then we begin. My heartbeat clicks double time in my chest. I will it to slow down. We can do this.

Sayrie was right, one good thing about the Droids is that they are highly predictable, rarely ever deviating from their regimented schedule. Already the telltale footsteps of evening patrol approach, vibrating along the cot's hard planks as I lie pretending to sleep as I know the others are doing as well. Closer now, I can actually hear them. In another thirty seconds, the cleaner Droid will enter the hatch. And then we'll have just one jaunt (or roughly five minutes as I figured out) to get the hellas out of here.

The cell hatch opens with a swish. Light floods in, and I will myself not to react.

Moments pass in eerie silence, then the light whining whir of metal on stone. *The cleaner Droid.*

Steady.

Something clinks to my left. It's just the rattling of a cup into the cleaner Droid's built-in bin. It's all I can do not to twitch. To pretend to be asleep. To pretend to be drugged by the evening's gruel. I know the others are trying hard to do the same. *Stay calm.*

Then suddenly, a muffled thump.

It's down.

"Okay now!" Sayrie whispers. Sayrie jumps up from the cot next to mine and uses the key to unlock my collar. An overwhelming sense of relief washes over me as soon as it comes off. But there's no time to celebrate yet. Quickly, I take the key from Sayrie and unlock hers as well. The others fall in line wordlessly behind her, stolen weapons already in hand. One by one, the collars come off. Allara, Jin, Ehi, Claris. We're making good time. Fina, Chee, Aok, Wendolyn. And finally Telisad. I pull the key I found from the seam of my shift. She trembles slightly as I insert the key into the collar's rigid notch. "Don't worry, it won't hurt," I reassure her as her throat bobs. And with a satisfying click, her collar drops as well. She and I let out a sigh of relief. Jin hands me a hazar.

Sayrie and I nod towards each other, crouching at the ready at the cell hatch. The others line up closely behind us. Sayrie mouths the countdown. Three. Two. One. I lurch out the door. Hazar and hand connect with the first guard Droid at the post. He comes down with a thud, but when I turn, I find that the others are in a black hole of trouble.

Sayrie and Jin struggle to take out their Droids. Their jabs with the batons meet nothing but air. And Chee is even worse off. The Droid grips her by the neck. Her face rapidly turns a dark shade of purple. Her feet kick uselessly as the Droid lifts her off the floor. The others look on, frozen in fear. If I don't do something quickly, we're not going to get very far.

I retrieve my hazar and lunge for the Droid who has Chee in a choke hold. I unleash my hazar and drive it into the Droid's back. The Droid and Chee collapse in a heap onto the cold stone floor. In the next motion, I sweep my leg low, connecting with hard metal but throwing both the other Droids off balance and allowing Sayrie and Jin to finally find purchase with their spiked batons.

"You all right?" I roll the Droid off of Chee and help her up.

"Yes, thank you." Her eyes are wide as she rubs at her neck. Her voice is raspy. "How did you do that?"

"Practice." I smile.

From behind, Sayrie claps me on my shoulder. "Yes, and let me say for the record that I'm *very* glad you are on our side." Sayrie then turns to Jin. "Quickly now, the backup Droids will be here any minute, so we've no time to waste. Here's where we split up. Use the homing device, and remember to take the perimeter tunnels. You're not likely to run into many more Droids there. Remember what Brevia told us about where to find the Pherrings. Once you find them, get everyone inside and get the craft ready for takeoff." She puts a hand on Jin's shoulder. "If Livi and I do not reach the Pherring by nightfall, you will have to pilot the ship. I want you to get yourselves off this rat's pit. Keep the camouflage device on and use the cover of night for takeoff. Don't wait for us. Do I have your word?"

"Yes, Sayrie." The old friends grip each other's arms tightly a split second before letting go.

Sayrie and I sprint down the tunnels, but I'm careful not to outpace her. I know my way to Nesting just as well as she, but I can't very well leave her behind. We encounter three Droids and two Dogger bots patrolling the tunnels, but I quickly disable them with rapid-fire shots from my hazar.

Sayrie looks at me in wonder. "You weren't kidding when you said you had combat experience, were you?"

I smile at her. "Just wait until you meet my friends."

LXXXIII

LIVI: THE RESCUE

SAYRIE AND I SNEAK up to the overlook above the Nesting, scanning the situation below.

We peek over the edge, and Sayrie quickly locates Rhyton at the far end. Keenon's and Eppel's pods are situated close to Sayrie's brother, still in the same location I spotted them last.

But there is no sign of Triton. Where in hellas could he be? Then I remember. The small antechamber with the glowing pods. *Please, please let him be there.* Because the alternative would be too hard to handle.

From our overlook, the entrance to the antechamber is just below, a Droid guarding it. With my Bionic eyes, I count twenty Droids hidden under the shadow of the eaves. Not great odds, but we have a plan.

"Ready for me to clear this place out?" Sayrie asks.

"Ready," I say with as much confidence as I can, though inside I don't feel ready for anything.

"Okay then. Let's go get them." Sayrie flashes her teeth at me before disappearing down the tunnel towards the main entrance of Nesting, hazar in hand. I perch myself just beside the open wall of the overlook.

Moments later, the ground shudders with an explosive boom. *That Sayrie sure is one heck of an elematician.* She managed to make a diversion device out of fermented gruel. Not only that, it's supposed to be powerful enough to temporarily disrupt local communication within the Droids' neural network.

And as Sayrie predicted, the Droids clear out below, rushing towards the explosion.

That is, all save for one.

And he remains guarding the door to the antechamber. *That figures.*

I catapult over the metal railing of the overlook, landing squarely on the Droid below, and with one quick jab of the hazar, disable it. Never have I been more thankful for my Bionic strength and agility.

Quickly I run through the antechamber, passing pod after glowing pod, until finally what I see through one of the pod windows makes me skid to a stop.

Charcoal-black hair with a lock of white. The remains of old bruises at his temple, along his angular jaw. I crane my head to get a closer look as my heart rate starts an even more rapid ascent. *He is here. It really is Triton. That draggart Gardurak wasn't lying.*

His pod is enveloped in glowing electrical currents of blues and golds. As I reach for the lever to open the pod, a sudden arcing bolt of electricity strikes my hand sending an excruciating pain zinging through my arm as I snatch my hand back.

"Crimeny," I curse as I cradle my hand, red welts already forming on my palm. But I have no time to dwell on the pain. Quickly I snatch the rope Sayrie gave me out of the makeshift satchel at my back, the one we made from the hems of my shift. One quick loop and knot later, I lasso the rope over the lever with my good hand and yank as hard as I can. The lever clicks with a resounding snap. The cover of the pod slides open as the electrical currents sizzle out, revealing Triton's sleeping form.

"Triton!" I grab him by his broad shoulders. "Wake up! Triton!"

But something is wrong. Triton's face pales, then turns ashen. I feel for his carotids. Nothing. Absolutely nothing. *No.* What have I done? What if he's dependent on the pod? But this is not supposed to be possible. He's a Bionic, for star's sake.

I start pounding on his chest. I'm no medicus, but every Galactic cadet knows basic resuscitation maneuvers. Thirty compressions. I pinch his nose and tilt his chin. Two breaths. His lips feel like ice against mine. *Come on. Come on. Please help me. This can't be happening.* Thirty more compressions and two more breaths. I put my ear on his chest. Only an empty echo answers. *Keep going, for star's sake. Don't stop.* More compressions and more breaths. *I can't lose him.* I continue the relentless pounding at his chest, throwing a call out to the unfeeling universe. *Help me. Please. Help me. I can't lose him. I just can't.* I pinch his nose and force another breath.

"He needs the antidote." A voice pierces my thoughts, the pitch foreign and strange but the rhythm hauntingly familiar.

I startle back and scrabble for my hazar as my eyes scan long to the antechamber entrance. A Sensate Droid. But not just any Sensate. The one with the honey-golden eyes. I know this Droid. One never forgets kind eyes.

"Quickly," he repeats more urgently as he takes a step towards me and holds out a metal device. "He needs the antidote. Your friend will die otherwise." His voice cuts through the haze in my head.

Is he telling the truth? Can I trust him? My whirling thoughts are interrupted by a shout.

"Get down, Livi!" Sayrie is at the chamber doorway, her hazar aimed at the Droid's back, finger on the trigger, breathing hard. Her arms shake, and there's an angry red welt on her arm.

"Wait!" I shout as I lurch forward to shield the Droid with my body.

"Are you crazy, Livi?" Sayrie shouts back between heaving breaths. "Get out of the way!" Her brows arch to the sky.

"No, really. Wait. I-I *know* him." I throw my arms wide. The Droid behind me stills. I need time to think. To sort things out. But there is no time. I've got to rule with my gut. "He saved me, before. He's trying to help us. Please. We can trust him." I say these words to convince Sayrie as much as myself.

A few precious seconds tick by. Her eyes search for the meaning in mine. Finally, Sayrie drops her hazar to her side.

And before I can say anything, the Droid surges behind me, metal arm arced through the air, and stabs Triton in the chest.

"No!" I scream as I whirl around and charge at the Droid, but in the next moment Triton jerks alive, his breath sputtering, color returning to his lips. Stunned, I rush instead towards Triton.

Triton swings his arms wildly, nearly knocking me over.

"Triton! It's okay. I've got you." I grab hold of his hands, stilling them. "You're okay," I say in wonder. I feel about ready to laugh and cry at the same time.

He shakes his head as if clearing the crust from his mind. His eyes crack ever so slightly open, but enough for me to see the steel-grey that I know so well.

"Livi?" His voice is weak, raspy.

"Yes. Yes, it's me."

"What happened?" Triton asks as he heaves himself slowly up, his hand coming up to rub at his temple.

"It's a long story. We just extracted you from the mind meld. I'll explain more later. But right now we've got to get Eppel and Keenon out as well. You think you can walk?"

"His Bionic body will help him recover," the Droid's voice interjects.

Now I have time to process it. To remember. The cadence hauntingly familiar, but the pitch all wrong. I turn to the Droid. "It was you, wasn't it? You helped me. Before."

"You weren't supposed to come back."

That voice. A reply so simple, yet it resounds in my head, jostling a cog loose, a distant memory. But I just can't place it.

"Why?" I ask. "Why are you helping us?"

"Because you called me."

LXXXIV

LIVI: A DIFFICULT DECISION

"**Y**OU MUST HURRY. I can only keep the guard Droids at bay for so long before the Master Sensate notices."

The Droid's words jerk my thoughts back to the present.

"But I have others I need to help. Do you have more of the antidote?"

The Droid nods. I look on in utter disbelief as he opens up a compartment hidden within the thigh of his leg. Several more of the same metallic antidote devices lie hidden there.

"Then, will you help us?"

The Droid's voice is like a flowing river, feeding into my mind. "As much as is possible."

"Thank you." I help Triton stand, then turn to Sayrie, who is still wide-eyed. "Any luck with your brother?"

"I couldn't get past the electrical currents of his pod." She points at the red welts running up her arms, confirming what I already guessed.

"The Droid says he will help us get the others. But we must do so quickly, before he loses his hold on the guard Droids."

Sayrie gives the Droid a wary glance but nods and hurries out of the antechamber.

I start to help Triton, but to my amazement, he takes a step forward on his own, waving my hand away. "I'm all right, Livi. Just lead the way."

"You sure?" I ask, my arm still out ready to catch him.

"Yes, I'm very sure. Now let's get the dark infinites out of here."

We dart back out to the larger chamber. The nanobot technology amazes me yet again, because Triton even manages to break into a slow jog despite almost dying just a few moments ago. When we reach the outer large chamber, I'm relieved to find that it's still clear of the guard Droids. We've taken so long that I'm certain the Droid with the golden eyes really is somehow keeping the other Droids away. We head to the far end of the chamber where Keenon, Eppel, and Sayrie's brother are all located. We come upon Eppel's pod first.

I start to loop the rope around the lever of Eppel's pod, as the Droid's voice pierces through my thoughts again. "The antidote needs to be injected directly into the heart. But we must be careful. If the individual is already fully bonded with the Quadrati collective mind, the antidote can't reverse the mind meld. And once the pod's seal is broken, there is no going back."

No going back. My hands still. "You mean he could die?"

"Yes." The Droid's answer is frank, unguarded.

"But how do we know if they're fully bonded or not?"

"There is no way to tell for sure. Usually the process takes several weeks, but in some individuals can take up to several star months depending on how strong their core sense of self is."

Infinite black holes. Then it may be too late for Sayrie's brother, for Keenon, maybe even for Eppel.

"What is it, Livi?" Triton catches up from behind, his face lined with concern.

Sayrie stands on the opposite side of Eppel's pod.

"According to the Droid, if we break the pod's seal and the individual is already fully bonded to the mind meld, then even the antidote won't save them. And we don't have much time, this Droid can hold back the other guard Droids for only so long." I turn to Triton. "What should we do?"

Triton looks back at me grimly. "I've known Eppel since my first day at Atlas. He has been like a father to me. And I can tell you that he would rather die than stay imprisoned in the Quadrati neural network. I have no doubt he would want us to try the antidote." He turns to me. "Here, Livi. Let me take that rope. It should be me who pulls the lever. The decision will be on my shoulders."

Triton takes the rope from my hand. There's only the slightest moment of hesitation before he jerks his hand, flipping the lever. The pod's clear cover slides open as the electrical currents blink out. The Droid is already by Eppel's side and injects the antidote into his chest. Not even a second goes by and Eppel heaves in a large breath. His eyelids flutter open.

"Thank the stars." I let a breath out as Triton helps Eppel sit up.

Triton turns to me. Despite his stoic exterior, his eyes are glistening. "I've got him, Livi. Eppel and I will go get Juki and Phlynnt. I know where they are. Go help your friend Keenon." Wordlessly, the Droid hands Triton two antidote devices.

I nod to him gratefully and rush to the pod where I last saw Keenon. The Droid and Sayrie trail not far behind.

Sayrie calls out to me between heaving breaths. "We don't have much time left. We've got to split up." She spins towards the Droid. "Can you give me one of the antidote devices?"

Without hesitation, the Droid reaches into his thigh compartment and hands her a metal device. In the meantime, I take out the rope, slicing it in half with my hazar, and press one end into Sayrie's hand. "Remember, the antidote needs to be injected directly into the heart."

"Got it. Thank you, my friend." She then spins towards the Droid. "And thank you as well." With that, she sprints towards her brother's pod.

When I get to Keenon's pod, seeing his familiar form so deathly still makes my insides shudder.

The Droid has followed me, and his voice pulses against my mind. "It may already be too late to save this one. Do you still want to proceed?"

I look upon the wavy jet-black hair and strong brows that I've known since childhood. Keenon appears almost peaceful under the purple and green currents flowing over him. The decision tears at me.

What if this doesn't work? What if he's too far bonded to the mind meld? What if I end up killing him instead? Could I live with that kind of guilt for the rest of my life?

But then images from what seems now like a past life flash in my mind, briefly taking me back.

I weave over the frothing crests of rushing waters, racing Keenon next to me. The surrounding underbrush glows violent purple and flaming red under the sunlight. Keenon flashes a mischievous smile at me, then spins his Kiok out in front, spraying a mist of cool water on my face with the dual spinning balls of his watercraft. When I catch up to him, he is laughing, beaming, a smile that could light up all of Cerulea. And carefree.

Yes. The answer comes to me just like that. That is how he would like to be. *Free. No matter what.*

I nod, my eyes pricking at the memory. "Yes, let's proceed." The rope is already looped around the lever on Keenon's pod. I throw a quick wish to the stars. *Please let this work.* And pull. As hard as I can.

The pod's clear cover slides away as the electrical current dies out, and even before I can reach him, the Droid already has injected the antidote. Keenon's chest heaves in an uneven breath. Then stops. His face rapidly turns a dusky blue.

Oh stars. No.

I rush over to Keenon, feel the lack of pulse at his neck. And start resuscitation maneuvers. *Stars, not again.* One, two, three, four, five—"Please he needs more antidote!" I call out to the Droid.

"I'm afraid that won't work."

—eleven, twelve, thirteen, fourteen—"Please. Just try again." —eighteen, nineteen, twenty—"Please." Keenon's lips are turning bluer by the second.

The Droid plunges a second shot into Keenon's chest. Keenon heaves another breath in. And then another. I put a hand on his neck. And this time I feel it, thready, but a pulse nonetheless.

I slump back, my arms shaking. Thank the stars. I don't know how much more of this I can take. In the next several moments, Keenon's breathing evens out. His color returns. His pulse grows stronger. But—but his eyes remain rigidly closed. "Why is he not waking up?"

"He doesn't have the nanobots to expedite the recovery," the Droid replies.

"Will he be all right?"

"Only time will tell. The reversal is not supposed to require double doses of the antidote. In the meantime, we must hurry."

As if they can hear the Droid as well, the others rush towards us almost all at once. Sayrie has one arm around Rhyton's waist supporting him, but to my utter amazement he's awake, his recovery so much faster than Keenon's. But I'm not too surprised when I see that Rhyton also has a slash of white through his lavender hair, just like his sister. The Mark of Dresden.

Triton guides Phlynnt forward, followed by Eppel and Juki walking on their own.

"Thank the stars," I say.

"Can't leave this old man behind even if you wanted to," Eppel replies. He looks tired but winks at me.

"We'll have to do introductions later," Sayrie says. "It's time to get out of here."

"But what about all these other people?" My arms spread wide. "We've got to help them."

The Droid turns to me, actually speaks out loud. "I can't hold off the guard Droids much longer. You've got to go."

"But we can't just leave them here. Let's try to save as many as we can. You've got that antidote, for star's sake." My eyes alight on the face of a young girl in a pod close to me, from the looks of it, barely a teenager. I can only imagine—someone's sister or daughter. My insides twist at the thought of leaving all these innocent people in the clutches of those metal beasts.

Triton puts a hand on my shoulder. "The Droid is right, Livi. As he said, most of these people are likely too far bonded to the Quadrati neural network to be saved anyway. We've got to get out of here. It is imperative that we make it back to Atlas to let them know what we have found. To warn them. If the Droids are allowed to unleash that new army of theirs, there is no telling how much more destruction they will wreak. The whole of the Ritarian Gateways is at stake. We'll find a way to come back and see if we can help these other people. I promise."

"Hurry." The Droid's voice is more urgent now. "Gardurak is already on his way. You've got to go. *Now*."

And as if in confirmation of that, I start to feel it—that intense buzzing at the base of my brain.

LXXXV

LIVI: DISCOVERY

HE DROID scoops Keenon up from the pod and slings him over his shoulder as if he weighs nothing at all.

Sayrie starts to head in the direction of the Nesting chamber entrance, Brevia's tracker in her hand, but the Droid sweeps out an arm stopping her. "You shouldn't go that way. Gardurak just mobilized his Droids around the core tunnels."

Sayrie backtracks reluctantly. "But we need to get to the northern tunnels." Her voice climbs ever so slightly higher. "Our escape crafts and the others are waiting there."

"Is there another way out?" I ask the Droid.

The Droid thinks for a brief moment, then gives a simple nod in confirmation. "Quickly. Follow me." The Droid rushes us back to the antechamber past several pods and inserts his hand into a panel by the far wall. The ground yawns open just an arm's length in front of him, revealing a steeply descending tunnel underneath. "Based on my neural map, this should work."

"Well, I'll be a fleefluff's behind," I say.

Sayrie looks at me, her eyes round. "You took the words right out of my mouth."

"This way," the Droid orders.

The Droid leads us down into the subsurface tunnel. I have to duck my head just to fit through the entrance. As soon as we're all in, the entrance zips closed behind us, pitching us into complete and total darkness, followed by a few curse words echoing down the tunnel. Even my Bionic eyes can't see a blasted thing. But a moment later, a shock of light erupts ahead. Of course. The Droid. A beam projects from the middle of his chest, lighting the way. *Is there anything he can't do?*

The Droid still carries Keenon slung over his shoulder as he leads us down the narrowly carved tunnel, so narrow that we have to go single file. Rhyton has recovered enough now to just need Sayrie's guiding hand. Otherwise, he manages to walk on his own. Triton follows right behind me, with Juki, Phlynnt, and Eppel bringing up the rear. From the thick layer of dust covering the walls and ground, it's clear these passageways aren't used—at all. A multitude of long pipes with diameters as thick as a giant Psyla tree's trunk run along the walls of the tunnel. As the ground dips lower and lower, the air grows colder and strangely more— more damp?

We descend rapidly into what seems like the endless maze of a molerat's burrow. Finally, the path widens just enough so that we no longer need to walk single file. Though my Bionic body protects me from the cold,

Sayrie and Rhyton are not so lucky. Sayrie wraps a protective arm around her brother, trying to keep him warm. We're so deep underground now that I can feel my eardrums squeeze. Just as the pressure in my ears starts to build to an almost painful ache, the tunnel flattens out and opens up to a sight that makes all of us stop dead in our tracks.

Water.

Not just a small, stingy puddle.

But instead, a vast, underground lake.

Its surface blanketed with cool mist.

"Dark infinites," Triton mutters from behind me, his breath curling in front of his face. "What is this place?"

The Droid answers out loud. "These are the underground aquifers that help keep the people in the pods alive, recycled for over a millennium now. You may not want to drink it."

Did the Droid just make a joke? But now I understand the pipes and tubes lining the tunnels. They supply the pods in the Nesting from here. I had no idea water could even exist on such a dry and desolate planet.

In the dim light, I can make out a narrow perimeter path weaving around the lake, with various other tunnel openings similar to the one we just exited.

"Will one of these passageways take us to the northern tunnels?" Sayrie asks.

"According to my neural map, yes," the Droid answers. "But the majority of these tunnels are no longer in use. The grounds are sometimes rocked by seismic shifts. They may or may not still be traversable."

Suddenly, a faint clanging echoes down the tunnel we just came down.

"Let's get going. Gardurak has discovered our escape route." The Droid forges ahead, resuming his breakneck pace. "The Dogger bots will catch up to us soon if we don't hurry. If we can make it to the other side of the aquifer into one of passageways, we may be able to lose them in the maze of tunnels. Their tracking signals are blunted this far underground."

Quickly he leads us around the narrow path skirting the lake edges. In some areas, the ledge dips underwater and we're forced to splash through knee-deep water.

"St-stars alive, that's c-cold," Sayrie exclaims. Her teeth chatter uncontrollably now.

"I don't know what's worse, being stuck in the Quadrati mind or freezing to death in their watering hole," Rhyton adds, his Rs curling and Ts blunted, just like his sister's. His lips are almost as blue as Wintron's summer lake, and I'm almost glad Keenon is still asleep so as not to feel the frigid cold.

We pass tunnel entrance after tunnel entrance. The whirring of the Dogger bots echoes down into the cavern, louder, closer.

"Faster, Rhyton." Sayrie encourages her brother forward, who seems to be tiring.

We've made it almost halfway around the lake, when finally the Droid turns. "This should be the one." His light shifts into the tunnel while the rest of us follow closely behind. Up and up we climb. The air warms as we ascend rapidly, the tension in my shoulders loosening as the sound of the Dogger bots fades and eventually dies out altogether. Finally, when I'm just be able to discern a faint light glowing ahead, the Droid stops.

"Head around the bend, and the path should take you where you want to go." Carefully, he lays Keenon down.

It takes me a moment to realize what he's implying. "You're not coming with us?"

"If I stay with you any longer, Gardurak will notice the irregularity in the neural network. At the moment, he still doesn't know that I am helping you."

"Please. You're not like the other Droids. Come with us. We can help each other. We'll offer you protection, and you can teach us about your antidote, how to free all those people from the Quadrati neural network."

"I'm afraid that's not possible."

The others shift uncomfortably, eager to get going. But I've been wondering about this Droid since the day he helped me. He's more of a puzzle to me now than before. I can't let perhaps the only opportunity to find out more escape again. I take a step towards the Droid. "How did you know about the nanobots? About the Mark of Dresden?"

"I can't explain that to you."

"Can't?" I look him square in his honey-gold eyes. "Or won't?" The subtle things he says, the haunting cadence of his voice pulls at me. I look at him more closely, but nothing in the ashen metal mask, the gleam of tinston, spell familiarity. "Wh-who are you really?"

The Droid's eyes pivot away for a long moment, searching for something I cannot see. Just when I think he's not going to answer at all, he turns back to me. His voice pierces directly into my mind. "Livinthea, it's me. Tomas. Your father."

"F-Father?" My own words sputter out like jagged rocks. The ground slides out from under me, though I haven't moved. How can the metal Droid before me be the same man who rocked me in his arms back to sleep, nightmare after nightmare so many years ago? The same one who taught me about the constellations of Erlion, naming each and every twinkling of light that I pointed to without fail? The one whose hair grew as dark as the midnight sands of Dresden, in the same shade I inherited? No. It was *impossible*. It must be a *trick*. I can see nothing of my father in this metal husk before me. *And yet*—and yet something about the eyes is achingly familiar. Something about the way he looks at me, the way he speaks. "I-I don't understand," I stutter.

"I'm sorry, my Comet. I didn't want to tell you. I didn't want to hurt you. I know it's hard for you to believe."

My father's pet name for me makes my mind go still. No one else has ever called me that. *No one.* The last day I heard that name, the world I understood splintered and frayed under a merciless wind. My gaze jogs up the gleam of his mask, *to the eyes*.

"But sooner or later you would have found out the truth. Better to know now. It may be the only way to help you out of this." He angles towards the side of the tunnel that leads to the aquifers, then back again. "But there is so little time to explain. I can only separate myself from the Quadrati collective mind a short time before Gardurak notices. Soon the pull of the neural network will become too strong, and I will not be able to hold on, so I need to help you see."

He steps towards me and touches my forehead gently. Triton, who has been waiting in the wings patiently until now, instantly descends upon the Droid, deflecting his hand. Eppel, Juki, and Phlynnt surge forward, not far behind.

"No, wait. It's okay," I reassure them quickly. "He means no harm."

Triton hesitates, but after a moment releases the Droid's arm, though he still remains rigidly by my side along with the rest of his squadron.

The Droid again places a hand on my forehead. A tingling sensation niggles there all the way to the base of my brain as snippets of time cog together, recollections and imaginings that are not my own weld into a map of memories.

It's raining ships. My father scans the sky. We've been attacked by Quadrati before. But this time is different. This time, worry lines my father's usually placid face. "Livinthea, go with your mother." His voice is low, urgent.

"But I don't want to leave, I want to fight. With you," I protest, grabbing at the tail of his shirt. Even then, I'm as bullheaded as a longhorn's cud, but so small that my father has to kneel down as he cups my face gently in his strong hands.

"I know, my Comet. Next time you will. But right now, I need you to look after your mother. Do you think you can do that?" My father was always good at that, bridling the wilderness inside of me, infusing the light into the dark.

I nod reluctantly, for I do not want to disappoint my father. He then stands and turns to my mother, a soft look in his eyes.

"Dalin, it's time. Head towards Fila's Tress. Stay close to the streams and underbrush until you get to the hideout."

Despite the commotion, my mother stays as calm as Wintron's summer lake, her shimmering hair alight against her beautiful face.

"Go, Tomas. I will keep her safe. We knew this time would come, and we are prepared. Let's do what we need to do."

He nods to my mother, placing a tender hand on her cheek. A thousand unspoken words pass within their look, but he only says, "For the love between us, whatever comes."

And despite my mother's brave words, despite the stoic way she holds her shoulders, her eyes glisten under the dying light. "For the love between us." They embrace for a long moment until my father turns to me. "Take care of your mother, Livinthea, and remember that whatever comes, my love for you is eternity itself. One day, my Comet, we will be together again." He graces the top of my head with a lingering kiss.

The Droid's hand comes away, the images evaporating.

I blink my way back to the present. The memory of that moment makes the corners of my eyes prick. The dusty floorboards creak back open. And as the metal Droid before me who seems the farthest thing in the universe from my father continues to stare down at me, somehow I understand, understand that he is speaking the truth. My throat squeezes at the exact point where air gives way to sound. I can barely speak. I can barely breathe. *Stars, he really is my father.* "The day you left, you ended up here?"

He nods. "It's a long story."

My voice pinches out in a stifled stutter. "Th-then it was you the whole time?" Starlock. My beacon in the dark. "You saved me?"

His honey-gold eyes lock onto mine. "No, Livinthea, *you* saved *me.* I had been lost. So long. Unable to find my way back. Until you found me. Now we must get you out of here. Quickly, before Gardurak senses what is happening."

I must look like I've just been slapped in the face because Triton steps between the Droid and me. "I don't know what you're doing to her, but I think that's enough."

"No, Triton. It's okay. The Droid has just revealed something terribly important. I'm just a little shocked. That's all."

"What could affect you so?"

"This Droid is my—my father."

Now it's Eppel's turn to stutter in surprise. "T-Tomas?" His eyebrows arch. "Is that really you?"

The Droid finally speaks out loud, his voice raw. "I'm afraid it is, my old friend, Eppelsoff. It's been too long."

"Stars alive. It really is you. No one but you would dare call me by that nickname. But how did it happen?"

"There's just too much to explain. That day at Finlan's Point, there was an ambush. The Quadrati captured me then. And brought me here. I managed to escape in the beginning, stayed hidden in the aquifer cabins for a long time and sneaked up to the pod chambers when I could. For many years I did this, and managed to work on an antidote to help all those people. Perfected it even. But they caught me the day I was going to try using it. The rest well"—his arms point to his own metal torso—"you can see for yourself."

"If I had only known what happened to you, all these years. How you must have suffered." Eppel shakes his head, his eternally strong and assured demeanor suddenly broken. "I'm so terribly sorry, Tomas. I should never have stopped looking for you."

"There's nothing to be sorry for, my old friend. We each have our own lives to live. I made my own choices fully aware of the possible consequences. I've found my way back again, and this reunion is more than I could have ever hoped for. But now, I'm afraid we must part again."

"I'm not leaving you like this," I say.

"Surely, Tomas, there must be a way to extract you from those draggarts' neural network," Eppel says.

Tomas turns to both Eppel and me. "The unfortunate reality is that I can no longer survive outside of my Droid body."

"But maybe we can find a way to help you. Please. Just come with us. Come with *me*," I plead. *Because I need you—* I want to say—*now maybe even more than when I was a child, just like that day I needed you so long ago.*

He looks at me for a long silent moment, as if memorizing the lines of my face.

"No, my Comet. I need to stay here to ward them off, maintain the block. Otherwise you'll have no chance." He picks Keenon back up and passes him over to Eppel.

"But Gardurak will put you back under his control."

He shakes his head. "Now that you've brought me back, Livinthea, I won't be lost again."

"But how can you be sure of that? Just come with us, and we can figure things out." I'm not too proud to beg. "Please, *father*." I believe him now, with the whole of my pitiful heart.

He tilts my chin up gently to look at him, just like when I was a child.

"You and I, we each have very important roles to play, more important than you can understand. The survival of the Ritarian Gateways depends on it. So for now, you must go, and I must stay. The Bionics need you." His metal finger drops from my chin.

He's absolutely right. I *don't* understand.

How could measly me possibly make a difference in this big wide gaping hulk of a universe? "What role?" I ask, desperate for an answer to help me make sense of this life that is doing its best to spin out of control.

"Don't you see, my Comet? Only you have the double Mark of Dresden mutation. The civilizations and worlds of the Ritarian Gateways need you. Only you have the power to overcome Gardurak and free the Gateways from his wrath. But it's not something I can tell you how to do. You must find the way yourself. Now go. Please. Before it's too late."

What about what I need? I want to say. How can the universe be so cruel? I have only just found my father. I have so many things to ask. So many things to say. And I can't just abandon him to the Quadrati like this.

He seems to sense my unspoken words, for in the next moment, he puts his cool metal hands over mine. I'm forced to look into his honey-gold eyes. "But know this, my Comet. The universe is not as unfeeling as you might think. *Love* is the life blood of the universe. It twines through the very fabric of space and time, holding it together, connecting *us* together. So no matter where we are in the far-flung reaches of this vast universe, know that I *will* always be with you.

"Now *please,* Livinthea. I need to get back to the aquifers, and you and the others must go. Gardurak is getting too close, and I can only maintain the encryption for so long. Do it for me. *I* need *you* to survive."

And with a light touch on my cheek, he disappears back down into the tunnel.

LXXXVI

LIVI: HARD TO LET GO

TRITON'S IRON GRIP on my arm is the only thing keeping me from running after my father. The Droid with the honey-gold eyes. The others have already gone ahead.

"Come on, Livi. We've got to get going."

I know Triton is right, but it still doesn't make my feet budge. My heart is like Juthri's stone, weighing me pitifully down. I'm on a cruel time loop back to when I was a little girl, losing my father *again*. The dismal hollows carve their way into my core. My vision blurs over.

Triton takes my hand, his large hand practically enveloping mine. "Look at me, Livi." He steps in front of me so I can't avoid his eyes. His gentle finger catches a traitorous tear. "Let's use the chance that your father is giving us. Let's not waste all that he has sacrificed. We'll figure out a way to get him back. But right now we have to get out of here. Okay?"

The kindness in Triton's eyes blunts some of the pain. He's right. I've just got to keep going. And yet it's so hard, to reach the apex of light, only to fall into the dark again.

But then I feel it, a gentle nudge at the base of my brain. *Keep moving forward, my Comet.* A strange sense of comfort touches me like a ray of sunshine through the clouds, an unbreakable connection. *I will always be with you no matter how far the distance.* The tightness in my chest eases to a tolerable ache. I look around in wonder. But my father is nowhere to be seen.

Finally, I nod to Triton and start moving my feet.

"The others went this way. Hurry!" Triton breaks into a sprint down a widely carved tunnel, pulling me along. Unlike the smooth base tunnels, the perimeter's passages seem ancient, uneven, and unused. I have to be careful not to trip. A dim light in the distance casts a shadowy glow, barely enough for us to see by. Just before we round the bend, I throw one last backwards glance. My heart already knows what my eyes will see. An empty tunnel.

Each step farther away from my father feels like the taut stretching of an elastic band, but I know I've got to keep moving. *Don't let the others down.* I force myself forward faster and faster. Just as we break out of the tunnel, Triton comes to a stuttering halt. Rocks and pebbles at his feet skitter over a sudden edge. I would have tumbled after them if it were not for Triton's quick reflexes, jerking me back. My stomach lurches into my throat as the rocks whistle down to the empty canyon floor far below.

"Easy there!" Seemingly out of nowhere, Eppel puts a steadying arm out in front of me as well. "I know you're in a hurry, but there's no need to take the shortcut down. We'll get there soon enough."

My eyes adjust to the bright light, and I use my hands to shield against the sandy wind blowing into my face. The others are perched close by on a behemoth of a bridge. Or at least what used to be one. Only crisscrossing beams of old rusted metal rafters and buttresses are left. It spans a heck of a drop down to the canyon floor. A rock kicks loose over the edge, and I almost get dizzy as my eyes follow its plummeting path. Even with my enhanced Bionic senses, I don't hear it strike bottom.

"We're going down there?" I ask.

Sayrie nods to me. "Brevia's tracker is picking up a signal just over there." She points down into the canyon, towards a broad stretch of flat sandstone.

Carefully, I peer over the edge again. "But there's not a darn thing down there."

"That's what we thought too, but take another look." Eppel scoops up a handful of pebbles. Then with a powerful arc of his arm, he showers them down into the canyon below.

Instead of bouncing off the flat surface below, some of the pebbles ricochet at odd angles, before they even reach the cavern floor.

"Camouflage device?" I ask.

"Quick learner isn't she, Comstadt?" Eppel quips at Triton.

"You have no idea," Triton says. He turns to Sayrie. "But where are the others you spoke about?"

"Inside the craft waiting, I hope," Sayrie replies, then turns to me. "Are you ready to go, Livi?" she asks, though her eyes pose a deeper question.

"Yes, for now," I answer.

Triton gives my hand a reassuring squeeze.

"Very well then." Sayrie turns and starts heading towards a narrow path etched into the steep cliffside that snakes down to the canyon floor.

Carefully we pick our way down, Sayrie and Rhyton leading the way. Triton and I follow closely behind. Eppel carries Keenon slung over his shoulder. Juki and Phlynnt bring up the rear, guarding our backs.

When we reach the canyon floor, I still can't see the spacecraft. But the next moment I blink, and suddenly, Sayrie and Rhyton are no longer in front of me. "Sayrie!" I call out.

"Still here!" Her voice floats back to me from out front. And sure enough, as I put my foot forward, it disappears into the empty air before me. I bring it back, and it reappears. Finally, I take a deep breath and step all the way through. Sayrie and Rhyton are standing there smiling, with the most odd-looking spacecraft I have ever seen behind their backs.

"Nice trick." I marvel.

"Isn't it though? One of my best inventions if I don't say so myself," Sayrie replies.

"You developed that technology?"

Sayrie nods. "That and many of the devices you see on the Pherring."

Rhyton smiles proudly beside her. "They don't call my sister Pantoc's best elematician for nothing."

In the next moment, Triton pops through the camouflage bubble, followed in quick succession by Juki, Phlynnt, Eppel, and Keenon.

Triton's eyes glom onto the odd-looking craft. "It's like a hybrid between a seafaerie and a fairlot. You sure this thing can fly?"

"Hellas yeah. I sure didn't help design this thing to swim. Now, let's hope Jin and the others are waiting for us inside," Sayrie says and heads towards the hatch door.

***

The minute we enter, I know something is wrong. It's too quiet. We can all feel it. Slowly, Eppel lays Keenon down.

Her foot halfway through the inner hatchway, suddenly Sayrie freezes. My eyes follow the line of her gaze. A body. Oh stars, it's Jin. A skyver in one hand, while her other is stretched towards the craft hatch as if she were trying to reach for it. Her head lolls to the side, the color leeched from her face.

Sayrie shakes her frantically. "Jin! Jin!"

I feel her neck. "She's got a pulse, just barely." Quickly, the rest of us disperse to various areas of the ship. But it's the same everywhere. Claris, Chee, Wendolyn. Barely breathing. More dead than alive. Even Telisad. Her poor little body curled next to Allara's.

We congregate back in the main holding area.

Triton shakes his head. "What in all hellas happened here?"

Eppel scratches at his temple. "It's as if something poisoned them, *all at once*. Look how they are strewn all over the ship. Whatever it was. It came on very quickly."

Suddenly, beside me, Rhyton starts dry heaving. Sayrie follows only a split second later. Both of them collapse practically on top of each other moments later, clutching at their stomachs. Triton and I barely have time to catch them. And when I look towards Keenon's face, the color which had finally started coming back starts to pale, becoming a sickly green right before my eyes.

My mind whirls for possible explanations. My eyes lock with Triton's, the answer dawning on us at the same moment. "Carbon tetron poisoning."

Odorless. Quick onset. Rapidly lethal. We've all been trained as cadets to recognize the first signs of the poison, a vaporous byproduct of burning hyponium propellant. It can build up if the output valves malfunction, and the Pherring has probably been sitting here for weeks, maybe even months now. No doubt its output valves are thoroughly clogged by the copious sand that seems to drown this stars-forsaken planet. And when Jin readied the craft in preparation for an immediate takeoff, likely the poisonous gas built up very quickly before they could even become aware of it. They wouldn't even know what hit them until it was too late. Because of the nanobots in our system, the other Bionics and I are protected from the lethal gas. Sayrie, Rhyton, and Keenon are not so lucky.

Triton grabs the skyver and turns to the rest of us still standing. "Hurry, let's get Sayrie, Rhyton, and Keenon off this ship."

Within moments, we have the three of them back outside. We lay them down on the rough dirt, careful to stay within the camouflage bubble.

Triton kneels next to Sayrie, his voice urgent. "Where is the environment panel on this ship?"

Sayrie clutches at her stomach, barely able to answer. "B-black panel—hatch door."

Triton tosses the skyver to Phlynnt. "Phlynnt, Eppel, Juki, perimeter defense protocol. Disable on sight. Livi, come with me." He rushes back towards the Pherring, calling back over his shoulder, "And keep those three on their sides in case they seize!"

I scramble up after him. "What are you going to do?"

"Sayrie's comrades have been exposed to the poison far too long. I'm going to do an air sweep and try to clear the ducts. Purify the air. Overpressurize the cabins with one hundred percent oxygen. Create a hyperbaric chamber of sorts to give the others a chance. And it's nearly nightfall, our best chance to take off undetected. We need to be able to use this ship to fly us off this planet by then."

"What about our own Hawwks?"

Triton shakes his head grimly. "We can't possibly get there in time. Not without our darkwing suits. No, I'm afraid this is the only way we even have a sliver of a chance of getting everyone out of here alive."

LXXXVII

LIVI: NOT NOW

"CABIN SHOULD PRESSURIZE to one hundred percent oxygen in ten. Shutting off basic engines now," Triton calls out to me.

He has been working furiously over the environment panel for the last few minutes.

"Okay," I shout back from the cockpit. "Purging outflow ducts. Let's hope this works."

"You can say that again." Triton nods. "Oxygen sensors reading one hundred percent. We're at six atmospheres of pressure. Your ears feel okay, Park? You can step out now if you want. I'll stay here with the others."

My ears feel boxed in, but I can tolerate it. "I'm good for now. How about we move everyone to the sleeping nooks while we're waiting."

"Good idea," Triton says.

Quickly, one by one, Triton and I move Jin, Allara, Telisad, and the others to the sleeping quarters on the craft, a spacious room with at least twenty nooks built into the wall.

After we leave the last of them in the sleeping quarters, I turn to Triton. "If this works, how long will it take them to—" The sudden release of air pressure stops me midsentence. The hatch door bursts open.

"Droids! On the ridge! They're coming down fast!" Eppel practically crashes in, Keenon slung over his back. "With the camouflage, they don't see us yet. But it won't be long before they're upon us."

"Hold them off then!" The Comstadt runs over to the environment panel, scanning it. "We're only fifty percent clear on the outflow ducts. Air's safe enough to breathe, but engines will overheat if we launch right now. We won't even make it out of the atmosphere."

"We can bypass to the Pherring's outjack pipes. It will only give us a temporary heat outlet, but enough to get us off of this rat's pit." Sayrie's face appears behind Eppel, Rhyton not far behind. Dark circles rim the siblings' eyes, but at least they're both upright.

The Comstadt's brows arch up for a split second before he commands. "Do it then. Quickly." He turns to Rhyton. "And get Keenon to the sleeping quarters. The rest of us will try to hold the Droids off." Triton barrels towards the cockpit door, grabbing a hazar.

Keenon lets out a soft moan as Eppel passes him over to Rhyton, but there's no time for me to see how he's doing. I rush after the Comstadt. Eppel follows not far behind.

Outside, Phlynnt is perched at the ready behind a large boulder, eyes cast skyward. I follow the line of his gaze, but *they* are already easy enough to spot.

Ten Droids. A line of lethal metal snaking its way down the narrow path etched into the cliff, the same one we came down upon.

Triton's voice rumbles low as he crouches down beside Phlynnt. "Once they get into range of our skyver, we take them down all at once." The Comstadt points towards the cliffside. "There, Magnar. Wait until they are all on that part of the trail where the ground thins. Aim right at the buttressing point of the trail."

"I see it, Comstadt." Phlynnt nods once as he adjusts the aim of his skyver.

"Steady." The Comstadt breathes low.

Closer and closer they descend. Though it's warm outside, a cold chill runs through my body. The Droid out front now looms barely a few dozen meters above us.

"Now!" the Comstadt barks.

Boom! Crack! The ground shakes as the side of the cliff shatters explosively. Shards of rock fly at us as metal bodies and dirt come crashing down. The avalanche of crumbling rocks and billowing dirt buries the Droids deep. Slowly, the dust clears.

We got them.

All of them.

Except for—

"Again!" the Comstadt shouts beside me.

Phlynnt takes aim at the flash of metal that scrambles back up the cliffside. "Come on. Come on," he grumbles as the skyver recharges.

But it's already too late. Before Phlynnt can shoot again, the lone surviving Droid has already disappeared beyond the upper ridge, out of sight.

"Burning black holes," Phlynnt curses, *because now the Droids know exactly where we are.*

Several long wretched moments pass as our eyes scan the broken trail and cliff face above. We hold our breaths.

Not even a jaunt later, a throng of Droids appears above us. They converge on the overhang of the broken bridge.

Then it starts. The buzzing at the base of my brain. *Stars. Not now.*

I know what will happen next.

On the bridge, a slash of red across tinston slices its way to the very front. The buzzing at the base of my brain surges painfully.

Gardurak.

Despite the camouflage, it seems as if his greedy red eyes pulsate directly into mine, then pivot away. Quickly, Gardurak motions to his Droids. A flurry of activity erupts above. *They're up to something.* It's of little comfort that the trail down to the canyon floor is obliterated.

"Livi! Get back inside," Triton orders beside me. "Jam the doors and help Sayrie and Rhyton get the craft back up and running. Take off as soon as you can. We'll try to buy you some time."

I dig my feet down into the dirt. "With all due respect, Comstadt, but—there is no way in all hellas I'm going to leave you all behind."

"This is *not* the time to be stubborn, Park," Triton barks at me.

"This is *exactly* the time to be stubborn. I'm a Bionic now too, remember?" I volley right back.

The Comstadt throws me an exasperated look, but it's too late now. The Droids have found another way down.

To my horror, the Droids rappel their way rapidly down the cliff face as if it were nothing at all, descending upon us by the dozens. There are far too many of them now and they're too spread out. Our one skyver is useless.

"Park, stay in back. Phlynnt, Eppel—rear flank positions," Comstadt orders in rapid succession. "Stick together. Hit them where it counts," the Comstadt shouts to us before surging forward.

The Comstadt takes a running leap into the air onto the back of a Droid and, in one swift motion, strikes it between the shoulder blades. The Droid tumbles out of the air, clanking hard right in front of me. But the Comstadt manages to hold onto the rappel rope, and now uses it to swing himself from side to side, his hazar coming to life. A second and third Droid fall from the sky before I can even blink.

What am I waiting for?

I jump into the fray simultaneously with Eppel and Phlynnt.

My training takes over.

Pivot, jump, kick. One Droid down. *Spin and leap. Hazar hard into the back.* Another Droid thuds down hard at my feet. All of those hours spent in Hemlock *are* worth something.

Beside me, the other Bionics are a whirlwind of well-choreographed movement. Every motion precise. Every motion lethal.

Three Droids converge on Eppel, but he doesn't even blink. A wide spinning sweep with his legs and the Droids are down all at once. Three more attack Phlynnt, but a backwards flip puts him at the advantage. Three more disabled.

Together, Eppel, Phlynnt, the Comstadt, and I take out Droid after Droid. Metal bodies start to litter the ground beside us, so thickly that I have to be careful not to trip over them.

We take down the first thirty, but just as quickly, forty descend to take their places.

"There's too many of them!" Phlynnt shouts between heaving breaths. The next instant he curses loudly. "Crimeny!" Phlynnt goes down, a long bloody gash on his leg. The Comstadt springs to his side, deflecting two Droids who come charging through.

But there are clearly too many of them, and too few of us.

"Aargh!" Eppel's legs buckle, a hand clutched at his thigh.

I take a running jump, landing between him and the fray.

This is it then.

A Droid barrels full speed towards us, metal baton aimed right at my gut. But just before the Droid takes out my innards, inexplicably, it hesitates for a split second— but long enough for me to somersault over it, and jab my hazar into its back. *What was that?*

Another Droid comes charging at us. But again, at the last moment, its solid metal legs stutter, movements unsure. I disable it again, this time even more easily than the last. *What's going on?*

I glance up towards the broken bridge. And then I see.

A struggle.

Metal tangles hard with metal.
Gardurak swipes at something behind him.
Dirt and rocks rain down.
His pulsatile red eyes flicker for an instant.
A second flash. Tinston.
The arc of a metal arm,
stabbing deep into the slash of red across Gardurak's chest.
The Master Droid collapses.

The buzzing at the base of my brain wanes.

A moment later, another Droid stands tall.
The Droid with the honey-gold eyes.
My father.
Looking down at me.
He's given us a chance.

A clang of metal to my left. Fifteen Droids descend upon the Comstadt and Phlynnt. Another fifteen surround Eppcl and me.

Oh stars. Though the Droids are slower, less coordinated even, they still attack us. There's still too many of them.

Command them, Livi! You have the power within you. Do it. Now, my father's voice pierces my thoughts.

And though the buzzing at the base of my brain is still there, it's much weaker now. I can think clearly again.

And deep down, I know what I have to do, what I've been afraid of doing all along.

I can't be afraid anymore.
I let myself go.

I let go of the tethers that tie me to the reality before me, into a second one that is just as real. I follow the path of the angry red light, jumping from node to node, from one artificial dendrite to another. A storm of voices and thoughts assail me, but I push through.

Starlock is there to lead the way.

Then I see it. A node that flares more intensely than all of the rest, pulsating in red-hot anger. *There. That's the one.*

The voices rage. Thoughts seethe furiously as I get closer. The void around me sizzles painfully. But there is no going back.

It's either now or never.

Now! I launch myself at the node and latch onto the fire. A searing pain wracks the whole of my body, but I hold onto it with all of my might—no matter how much it burns, how much it tries to repel me.

And then the strangest thing happens. *I feel it coming.* Suddenly, a blast of multicolored light surges forth from my fingertips. It arcs out and around the red beast of fury, pushing back, dampening the pain, quelling the anger.

But it's still not enough. Still, the red pulsates.

More, I urge. *Stronger.*

The rainbow of light flares again, this time so brightly that I gasp. It surges from my very core and spreads across to the other nodes, transforming what was once a sea of angry red dendrites into an ocean of dancing colors as far as the mind can see. The red rage falters.

And I know, *this is my chance.*

Stand down. Stand down now! I order, with all of the stubborn willpower that I've built up since the day I was born. *Stop fighting, you draggarts.*

I open my mind to the other reality before me. Two droids charge towards me, then stop suddenly in their tracks. The chaos of sound and battle abruptly stills. A long breath of a moment passes.

I'm afraid to look, but I do anyway.

To my amazement, all around us the other Droids hang lifelessly in their spots, as if frozen in time. Droids on the cliff face dangle mid-descent. Those surrounding the Comstadt and Phlynnt seemingly turn to stone. Wide-eyed, Eppel disentangles himself out from under a Droid, away from the lethal tip of a metal baton perched directly over his heart.

It worked.

"Hurry!" I call out as I grit my teeth against the buzzing in my brain that is slowly starting to build again. "I can't hold them for very long."

Triton, Eppel, and Phlynnt all turn to stare at me, shock and disbelief clear in their eyes.

But Triton quickly recovers. "Everyone back on the ship! Now!" he orders.

And I wonder then whether it's just luck or if the universe is actually looking out for me. For at that very instant, Rhyton shouts from the cockpit door, "Sayrie accessed the outjack pipes! We're good for takeoff!"

As we rush back into the craft, I take a glancing look back up towards the broken bridge.

But the Droid with the honey-golden eyes is already gone.

My heart squeezes so tightly I can barely breathe. But all I can do now is hope that my father got away.

LXXXVIII

LIVI: WHERE ONE PATH LEADS TO

ANOTHER

"**H**OW LONG CAN YOU hold them off?"

Triton slams the door closed behind me as we scramble back on board.

"Not long," I say in a rush. Already I can feel the buzzing at the base of my brain surging, my grasp of the raging fire unraveling. *It's fighting back*, thoughts and voices not my own, clawing to get out.

Triton spins towards Rhyton. "You know how to pilot this beast?"

Rhyton snaps forward with a nod. "My sister may be Pantoc's best elematician, but I'm their best pilot."

"Then do it," the Comstadt barks. "Get us off this rattling planet before it's too late. We don't have much time."

"Don't need to ask me twice," Rhyton calls back over his shoulder as he disappears into the cockpit.

The Comstadt turns to Eppel and Phlynnt. "Work the ship's defenses. Get the shields up. Rhyton's going to need all the help he can get."

Then Triton turns to me and grips my hand. "Hold them off, Livi, just a few minutes longer, okay?" The concern and intensity in his eyes drill into mine.

I nod, balling my fists against the burning pain, diving back into the void. I hold on as the raging storm kicks and bucks, hold on to Starlock with all of my might. I tread water in an ocean of multihued dendrites that threatens to carry me out and away from shore, dousing me with wave after wave. Seconds seem like minutes. And minutes seem like forever. Whether it has been only a moment or an eternity, I can't tell. The two realities twist together, intertwine, and I am getting lost between the two.

Getting lost.

"Livi!"

So lost.

"Livi!" *Triton's voice.*

"Stay with me!" Triton grips the sides of my face and makes me look at him. The warmth of his hands on my cheeks, his steel-grey eyes, pulls me back from the void.

I nod at him. "I'm all right."

The muscles at the angles of his jaw relax.

But the ground sways.

No. It's a good thing. The ship's thrusters are flaring. I can feel the pressure at my feet, gaining altitude.

We're in the air.

Thank the stars.

Just in time, because at that moment, I can feel it break. My bond with the Quadrati neural network snaps like a dry twig, and I'm almost thrown off balance as I lurch back into the here and now. The two realities collapse back into one.

Boom! Crack! The walls of the ship shudder violently.

Triton rushes us towards the cockpit.

"Status?" the Comstadt calls out.

"We're at full thrusters, maximum ascent. Shields up ninety percent thanks to your men," Rhyton yells, his voice just audible above the raging engines. "Sayrie's gone to check on the others."

Boom! Another bone-numbing explosion. My stomach sinks like Juthri's stone.

"A fleet of Buggards and a Hellion less than ten kilometers back!" Eppel cries out next to Juki from the lookout port.

"Give us more time!" the Comstadt yells to them.

Juki and Eppel rain lasering fire upon the Buggards that follow in our wake, taking out ship after ship.

The Pherring's walls rumble as we burst through the thin atmosphere. Buggards litter the space beyond.

"Which one?" Rhyton calls back over his shoulder, as he banks the Pherring abruptly, narrowly avoiding a crimson fireball that hurtles past us. Sweat trickles down his forehead as he works the controls furiously, dodging fireball after fireball.

My eyes follow Rhyton's out the cockpit window. Before us blaze multiple rings, *too many gateways to count.*

"There!" Triton points to a ring in the far distance. "Head for the wormhole with the blue aura, that's our gateway back to Atlas."

Boom! Another flash of crimson, barely missing the Pherring's right wing.

Suddenly, a familiar baritone voice calls out from behind me. "No! We'll never make it. You've got to head for the closest gateway. Lose them first!"

I spin around. "Keenon!"

Keenon staggers forward into the cockpit, eyes bloodshot, face pale as stone. His hands are white-knuckled around the wall bars for support, but he is awake.

Triton's eyes widen momentarily at the sight of him. "We don't know where any of those other gateways lead. We would be lost to the dark ethers."

"Better lost than dead and blown to bits. Those Buggards are right on our tail!" Keenon argues.

"If we get lost, we *are* as good as dead." Triton volleys back above the roar of the engines. Then turning back to Rhyton, he shouts, "Get us to that blue gateway!"

Another blast makes the Pherring shudder violently. *That was too close.*

Despite his weakened state, Keenon doesn't back down. "They're almost on us. We've got to lose them in the other gateways. We'll find our way back."

This is not the happy reunion I envisioned. I turn to Keenon. "But how? Triton's right. We *don't* know where those other gateways go. It's too much of a maze. We'd never find our way back to the Erlion system."

The flash of hurt in Keenon's face is apparent as he spins towards me. *Siding with the Bionic?* his dark brown eyes accuse. But he only says, "Trust me, Livi."

But in the next moment, the horror unfolds as if in slow motion. A hellion ship and three Buggards circle ahead of us. Laser fire erupts from their ships, aimed directly at the blue ring in the distance. Only a second later, a powerful explosion of pure white light, and then our only way home collapses into nothingness.

"Dark infinites," Triton curses.

"What now?" Rhyton's voice is in a panic.

"We have no choice now," Triton states grimly. "The dark ethers it is then."

LXXXIX

LIVI: NEW DISCOVERIES

"HOLD ON TO your fleefluffs!" Rhyton calls out.

The Pherring dives so sharply that I almost lose my balance despite the ship's gravity stabilizer. I grip the wall holds tighter when I see where Rhyton is taking us—directly into the mouth of a flaming white ring.

"Four Buggards—coming at us like the Dark Skythes!" Eppel yells from the lookout. "Can't this ship go any faster?"

With a sudden burst of acceleration, Rhyton pitches us through the ring. And it's even more turbulent than before.

"Those rattling Buggards are following us through!" Juki shouts.

Triton scrambles up to the lookout. "Eppel! Juki! When I give the word, fire all that you've got back towards that wormhole." He calls back down, "Rhyton, the moment we're through, redirect as much energy as you can to the Pherring's weaponry systems. We're going to destabilize the wormhole as soon as we're clear. Two can play their game."

Electrical currents storm around us as we pitch and yaw through the wormhole. How the Pherring remains in one piece, I don't know.

"Get ready," the Comstadt growls, his eyes laser-focused on the path before us. "On my count—three, two, one—Rhyton! Divert all energy to our weapons. Juki and Eppel! Fire! Give them all you've got!"

The lights of the Pherring flicker as Juki and Eppel send an intense beam of energy back towards the wormhole. The edges of the wormhole ring glow brighter, expanding, undulating. And just as the nose of one of the Buggards breaks through, the gateway erupts into a blinding flash of light, so bright I have to turn my head away. I look back just in time to see the wormhole collapse, sucking the Buggard backwards into it, then vanishing into the ethers.

All that's left of the gateway—unadulterated, empty space.

A moment of disbelief blankets the air until Juki lets out a big whoop. "We did it! Good call, Comstadt!"

"Those were some rangtang moves, Rhyton. You can be my pilot any day," Eppel adds from the lookout.

"Thank you," Rhyton replies. "And I commend you on your very impressive aim with our chivs. We could use some clean shots like you on Pantoc."

They continue to chatter in relief, and I'm almost caught up in their revelry when I realize that Triton has not uttered a single word. When I peer up to the lookout, he's leaning forward, eyes trained on something in the distance.

The others notice as well, and suddenly all is quiet again as our eyes follow the direction of the Comstadt's gaze.

Two suns.

"Looks like a binary system with five orbiting planets," Keenon observes.

"Yes, a main sequence and a white dwarf star. I'm guessing the largest planet is likely a gas giant," I add.

"Yes, but look closer," the Comstadt urges. "The fourth planet out from the main sequence star."

That's when I see it.

Flashes of metal, rotating spheres to be more exact, orbiting the lovely azurean blue of a planet.

My eyes lock onto the Comstadt's as I say out loud what he has realized well before the rest of us. "It's inhabited."

Listen. It whispers. You've got to listen to the song of the universe that courses through each and every one of us. Don't let go, and you will always find your way. No matter how much noise there is.

(Excerpt from *The Thoughts and Memoirs of Livinthea Park*, star year 8117)

GLOSSARY

Altheria - The largest of the three Gliese sister suns that shine on Cerulea.

Atlas I - Bionics' space station.

Bionic - Humans with the Mark of Dresden mutation, who have received the nanobot transfusion giving them special superhuman abilities and infinite ability to self-repair.

Buggard - Quadrati patrol ship.

Cerulea - Livi's home planet.

Comstadt - A term of respect referring to the Bionics' top officer. Head of all of the Magnars.

Dark Skythe - A four-legged herd animal native to Cerulea, similar in appearance to a buffalo but with dark

489

brown and black stripes, spiraling horns, and a massive, spiked tail.

Domseis - The Elder Bionics.

Erlion System - Galaxy where Ceruleans live.

Fairlot - A small birdlike animal, native to Cerulea. Instead of wings, its mechanism of flight is akin to the rotor blade of a helicopter. The bird is rarely seen and even more rarely heard.

Hawwk - Bionics' long-range patrol craft.

Hazar - Weapon used in hand-to-hand combat.

Hellion - Quadrati mother ship.

Hespera - A descendent of the falcon, brought over from Earth by the first colonists, but larger than its ancestors with oversized claws that are adapted to preying on large animals.

Hurako - One of the planets in the Erlion system that is inhabited.

Jaunts - Unit of time that equals approximately five minutes by ancient standards.

Magnar - A Bionic officer.

Mercatorian lines - The three-dimensional gridwork of lines in space used by the Bionics to map out the Ritarian Gateways.

Meridiae - A unit of length, approximately ten miles by ancient standards.

Nadir - "Midnight" on Atlas Station I. Since Atlas does not cycle through a normal day, they have set up an artificial cycle to track time.

Nanobots - Microscopic robots with the ability to repair all aspects of the human body.

Nullification - Process by which a Bionic is stripped of his/her nanobots.

Pan - The largest of the five oceans on Cerulea.

Pantoc - One of the habitable planets of the Ritarian Gateways.

Petronian wildebeast - Large four-legged long-haired mammal with a humped back. The animal grazes very slowly, but has a bad temper, and when threatened, charges ferociously.

Pherring - Spacecraft with a two-pronged propeller at its head and broad wings. Used by the people of Pantoc.

Prismei - Top speed of the Hawwk. Half supraluminal speed.

Psyla tree - A tree native to Cerulea with a thick canopy, wide trunk, and broad and glossy leaves.

Quadrati - Droid-like race invading Cerulea.

Ritarian Gateways - An ancient secret wormhole network connecting the various civilizations that dispersed from the World of Origins during the Great Dispersion.

Sar - Bionic officer who is second in command.

Skyver – Long-range, high-energy weapon used by the Quadrati.

Talon - Bionic's short-range patrol craft.

Tully - Galactic aircraft.

Yentian Belt - Asteroid belt within the Erlion system.

Young Blood - A Bionic who is less than twenty-one star years old and newly transformed.

Zenith - "Noon" on Atlas Station I. Since Atlas does not cycle through a normal day, they have set up an artificial cycle to track time.

Acknowledgements

Leaning on Water has been quite the journey, born from my love of space and all things sci-fi. It has taken nine long years of writing, but never lonely because of the wonderful people in my life.

Thank you most of all to Ken, my husband and fellow life adventurer, my first beta reader, my sounding board even in the late hours, without complaints and always with words of encouragement, humor, support, and love.

Thank you to my children, Dylan and Vivian, for your enthusiasm and your patience, for letting me fulfill this dream while you pursue dreams of your own. But thank you mostly for the immense joy you bring to my life.

And of course thank you to my parents, Ming and Wen Hwa, and my brother, Rich, for always being there for me, for all of your love and support throughout the years in all capacities.

A thousand thanks to my amazing copyeditor, Lisa Gilliam, for your attention to detail and keen eye, for going through my manuscript with a fine-toothed comb and giving it the extra tune-up it needed.

Lastly, a special thanks to Aimee, for your suggestions and encouragement, for spending your winter break slogging through my draft despite your very busy schedule, and for being the best sister-in-law ever. Thank you!

Love you all!

JOAN JUNE CHEN MD obtained her undergraduate and medical school degrees from Stanford University, then went on to complete her anesthesiology residency at UCSF. Though she may be a full-time anesthesiologist, when she's out from under the bright glare of the operating room lights, her other passions are writing and letting her creative juices flow free. She currently lives along the gently rolling foothills of the Bay Area with her husband, two children, and two hamsters—Livi and Jia.

Made in the USA
Columbia, SC
06 July 2020

13249883R00302